THIS

WRETCHED

DAWN

THIS WRETCHED DAWN

KEYLIGHT BOOKS
AN IMPRINT
OF TURNER
PUBLISHING

MELINDA GONG

KEYLIGHT BOOKS
AN IMPRINT OF TURNER PUBLISHING COMPANY
Nashville, Tennessee
www.turnerpublishing.com

Cover illustration by Addison Green
Book design by Ashlyn Inman

Library of Congress Cataloging-in-Publication Data
Names: Gong, Melinda, author.
Title: This wretched dawn / by Melinda Gong.
Description: Nashville, Tennessee : Keylight Books, 2025. |
Audience: Ages 12-17. | Audience: Grades 7-9.
Identifiers: LCCN 2024033894 (print) | LCCN 2024033895 (ebook) | ISBN 9798887980294
(hardcover) | ISBN 9798887980300 (paperback) | ISBN 9798887980317 (epub)
Subjects: CYAC: Romance stories. | Mystery and detective stories.
| Conspiracies--Fiction. | Shanghai (China)—Fiction. | LCGFT:
Romance fiction. | Detective and mystery fiction. | Novels.
Classification: LCC PZ7.1.G652183 Th 2025 (print) | LCC
PZ7.1.G652183 (ebook) | DDC [Fic]—dc23
LC record available at https://lccn.loc.gov/2024033894
LC ebook record available at https://lccn.loc.gov/2024033895

Printed in the United States of America

*To my sister, who has supported me
(against her will) for 22 years.*

如今俱是异乡人，相见更无因.

Now all are strangers in a distant land;
no more chance of meeting again.

—"Lotus Leaf Cup" by Wei Zhuang (Late
Tang Dynasty Chinese poet, c. 836–910)

CHAPTER 1

I was six, I think, when I discovered that the best place for spying on inner circle meetings was the balcony.

The meeting room is a rotunda capped with a gilded dome. There are no rafters to hide within and no door close enough to the giant oak table that would allow for the escape of sound louder than a mumble.

The balconies wrap perfectly around the rotunda, just below the dome, meaning you can choose a place anywhere and listen in on whatever private conversation is happening down below.

Today, they are discussing the Dawn Court.

"This cold peace is not sustainable," Lord Fei is saying, his voice carrying easily to where I'm perched on the balcony. "It's been less than a decade and things are no better than they were when we were in all-out war."

He is one of twelve members of the Midnight Court's inner circle, the Emperor's Council.

"That's ridiculous," Lady Zhao snaps. "What's better is that we no longer have dozens of deaths every day. A political rivalry with London is still an improvement from the war years."

I'm not surprised they're arguing over this. The Dawn Court, headquartered in London, is one of the most powerful empires in the West. The Midnight Court is its mirror in the East, meaning it's practically inevitable that they've been at each other's throats for centuries, the feud exacerbated by constant territorial conflicts. Nine years ago, King Ateş and Emperor Xia signed a peace accord that basically established some surface-level civility between the two courts.

But it was not so long ago that I have forgotten the days when it didn't exist. The days when there was the constant sound of gunfire outside, when coming across a limp body on the street meant very little. Was of no surprise.

It doesn't fool anyone either. These years of accorded peace are just the courts biding their time. Waiting for a chance to strike again.

"I disagree," Fei answers. "At least we knew what they were doing during the war, what they were planning. Days ago, we heard a rumor that they were planning an attack. What would we have done if that rumor had been true? Right now, we're sitting here like lambs before a slaughter."

He's not wrong. A week ago, someone sent an anonymous message to the Council warning of a Dawn Court attack on Shanghai in three days. Thankfully, it had been a false alarm, but the scramble to prepare for it had shined a garish light on just how complacent we've become. Lambs before a slaughter, indeed.

"So, what is it you're proposing?"

"We attack first." Fei's voice is urgent, animated. "We send a spy, someone trustworthy, to scope out the situation first. Gather as much information as possible. And then *we attack first*."

"Anna!"

I hear the fierce whisper from behind me and turn carefully so I don't make any unintended noise.

Josephine Jiang, my best friend since we were both three years old and walking on still-shaky legs, is standing a couple paces away, an expression on her face that I can read immediately. I've probably seen it hundreds of times by now. It screams: *What are you doing?*

I motion her over, and hesitantly, she makes her way to me.

"What's going on?" she quietly asks.

"I think they're planning an attack," I tell her in a hushed whisper. "On the Dawn Court." As if that last part isn't obvious.

"What? What about the accords?"

"Listen," I say, angling my head toward the twelve Midnight Court members sitting around the table.

"You really want to be responsible for breaking the peace accords?" This is my mother.

"It is not something I want to do, Lady Liang, more like something I feel we are compelled to do. Isn't it always better to be on the offense rather than defense?" Fei replies.

He's not wrong there, and I suspect my mother knows it because she doesn't argue. Just nods.

"Does anyone else have opinions they'd like to share?" my father asks. He's sitting at the head of the table in the seat usually reserved for the Emperor. But since he's absent today, it is my father's job as deputy to step in as regent in his place.

"I think this is completely absurd," Lady Zhao shoots. "We finally have peace and now you're choosing to voluntarily break it. Absolutely ridiculous!"

"If this is what we elect to do, it needs to be something that's thought-out. Planned in detail. Not some spur-of-the-moment decision," Lord Jiang warns. He's Josephine's father; a stocky man whose salt-and-pepper hair betrays his age. I think out of all of them, he's been on the Council the longest. He has lived through war and peace, and it has made him cautious. Rightfully so.

"Of course," Fei assures. "The spy will go in first, and then we can decide our next course of action."

A sudden flash of silver catches my eye, momentarily distracting me from the conversation below. I squint, peering down into one of the windows. But if there was anyone there, they aren't there now.

Strange.

"Hold on," I say to Josephine. "I think I saw someone."

She looks at me. And without hesitation, simply says, "Be careful."

My heart is pounding as I stalk down the stairs, out the entrance. I can hear it in my ears, how loud it is, like drumbeats.

My fingers are twitching, itching for a fight.

I know what I saw. I know it. And if there's a Dawn Court spy in our territory hearing everything the Council just discussed, we're screwed. We lose the element of surprise, and just like that, we're on the defense. I make a mental note to remind my father to increase security around the building during meetings. Just because we're in a period of peace doesn't mean we're safe.

It's warm outside. The humidity is suffocating me like a film of plastic, but after eighteen years of hot, muggy Shanghai summers, I'm used to it. Near the Bund—the waterfront on the Huangpu River's west bank—it is a hundred times worse, but it rarely bothers me anymore.

I make my way toward the window where I spotted the spy, the blade of the knife tucked in my sleeve cold against my skin. If I was smart, I would've notified the guards as soon as I'd seen the flash of silver. Or, better yet, I would've notified the Council. But then again, I am not exactly known for doing the smart thing. I am not my sister.

The side of the building touches a narrow alleyway, dimly lit except for a single streetlamp whose bulb ought to have been changed years ago. The asphalt of the road is wet, glistening like a sheen of resin after the recent rain.

But when I get there, I see nothing. No footprints, no scuffed dirt, no sign anyone was ever there. I'm preparing to turn around and head back inside when I feel it.

The cold steel kiss of a gun against my temple.

"You shouldn't have come out here." The voice is undeniably masculine. Cool, precise, articulate. Speaking perfect Mandarin, but the checkered barrel pressed to my head is very clearly British. Clearly Dawn Court.

"And you shouldn't have been spying," I retort in English. The gun presses harder against my skin, a faint ache beginning to radiate out. His grip is like iron.

"You're not exactly in a position to be telling me what I should or shouldn't do."

"This is Midnight Court territory, if you haven't noticed," I hiss, palming the knife from my sleeve. "What's a member of the Dawn Court doing here?"

Quickly, I move to jam my elbow into his side, but he's too fast, shifting out of the way before I can make contact. Obviously trained.

"You are also," he replies, "not in the position to be asking questions." He taps the barrel of the gun for emphasis. "Come on, we're walking away from the windows."

And then I'm being pushed. We head down the alley and to the right, into some random building where he shoves me into a chair and ties a rope around my wrists. Just tight enough that I won't be able to slip loose.

And then he finally comes into view and I think I've lost it. Truly, completely lost it. Hit my head one too many times in a fight and now it's caught up to me.

I can't quite believe my eyes. Can't quite trust myself. Because standing in front of me, dressed in all black like he isn't an integral member of the enemy court, is the youngest prince of the Dawn Court.

Running my eyes over his face is like remembering how to ride a bike again after years of not doing it. After years of leaving it in the garage to collect dust and finally, it's taken back out. At first, it feels foreign—strange—but slowly, it all comes back. Muscle memory.

I haven't seen him since I was fifteen years old—six years after the Midnight Court relinquished him to the Dawn Court, to London, to his father, after his mother passed away. This aberration of both courts, a welding of two bloodlines.

He looks exactly the same and yet completely different. Same gold hair, same strange, strange eyes. Green with the Dawn Court circle of gold around the pupil, but slightly more angular than those who are full-blooded Dawn Court. It betrays who he really is. And the Midnight Court half of him is reflected in other ways as well: in the fullness of his lips, the width of his cheekbones.

But he is older now, less of a boy. There is no more extra childhood-chubbiness, no more expressions that are open like a book. He is tall and shuttered and so very, very foreign to me.

But still I say, "Paris."

"Hello, Anna," he says. "It's been a while."

I can't breathe.

CHAPTER 2

The last time I saw Paris, he might as well have stabbed me in the back, twisted the blade, left me to bleed out all over the dying grass.

For three years, I have sworn to return the favor.

CHAPTER 3

"I haven't seen you in three years. Why are you back?" I can't seem to wake up from this dream. This nightmare.

"It's peacetime, isn't it? I'm allowed to be here." There's a glint in his eye that tells me he doesn't believe it any more than I do. Any more than the court leaders do.

"That isn't what I'm talking about, and you know it. And since when does peacetime involve spying on the Midnight Court Council?"

"Spying," Paris says, "is such a loaded word. Besides, I assure you I didn't hear anything. Your court is wise enough to soundproof the walls of its meeting room." He keeps avoiding my question.

"Stop," I say. "Stop playing games." I think my heart has never pounded this hard. I am a test tube of emotions—shock and pain and disbelief and this overwhelming, *stupid* urge to cry.

"Okay," he says, leaning against the wall. I wish he would move farther. I wish he was closer. "What exactly would you like me to say, Anna?"

Why you're so cold. "What happened?" *To you,* I want to add. "In the past three years?" I think I know.

Paris spins the gun that was just jammed against my temple around his fingers. "If you're looking for some storybook tale," he says, "there isn't one."

"And, what? You've completely forgotten about the complete other half of your life?"

"Inconsequential," he answers. Just that. One word.

I let it sink into my skin like an arrow, wait for the stinging to fade, and then yank it back out.

"Right," I say. "You're Dawn Court now. You always have been. So why did you come back?"

Paris doesn't flinch, doesn't even twitch. Isn't fazed. Just looks at me, sighs, and says, "You'll see soon enough."

What the hell does that even mean?

His lack of emotion and my complete inability to read him is beginning to irritate me.

I twitch against the rope binding my wrists. "If you're going to kill me," I say, "just do it already. Stop with the theatrics."

He throws me a look like, *Oh please.* "For the record, out of the two of us, I'd argue you're the more dramatic." Taps a finger against the grip of the gun. "Besides, I'm not going to kill you. Can you imagine the riot it would cause, me murdering the daughter of the Midnight Court deputy?" He shakes his head. Smiles mirthlessly.

I lean back in the chair. "I was beginning to worry you'd forgotten who I was." Beyond just my name.

His lips twitch. "I'm not an idiot, Anna," he says, and I'm trying to understand why my name suddenly sounds so strange falling from his lips. "I didn't get where I am from good looks alone, you know."

I open my mouth. Close it. Speechless for probably one of the few times in my life. Suddenly, I'm struck by the reality of what I'm doing, by the fact that I'm sitting here talking to a Dawn Courter—the king's son, no less—as casually as if he were a member of my own court. As if three years ago, he didn't completely break my heart. Break *me.*

"Okay," I say. "What, exactly, is the point of this then?"

He stalks closer, crouches down until he's face-to-face with me, until there are only inches of air between us. I think I've forgotten how to breathe. My lungs have forgotten how to function. Only my eyes still work because I can't stop staring.

All I can think is, his scent is still the same. Amber and musk and something that is all his own. It is a heady mix of nostalgia and wariness. My heart is pounding so hard I'm afraid it's going to jump straight out of my chest.

I'm afraid he's going to hear it.

Every cell in my body is screaming *enemy*, is screaming *friend*, is screaming *make up your goddamn mind*. I don't move a muscle. My gaze falls from his eyes to his lips, back to his eyes. He is too close, too close, too close.

Paris won't stop playing with the gun in his hand. He rests his elbows on his legs. Leans forward. Looks at me.

"I want to know what they're planning," he says, seemingly completely oblivious to the fact that my mind is tearing itself apart, trying to reconcile this new Paris with the old one, the one I knew.

And then I'm distracted. I'm staring at his left wrist, at the red string bracelet there. It looks simple enough, these few strands of thread braided together, but I know what's on the other side.

The Chinese coin. It's supposed to be a symbol of luck, of wealth and good fortune. I can't believe he's wearing it. I wonder how he hides it from the Dawn Court king, or if his father knows but tolerates it anyway.

"Your bracelet," I say. "It's a Midnight Court relic."

"Yes, I know," he responds, mildly irritated. Not even irritated really, more impatient. He acts like it's no big deal that he's wearing this thing on his wrist that shatters the entire new identity he's built.

"It was my mother's," he says. "Now, please, give me what I want so we can both stop wasting our time here. I have more important things to do, and I'm sure you do too."

And then—I'm so stupid, I realize. I am so incredibly laughable because Paris didn't check for weapons. I have been sitting here in this chair for the past ten minutes so completely distracted that I've forgotten about the fact that there is a knife in my sleeve with a blade that can cut through rope. Easily.

In one swift motion, I've slipped the knife free and sliced through the rope. In another second, I have Paris pressed to the wall with the blade at his throat.

Oh, how the tables can turn.

He's eyeing me warily, but he isn't nearly tense enough for my liking. I can't stop thinking about how I can feel the warmth of his skin where it touches mine. Too human. Too like me. And that I can see his pulse in his throat.

I convince myself it doesn't matter. He's a threat—to my family, to my home. My sworn enemy from the moment I was born, as dictated by both our birthrights. I press the knife harder, mirroring his every move from earlier.

"This is why you don't wander into Midnight Court territory," I say. And then I drag my knife across his throat.

But he's too fast. Too quick, and part of me is wondering if I was simply too slow, or if something was holding me back.

I don't stop to examine it too closely.

In a second, he slips out of my grasp and then it becomes a full-on fight. I duck, narrowly avoiding the butt of his gun, and stick out a foot to trip him, but he dodges easily.

I have two advantages in this: the knowledge that he isn't trying to kill me (because if he did commit murder on Midnight Court soil, he'd effectively be restarting the war), and the knowledge that I am most definitely trying to kill *him*. That I can because: 1. I am fully within my rights to do so because I'm pretty sure this counts as self-defense, and 2. I know my court's about to reignite the war anyway.

I jump, spinning in the air, using my momentum to send a kick at him. It hits, my shin colliding hard with his side, and I hear a quick intake of air. But my satisfaction is fleeting. In another moment, there is a blinding flash of pain in my upper thigh, and I bite back a scream as fire lances its way through my leg. The muscle tears apart and blood soaks the fabric of my pants, somehow turning the black even blacker.

And then, an odd sensation—like my bones can no longer support my leg, like my cells are committing mutiny and no longer wish to work. I stumble, catching myself against the wall.

"It's poisoned," he says with eerie calm. "The blade I just cut you with." So stupid of me not to realize that he had a knife too. "You might want to go get it checked out before you either bleed to death or it spreads to your heart.

"It was nice to see you again, Anna." Paris makes to leave, then stops by the door. "Oh, and if you tell anyone about this, I won't hesitate to kill you next time. And Josephine."

And then he's gone.

CHAPTER 4

The poison, it turns out, was viper venom. Disgusting symptoms, but easily curable. I'd expected it, anyway. I told my parents it was a spy from the Dawn Court but not that said spy was *Paris*—the truth, with a couple omitted details.

"You need to be more careful, Liang An Na," my father is saying. "Even you are not invincible."

"Yes," I sigh. "I know. I'll be more alert next time."

"And you shouldn't spy. I can't remember how many times I've told you this, already."

At this, I am silent.

I'm lying in the infirmary, taking up one of the many identical white beds in the space. The Emperor and the Council exist in one singular building here in Shanghai. It houses the meeting rooms, the armory, the living spaces, and the infirmary.

"You're eighteen years old, Anna," my mother adds. "Don't throw away the next eighty years of your life."

I roll my eyes. "Mom, I'm not going to live to be ninety-eight. You have too high hopes for my lifespan."

She just smiles, says, "You're sure you're okay to leave? No one will judge you for taking a few extra days to rest."

"I've been in here too long already." I have. I've been sitting in this bed for two days for nothing but the gash in my leg that's now scarred over. Yet another blemish added to the map on my body.

The only reason, I suspect, that I'm finally allowed to get out of bed is because the Emperor and the Council want to talk to me. It's nothing bad, my father assures, just a request. But I'm nervous anyway. I'm nervous because this is a man who holds more power than anyone I know—so much so he shouldn't even be considered human. I don't know how the Council can work with him every day knowing he can order their deaths, end their existence, put a period to the sentence that is their entire life with a single word. A single order. It almost nauseates me. Sometimes I wonder if I am strong enough to survive in this world. But I know my place. I know who I am, my position as a soldier for my court. I do what is asked of me.

Slowly, I slip off the bed, standing on too-weak legs—legs that haven't stretched, haven't breathed in days. And I make my way to the Council Chamber.

Almost everyone is already seated when I arrive. Swiftly, my parents take their seats to the right of the Emperor. I am the only one left standing—straight-backed, hands clasped in front of me, *qipao* completely wrinkle-free—in front of the Council. Directly facing the Emperor.

"Welcome, Anna," he says. "It has been a long, long time. You are looking more like your mother than ever."

I don't know why adults always talk about this, debate over whether you look more like your mother or your father. Whether you've inherited your mother's double lids and straight nose or your father's strong features.

My mother smiles. Demure in a way I can never be.

"Thank you," I say. "Sir."

I think the last time I spoke to the Emperor was six years ago—when I was twelve years old and all gangly limbs and braces.

Unlike me, he has hardly changed at all. Emperor Xia is a broad-shouldered man; power is etched into every line of his body, into the thickness of his fingers, into the very way he holds and carries himself.

In the old days, in Ancient China, people used to believe emperors were the Sons of Heaven. That they carried the Mandate of Heaven that justified their rule. I think that even though Shanghai is just a city—not the nation that emperors used to rule—Xia still believes he carries Heaven's will. That the Midnight Court does. And that Dawn is the embodiment of Hell.

It is so ironic that in so many places in the West, light is considered good. It is considered pure and innocent, while darkness—night—is considered evil. I think Emperor Xia would laugh at the idea of this black-and-white dualism, say it's the other way around. Sometimes, I'm not so sure.

"Have you wondered," he asks me now, "why we have called you here? Why I, specifically, have called you here?"

"I have."

He plays idly with something on the table. A jade pendant.

"The peace is crumbling between our two courts. I'm sure you know this. In the West, our spies are telling us that whispers of an end to this *alliance* are beginning to surface.

"But," he says, raising his head, eyes, to mine, "we are still in an alliance—for the time being. We are still bound to the accords as much as we are bound to our own blood. And until it is dissolved, until an act of war is clearly declared, we are obligated to provide aid."

Wait, what? This wasn't the conversation I had been expecting. I blink. Stare. Wait for him to continue. The silence of his pause is beginning to flood into the room like water from a dam. Like blood from an open wound.

Bewildered, I venture, "I'm not sure I understand what you're saying, Huang Shang."

"The Dawn Court has been attacked."

"*What?*"

"Not directly. Not physically. A vial of poison—created by our two courts long ago as a safeguard against the royal families ever becoming too powerful—has been stolen from their laboratory. Up until nine years ago, until the accords, we were in possession of their vial, and they were in possession of ours. As a gesture of peace, we gave them back to each other.

"Now someone has stolen theirs. Intriguing, because very few people know where it was kept. Even more intriguing that not a single attempt has been made on ours, which means if they didn't suspect us before, they most definitely do now.

"However." He smiles a little. Picks up the jade pendant again. "There is one absolute fact I know. This was not the work of the Midnight Court."

"No offense, sir," I interrupt. My parents throw me a quick, cautionary glance that I ignore. "But how are you sure that it wasn't?"

"I'm sure you've heard about the old Midnight Court in your classes," the Emperor says. "You remember how it died out?"

"Of course," I answer, a little confused as to where he's going with this. Shanghai was once ruled by another family, another blood lineage, but they were all wiped out almost a century ago by a brutal attack reminiscent of Julius Caesar and Brutus.

"It's necessary that I watch my people very, very closely, Liang An Na," the Emperor tells me. "I know everything that happens in my court. And regardless, my Council has absolutely no motive. I confess we were planning to launch an attack sometime in the near future and unfortunately, this has completely disrupted our plans."

"I see," I say. "And what is my place in all of this?"

"I've talked to the Dawn Court king. Struck a deal. We will pool our resources into finding who's responsible. Otherwise, the cold peace is over and they will declare war."

I'm so confused. Really, truly confused. And I'm beginning to wonder if the poison has actually affected my brain, impaired my understanding, without anyone knowing it.

"I thought you didn't care about the peace? I thought you were going to launch an attack anyway."

The Emperor sighs. Heaves it. Says, "How do I explain this? We want you to work with Paris. Enroll you in Eladine Academy—"

My eyes are shooting out of my head. All the nerves in my brain are jumbling together into one tangled mess because I am shocked right down to my very roots.

Paris? Eladine Academy?

"The one in *London*?"

"Yes," Emperor Xia says. He pauses for a moment, as if he's waiting for me to process, but I am not processing. I am frozen except for

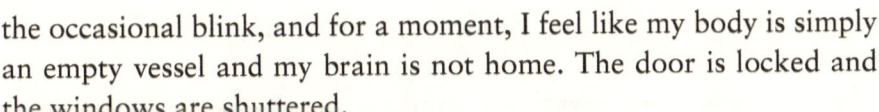

the occasional blink, and for a moment, I feel like my body is simply an empty vessel and my brain is not home. The door is locked and the windows are shuttered.

Eladine Academy is the Dawn Court's most infamous spy school, an institution that teaches espionage like no other. And it is in the very heart of Dawn Court territory, right next to Green Park and minutes from the Thames. It is also where every Dawn Court prince has trained, where all of the sons and daughters of the Dawn Court's inner circle attend.

When they opened up enrollment to the Midnight Court back in the beginning of the peace process, both governments faced extensive backlash from their people.

I can't believe he's sending me there. *And to help the Dawn Court?*

And then he continues, and I finally understand. Finally see his end-game. And this, this seems much more like our Emperor, our Huangdi.

He says, "But while you are doing this, I want you to do something else as well. You are, effectively, infiltrating the Dawn Court at their very center. I want you to gather as much information as possible. Make use of your *arrangement* with Paris. We would expect you to check in with a member of the Council every week or two, so that we may ensure you are making progress, and to collect the intelligence you have gathered. Once you are done, once you are confident you have obtained as much information as you possibly can, kill him. Our people at the embassy in London will guarantee you safe passage home."

I blink. "Apologies for asking, sir, but why me? Why not Katerina?" My sister is the one they usually go to for this. She is almost notorious for her aptitude for spying.

"As I'm sure you know, this truce has always been temporary. And in this age of cold peace, spies are the lifeblood of our court. You are eighteen years old now, Liang An Na, the age Katerina was when she began to take on assignments. Your parents and I believe it is time for you to take your seat in this court. To create your own position. We are giving you your opportunity to do so."

There is a very large part of me that is anxious—that is wary. That has just processed that I am being tasked with killing not just another human, but *Paris*, and am wondering if I have the strength to follow through.

But there is also a part that is thinking *yes*, that is thinking *please*, that is beating to the tune of *revenge*. The part of me that recognizes that no matter what my heart is saying, my brain knows that I have been born into this position whether I wanted to or not and I can't change that. That my life is the property of the Midnight Court, and my priority is to defend it. At all costs.

I am being given an opportunity to effectively kill two birds with one stone.

So I say, "When do I start?"

And he says, "Good girl."

CHAPTER 5

Two days.

I have two days to prepare, to pack up my entire life into one suitcase and ship it—and myself—halfway across the world to a city that will not welcome me. That despises my very existence.

My consolation is that Josephine is coming with me. She volunteered, because no matter what, we don't do things alone. She might as well be a part of my identity.

"What are you bringing to London?" Jo's asking me. We're sitting on the floor of my room, suitcases yawning open like gaping mouths. Mine is already half-filled with clothes, packed neatly with shoes and weapons. Hers is empty.

"Necessities," I say. "Clothes, shoes, weapons, toiletries, et cetera."

"Weapons?" She wrinkles her nose at me. "Seriously? We're going into Dawn Court territory and you're bringing *weapons*?"

"...Duh?"

"No, I mean like—" She lets out a frustrated huff. "They already see us as a threat. And then you're going to increase that threat with a suitcase full of weapons?"

I roll my eyes. "It's not a suitcase full, Jo. A couple knives, *tie shan*—"

"You do love your iron fans."

"—throwing stars, balisongs," I continue, ignoring her interruption.

I look at the long, double-edged blade on my bed. "*Jian.*" No guns because that has never really been a Midnight Court thing.

"Okay," Josephine says. "Fine. I hope you didn't pack up *all* your clothes, though. Don't forget we still have to attend the celebrations for the Moon Festival tomorrow."

It used to also be known as the Mid-Autumn Festival, a celebration of the harvest during the autumn full moon. But ever since the Midnight Court rose to power centuries ago, they thought it'd be more apt to just call it the Moon Festival.

"I know." I point at the qipao hanging in the closet. It is dark red—the color of blood, the color of rage and wrath—embroidered with gold.

"Nice," Jo says approvingly. "Maroon is so your color."

"Black is supposed to be our color," I respond. "Black and some dark shade of purple. Eggplant."

"Indigo?"

I frown. "Isn't indigo like a blue-purple?"

A sigh. "I don't know. So, remind me again what Huangdi wants you to do?"

I cast a sidelong glance at her. "Infiltrate the spy school. Get intel. Kill Paris."

Three simple steps.

So why does it feel so difficult?

"Isn't killing a little extreme? We're eighteen. As aware as we are of the world we live in, we haven't actually killed anyone before." This is a rare instance where Josephine is being serious. A novelty.

"I know," I say. "But we don't question orders, right? The Emperor's word is law."

"I don't know, Anna," she says. "Killing isn't something you can come back from. It's like stepping off a cliff: You can't just decide to go back. To change your mind."

I know this. It has filled every crevice of my mind, consumed all the oxygen and space in my brain until I have exhausted my entire capacity to agonize over what this will do to me.

It is easier, I think, to just follow orders. There's a reason why only some people choose to lead; others are content just to follow. To be led.

It is a hundred thousand times simpler.

"I'll be fine." Lying, it seems, almost comes more naturally than breathing these days. I poke her. "What are you wearing tomorrow?"

In an instant, Josephine has completely forgotten about the mission. Completely forgotten about this life-and-death debate. Wholly focused on the festival tomorrow. There is nothing Josephine likes more than parties, dressing up for events, forgetting—no matter how temporarily—this world we live in.

Sometimes I wish I was more like her.

"A pink qipao," she says, grinning ear to ear. "Not a Midnight Court color, I know. Girly, I know. But I *hate* that stereotype. I'm so over it. I'm going to make pink the new black."

I laugh. "That is so like you."

Josephine could turn the world on its head if she wanted to.

The festival is, I suspect, just another way for the courts to spread their feathers, show off their patterned plumage. A way to put their wealth and power on display.

The main event is held in the Midnight Court building. The ballroom is an explosion of red and yellow. Everywhere, there are paper lanterns hanging from the ceiling, the lights inside flickering in some imitation of real fire. The entire room is bathed in a warm, diffused glow that is so at odds with the people here tonight.

Mooncakes are laid out by the dozens in the back where tables have been set up, Chinese characters engraved like runes on top. I don't even know where they've gotten so many.

The room, as large and grand as it is, is almost completely packed. Filled to the brim with people from both the Midnight Court and the Dawn Court. Even after nine years, it is still so strange to see.

"Anna, mooncake!" It's my cousin Willow, waving her arms to get my attention as if we're the only ones in the room. As if people from both courts aren't staring at her like she's lost her mind. There's mooncake in her mouth; I can tell from the way the left side of her cheek is bulging where she pushed it aside to speak.

I laugh. Shake my head, mouthing *I'm okay*. I am not loud and brazen enough to do what she did. I hope she can read my lips.

She shrugs, stuffing another one in her mouth as if to say *More for me, then.*

In one corner of the room, almost all of the children are piled around a circular table. Dawn Court and Midnight Court alike, seemingly uncaring that they owe their allegiance to different kings. Different empires.

I find that I can't stop staring at them—can't stop staring at the ease and childlike wonder that comes with youth, and suddenly, I'm wondering where mine has gone. I am struck so cogently by this feeling of *missing*, of longing for days when I was still too young to understand what living meant, for a time when I thought that good deeds and pure thoughts could be currency to live by and when the lights and glitz of this city did more than just emphasize the shadows.

Sometimes I wonder if you ever really let go of your childhood. If you can set yourself free from it, if you really want to. Or if it just lingers inside you forever—like wingless birds, like broken memories. Fragments because you can never really remember it all.

The Emperor's voice pulls me back to reality with an abruptness that makes me blink. "Anna." His voice is booming, and he's not even trying to be loud. "Come, I want to introduce you to a few people."

Right now, I'm wishing I had the affinity for politics that my parents have. Unfortunately, my political interest extends to about the same level as my interest in embroidery. Read: none.

For a weak second, I debate pretending I simply didn't hear, but it is an empty consideration. It wobbles and breaks down even before the thought fully makes its way through my brain. I make my way over. I'd rather not find out what my parents would say if they heard I had *ignored* the Emperor.

"Yes, sir, I'm—"

My words die in my throat. Dissolve, like they were never meant to exist in the first place. Time dies next. Seconds fading away and I swear I can hear the clock ticking with each one that disappears.

Tick, tick, tick.

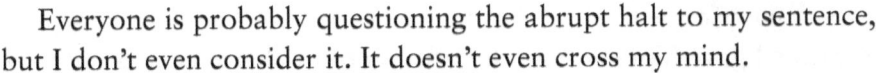

Everyone is probably questioning the abrupt halt to my sentence, but I don't even consider it. It doesn't even cross my mind.

The only thing I'm thinking is, *What the hell is Paris Ateş doing at this Midnight Court event?* But of course he would be here.

It is just my luck that I don't see him for three years and then, in just the past three days, I've seen him twice. And the first time he poisoned me.

My first instinct is to open the *tie shan* in my hand and throw it at his face—maybe mar its beauty just a little—but I force myself to hold still. Remind myself that the Emperor has no idea what happened three days ago, and he can't know.

"Sir," I say. "You summoned me."

"Yes." He continues, as though the mildly awkward pause didn't just happen. He extends an arm out to Paris and to a man who, I assume, is his father—the Dawn Court king.

"This is Gideon Ateş, the...leader of the Dawn Court. He wanted to meet you before you are to head into his territory." There is an undercurrent in his voice, something a little lighter than mocking, than hostility, but there, nonetheless. Reminding me that as cordially as these two men stand side by side, they are still enemies. Reminding me to be cautious.

"It's a pleasure to meet you, sir," I say, reaching out to shake his hand. I am agonizing over this handshake. How do people decide on the correct degree of firmness? I can't tell if I'm squeezing his fingers too tight in an attempt to seem more confident than I am.

"The pleasure is mine." He is so smooth, so self-assured. I can't read anything in his face and I'm beginning to realize where Paris gets it from—just how similar they are. "Annabella Liang, is it?" he asks.

I haven't heard anyone call me by my full name in so long it startles me for a second. I blink. "Just Anna is fine."

"Anna." He repeats it with some tone of finality. I just nod.

"And it's been a while since you two have seen each other," Emperor Xia cuts in, ironically echoing words I heard too recently. "I'm sure it must've slipped your mind already, but his son, Paris. You two will be working together for the next few months."

Months? Something unsettles in my stomach. A very substantial part of me is remembering that the last time I worked with Paris, the last time I gave him my trust, he left it and the shattered pieces of my heart all over the ground.

I swallow and say, "I remember." Paris doesn't reach out a hand and neither do I—my heartbeat is already out of control, and I don't want to know what will happen if I touch his skin.

"I look forward to it," Paris says. The corner of his mouth twitches slightly and something red-hot is burning its way through my chest.

"Yeah, me too." It is an Olympic effort to keep my voice from shaking—from anger or something else, I can't tell.

He smiles.

I can't stand it anymore. I can't.

"Excuse me," I say. "Paris, would you mind walking with me? Just to discuss our...plan for the future."

His eyebrows raise. I've caught him by surprise—a rare moment. Then, "Of course."

"We'll be back soon," I tell the Emperor with a curtsy, and then loop my arm around Paris's, plastering the most artificial of smiles on my face.

"Why—"

"Outside," I say.

His arm, even through the layer of fabric, is burning a hole into my skin. My hand is itching for the *tie shan* or the knife in my dress, as if I'm going to use it. I know I'm not. Not now, anyway.

Memories are flashing through my mind, every little thing bringing flashbacks that burn through my brain, and it is like I am playing "remember the last time" by myself.

It has been barely two minutes, and already I am questioning my ability to actually kill this boy, actually go through with the assignment the Emperor gave to me—and this is really,

really

not good.

We walk down several escalators, stride past the guards in the lobby, push through the front doors. And then Paris lets go of my arm. Turns to me with narrowed eyes. Says, "Okay, *what?*"

I shove the iron-coated edge of my *tie shan* to his throat.

CHAPTER 6

"**I** should kill you," I say. "For what you did three nights ago."
What I don't say is: *and three years ago.* "You have a lot of nerve coming here."

He stares straight back at me. "No offense, Anna, but if it was my choice, I would be very, very far from Shanghai."

"You poisoned me. You threatened people I care about! Don't you ever threaten Josephine. *Ever.* Do you understand?"

"It's not that I don't understand, Anna, but I'm afraid I can't agree to your demands. Threatening is a relatively effective way of protecting my interests. And I would really appreciate it if you could remove your fan from my throat."

"I would've really appreciated it three days ago if you had removed your gun from my head," I say, but I drop my arm anyway. "Why did you agree to this? Why you, and not one of your siblings? Or someone from your inner circle?"

Do you know I have to kill you? It suddenly occurs to me that the Dawn Court might be planning something similar. That Paris might have orders to kill me just as I do for him.

"It's not like I have much of a choice," he says, crossing his arms. "Come on, keep walking. Everyone can hear us here." He leaves without waiting for me to respond and I'm stuck hurrying to catch up. I shoot daggers at his back.

It's amazing how much the city is transformed on this one day.

The Bund is almost completely illuminated, alight with the same lanterns that decorate the ballroom. But there is so much more.

Out on the water, giant inflatable dragons and light-up lotuses float on the river, casting a rippling reflection on the black. The streets too have not been spared. There are parade floats and lantern shows and people streaming by with flaming torches and such outrageous costumes that I almost laugh.

Sometimes even I still find this city incredible.

Paris isn't looking at me when I finally catch up to him. I wonder if standing on this Shanghai stone is bringing back the ten years of memories, ten years of living here. I wonder what it must feel like.

This feels, I suddenly think, so peculiar. It is like walking in a fever dream, everything hazy and distorted under a film of oil. It does not feel quite real.

In my head, I'm thinking it's almost like we've gone three years back in time. Not like we've been transported from the present to the past, but more like this *is* it. Like we are still fifteen and sixteen.

It is almost déjà vu, what we are doing right now, because three summers ago, we were in this exact same position. Walking down the Bund, side by side. I was hyperaware of *everything*—the kiss of the breeze coming in from the river, the chime of laughter from the children playing by the water's edge, but most of all, I was aware of *Paris*. His presence, his proximity, the heat of his skin where his fingers entwined in mine, and I remember thinking, *This is what bliss is made of.*

That summer was the hottest it had been in the past decade, and because of it, somehow, it felt like a break from reality. Like nothing mattered and nothing would and this age-old rivalry between our two courts was on the back burner. Like it never really existed at all. We knew the consequences, the implications of what we were doing, Paris and I, but it was almost inconsequential. At that point, it felt like integration, like lasting peace was so close on the horizon we could touch it. Taste it. Reach out a finger and feel it on our skin like some tangible thing. It was peace as we had never known it.

The city itself was full of hope, glittering and golden, and for the first time, it felt like the door was open. That the end was in sight, and it made us giddy. It made us heady and drunk. And that, I think, that was our downfall.

Without preamble, Paris says, "My father thinks Eladine Academy is a good cover." Three years ago, he always referred to Gideon Ateş as *the king*. Now, it is *my father*, and I suppose Paris has finally assimilated. Really become one of them. I have no idea why the thought sends another pang echoing through my stomach.

"Everyone else except for me and Talia have graduated," he continues, "and she's years too young to even start, so it has to be me. Besides, what would you have me say to him? No?"

"You don't seem particularly concerned that someone's holding a vial of poison that could murder your entire family."

Paris ducks his head to avoid walking into a hanging lantern. "We face threats to our lives every day, don't we? It is, very simply, just what being born into this life entails. I could be poisoned anywhere, anytime. It doesn't make a difference that this one was created just for my blood."

"It does mean someone's intent on killing you, though," I point out.

He shrugs. "That doesn't exactly constitute a difference."

I am suddenly struck by how absolutely ludicrous this entire situation is. That I have not seen Paris in so many years. That three days ago—probably to the hour—I was tied to a chair by this boy I am now having a casual conversation with. That in a couple of months, I will have to stab a knife into this same boy.

"And you're okay with this? Us working together? *Me* moving to London?"

He shoots me a look I can't quite interpret. "Why wouldn't I be?"

I rub at my eyes, suddenly exhausted by this verbal dance we're doing. "Can we just talk straight for a minute?"

He makes a gesture as if to say *go ahead.*

"What are you doing here, seriously? Why is this the first time you've come back?"

Paris stops, rests his forearms on the black railing. He chooses his words carefully. "After I left, I admit I didn't quite have a desire to come back to this city. To Shanghai. Everywhere and everything felt tainted to me. Every memory of mine that I had made in the ten years—and then some—of my life that I spent here.

"And London." He smiles. Shakes his head. "London was something new. It was a completely blank slate with absolutely no one that I knew, no one who knew who I was. And that was beautiful to me." He throws me a glance. "You've been to London. I assume you know what I mean."

"Shanghai," I say, "is also nice." I'm not sure why I feel so defensive. Really, I'm still stuck back on the *everything is tainted*.

A faint smile drifts across Paris's lips, an almost sardonic smile. "Shanghai will always be a part of me, but my loyalty is to the Dawn Court now."

I'm not sure what to say to him now. I've forgotten everything I wanted to ask him; it's slipped from my mind like it was made of water and now all that remains is mist. Evaporated. I keep getting the sensation that we're tiptoeing around something here, but I'm not sure what it is.

A couple yards down, a group of kids are chasing each other around the street with glow sticks. Their laughter carries to where we're standing, drifting into the quiet.

And then Paris says, "Can you believe we were ever that young?" He's observing them, not looking at me; the question feels more to himself than it is to me, but I answer anyway.

"No."

I can't resist studying him, studying his face when I know he's distracted. The lights of the city are reflected in his eyes, casting a glaze over the green and gold.

It hurts to look at him like this. Inches away. Asking the questions I have wanted to ask him, and it is

too painful.

Brings back memories I don't want to remember, don't want to take out of the box I stuffed them in years ago and run a finger over their surfaces like they haven't been sharpened to the edges of blades, like they haven't already cut me before.

I realize with an intensity that startles me that I don't know him anymore, this boy standing next to me. I haven't the faintest idea who he is any more than I know his father, or any of his siblings.

It is a weird sensation, I think, to see two different people in one face, and not one easily explained. I wonder what he must think about me.

Suddenly, he stills, muscles tense and eyebrows drawn in concentration.

"What is it?" I hiss.

He shushes me. Then, "Someone's watching us."

"What? How do you know?" I cast a quick, furtive glance around, but I don't see anything.

Paris rolls his eyes. "I can feel it with my sixth sense. Can you just trust me?" And then he says a quick, "Come on," and he's gone again, melting into the crowd so rapidly that I lose him for a minute.

I think, *I'm going to kill him too early and ruin my entire assignment if he does this one more time.* And then I plunge in after him.

I am eternally grateful for the training my parents made me go through if only for this moment. For the fact that I'm able to weave through the crowd without unintentionally slamming into some lit-up paper lantern or costumed body, and make it to the other side decently unscathed.

Paris motions with a quick jerk of his head toward a narrow alleyway, and then we're off again. He turns corner after corner, strides down winding street after winding street and I'm beginning to wonder if he even has a destination in mind or if we're just lost before he slips past a gate and disappears into the darkness.

"Where are we?" I whisper, but—oh.

I recognize it. It's one of the gardens located near the Midnight Court building, one that we kids used to go to all the time. One that Paris and I went to together years later. It's been a long time since I was here.

I have to blink seven times before I process it.

"I'm surprised you still remember how to get here," I say, twisting around.

"Yes, well, so am I." Paris glances behind me, at the entryway we just passed through. "I can't see if they're still there or not."

I look too, but considering I didn't even see the person to begin with, I'm not sure how helpful it is.

"I doubt it," I say anyway. "You turned so many corners I almost lost you."

"Added bonus."

If I were my sister, I would've stabbed him with my knife by now. Anything not too close to major arteries wouldn't do too much damage.

Who am I kidding?

"Who do you think it was?" I ask.

"I don't know. They were standing too far to hear anything, so it's not like they collected anything of much value."

"They saw us talking," I point out. "That's plenty."

"Is it? Perhaps we're simply stepping out. Taking a pleasant stroll. Enjoying each other's company." Even Paris can't mask his sarcasm with that one.

I don't know why I'm blushing. I'm thankful for the darkness and the fact that he isn't looking at my face.

"Right. Sure."

I'm glancing around the garden now that the immediate danger has dissipated. It looks almost exactly the same, willows and miniature bridges and lily pads floating on water. Same persimmon trees. I look away.

In the Moon Festival fervor, carnation-red paper lanterns have been hung from the trees and multicolored lotuses placed in the ponds. It's so artificial looking it's almost a style all in itself.

"I haven't been here in years," I say, running my eyes across everything as though they are fingers, stroking.

Paris doesn't say anything for a moment, just looks at me. And then leans back against the fence and asks, "Why?"

I glance at him, feeling the incredulity in my own eyes. "Why do you think?"

Silence. Seconds whizz by like flies near my ears and I'm thinking, maybe it was too soon. Maybe I should've just left it alone, continued tiptoeing around it like both of us are not walking on eggshells but avoiding them, until finally,

quietly, he says, "Right."

Not an acknowledgment of anything. Not a dismissal of it either.

It's hanging in the air between us, a very real, very dense thing that I am terrified to touch.

Suddenly, I think, he is so close. Too close. This position, *everything*, is too intimate. Too familiar. It is terrifying how easily we fall back into these same patterns, how easily my mind forgets everything that has happened, and for a moment, I want it back. This. Him. With an intensity that makes it hard to breathe. It is like something in my brain has been hardwired to love him and no matter what I do, no matter what I tell myself, I can't change it.

He's watching me, an expression in his eyes I can't read. Watching. Waiting. Waiting for me to do something, pull back, lean in—except I'm frozen. Every cell in my body has been iced over, turned to stone, refuses to move, and I am trying my hardest to pull away, but whatever force, whatever magnet is drawing me here won't let go.

Except then he says, "Anna," and the spell is momentarily broken. Within a second, I've slipped the *tie shan* out of my sleeve and pressed it against his jaw, the blade glinting coldly in the moonlight, and he doesn't move. Doesn't even react. Just stares at me with a look that is half-challenge in his eyes, and I am overwhelmed by this barrage of emotion.

Longing and hatred and shame and nostalgia all in one. We're so close I can see the pulse in his throat, can see the ring of gold around his pupil bleached silver in the darkness.

His eyes haven't changed.

They are exactly the same as they were three years ago, green and gold and fringed with eyelashes that are like soot against his skin and it knocks the breath straight out of me. Everything about him is too much, too intense, tugs too many emotions from my body and I feel ready to break, ready to explode.

My heartbeat is colliding with his, a chaotic rhythm of beats that twine around each other, so entangled I can no longer even differentiate his from my own, and I'm thinking the physical expressions of fear and hatred are too much like love and lust and yearning that I'm afraid my body is going to forget which is which.

Paris doesn't step back, doesn't move away. Instead, he steps closer until the razor edge of the *tie shan* is pressed into his skin, until it draws a crimson bead of blood that is entirely too human.

"Do it, then," he says. "Kill me. I know you've thought about this moment more than once in the past three years."

I'm trembling. My entire body is shaking except for the hand that is holding the *tie shan*, and I am trying so hard to push it in. Just a little further. I should, after everything that he has done to me, to my family, to my court.

But I have never been able to kill Paris, despite how much I desperately wanted to three years ago. Despite how much I should have.

In an abrupt movement, I've stepped back, flung the *tie shan* onto the ground, and my knees are suddenly so numb they won't hold me up anymore. All the bones have dissolved in my legs and I sit down, heavily, on the raised curb.

Drop my head into my hands.

Whisper, "Oh god."

I'm so weak. I have always been weak where Paris is concerned, and it is this weakness that threatens to kill me. It is this weakness that killed twelve of my people, took their lives and threw it six feet underground, and I'm still trying to process what happened. Still trying to understand.

I have been reeling for three years.

"Anna," Paris says. He's kneeling down, at eye level with me.

"I should hate you," I interrupt. "It's because of you that my hands are stained with the blood of my own people. And *yours*," I add, fiercely. "Yours are too, and I should hate you all the more for it."

I raise my head to meet his gaze and he's looking steadily back at me. His face is closed off and this distance between us suddenly feels like miles.

Calmly, he says, "It had to be done. And no one stained your hands but you. You chose to make yourself responsible."

"It wasn't a *choice*," I hiss. "It just *was*."

I stand up. "Unlike the decision you made."

He looks at me. Sighs. Says, "It's been years. We might as well just agree that we're never going to see eye to eye on this, that it's just not something we're going to get over and move on. Don't forget we have to work together for the next few months."

Right. That.

"Don't worry," I say. "I've learned my lesson."

His expression is unreadable. "Yeah, so have I."

Paris stands up. Brushes nonexistent lint from his pants and says, "We should head back. We've been gone awhile."

I don't argue. All I want to do is get away from this, this too-tight feeling in my chest, this sensation like the air around us is too full of cotton, this *confusion* in my brain.

He doesn't say another word until we're back, until we're standing on the steps of the Midnight Court building.

"I just want to stress that this doesn't automatically imply friendship," he says. "We do this, we find whoever is responsible for stealing that vial so that my court is safe and yours proves its innocence, and then we're done. As clean as possible. It's easier that way, right?"

"Right," I say. It won't matter in the end, anyway. I hope it doesn't show on my face.

"Good," he says, and then he's gone.

I'm left standing on the top of the stairs wondering what in the hell I've signed up for. Thinking I've really done it this time.

And then I take a deep breath and follow him in.

CHAPTER 7

Leaving, I think, is such a strange sensation. In the moment, it almost feels as if the people, this lifestyle you're leaving will never fit together in the same way again. It feels like the end, even though it isn't.

I've never left Shanghai for more than a few weeks at a time. And now that I'm going to London for the four months that is the duration of the semester, it feels like the death of this way of life that I have known for so long.

Leaving, in short, is the epitome of melodrama.

This isn't the first time that I'm going to London. It's not even the second. Katerina and I have accompanied our parents there every time the Dawn Court has held a summit in the nine years since the accords were signed.

But I have to admit, there aren't many specifics that I remember about it. The memories I do have are fragmented, fractions of a whole that align in a way that doesn't quite make sense.

"I just don't understand why we have to leave so early in the morning," Josephine complains, eyeing one of the workers as they drag her preposterous number of suitcases onto the plane.

"Well, if we left any later we would get there in the middle of the night," I say. "Besides, six a.m. isn't *unthinkably* early. Some people even get up at five just for fun."

"I know *that*," Jo returns. "But it doesn't take into account the

fact that there are a million things to do before we even *get on the plane*. Like, for example, I had to finish packing, had to get dressed, had to shower, had to brush my teeth. It's a tightly packed schedule, Anna."

"You could've, as an alternative, finished packing last night like I did. Or shower at night instead of the morning like I do. Would've saved you a lot of time."

"Yeah, yeah. Your way is the right way—I got it."

"Exactly."

Five minutes later, we're on the plane ready for takeoff. Josephine despises flying with a passion that I have never really understood.

I love it.

The feeling of leaving the ground, positioned completely in the air, hurtling toward a place that no human being was ever meant to go. Above the clouds with a view that no human being was ever meant to see.

It's a special kind of thrill.

Today feels more bittersweet than anything. Rising into the sky until Shanghai looks smaller than it ever should, the Pearl Tower looking like a Monopoly board piece and the Huangpu River like a thick segment of string.

From up here, it's hard to ignore how similar Shanghai looks to London. Just another city built on the banks of a river; no one really cares that the names are different, just that they look almost identical. This high up, it's almost impossible to be bothered by everything that's going on down below. In this little pocket of space, I feel almost removed from time. Caught in honey, in amber.

The flight time from Shanghai to London is twelve hours, give or take. Extremely inconvenient for dual-court meetings, but I have never minded the long flight.

"God, I *hate* flying," Josephine says. She's reclined her seat back all the way and her fingers are repeatedly tapping against the armrest. "These planes are so small and slow and give me claustrophobia."

Claustrophobia. Yet another reason Jo hates flying. It's almost as if this activity was specifically tailored to incorporate every one of her fears and dislikes.

"Sorry," I say. "You technically don't even need to be here."

She waves a hand at me. "Oh, stop. Where you go, I go. I'm latched onto your ass forever, Anna."

I snort. "Exactly what I wished for in life."

"As you should. Besides, if I blame anyone, I blame Huang Shang."

I bite my lip. "Don't let anyone else hear you saying that."

"Yeah, yeah. There's no one else here anyway except the pilots in the cockpit. Besides, what is His Majesty the Emperor going to do to me, anyway?"

"Anything," I say. "Make you eat an entire chocolate cake, like in *Matilda*. Or make you clean the entire Midnight Court building like his own sick version of Cinderella."

"I'm so scared."

"He could also execute you with any absurd reason he comes up with."

Josephine scoffs. "When was the last time someone was executed?"

Sometimes I think she's brave, bordering on reckless. She takes the world—and its very real consequences—a little too cavalierly for my comfort. Just because things have been quiet recently doesn't mean they're going to stay that way.

But I don't bother to say anything to her. Josephine is more *talker* than *listener*, and I suspect it'll be a very cold day in hell before that changes.

By the time we arrive, it's 6:00 p.m. in London, meaning it's 2:00 a.m. in Shanghai. God, time zones. I hate them almost as much as Jo hates planes. Thankfully, I was able to sleep a bit on the plane—and am wide awake for whatever is to come.

By some miracle, or careful planning by the Council, our arrival coincides exactly with move-in day for the first-years, so we don't stick out like sore thumbs. The plane touches down on some landing strip we've been told is near the school, and then the ramp is being lowered and we're stepping out onto Dawn Court soil. I almost feel like I'm committing treason just by being here. Just by breathing this air. And then I hear a "holy shit" from Josephine, which makes me look up.

Holy shit is, in fact, the correct phrase in this particular situation.

The Dawn Court has truly outdone themselves this time. The landing strip isn't just near the school, but on the campus itself, and the school is a giant *glass* structure edged in bronze, carved in a lotus shape oddly reminiscent of the artificial lotuses I had seen just yesterday. It's probably three to four stories high and surrounded by a sprawling garden that I assume functions as the school campus.

There are little *bridges* and *flowering trees* and *ponds* and I can't quite believe my eyes.

Behind the Lotus, I can just make out a square that's outlined by identical short buildings, which I think might be the dormitories. Like a little quad.

They really did their best to make this seem like some university.

"Holy Jesus," Josephine mutters.

"Yes," I say. "Exactly that."

"Now, why doesn't the Midnight Court have one of these?"

"Maybe the Dawn Court is richer?" I suggest.

"Yeah." A snort. "Right."

A man with salt-and-pepper hair cropped close to the scalp strides up to us. He looks to be in his mid-forties, dressed in a casual white button-down with gray pants. He stretches out a hand as he approaches us, and Josephine and I shake it cautiously.

"Hello," he says, pleasantly. "My name is Harold Yates. I'm one of the administrative assistants here at Eladine and I'll be helping you get settled in." Before either of us can respond, he points at the structure behind us and continues, rapid-fire. "That's the main building. We call it the Lotus. Virtually all of your classes will be there. The dormitories are just a little ways away.

"Move-in technically began a couple hours ago, so everyone has already mostly moved their things in, but the two of you can just leave your suitcases here and I'll have someone bring them to your dormitory for you." Mr. Yates is speaking so fast I can barely even process what he's saying before he moves on. "For now, you should attend the assembly for incoming students in the main hall. You can just follow everyone else into the Lotus. Any questions?"

I blink at him. Josephine squeaks, "No."

He nods. "Well, in you go, then. I'll meet the two of you after the assembly to guide you to the dormitories."

We follow the stream of students heading into the building. The Lotus is, in reality, a lot larger than it seemed on the outside. There are dozens of hallways that branch off from the lobby—which is also offensively gigantic—and a section that connects to the Lotus that looks like a large horizontal balloon.

We file into a hall that I assume is the dining area. True to form, it's similarly massive. Great, crystal chandeliers hang from the ceiling, throwing warm light onto the wood walls and flinging intricate patterns onto the vaulted ceiling. Four long columns of small tables of four fill the majority of the space with students crowded one next to the other on the benches. Everywhere, chatter in varying degrees of volume fills the air, flooding pockets of space. My brain, I think, is failing to process it all.

It seems, though, from the almost awestruck expressions and giddy chatter, that everyone here is a first-year. Not a single upperclassman in sight, which calms my nerves a little. At the very least, I'm guaranteed no accidental collision with Paris.

Josephine and I are met by another member of the Eladine staff who asks for our names and then guides us to our seats. The seating must be assigned somehow, I think—by last name? She weaves through the tables with the practiced air of someone who has been doing this for years, stopping at a table on the edge where two girls are already sitting. They wave to us shyly as we sit down.

"Is this all first-years?" the girl sitting across from me asks, echoing my thoughts. She has brown hair and a soft face, the kind that has no hard edges to its features.

"I think so," the other girl answers. "Didn't the upperclassmen move in a week ago?"

"Something like that, I think." She sounds unsure. "Are you guys Dawn Court or Midnight Court?"

The question startles me. I'd known that the school has been open to students from both courts since the accords, but I hadn't really thought Midnight Court students would attend, being so far from Shanghai.

"Midnight Court," Josephine says, and I just now realize the girl had been directing the question to all of us: Josephine and me, who are across from her, as well as the other girl sitting to her left.

"Oh, wow! I've never actually met a Midnight Courter in person before. Sorry," she says, blushing. "I didn't mean for that to sound like you guys are animals in a zoo."

I stifle a laugh.

Josephine says, "You didn't. And to be fair, I haven't met many Dawn Courters either."

We're interrupted by a noise that cleanly slices through the chatter in the room.

"May I have everyone's attention, please!" We all look in the direction the voice came from. A man is standing at the front of the room, short with round silver spectacles that keep slipping down his nose. He pushes them back up.

I make eye contact with Josephine, struggling to hold in my laughter.

"Hello, new students," he says. "I wanted to extend a warm welcome on behalf of all the faculty and myself to all of you who have made your way here today. Congratulations on being accepted into Eladine.

"My name is Gerard Eladine. My great-grandfather founded this school many, many years ago as a place to teach young people like yourselves the art of espionage. Gathering intelligence, hand-to-hand combat, six hundred and seventy-two ways to kill a man. Of course, as you all know, this was long before the relative period of peace we know now."

At his pause, there is a sudden rush of chatter in the room. I hear snippets of whispers, excerpts of conversation dancing in the air—*"Eladine?" "I didn't know there were descendants." "I didn't even know Eladine was the last name of a person."* Gerard waits for the noise to die down before continuing.

"Today, this school is meant to train you for royal service. My colleagues will touch on that more later. Now, you will be assigned to teams. For those of you who don't know, all Eladine students are divided into fifty different teams. It is these teams that you will work with, sleep with, live with."

Jesus, fifty.

"I hope you use your time here wisely. It is absolutely up to you how much you learn. Now, I'd like to introduce Professor Song to speak about the program a bit more in depth."

A woman steps up this time. She's Asian with thick black hair held up in a chignon at the back of her neck and a stern, kind face. I stare at her, mildly curious because it is rare to see Asian people in the Dawn Court.

"Thank you, Gerard," she says, "And hello, students. I am Eleanor Song, professor of Poisons and Potions. It is very, very nice to meet all of you.

"Tomorrow, you will meet your cohort leaders. They are collectively known as the *praefectus*. There is one per individual team. Each of them was the best and brightest of their class. Ask them your questions. Go to them with your concerns. They are resources for you. Remember, they were once in your shoes as well.

"Any questions before I continue?"

The room is so silent it's like all the sound has been sucked out of it by a vacuum. And then slowly, slowly, someone raises a hand.

It's a boy in the front. All I can see is the back of his head—black hair.

"Are they all second-years, the praefectus, I mean? Or are they other years too?" He has an accent that doesn't quite sound like it's from the city. I'd figured everyone here would be from London proper, or at least around it since the Dawn Court itself is in London city, but I guess not.

I almost miss Professor Song's response. "All second-years," she's saying. "Your cohorts will change every year. First and second-years are together. Third and fourth-years are together. As such, your cohorts are led by second-years. Next year, some of you may become cohort leaders. Once you enter your third year, those will be fourth-years. Clear?"

I think I see him nod.

"All right, one more thing before I let you go. All of you are required to undergo Initiation the day after tomorrow. For those of you who don't know what that is, ask a friend or an upperclassman to explain it in more detail to you. But in very, very simple terms, it is a test that analyzes the most basic skills necessary for survival here at Eladine. You must meet a specific benchmark to be allowed to continue.

"Now, take a look at your tables. Each is divided into sections of four people. Whoever is in your section are the ones you will spend the coming year with. I promise by the end, you will know each other almost as well as you know yourselves."

With that, she dismisses us. The hall is abuzz with noise—voices, mostly, and the grating scrape of chair legs against the floor as everyone scrambles to leave.

"How does everyone just know where they're going?" I ask in wonder, watching the stream of people leaving the room dwindle until it's almost a trickle.

"Older siblings, maybe?" Josephine suggests. "Or friends? Or maybe it's just something you know, like, as a Dawn Courter."

"I feel behind already."

"It's not like we're actually in this school."

I shush her, quietly. *"Undercover, Jo!"*

"Oops," she says, not looking apologetic in the slightest.

Out of the corner of my eye, I spot Mr. Yates walking toward us, sidestepping the steady line of students exiting the hall. I nudge Josephine with my elbow.

"How did you like the assembly?" he asks us, stopping in front of us with a courteous smile.

"It was nice," I say. I never know how to answer when people ask these things.

"Informative," answers Josephine.

"Good," Mr. Yates answers. "I'll show you two to your dormitory now."

As we fall into step behind him, Josephine whispers, "I can't believe you have to work with Paris."

It's almost dark already. The whole speech inside the dining hall must've taken longer than I thought. In the distance, the dying rays of the setting sun are reflected in the glass and bronze of the Lotus until it's set ablaze, awash with colors of orange and crimson and indigo.

The glare is killing my eyes. I look away.

"Have you guys even talked about this?"

Josephine knows everything—what happened three years ago, four days ago, and the assignment. She is the one person I tell everything to, who I trust with my whole heart.

In truth, Paris and I did talk about it—but only briefly—after the whole garden fiasco. We're supposed to meet; tomorrow, I think. To discuss—whatever that means. I don't even know how to start. How do the Emperor and my parents expect me to work with him and conduct my *activity on the side*? I have no idea how I'm going to pull this off.

"A bit," I answer, and Josephine doesn't press me.

Mr. Yates leads us to the square of buildings I saw earlier, the ones I figured were dormitories. I was right. People are piling into them, disappearing behind oak doors until there is almost no one left out on the quad. He stops, pointing to one of the buildings to our right. "That one's the dormitory you two will be living in. Your suitcases are already there, so you can just go straight in and unpack."

"Got it. Thanks, Mr. Yates," Jo says.

He nods to both of us and then disappears back the way we came.

It's a two-story building. That much I can tell. Standing in the entrance, I can see that the entire downstairs is actually one giant room, and it is so much larger than I thought it was from the outside. A recurring theme today, it seems. The ceiling is warm wood, punctuated here and there by brass chandeliers that throw dancing shadows onto the wall. The walls themselves are white, or some variation of it. Ivory. Cream. Across, brass sconces blaze, two per side.

"Does it seem particularly symmetrical to you?" Jo whispers to me.

It is. Very symmetrical. Very, very square. There are two couches to our left and right, two wrought iron and glass tables in front. Exactly the same.

Directly in front of us, two enormous windows consume most of the wall space. Although it's dark out, the gleaming, burnished gold curtains are open wide. Nestled between the windows, a giant fireplace blazes.

"They must've had to come up with an efficient design for the entire school," a girl—the one without the brown hair—says, having heard Josephine's earlier comment to me. I should really learn their names. "It's a wonder they did it so well."

I don't disagree with her. It *is* nice.

"I wonder who else is in our cohort," the brown-haired girl says. "Although I guess we won't find out until classes start. What are your names, by the way?"

"Josephine," says Jo.

"Anna," I say.

"Oooh, my cousin's name is Anna too. But hers is short for Annabeth—you know that famous Percy Jackson character? Is yours short for something too?"

"Annabella," I say. "But I don't really go by that."

"Just Anna, then." She nods. "What about you?" Now she's talking to the other girl in the room.

"Mariam," she says.

The brown-haired girl nods. "I'm Cassie."

The four of us spend the next two hours unpacking suitcases, exploring our suite, and then the entire building until we've seen probably every inch of the white marble.

They really do take the whole white versus black thing seriously here. I've barely seen a spot of black since I walked into Eladine.

It's 10:00 p.m. when everyone leaves for their respective rooms. 5:00 a.m. in Shanghai. I think about taking this time while I'm alone to report back to the Midnight Court, but I doubt anyone's awake anyway. I settle in, hoping sleep finds me.

By 5:00 a.m. London time, I'm wide awake. Sometimes I envy how easily Josephine sleeps—the way she can sleep, if left undisturbed, into the early afternoon. I head outside where the air is crisp and the sun has just barely crept over the horizon. September in London, and summer is already giving way to autumn. The musky-sweet scent of fallen leaves permeates the air like cheap perfume, suffocating me. I need to get out of this garden. Get away from this fake representation of a fake peace and cordiality, so reminiscent of that garden back in Shanghai. Amazing how things don't change even when you fly almost six thousand miles somewhere else.

I wander south. Eladine is a little ways from downtown, but I walk for so long I find myself passing by Buckingham Palace and Westminster, walking down Parliament Street back toward the Thames, somehow finding my way there even though I have no conscious memory of London's geography.

It's unsettling, sometimes, how our unconscious minds work.

In the early morning silence, I make a phone call to report to the Midnight Court—my mother answers. I give her the layout of Eladine and information about the cohorts and praefectus. Probably not actually very helpful information at this point, since Midnight Courters have been attending Eladine for years now, but I want her to know that I'm taking this assignment seriously. That I can be just as competent as my sister.

At the end of the call, right before she hangs up, she tells me, "Good job so far. Keep it up." And I feel a quick pulse of warmth through my chest.

I told myself I'd take a walk to clear my head, collect my thoughts, whatever it is that people do to be productive on walks, but I don't actually manage any of that.

Instead, I find myself staring at the buildings and the red buses that are like bright red candy hearts chugging down the street. The sounds of the city waking up surround me—the huff, and occasional honk, of the cars and buses, the footsteps and voices of thousands of people up and down these streets. I can smell the scent of candied nuts hanging in the air, adding just a tinge of sweet to the always present acidity of exhaust and the salty-sour tang of the Thames.

It's so strange, I think, to be in a certain place one morning and then wake up the next morning half a world away. I wonder if it ever bothers anyone else. Here, every street sign and building and tube station—their underground subway—is screaming *Foreign! Foreign! Foreign!* at me. It's so loud inside my head.

I keep walking. I walk all the way down the bridge, all the way past the Eye and South Bank and back up Blackfriars and I keep looping around, as though I can somehow walk off this feeling of strangeness, of foreignness. I can't get used to it. It's like a second skin, and no matter how hard I scrub at it, how hard I try to wash it away with soapsuds and water, it won't come off.

It's 7:00 a.m. by the time my feet finally tire of walking, tire of repeating the same actions over and over again.

Deciding that I might as well text Paris and ask him where he wants to meet today, I swipe open my phone. I've just started texting *we need to get started* when I hear a voice say, "Amazing. This city is six hundred seven square miles and I manage to bump into *you* at seven in the morning."

I whip around so fast I'm dizzy for a moment.

I blink. Blink again. I'm about to open my mouth to say something—I don't even know what—when Paris continues. "Is speaking no longer a natural function of the human body or is it just you?"

I ignore his remark. "I was just texting you," I say.

"Oh, were you?" He sounds uninterested.

Fighting the urge to roll my eyes, I ask, "Why are *you* awake this early? I'm jet-lagged. What's your excuse?"

"Do I require an excuse to wake up at seven? It's not like it's excessively early. Some people get up at four, you know."

"Some people aren't human."

"*People* is synonymous with *human*."

"Oh, get that stick out of your ass."

He laughs. Actually laughs. Says, "Yes, sure. Just for you."

"We need to figure out what the hell we're doing," I say. "I would really prefer to go home as soon as possible."

"Yes, fine. The faculty's going to call a meeting for all you first-years later today. Find me after. There are some people you need to meet."

I feel my eyebrows crease. "Where?"

Paris waves a hand. "I don't know. The lobby."

"Fine."

He seems amused at that. "Fine. I'll see you later." And then he's gone.

The so-called meeting for first-years lasts half an hour. It can barely even be called a meeting—just time set apart for us first-years to get to know each other more formally after the welcome dinner last night.

I find Paris in the lobby afterward. He's standing against one of the pillars, talking to a group of praefectus, laughing. And I realize I've never really seen him laugh before—well, not counting when he's laughing *at* me. Not in the genuine, carefree way you do with friends.

It's disconcerting.

I have to kill him.

The Midnight Court sent me a message last night—a letter through the embassy—reminding me of the assignment. Reminding me, in no uncertain terms, to stay focused and not to stray. As if I needed that reminder. It never leaves my head.

Paris catches my eye over the blonde head of the girl standing in front of him, across the fifteen feet of distance that separates us.

He makes a gesture like, *Hello? Why are you just standing there?*

I make some movement with my head that I hope conveys *I'm waiting for you to finish chatting, dipshit.*

And then he's walking toward me with a sigh. "Are you serious? Next time just come up to me."

"How was I supposed to know whether or not you'd mind being interrupted?"

"You can ask."

"That would be interrupting."

He heaves another exasperated sigh. "Okay, fine. I'm telling you, next time *interrupt me.*"

My "Jesus, okay, pushy" earns a roll of his eyes.

"So, where are we going, exactly?" I ask as we turn down one of the many hallways of the Lotus that all seem interwoven. It's like a maze, or some gigantic spiderweb, and I just don't understand the point of making a floor plan so complicated.

"You'll see."

"Give me that as an answer one more time and I *will* take a finger off." Paris looks at me like I've gone insane. I shrug. "Fair warning."

"Have I said it another time?"

"Ah," I say. "I can refresh your memory. Easily. Let me just say, I was tied to a chair."

"Oh, that," Paris says like I brought up some pleasant mutual memory. "I'd apologize to you, but I'm not quite sorry for it and it'd be unfair to lie to you, I think."

I feel myself blanch. "You think it's unfair to say sorry when you don't mean it, but it's perfectly fine to tie someone to a chair? And hold a knife to their throat? And *poison them? And threaten their friends?*"

"Didn't we already discuss that last part? Yes, I'm not sorry. I believe it was justified."

Before I can argue, Paris says, "We're here."

Here is staring at a stretch of blank wall that looks no different than the five inches following it, or the five inches preceding it, for that matter.

I stare. "The wall?"

"Patience, Anna." He pushes on it gently and it slides open like a door.

CHAPTER 8

We find ourselves standing in what seems to be a common room. It *looks* exactly like one, anyway. There are two white couches on the left in an L-shaped formation with a giant navy beanbag across from them, all situated in front of a wall of warped glass.

On the right is a pool table. I assume it's the actual glass that forms the outside of the Lotus. But the common room isn't what Paris brought me here for—at least, I hope.

There are three boys piled around the pool table—two playing, one sitting down. I have no idea what distinguishes first-years from second-years or even fourth-years, so I also have no idea what grade they're in or how old they are, but the logical assumption would be that they're the same as Paris. They're his friends, after all.

The three of them turn toward us when we walk in, heads swiveling until all three sets of eyes are on us. On me.

One

two

three seconds of silence.

Then, "Bro, have you already forgotten what happened last time you brought a girl in here?"

I blink. "What?"

"He's kidding," says Paris, by way of response. He waves a hand at them. "Devaj, Max, and Kyan."

"Spelled with a *Y*, not an *I*," says one of the boys at the pool table. "Not me—him." He points to the one sitting.

I blink again. "Okay."

"I'm Max."

"They're going to be working with us and Professor Song, as well. You'll meet her later." I recall Professor Song from the welcome. I'm almost grateful that it's her.

Paris leaves my side, walking over to the pool table so that he can see the game. He looks so natural there, so much like he completes whatever odd painting I'm looking at that I just keep staring.

"So, who's winning?" he asks. And just like that, their attention shifts resolutely back to the game.

It's Kyan who finally speaks to me. The first thing I notice is that he's pretty. Not handsome-pretty the way some men are, but actually, sincerely, pretty. Like he could pass for a girl if he wanted to—if he just grew out his hair, even.

He looks at least part Asian, I think. Maybe even full Asian—East, like me. I can tell by the black hair and brown eyes and the shape of his features. His parents—or someone somewhere in his line of ancestry—must've moved from a part of Asia far removed from the Shanghai Court to London before he was born and joined the Dawn Court. Rare, though it still happens. Even though I know he's Dawn, I feel inexplicably more at ease.

"You're Anna, right?" he asks me. His voice is soft.

I nod. "Has Paris told you about the"—I have no idea what to call it—"the assignment?"

"Most of it," Kyan says. "I know you're meant to find whoever stole the poison. I'm not exactly sure of the details, but I've never been interested in politics."

He says it with no inflection. Merely stating a fact.

"Me neither," I say. Confess. "Not really."

"You're from Shanghai, aren't you? You're Chinese?" He sounds genuinely curious and not at all hostile.

"Yes," I say. "A–are you?"

Kyan smiles slightly. Shakes his head. "Korean. My original name's Kang Kyung-Sun. Lots of *K*s."

I laugh, finally feeling a little less out of place here.

"Kyan!" one of the boys shouts from the pool table. "You gotta watch this shot, mate!"

We glance over just in time to see the cue ball shoot quickly past the eight ball, widely missing its target.

Silence. I see Paris struggling not to laugh out loud, turned away, shoulders shaking.

"Amazing shot," I say, deadpan. "You should try out for the national league."

The other boy is laughing. The one with brown skin and hazel eyes that I distinctly remember is called Devaj.

"She got you there, dude," he says, slapping Max on the back. "That might've been the worst shot I've ever seen."

"Shut up," Max says. "I'm still winning, anyway." He turns to me. "I'm playing you next, Anna!" he shouts.

I gape at him. "I don't play pool."

Max smirks. "I'll teach you."

Paris cringes.

Kyan says, "Please, no."

Devaj agrees. "Don't do it, Anna. Max does that stereotypical pool table flirting because he can't devise an original method."

"Shut up, Dev," Max says again.

"Oh, don't worry, I have no intentions of playing!" I'm laughing. And just for a moment, I almost forget what I'm doing here, the reality of my situation.

I can't keep doing that. I can't *imagine* what the four of them would say if they ever found out the truth of why I'm even here. Nor do I want to know.

"Anna, come closer," Dev says. He waves me over. "You don't want to miss the entertainment that is Max Williams playing pool."

I do, coming to stand next to Paris at the table. He watches me approach, face neutral, eyes unreadable. Watches until there is a painfully thin inch of space that separates us. Separates my left arm from his right arm.

I can feel his body heat.

Neither of us moves.

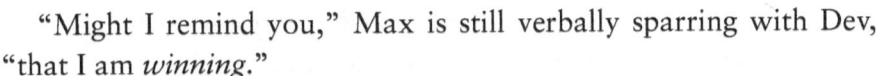

"Might I remind you," Max is still verbally sparring with Dev, "that I am *winning*."

"Yeah, yeah, for now. Talk to me again in five minutes."

"Well?" I ask, voice pitched low to Paris while Dev and Max continue bickering.

"Well, what?"

"Is there a point to this? Or did you bring me here just so I can watch a game of pool?"

Paris looks like he's trying hard not to roll his eyes again. "God, Anna, is it at all possible for you to refrain from obsessing over this for *one single minute*?"

"No!" I shoot back, indignant. "I would like—"

"To return to Shanghai as soon as possible. Yes, I know. But this isn't exactly as easily solved as going out and killing someone."

I huff out a breath of frustration. "I *know* that. But we can at least get started on something. A plan, at the very least. To be clear," I add, "the stakes are higher for you. This poison was created for your bloodline and yours alone. The Midnight Court only agreed to help to prove our innocence, which we aren't even obligated to do. Honestly, I don't even know why the Emperor agreed in the first place." That's a lie. "If you attack us, we can attack you right back. Both sides will hurt."

Paris sighs. Turns away from me to rap two short knocks on the table. "All right, wrap it up, gentlemen. Her Majesty the Queen has demands."

I glare daggers at him. He ignores me.

Five minutes later, the four of them are all sprawled on the couches with a casualness that speaks volumes to the ease they feel in this room. With each other.

The sudden change in the atmosphere throws me off-balance. Off-kilter.

There's this feeling of uncertainty, of being acutely aware that you don't belong when stepping into someone else's house. A feeling that blares *out of place* in the recesses of your brain.

"Anna, are you going to take a seat, or would you like to remain standing for the next half hour?"

I blink. Ironic that Paris's quips are what restores balance. I fold myself into the space on the couch next to him.

"We should get a whiteboard," Max says. "You know, create one of those detective spreads."

Dev snorts.

Kyan says, "This is serious, Max," but he's smiling faintly.

"All right." Paris turns toward me, an eyebrow raised. "What are you thinking?"

"Me?"

"You called this meeting."

I sigh. "Fine. I was thinking that first we can make a list of everyone who knew where the vial was. That way we can narrow down the suspect pool."

"That would be a great idea," says Dev. "Except we have no idea who had knowledge of the vial's location."

I stare. "None?"

"They hold meetings every year to discuss where to move the poison next, but everything's in code names," Paris explains. "And disguises." His mouth twists into a wry smile. "My father used the utmost caution—not that it mattered in the end."

"Is there anyone that you guys know for sure would be in that meeting?" I press. "Just one person."

"Probably the keeper of the grounds," Max says. "Because there's not a single nook and cranny of that wretched place that he doesn't know about. But he's not anywhere near the security clearance he needs to be of any use."

"Well," I say. "At least it's a start. How do we get to him?" I glance at Paris. "Can you—"

"We infiltrate the Dawn Court headquarters."

I gape at him, not sure if I just heard him correctly. "You want to infiltrate your own court? You're the king's son, why can't you just walk in?"

"Anna," he says patiently, as if he's explaining some sort of advanced concept, like multiplication or the rule of parentheses, to a toddler. "We're investigating something. We're trying to find someone, and we have no idea who this person is. For all we know, they can just as well be from the Dawn Court as the Midnight Court. I would rather not broadcast our every movement to the hundreds of people my father employs."

"Oh," I say. "Right. Okay, so I guess we...infiltrate?"

Paris's smile is self-satisfied. "I've never tried to sneak into my own house before. My father is not going to be amused."

"And that's a good thing?" I think I'm maybe looking at him like he's lost his mind.

"Of course. Can you imagine the look on his face when I inform him that his security is inadequate? That I was able to walk in unde-tected?" The corner of his mouth twitches.

A laugh escapes from Devaj.

"*Ookay*," I say. "For those of us who don't have a death wish, how exactly is this infiltrating going to work?"

"Paris knows the entire schedule of the guards," Kyan says, intently. "And probably every unguarded back door as well, I assume. That part won't be difficult."

"And what part will be?"

"The part where five people are inside a building full of guards and somehow need to stay unseen."

I think about it for a minute, pulling my legs into a crisscrossed position and leaning forward. "Okay, then we split up. We don't need five people to torture some information out of one man."

"*Torture*," Max repeats. He sounds impressed.

Dev lets out a snort and Kyan bites his lip to keep from laughing.

"Anyway," I continue. "I say two of us go find the groundskeeper, the other three find out the location of the vial when it was stolen. If we know that, we can narrow it down to who could've had access and figure it out from there."

"Sounds like a solid plan," says Max.

"As long as we don't get caught," Dev adds, shuddering. "I might get killed if we do."

I open my mouth to ask why, but a light nudge to my side stops me. "Dev's here on scholarship," Paris murmurs to me under his breath. "He always has to make sure he doesn't step a toe out of line because his family can't afford for him to get kicked out."

I swallow. I can't imagine what that's like, constantly worrying about being inside the lines, sticking to the rules. Faintly, I hear Max speaking quietly to Dev. "You know you don't have to go if you don't want to. We'd all understand."

But Dev just shakes his head. He clears his throat and says, loudly, "How are we doing the assignments?"

"I'm finding the groundskeeper," I answer. "No offense, but it's the more important task and I trust all of you about as far as I can throw you, as they say."

"I'm going with you," Paris says.

I stare at him, startled. Unsure if the sudden twisting in my stomach is anticipation or wariness.

"Why *you*?"

"Why *not* me?"

"I don't trust you! I don't trust you not to kill me or—or set me up or hand me over to your father as some sort of hostage or something."

Paris looks at me wryly. "And you trust them not to?"

"I trust anyone more than I trust you," I tell him. "I would trust a stranger on the streets of *London* more than I trust you."

"Oof," says Devaj.

Paris sighs. Exasperated seems to be his resting state with me these days. He says, flatly, "Well, I'm sorry to disappoint you, but you aren't worth nearly enough for me to put all that effort in. And while we're on the subject, I don't trust you either. So whatever Edenfield tells you when you find him, I'd rather hear it directly from him."

Dear god. "Fine," I snap. "Have it your way."

"Great." He smiles pleasantly. "Dev, Max, Kyan, you might want to look into my father's office. He most likely discussed the theft in his correspondence, which might be a useful place to start."

"Got it," says Max.

"When are we doing this?" I ask.

"Tomorrow," says Paris. "Obviously."

CHAPTER 9

Last night we ironed out the details of the plan. We go this afternoon at 4:30, after classes, and if anything goes wrong, it'll be the weekend anyway so we'll have a bit of extra time. The five of us will take one car to the Dawn Court together and split up half a mile away. Paris and I will go to Edenfield's house in the middle of the grounds and the rest of them will sneak into the main palace. And although I told Josephine the entire plan, I didn't want to involve her in this. Didn't want to put her at risk, especially since this assignment was never her responsibility in the first place.

It's not exactly a well-thought-out plan—most definitely not foolproof—but it's the best we have. The best we can come up with on such short notice.

I only hope it all goes smoothly.

I'm nervous all through classes. Today's the first day, so every new class starts with introductions—introductions both of the course and of ourselves.

It is both exhilarating and exhausting all at once.

My first class of the day is history, one of the many I share with Josephine. The two of us woke up at 6:00 for this 8:00 class to get ready—me out of stress and her out of excitement. She practically bounces out the door.

"Come on, Anna, we're going to be late!"

I check the time on my phone: 7:30. It's a ten-minute walk to the classroom, but I indulge her anyway. Plus, better safe than sorry.

The September air is already brisk. We walk through the gardens, appreciating the riot of colors in the leaves that are already beginning to change—green giving way to bold brushes of orange, scarlet, and gold. The transition to fall happens so much earlier here than it does in Shanghai.

We walk together in comfortable silence, and I lose myself in thought, so entranced by every difference and every similarity I see between this city and the one I have always known. A million comparisons. A million new feelings.

Fall has always been my favorite season, maybe because of just how ephemeral it is. How even though they say it starts in September and ends in December, even though it's meant to last three months on paper, it doesn't. There are only a few weeks in Shanghai where it really feels like fall. Fall the way it is meant to be—watercolor leaves and crisp air, and buttery, golden afternoons.

In London, it is not so transitory. We walk out from under a canopy of leaves, and there it is: the Lotus. In the weak light of the still-rising sun, the bronze is set ablaze, gleaming in the early morning.

It is absolutely stunning.

We end up waiting half an hour for class to start—8:10 to make sure everyone shows up, that no one got lost in the maze of hallways within the Lotus.

Our professor is Howard Larne, a man in his late fifties with already fully gray hair. He's dressed in a suit so very clearly old, so worn, that I almost smile.

He says, "Good morning, everyone. Welcome to, I believe, your very first class here at Eladine and indeed, the first of the term. My name is Howard Larne—that's 'Larnee,' not 'Larn'—and, as you've likely gathered, I'll be your professor. So, the plan for today: I'll begin with a brief introduction to the course, go over what we'll be covering, and then we'll move on to a few icebreakers. A chance to get to know each other a bit, as we'll be spending the next four months together. Sound good?"

Nobody speaks a word. A couple of people nod.

"Brilliant. This class," he takes a marker and scribbles on the board, "is, quite simply, history. It's the introductory history class that's required for all of you. You're welcome to take any history elective you so choose in later years.

"I'll be sending you all a copy of the syllabus later, but to save a bit of time, I'll just briefly go over the topics now. We'll be covering three time periods: the prewar era, the period of war, and the postwar era. We'll be studying both courts—"

At this, someone raises their hand and doesn't even wait for him to call on them before asking, "Why both courts? Why care about Midnight Court history?"

"Because," says Larne, turning around. "We are not isolated. Each court influences the other, and we are intertwined by years and years of history. Understanding history, and understanding each other, prevents mistakes from being repeated. Mistakes we'll be examining in depth later on."

He continues, discussing the topics in more detail, and I'm already beginning to zone out, already distracted, and it is only day one—class one.

I'm watching the second hand tick on the clock, watching the minute hand jerk forward one click every sixty seconds, and my mind won't stop drifting to this evening.

My heartbeat quickens as the day progresses, until, mercifully, the final bell rings.

Classes are over.

It's finally time.

CHAPTER 10

The Dawn Court, it appears, is housed in a building that is practically a palace, just north of Victoria Park. I have no idea why they chose this location.

It's hilarious to me, suddenly, how the Dawn Court stereotypes all Midnight Courters as chaotic, evil, out of control; and the Midnight Court, at the same time, stereotypes Dawn as some cruel, calculating species, but it is almost the opposite with the buildings they chose to house themselves in.

The Midnight Court building was chosen for the sole purpose of functionality, its location in the very heart of Shanghai and the space able to fit everything and everyone they needed into one place. It is not flashy, nor ostentatious.

The Dawn Court building, on the other hand, seems chosen for its flashiness, to project the Dawn Court's image of royalty, to broadcast who they are so that no one can even question who lives here. Who inhabits these grounds.

It is a wholly white and gold building, complete with a gold dome and Grecian columns. The grounds stretch out half a mile on all sides, undoubtedly modeled after Versailles.

"You're kidding," I say.

"Before you somehow manage to assign blame to me the way you seem to be able to do with all things, I would just like to remind you that this was built years before I was even born," Paris says.

"I wasn't going to blame you for this."

"Sure."

We stop half a mile away, at a crossroads between the small cottage—small only in relative terms—and the Dawn Court main building.

"All right, let's split up here," Paris says; he's addressing Kyan, Max, and Devaj. "The three of you go through the palace back entrance. If there's a problem, shoot some signal."

"Or text?" suggests Max.

Kyan shakes his head. "We should try to use our phones as little as possible. Our courts have access to everything, and we have no idea who can see it."

"What about setting off some sort of explosion?" Dev suggests.

Max frowns. "Dude, that's going to draw the attention of everyone in the fucking building."

"Yes," Dev says, dryly, "that is the point of a signal."

"Oh, fine."

"Okay," says Paris. "Good talk. Let's go."

I must, I think, be dreaming. I have to be, because there can be no other way that I'm scheming with four Dawn Courters or that I'm about to sneak into the *Dawn Court* with a Dawn Court *prince*, for god's sake.

This, this does not feel real.

"Okay, so what's the plan again?" I ask, following Paris down a paved path of packed white sand. He's dressed in all white, a plain shirt and trousers, in an attempt to blend in, to not draw attention to himself.

I'm in white too—white pants, white top—but my hair and my facial features are a clear sign that I'm not from here, nor do I belong here. I'm hoping people haven't seen my face enough to place me as the daughter of Midnight Court Council members and instead think that I'm just an anomaly. Strange, but not dangerous. Like Professor Song.

"We walk in, ask for the list, and walk out," Paris says.

Right. I have no idea why I even asked.

In the back of my mind, I'm thinking this would be a great opportunity for me to do some reconnaissance, collect some intel that I can send back to the Midnight Court and prove my usefulness. Prove that the universe did not make a mistake in birthing me into this position.

Except, if I really wanted to do that, the smarter choice would've been to opt to go with the other three. Sneak around the palace under the guise of searching for the location of the theft, when in reality, I'd be searching for information.

My reluctant conclusion is that I am not very good at my job. I should've thought about that earlier.

Paris snaps his fingers in my face. "Pay attention, Anna. This is really not the optimal place to be daydreaming."

"Sorry," I say, coming back to reality. "Were you saying something?"

He mutters something that sounds like *Good god* and says, "I was *saying* that the guards rotate at precisely 17:00 in front of the groundskeeper's cottage. That gives us about a three-minute window to get into the building without being spotted. Think you can manage that?"

I resist the urge to stab him with the needle knife in my boot. "Yes, Paris, it very much sounds like something I can do. And since you're not looking at me at the moment, I would just like to politely inform you that I am rolling my eyes."

"Thanks," he says, dripping sarcasm onto the floor.

I check the time on my phone: 4:54 p.m.

"Well," I say. "We have six minutes. Let's maybe walk a little faster."

"We're fine," he says. "Besides, if the guards do spot you, I doubt they'll know who you are. This is merely a precaution."

"Right," I say. "Also, just in case I didn't mention this earlier, if you do anything that I categorize as betrayal in any way, I will not hesitate to betray you first," I add. "Or shoot you."

"I'm sure you will," he says. And then, "I wasn't aware you were in possession of a gun."

"I'm not. You are."

"Right. You're shooting me with *my* gun."

"Of course."

Paris opens his mouth like he's going to retort, then shuts it. As if he's just remembered that we are not friends. Not even close.

And really, I should shoot myself for not catching it first. It scares me how easily we fall into this casual back-and-forth. How easily the last three years were not erased but covered over with Wite-Out. Neither of us forgets, but acting this way almost makes it seem forgiven.

And for that, I can't forgive myself.

"Stop overthinking. We haven't got time for this," Paris hisses. "You can do all your overthinking shit after."

It is disconcerting, to say the least, how well he still knows me. I feel utterly, completely bare. Wholly transparent. I hate it. My mouth tightens. "I have no idea what you mean." The lie blares so loud I'm certain we both hear it.

"Yeah, whatever," Paris answers.

We walk the rest of the way in silence. Silence, which stuffs the air between us with cotton balls and wraps a nylon rope around my chest until it's hard to breathe. The seconds tick by, seconds like swarms of butterflies that dive from the air into my stomach. I'm trying to deep-breathe away the sudden nerves, swat away the sudden awareness of what I am actually doing.

A very large part of me is thinking that if I get caught, there is a very, very real chance I could die for this. That the fact that I'm doing this accompanied by Dawn Court sons of nobility and one Dawn Court prince will be entirely meaningless.

I really should have run this by my father. Or my sister Katerina, at the very least.

I need to stop bringing *I should've*'s everywhere I go.

We get to the cottage a minute early. Two guards stand on either side of the door, dressed in white military gear. Rather excessive for grounds guards, in my opinion.

I am within moments of walking straight into their line of sight when Paris grabs my arm and pulls me back behind a tree. Both of us are pressed flat to the trunk, trying not to breathe too loudly.

His touch, his touch is *scalding*. Even through the two layers of fabric that are my shirt and jacket. I snatch my arm back so fast it's almost as if I was actually burned.

"Forty seconds," he leans over to whisper to me. "Remember, at my signal head straight down. *Walk*, don't run. Try to act normal," he says, and I nod. My heart is not even going *thud, thud, thud* anymore. It's going *duhduhduhduhduh* and I'm wondering how the tongue can be the strongest muscle of the body when the heart can beat this fast, this rapidly?

I'm thinking, *Oh god, I am really not prepared for this*, and I definitely should've spent more time planning—another *should've*—or, at the very least, mapping it out in my brain before actually going in. Should've asked more questions. Should've, should've, should've.

I am chock-full of them.

And then Paris gives a jerk of his head. We slip out from behind the tree, one after the other. I can feel his presence behind me like a brand: heat and a tingling *awareness*. I have never been so aware of anyone in my life.

We walk up to the front door, slowly, casually, and I'm thinking, *You always plan everything out step-by-step*, but in the heat of the moment, in the heat of actually doing it, there are no carefully distinct steps. There is barely time to think.

Thirty seconds later, we're standing in front of a small oak door.

I'm glancing around us, scanning the entire grounds behind us, making sure that there's no one there, that no one saw us walking to the door.

"Um, do we break in? Do we pick the lock?" I ask, studying the oak door.

Paris sighs. Raises his hand. Raps on the door, and I say, "Oh."

He knocks once. Twice.

On the third, a woman opens the door. She's older—maybe late sixties, early seventies—with a head full of wispy white hair and smile lines around her eyes. Right now, she's blinking at us in confusion. Her gaze fixes on Paris and she says, "Your Highness, can I help you?"

"Joan," Paris says. He looks surprised. *I'm* surprised he even knows her name. And then I realize that if he's startled, he wasn't expecting this. And that sends anxiety straight into my stomach.

He asks, "Where's Edenfield?"

CHAPTER 11

As it turns out, Joan is Edenfield's housekeeper. And the fact that she's answering the door—and he's not—means he's out.

"He should be back in a couple of hours," Joan says. Her gaze flicks from Paris to me. "You're welcome to stay and wait."

Paris looks at me. "What do you want to do?"

I blink. I wasn't expecting him to defer to me. Before I can start agonizing over the pros and cons and talk myself in circles, I say, "Let's wait."

"Okay."

The inside of the cottage looks more old-fashioned than I was expecting. As if it was built a century ago.

Directly to the left is a sitting area, with couches covered in worn cloth of mismatched patterns and colors, and bay windows with fraying dark brown curtains.

On the right is the dining area, six wooden chairs surrounding a scratched mahogany table. Further down, I can just see into the kitchen.

This house feels very, very lived in, and it makes me uncomfortable, almost antsy. It's as if I'm invading someone's privacy, someone's personal space without their knowledge or their consent.

And then I'm thinking about what my sister told me before I left. *Don't start thinking of them as too human.* This house, this man, feels very, very human.

"Feel free to sit anywhere you'd like," Joan tells us. "I'll let you know once he's back."

"Thank you," Paris says, and I murmur in agreement.

"Why isn't Edenfield here?" I ask as soon as she leaves. "Isn't the job of the groundskeeper to be on the grounds?"

Paris looks at me. "He takes care of odd jobs for the Court as well. Making deliveries, that sort of thing. Or maybe he's just on a different part of the grounds."

I make a noncommittal noise in response. "We should tell the others."

He says, "Right. I'll give them a call."

"Okay."

Paris is back three minutes later. Silence invades the space between us, warping the seconds. Making them longer—stretching them into twos and threes. I think, there has never been *awkward* silence between Paris and me. There has been *comfortable* silence, *tense* silence, silence that is just *silence*. But, never awkward silence.

Until now.

And it is yet another reminder of who we have become, another reminder that whatever is between us has been twisted and misshaped so many times it has become unrecognizable. Distorted. My three-year-ago self would not even recognize myself now.

It is a sobering thought.

We spend the next several hours in and out of conversation—little snippets that don't last very long, that are abrupt at the ends like cut string. We are two puzzle pieces that have been warped by water and time and can never be put back together the same way again.

At 10:00, Joan comes bustling back into the room.

"I am so sorry," she says, and she does look apologetic. "I've just received word that Mr. Edenfield won't be back until early morning tomorrow. You're very welcome to stay here. There's a guest room upstairs with twin beds."

"There's no need—" Paris begins to say, but Joan cuts him off.

"Please, I insist. I feel terrible to have kept you waiting this long."

I shake my head. "Don't worry about it. It was no bother."

She sends a grateful smile in my direction, and I send one back.

Joan almost reminds me of the housekeeper we had at our old house in Shanghai. Before we moved closer to the Midnight Court building for my parents' Council work.

That period in my life has always felt hazy, blocked off. There are the memories that I recall, the ones that are imprinted in me, the ones that I have held and admired in my hands time and time again. And then there are the ones that come to me in fragments, pieces of my life before my family became so involved in the court. And others still that have stayed in whatever far place my brain cannot reach. Maybe it's nostalgia, or maybe it's just my plain inability to say no, but I hear myself saying, "We'll consider it."

Paris is shooting me an incredulous look, one that says *Have you completely lost your mind?* I ignore him. Ask, "There's no requirement that we stay in the dorms every night, right?"

Through his teeth, he says, "No."

"I'd hate to make the two of you head back to school at such a late hour," Joan adds. "The city unfortunately isn't quite as safe as we'd all like it to be this time of night."

"She's got a point," I tell Paris. He just shakes his head. Sighs in defeat. I turn to Joan with a smile and say, "Show us the way."

Pleased, she answers, "Follow me," and begins walking toward the stairs in the middle of the house.

As soon as her back is turned, Paris whispers to me, "Really?"

"I felt bad for her! At least it'll make her feel better."

He rolls his eyes. "You're hopeless."

"I prefer *empathetic.*"

We follow Joan up the set of stairs and down the singular hallway that makes up the second floor. I count three doors before she stops and says, "This is it. If you need anything, please let me know."

I nod, say, "Thank you," and Paris pushes open the door, stepping into the room.

To be fair, it's not as bad as I'd thought. It's small, but it's not like we need space for anything. The ceiling is slanted with exposed beams that are the same cherrywood as the floor. The only furniture in the room are the two twin beds separated by a single nightstand in between.

We look at the beds. Look at each other.

"I'll take a wild guess and say you prefer the one near the window," he says.

Surprise is a sharp arrow to my chest. There is so much that he remembers. I almost wish he didn't.

"Your wild guess is correct," I say, and he just sends a half-smile in response.

I don't fall asleep immediately. The combination of this new, strange place and *Paris* not ten feet away creates the perfect recipe for insomnia.

I am hyperaware of myself, of every noise I make, every breath I take. I am afraid to move, afraid to turn over to see if he's asleep yet, overly conscious of everything this is and isn't. I can't stop remembering the last time we slept in a room together. In a bed together.

This, this feels so *wrong*. This new discomfort, this new uncertainty. It is everything I have been trying to avoid, staring me right in the face, and I don't dare to stare back. I can't.

My heartbeat refuses to calm down.

I'm gazing at the sliver of moon through the curtains, trying to push back every thought that materializes in my brain, trying not to overanalyze and overthink for what feels like eternity before I check my phone. Check the time. It's been forty-five minutes.

To my right, the sound of regular, deep breathing gives me enough reassurance to flip around and look at him.

Paris is asleep.

I'm suddenly understanding every book's description of people looking "peaceful" during sleep, because he does. He truly does look peaceful. It isn't an expression I have seen him wear since I was fifteen and he sixteen.

Lying in the shaft of moonlight that shivers through the dark, he is doused in silver, transforming his hair and his skin to a pale white-blue. I find myself tracing his face with my eyes, tracing the shape of it, of his nose, and his lips.

I can't stop staring at him.

There is a fluttering feeling in my chest, like a bird beating its wings a little too hard. A little too fiercely. But there is another feeling too—like a stone being dropped—dragging at my lungs, my diaphragm. And it is in this moment, as I stare at him there in peaceful slumber, that I realize that as much as I have lied and tried to convince myself otherwise, I have never let him go.

He—and our history—are as much a part of me as the color of my eyes, as the scars on my skin. And that is not so easily forgotten.

I'm not even aware I've fallen asleep until I wake up, moonlight still leaking into the room. And for a moment, one fleeting second, my brain is in the in-between state, half asleep, half still trapped in a dream, and I think I'm at home. In my bed in Shanghai.

And then reality comes crashing down like a bucket of icy water poured over my head.

I'm sitting up, rocketed upright and

I'm shaking. My hands, my arms are trembling, and my heart is *thud-thud-thudding* in my chest. So hard and fast that I'm almost afraid it will beat straight through—breaking through bone and skin and sinew—and leave a gaping hole in the center of my body.

I can't breathe. My breaths are coming in too tight, too short, and I'm vaguely aware that I'm gasping for air—trying desperately to haul it in through my mouth, but my throat is closed up, blocked off, not letting any air through and I can't *breathe*. I can't. My chest is heaving up-down, up-down, and it isn't until a few seconds later that I realize I'm crying; great, gasping sobs that shudder through my body. They are breaking my bones where they connect at the joints, turning them into a jumble of sticks and stones and dust. The tears are so thick I'm choking on them.

Disjointed scenes floating through my mind remind me exactly what I was just reliving as I slept. Snippets of my nightmare come flooding back to me, all of them in 4K, in HD. Shattered fragments of images: splatters of blood, wide eyes, limp bodies. And it is as if it happened not three years ago, but only yesterday. As if I woke up and suddenly, I'm fifteen again, experiencing it all for the first time.

There's a lingering feeling of *something* in my chest, grief or fear or some combination of both I can't discern. It feels heavy, weighing down my body like an iron anchor, and I can't get it off, I can't throw it off, I can't—

Movement catches my eye.

Paris is sitting at the edge of my bed, hands hovering above me like he isn't quite sure whether or not to touch me. He's looking at me with wide green eyes and he's saying, "Anna. Anna, it's alright. It was just a dream," and I'm wondering how I'm just now noticing him. It dawns on me that he was the one who must have woken me up.

There is unmasked concern on his face, and it is so unexpected that for just a second, surprise invades my brain, pushes away the grief. It is a second of reprieve. One second.

He's leaning over me. For a fleeting moment, I can't believe he's here. I can't believe this is the same Paris who, a week ago, held a gun to my head. Whose throat I held a knife to. It's almost as if no time has passed, as if the past three years and the past week have been erased and it is

so

confusing. I can't keep up with this back-and-forth, this hot and cold, this old and new. Right now, I am too disoriented to dwell on it.

I'm opening my mouth to speak, except I have no idea what I'm trying to say—not that it matters anyway because I can't get a single word out. My voice has collapsed and died in my throat, left to rot, and I am still trying to pull myself together—still trying to shake off this horrible, horrible feeling that is like a layer of grease over my skin.

Paris touches me lightly, tipping my head up. He says, gently, "Look at me."

I do.

"You're okay," he tells me, and his voice is firm. Reassuring. He grips my hand over the covers and the pressure calms me, slows my heart rate. Forces my body to still. "Try to slow your breathing," he suggests. "Breathe in through your nose."

When the tears finally stop and my breathing evens, he asks, "Would you like to talk about it?"

I shake my head. And then, before I can stop myself, before I can trap the words behind my teeth and never let them go, never let them out, I ask, "Can you...can you just stay with me?"

As soon as I say it, I wonder what the hell I'm doing. I'm almost ashamed of myself for how easily I fold, how quickly I come running back to someone who has hurt not only me but also the ones I love, someone who I know doesn't care for me, and god, I hate it.

I hate how weak I am. I hate how easily I betray myself. But in this state, in this in-between in the darkness that feels unreal, almost like an illusion, my brain is too battered to take it back. And I am too tired, too drained, too exhausted to care.

His surprise is almost palpable. I can feel it in the way his grip tightens on mine for a second, can see it in the way his head jerks up and his Adam's apple bobs hard in his throat as he swallows. His gaze catches mine, and for a second, I can almost read him, his eyes, before he schools his features back to neutral.

Paris hesitates for so long that I almost say, "Never mind," but then he gives me an almost imperceptible nod. "Of course."

I move slightly on the bed to make room for him, and I can feel the mattress shift underneath his weight as he lies down next to me. There is an inch of space separating us, an inch that holds the entirety of the giant, tangled mess of history that we are—all of the tension, all of the betrayal.

All of the yearning.

We haven't been close like this in years. This moment is bringing back every single memory—every midnight and gentle touch and whispered endearment—and I am almost drowning in them. Choking on them.

I'm shaking again, shuddering slightly with all of these emotions— the fading remnants of the horror and grief from my nightmare and now this new, added feeling of *missing*. Missing what we once were. What we once had. The devastation of realizing we will never get it back.

In the darkness, amid the chaos in my brain, I feel Paris shift a little closer and I almost forget to breathe. He is so close I can feel the solidity of his chest against my back, the rhythmic beat of his heart that is

just as fast as mine.

He wraps an arm around my waist and says, "Stop thinking about it, Anna. Just sleep."

And I do.

When I wake up the next morning, Paris is gone. It doesn't particularly come as a surprise—he has always had a habit of getting up at ridiculously early times, but it unsettles me nonetheless.

But also, in a way, it is almost a relief. Not having to face him now means not having to face what happened last night. In the darkness, in between sleep and wakefulness, everything is ill-defined. Every edge is blurred, and in the morning, in the sudden garish spotlight of the day, it is all painfully, embarrassingly clear.

A nightmare made me drop all of my walls, burn them to ashes. I promise myself it will never happen again.

Quickly, I brush my teeth with the disposable toothbrush and travel-size tube of toothpaste that Joan left in the bathroom. I straighten out my clothes, attempting to look as presentable as I can before I leave the room.

Paris is sitting at the kitchen table when I come down; he's on a barstool, a steaming mug resting between his hands, and he's laughing at something Joan is saying. He looks so *normal*, not like the prince of the enemy court but a nineteen-year-old boy. Unburdened. Not yet carved and sculpted by the cold blade of the past. I'm realizing how fiercely I'm wishing this image could be genuine, could be real, when in reality, I shouldn't even care. But emotions have never been something I could control, not in the way my parents and my sister do.

Joan sees me before he does. She says, "Good morning, Anna. How did you sleep?"

I don't dare look at Paris.

"Okay," I lie.

"Good." She gives me a smile. "I was telling Paris earlier that I believe Mr. Edenfield has returned, if you'd like to speak to him."

"Oh." I blink. "That's great. Thanks, Joan."

"Of course," she says. She points a finger down the hall. "Third door on the left."

"Ready?" Paris asks me. I slide my gaze to his; there's no indication that he is thinking about anything that happened last night. His face is carefully blank, carefully impartial.

"Yep," I say.

Paris slides down from the stool and we make our way down the hall in silence. Arriving at the door, he knocks. We wait.

Seconds later, we're stepping inside a relatively spacious room—a study, judging by the well-worn set of old bookcases and the table in the corner. I'm almost tempted to peek at the sprawl of papers strewn across Edenfield's desk until I remember we've come to find *him*. Meaning he's present here, somewhere.

Paris raps against the wall as we enter. "Edenfield? Are you there?"

One, two, three, four, five seconds of silence.

"Maybe he left again?" I suggest.

Paris says, "He hasn't." He walks further into the room. "Edenfield, need I remind you how hierarchy works in this court?"

There is a sudden crashing noise so loud I startle, hand going to the hilt of my knife out of pure instinct. I'm still waiting for my heartbeat to settle when a man walks out of the adjoining entryway.

He reminds me of one of my uncles. Actually, he reminds me of Gerard with the height—or rather, lack thereof—and the spectacles. Except unlike Gerard *and* my uncle, he has extensively mouselike features that immediately rouse my suspicion for no other reason than what the term *mouselike* denotes.

"Mr. Ateş?" he asks, squinting as if he doesn't quite believe it's Paris in the room. "I thought you were in school."

"I am," says Paris, "temporarily on leave. I need your help with something."

"My help? Wh—" and then he seems to just notice me, stopping abruptly mid-sentence to stare. And blink. And ask, "Who is this?"

"Um." Several thoughts enter and exit my brain in quick succession. First, whether or not I should tell him my real name—something that never came up during discussion. Second, that I should probably not look at Paris because if Edenfield wasn't already suspicious by us barging into his room, he definitely would be then. Third, I have never, ever been taught how to come up with random names on the fly.

Really, it shouldn't be this hard except I can't come up with anything that sounds remotely authentic. Not a first name and *definitely* not a last name.

I guess my lying capabilities don't extend to this.

"Elizabeth," I say, finally. "Elizabeth Spice." I have no idea why this is the first name that pops into my head. "We go to the same school," I add. Not a lie.

"Er, okay," says Edenfield. His gaze slides back to Paris and I almost breathe a sigh of relief. Damn my parents for teaching me 164 ways to kill a man, and not a single lesson on how to generate aliases on short notice. As if that isn't just as important a part of being a spy.

Edenfield opens his mouth to say more, except the quiet is suddenly marred by the sound of a telephone ringing. And by *telephone*, I really, truly mean telephone. One of the old ones that has a dial and a receiver and probably hails from the Victorian era.

Edenfield mumbles, "Excuse me for a moment," and then he retreats back into the other room.

Paris rounds on me. "*Elizabeth Spice?*" he echoes. "*That's* the best you could come up with?"

"Sorry!" I say defensively. "I don't do well under pressure! All I could think about was the Spice Girls and how every girl's first name in London is Elizabeth."

Paris casts his gaze heavenward. Exasperated, he says, "We need to work on your cover skills. It's essential, otherwise next time you're going to get us both killed."

I'm about to snap back but Edenfield chooses that exact moment to reenter the room.

He stops a few feet away from us. "What is it that you need my help with?"

"A couple questions," Paris answers smoothly, turning away from me as if nothing happened. "It shouldn't take up much of your time."

"Well, one question really," I say. "Who knew where the poison was?"

Edenfield gapes.

Paris shoots me an exasperated look that clearly reads *Way to have tact, Anna*. But he explains to Edenfield anyway, "We're investigating the theft. Knowing who had the location would be greatly beneficial."

Edenfield closes his mouth. Crosses his arms. He says, "I wish I could help, but that is, unfortunately, classified information."

"Classified," Paris repeats. "And who, exactly, is cleared to know it?"

Also classified, apparently.

Paris takes out his gun. In the silence, the click of the safety cracks the air in half.

Keeping his gun trained on Edenfield, he tells me, "Anna, I need you to please go over to the bookshelf."

I look at him, confused, but his expression says, *Just do it*. So I do.

"Grab the green book all the way on the left."

At this, Edenfield must realize what Paris is up to, because he glares at him and spits out resentfully, "I hope you know this is treason, son of Midnight. I always knew you couldn't be trusted."

Paris ignores him, just watches me as I pull the book from the shelf, and then I understand. I recognize the cold metal of the gun in my hand before I even see it. The Dawn Court must have them hidden all over the palace.

I'm surprised he's offering it to me.

Meeting Paris's eyes for a second, I can see the warning in them as clearly as if he's speaking to me. *Don't make me regret trusting you.*

I look away. Point my gun at Edenfield and say, "You might want to rethink your earlier answer."

Two seconds pass. Edenfield looks as if he's trying to determine whether or not I'm bluffing, but Paris says, "I should warn you she's quite violent. Very trigger-happy. And bloodthirsty. You know the

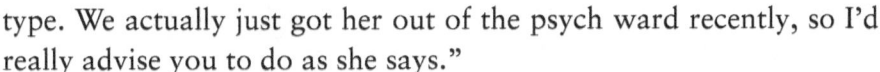

type. We actually just got her out of the psych ward recently, so I'd really advise you to do as she says."

I'm forcing myself to keep my face blank and not stare at Paris like *he* belongs in a psych ward.

Edenfield swallows. "I do attend the meetings, but I can't be of much help. Each attendee was asked to use a code name and wear a disguise, so no one could distinguish any part of another's identity."

When neither of us says anything, he adds, "That's all I know, I swear."

"You're lying," says Paris. His voice is so, so soft. "I think you're overestimating how much patience I have. Try that again because I promise you, this gun is not just for show."

Edenfield's face twists. "You dare threaten me? In two minutes, the guards will come barging into this room and have the two of you arrested. You," he says to Paris, "for colluding with the enemy and you," this time to me, "for trespassing."

In my head, I'm thinking, *Technically I'm not exactly trespassing considering the king assigned this task to us,* but if Edenfield isn't aware of it—and clearly, he's not—then the guards aren't either. And we can't draw this much attention to ourselves.

"How dim-witted do you think I am?" Edenfield continues, "It is almost insulting for the two of you to pretend that she is not who she is. As if I wouldn't recognize one of the Midnight Court's favorite daughters." He spits out the last part as if it is a poison. "Annabella Liang. How do you imagine your parents will react when I send them your head in a box?"

In a sudden, callous movement, Paris shoves Edenfield against the wall, pressing the barrel of his gun under Edenfield's chin. "I'll give you three seconds. Consider what you value more, your life or whatever it is you're hiding. One."

Edenfield glares.

"Two." His glare shifts to me. My heart is being strangled by wire, wrapped over and over again, and squeezed until it is threatening to burst. He can't possibly be willing to die for this. Paris can't actually shoot him.

This has escalated too fast. Spiraled too quickly out of control.

"Three."

"Okay, fine," Edenfield spits, and I almost heave a sigh of relief out loud. "There's a list. A key to the code names. You'll never be able to get it."

"We can decide that for ourselves. Where is it?"

"Where else? The king's study."

I gulp. You've got to be kidding me.

I see Paris's jaw tighten. He doesn't like it either.

And then, the muffled sound of footsteps outside—multiple boots against the ground—and I'm shooting Paris a look that's part alarm and part warning.

"We need to leave."

Paris nods, lowering his hand, and then—

They say it's like slow motion—the moments before you're about to die. They say your life flashes before your eyes like it's some sort of movie sequence, but all I see is Edenfield. His fingers reaching out to grip the barrel of Paris's gun that is no longer pressed against his skin. His fingertips touching the metal.

In this moment, I am vaguely aware that I have never, ever killed someone. I have hurt. I have wounded. But I have *never* taken the life of another human being.

But I can't stop to think about what I'm doing. Instinct grasps the grip of the gun with cold fingers. Fear aims at Edenfield's head.

My finger pulls the trigger almost before my brain processes what is happening.

The bullet hurtles from the gun straight through Edenfield's forehead. Paris jerks out of the way just before a spray of scarlet, scarlet, scarlet attacks the wall, tramples the air.

And all I'm thinking is, *Human beings' one talent is to kill.* To create the perfect weapon to destroy their own species in the most efficient way. That in the centuries and eons and millennia, this is the only thing that has improved without a hitch.

It is terrifying.

I can't even stop to process the gravity of what I've done before I hear the guards flood into the house, breaking through the front door with a crash. And, just as quickly, they're at the door to the study, shouting at Edenfield to open it. I'm thinking, *They must've heard the gunshot.* They must've.

Paris is pulling me away, through the other room and down a hallway that I don't even understand how we got to.

Shock, I've come to realize, is ice. It is the bitter wind when you step outside in the winter that numbs your entire body, the cold that invades your brain until you can't think.

Distantly, I'm thinking, *We need to get the list, we need to find the king's study.* I must have said it out loud because Paris is saying, "We don't have time. We have to go."

We've made it out of the house and halfway back along the path we came from before our luck finally runs out in the form of a voice behind us.

"Stop."

Paris ignores it.

"Stop or I will shoot." What is with the Dawn Court and threats of bullets?

I jerk Paris to a stop. He might have a death wish, but I don't.

Slowly, I turn around. I am hoping, praying that we can get out of this.

Then, "*Paris?*"

Startled, I glance back at Paris, and he doesn't seem concerned. Doesn't seem anxious. He is relieved.

"Darren."

It takes entirely too long for me to recognize the similarity. The same golden hair, the same green-gold eyes, the same straight nose.

It's his brother. I must've seen him at summits too.

"I had no idea it was you," Darren says. "They said that we'd been compromised, that there were two intruders. They didn't say you were one of them." He pauses. "They said you killed Edenfield."

News sure does spread fast around here.

"He attempted to kill me," says Paris. "We killed him instead."

He doesn't say that *I* killed him. Me, specifically.

I'm beginning to get antsy. We only have so much time before the guards catch up to us.

Darren turns to me, and there is a sudden jolt of panic that unfurls in my chest the moment his gaze lands on my face. Does he recognize me? Is he *allowed* to?

He asks, "Who's this?"

Paris shoots a glance at me so quickly I almost miss it before he looks away. Then, "Anna Liang."

Well, that answers my question.

"Ah," Darren says. "The infamous Anna. What's she doing here?"

He really does like to refer to me as if I'm not here.

"She enrolled in Eladine," Paris answers, smoothly.

I frown. So, I guess he can know my name, but Paris doesn't want him to know the real reason I'm in the Dawn Court.

"It's nice to meet you," I say, trying to act as normal as possible.

Darren says, "You as well." He glances at Paris. Glances at me. "I would love to meet you formally sometime, but I can see you two need to go. I'll attempt to hold off the guards for as long as I can. I'd advise you to use the passageways through the tunnels as they've currently put the entire palace and the grounds on lockdown. There are men everywhere."

"Thank you," Paris says, and in another second, we're moving again.

"I hope you know which passageways he's talking about," I hiss.

"I've lived here for nine years. How ignorant do you think I am?"

CHAPTER 12

We reconvene with the other three in the tunnels—Paris having called them after our accidental encounter with Darren—and I'm already thinking about what information I can send back to Shanghai later. This, I think, this is so perfect.

And then Paris says, "Just in case you're planning to reveal the existence of these tunnels to your precious Midnight Court, you should know that the only direction they go is *out*."

"What the hell does that mean?"

"The doors at the end only open outward. *Meaning*, you can't get in from the tunnels."

I grind my teeth. "I wasn't thinking about revealing it anyway, for your information. It's your own problem that you have a tendency to see the worst in people."

"Seeing anything else gets you killed."

"True," says Dev.

A scoff. "You guys are so morbid." Max's voice echoes down the tunnel in a low pitch. "What's wrong with a little optimism?"

"He's not wrong," I say.

"Let's not have a philosophical discussion when we're trying not to be executed for murder," says Dev. "Who did that, by the way?"

How did I forget?

In the chaotic terror of fleeing from the guards, the simple fact that I have killed another person had completely fled my mind.

And now it is back. With a vengeance.

In my head, I'm screaming, pleading with myself to *keep it together*. But my heart is pounding, beating double-time, so fast it's like a jackhammer in my chest.

And it really does feel like it too, like a jackhammer is pounding into whatever bones keep my chest upright, keep it from caving in and crushing me with the weight of all the sins I have ever committed in my life.

From what feels like a million miles away, I hear Kyan—Kyan?—telling Dev and Max to keep going, that we'll meet them back at the car, and then it's just us, just Kyan, Paris, and me alone in the corridor.

Flashbacks—from *then*—keep invading my head, burning into my retinas, my memory. The scars are so deep now I can never, ever forget it. Guns pressed to heads, blood splattering white walls like grotesque paintings, and in my head, their faces are flickering in and out, their faces are merging with mine and I am suddenly having trouble breathing.

Oxygen is fleeing from every part of my body, evaporating from my blood, my lungs, my brain, and I can't think.

Blood is shooting to my head, so quickly that I feel off-balance. Watching the world as it's stabbed by spots of darkness. There is a roaring sound in my ears and numbness in my fingertips and *God, I can't breathe.*

Everything hurts—pangs and flashes and aches in my chest, my stomach. My body is its own battlefield, inside and out, and I am almost certain I'm having a heart attack. In the back of my brain, I'm thinking, statistically speaking, I'm eighteen years old and relatively active, so the probability of me having a heart attack is low.

Then I think, *It's a panic attack.* The knowledge doesn't make me feel any better.

God, I wonder when I'll stop dying.

"Anna," Kyan says. "I need you to listen to me. Focus on the sound of my voice; can you do that?"

I'm counting numbers in my head, waiting for this to end. Wondering if it ever will, if I'm going to be murdered by my own heart and lungs and body.

I say, "Yes." It comes out as a gasp. I wasn't expecting a gasp and it startles me more than it should.

"Okay," he says. "Good. I want you to tell me five things you see."

"Um…" I don't even have the effort to question why. "Rocks," I say. "The walls of the tunnel. God, um, the lights. The ground." I squeeze my eyes shut. "I don't know."

"Come on, Anna. One more."

"Hair."

"Great. Now, four things you can touch?"

"Same thing."

Kyan sighs. "Sure, we'll go with that. Three things you can hear?"

"Blood in my ears. Breathing. Your voice."

"Good. Two things you can smell."

"Um, stone," I say. I close my eyes. Jab a finger to the other figure standing to the left, a couple feet away. "Paris."

I'm so conditioned to recognize his scent, and in this moment, I don't mind. It is almost comforting. So familiar.

A snort.

"Okay. That works. And one thing you can taste."

"*Blood.*" The metallic tang is all over my tongue, coating the roof of my mouth. But the pressure on my chest is beginning to lift. Minimally.

"What now?" I ask. "What's next?"

"Next, I want you to concentrate on your breathing. Focus on taking deep breaths, inhaling through your nose, counting to five, exhaling through your mouth. I want you to start from your feet and go up your body, focusing on relaxing one muscle at a time."

"You could be a meditation instructor," I gasp out. "Or like, be some Buddha." But I do as I'm told, working my way from my feet to my legs to my arms.

Breathing.

Inhale, count to five. Exhale. Inhale, count to five. Exhale.

By the time it's over, truly over, I am exhausted. I am post-marathon, post-getting-run-over-by-a-truck, post-seventy-eight-hours-without-sleep. I am sitting back against the wall, boneless.

"How did you know how to do that?" I ask.

Kyan is in a crouch. He smiles and says simply, "I used to do it for Paris all the time."

I raise an eyebrow. Look at Paris.

He's standing a couple feet away, half-hidden in shadows. At my glance, he shrugs and says, "I had them almost every day without fail back when I first moved here. Kyan knew relatives who had gone through the same thing, so he already had a rough idea of what to do. Thankfully."

Kyan smiles. "Yeah, you're welcome for that." He turns to me. "Do you need a minute?"

I shake my head. Struggle to my feet. I am insanely out of breath.

Kyan reaches out and offers me a steadying hand and I take it, grateful for the support.

CHAPTER 13

The moment I get back to the Eladine dorms, I tell Josephine everything. The words spill out of me, breaking through my ribs and streaming past my throat in an unstoppable torrent. I tell her about the grounds, the Dawn Court main building. I tell her about Edenfield.

How I shot him.

I leave out the part about last night. What happened between Paris and me. I'm not sure why, I just know I want to keep that part private. For now, at least.

Josephine has known me my entire life. She knows what effect that moment with Edenfield has on me.

"I'm not going to tell you that it's okay, Anna, because I know that to you it isn't. But it will be." She takes my hand in hers. "You did what you had to do."

"I don't know if I had to kill him, Josie," I say.

She shakes her head. "Think about what Katerina would say. What your parents would say. This world is ruthless. There's no room for hesitation, for weakness. Who's to say that if you didn't kill him, he wouldn't have killed you instead? Both of you?"

I have to believe she's right. "Selfishly," I say, "I wish you had been there. I hate doing things without you."

Josephine rolls her eyes and laughs. She says, "Yeah. I could've had a shot at him too, but instead you hogged all the fun." I know she's kidding, trying to make me feel better, and I love her all the more for it.

Since I have a couple hours before I have to meet with the group again, I switch the topic. Ask her, "How are you feeling about all of this? London?"

"Oh, you know me," she says, flashing me a grin that actually seems genuine. "I love it." Josephine thrives off chaos and new experiences. I've always known this about her. Ever since we were little, she was always on the move, always in search of the next adventure. Sometimes, I truly marvel at just how different we are.

"Do you ever miss Shanghai?"

She shrugs. "Not really. I think it's been too chaotic the past few days for me to even have had time to think about it. And we'll be back in a few months, anyway."

"Yeah. You're right," I say.

"Aren't I always?" Jo jokes. "But seriously, Anna. I'm glad I came with you. Thank you for letting me."

"Thank *you* for coming," I shoot back, nudging her with my elbow. "You know I couldn't do this without you."

By the time the five of us reconvene in the common room, it's already late afternoon. Sunlight is streaming through the warped glass of the Lotus's wall, bathing the room in a diffused sort of orange light.

I have never really liked this part of the day—the dying, tail end of it. The hour just before sunset, just before the sun gives way to night, gives way to darkness.

It is the death of the day.

Today, Professor Song is here. I see her as soon as I walk in, and she looks so out of place among the couches, beanbag, and the pool table that I almost smile, in spite of myself. She's sitting on a couch, but stands up as soon as we come in.

She greets the guys first, saying, "Hello, boys. It's good to see you're all still in one piece," before she spots me. Her face is kind, welcoming. She says, "And you must be Anna. It's very nice to finally meet you."

Her hand is outstretched, and I shake it. "You too."

"I hope they haven't given you too much trouble," she tells me, giving me a conspiratorial wink, and it is so unoriginal, but it makes me laugh anyway.

"Not yet."

With a smile, she says, "Good." And then to all of us, "So, anyone want to debrief me on what happened?"

"Max, Kyan, and I checked out the king's study," Dev speaks up. "Not much there that was useful, just the same conversations about the vial being missing, but nothing else. No location. We did find out that the first time they noticed was about two weeks back. They have no idea who it could've been, though."

At this, I frown. I'd forgotten that the three of them had already searched the king's study. Edenfield had said that the list was there, so they should've seen it.

Paris must be thinking the same thing because he says, "Edenfield told Anna and me that the list of people that were at the meeting is in the study. I don't suppose any of you saw it?"

This time, it's Max who speaks. "Unfortunately, no. We also didn't dig in too deeply—just the pile of papers that he had on top of his desk since we were kinda short on time. Sorry," he adds.

"It's no problem. I didn't think you would've if you didn't know what you were searching for. My father's desk tends not to be very... neat," Paris says.

"Understatement of the century," Max mutters under his breath.

A smile flits across Paris's mouth.

Professor Song speaks up. "All right, well, it seems we're on the right track—"

"Wait," Kyan cuts in, and it's hilarious how everyone's attention goes straight to him, as if they're not used to him speaking up, interrupting. He ignores it all, saying, "There's something I wanted to run by you, Professor." He shifts, obviously uncomfortable with this much attention on him, five pairs of eyes. "I was wondering if I could get permission to use the school lab. I want to try and see if I can formulate some sort of antidote for the poison that was stolen."

This piques my interest. A lab. The creation of an antidote. This would be great intel to send back to the Council.

Song blinks at him. Once. Twice. "I think that's a wonderful idea. You can go up whenever. It should be open as long as it's during regular hours."

"Thank you," Kyan says.

"Of course. Let's all meet back here tomorrow—" she turns to me—"after your Initiation, Anna, if you end up going tomorrow. And then we can discuss next steps."

Oh. Right. Initiation's tomorrow. In the heat and haste of everything, I had nearly forgotten.

"Wait," I say. "What exactly is Initiation?"

It's Max who responds. "Ha. Basically, it's this ridiculous exam that they make every first-year go through in the beginning of the semester. They need to test that you have certain baseline skills before they let you study in 'spy school.'" Air quotes at the end. "And also you get ranked and it pretty much dictates from the start who the most competent students are. People tend to get competitive."

"The first part is a physical test," Paris tells me. "They're scoring the quantity of exercises that you can do before you burn out. The second is a maze. Your score's dependent on how fast you're able to navigate through it. They're going to put obstacles in your way—I think in past years they've had simulation opponents that you had to fight through, or a poison mist that you had to make an antidote for before you were able to get through. I'm fairly certain they just reuse this stuff every year.

"Just don't die," he adds.

"Okay," I say. "Very helpful. Thanks."

"Don't stress too much about it, Anna," Professor Song tells me, kindly. I nod at her.

"All righty," says Max. "Shall we meet tomorrow, then?"

"Sounds good," says Dev.

"See you all later," Max says with a wave, and then he's out the door. The rest of them quickly follow.

And then it is just me and Paris left in the room.

Suddenly, I realize what people mean by "deafening silence." In an abrupt contrast going from three hundred decibel–level bickering to this absence of *everything*, the silence is almost a tangible thing. It is

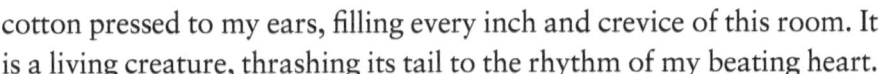

cotton pressed to my ears, filling every inch and crevice of this room. It is a living creature, thrashing its tail to the rhythm of my beating heart.

Tension too is a living thing. It almost pushes me straight out of the room except—

Paris is walking toward me, so very out of place with his black clothes and his gold hair and his grace in this room that is so mundane. So very ordinary.

"Can we talk?"

I'm racking my brain, scouring the past few days with a fine-tooth comb wondering what in the world he could possibly want to talk about. I hope it's not about last night. I hope.

"Um, sure," I say, but in my head, I'm wishing I could say no. I'm wishing I could just leave the room because this discomfort is enough to send me straight through the door.

He pulls up a chair, gracefully—too gracefully—and sits down in one fluid motion, the back facing me. And then he says, "I'm sorry. I—"

"For *what*?" I interrupt. Apologies, especially to me, after everything that's happened, are so out of character for Paris that I'm startled into silence right after my question.

He gives me a look like *If you would let me finish*. "For Edenfield." He laughs, humorless. Looks down at his clasped hands resting on the back of the chair. "I shouldn't have even given him the opportunity to try and take my gun. I'm sorry you had to shoot him."

"Oh," I say. Surprise has chased all the words out of my mouth in flocks. So I just find myself repeating, "Oh."

"Yes, well, good talk," says Paris, getting up to leave. "I'm going to assume *oh* means 'I accept your apology' in whatever language you're speaking at the moment."

"Wait," I say, reaching out to grab the air, the chair, his arm—I have no idea what. "Wait," I say again. "Sorry, I'm just...I wasn't expecting that. It wasn't really your fault." My gaze shifts to a particularly worn section of the couch. "I mean, I didn't have to shoot him in the head."

Paris is looking at me with an expression I can't quite parse. He says, "Well. I guess we're both at fault, then."

"I guess so," I say. Upgrade to picking at a frayed section of the couch. And then I ask, "What was it like for you? The first person you killed?"

Paris's gaze locks with mine. He looks discomfited, but asks, "Are you sure you want to have this conversation with me?"

Again, I am startled. Not from anything that he did or said this time, but rather from something that I did. That I'm talking to him about this. I feel a flush rising in my cheeks and I wonder why I get embarrassed so easily.

Then, "If you don't want to we don't have to," I say. "I was just curious."

"I was just making sure." Paris sighs. Taps a pen against the chair. "I was ten years old."

At this, I jerk my eyes upward to stare at him, pretty sure horror is etched into every line on my face, in the way my jaw almost drops wide open. *Ten.* I find myself wondering why we didn't talk about this three years ago.

He continues. "It was right after I was transferred to the Dawn Court. My father," he laughs. A sharp exhale of air that's really more of a scoff. Shaking his head, he continues, "My father thought it'd be a good learning experience. Killing someone. Better to get all that morality bullshit out of the way early before it comes back to bite you in the ass later, right?

"He said that all my siblings, except for Talia, of course, had already gone through this little ritual. That it was meant to make us stronger because emotions, morality, all of that is a weakness. A chink in the armor. Humanity's Achilles' heel."

"Who did you kill?" My voice is a whisper. I'm almost afraid to ask.

"A man suspected of harboring criminal thought. Allegedly, he was attempting to start an uprising, but knowing my father and his Circle, he most likely just said the wrong thing. An offhand comment to a friend.

"I shot him in the chest with three bullets. An inefficient kill, but I was overeager. I wanted to show my father that I was like him, that

I was just as strong as every one of my siblings. And not only could I *kill*, I could perform the action willingly. Without hesitation or misgivings. I wanted to prove I was the perfect soldier."

It's ironic just how similar his words are to what I have always thought about Katerina.

He laughs for real this time. "I ran straight back to my room and dry heaved for half an hour afterward. I couldn't even actually throw up, like the universe wouldn't grant me that mercy, wouldn't grant me even a semblance of comfort because I had committed the greatest sin a human could. I killed one of my own.

"The panic attacks started not long after. And the more my father made me kill, the more frequently I experienced them. They stopped, eventually," he says. "But that was almost worse. After nine years, I'm afraid I've grown almost numb to this. To the killing, the violence. And the worst thing is, it doesn't quite bother me as much as it should.

"I am afraid," he says, "that I am becoming more Dawn Court than I had ever planned to."

I am speechless. His sentences have robbed me of my entire vocabulary, of my voice. I am distantly aware that I must be staring at him with horror written into my eyes, but I just can't think of a single thing to say.

His story itself makes me want to vomit. Makes me want to upend the entire contents of my stomach because I cannot *believe* that this is real. That this is someone's reality, anyone's, much less someone that I know with frightening intimacy. I wonder again how I didn't know, how I could have known someone so intimately, and yet not know them at all.

I have been horrified of him since he betrayed me three years ago, but now, now I am surprised to find that I am also horrified *for* him. For what he has had to endure—and I hate it. I don't want to feel these emotions that haven't known daylight around Paris in so very long. These are emotions I want to reserve for my friends. My family. The people that I care about unconditionally. The people that deserve that emotional investment and expenditure.

But here they are, presented in front of me like platters at a feast, and for the life of me, I cannot force them back down. I cannot force them back into hiding, into the darkness.

"Killing is Midnight Court too," I say, quietly.

"Yes. Well."

"You never told me. Back when—" I cut myself off. "Three years ago, you never told me."

"You never asked," he says, simply.

A pause—long and overgrown and stuffed with commas, ellipses, semicolons—before I say, finally, "I wasn't aware you had quite so many layers."

Paris barks a short laugh. "Most people," he says, "are more complicated than you think, Anna. I'm not going to mince words here," he adds. "I admit, I'm surprised that Edenfield was the absolute first person you've ever killed, but I appreciate what you did. No matter how much you might hate yourself for it, I am grateful." He glances at me, a faint smile playing about his mouth. "Ironically, I think I might owe you a life debt."

I blink. Oh. "No. I don't want it," I say. "I think it's best if we keep ourselves very, very separate. It's better that way."

"That it would be." He cocks his head at me. "To be honest, I would've expected you to let him kill me. It would have benefited you, without having to dirty your own hands."

My stomach turns over, suddenly. Unexpectedly. He is far too close to the truth for comfort.

"Well," I say. "Maybe I'm a better person than you think."

"Most people are," he tells me.

"Can I ask you something?" I ask.

"You can ask," he answers. "I can't guarantee an answer."

"The panic attacks." I'm hesitant. "How long did they last?"

He smiles wryly. Looks down at his hands. "Three years with frequency. Another two years after that. By the time I turned sixteen, they had almost faded completely. I can't say I miss them."

"Oh. Wow." It slips out before I even have time to think.

"I assume you're asking me because of what happened in the tunnel today."

I shift in my seat, absentmindedly tapping my fingers on my leg. "Yes. I feel like I'm almost always in constant fear of it happening again."

"For what it's worth," Paris says, "Edenfield had to die, regardless of whether it was you or I who had to kill him. He possessed sensitive information which, in the wrong hands, would've jeopardized our entire assignment."

And with that, he's gone.

CHAPTER 14

Today is Initiation.

Though it's been two days since we arrived, this still feels like a fever dream—like some sort of skewed reality—and that at any time now, I'll be teleported straight back into real life. The entire dorm has been awake since 6:00 a.m., hovering on a triple espresso energy level like we are all on a joint caffeine high.

All morning, people have been scrambling to do last-minute prep—stretches, aim practice, textbook memorizations of common codes. The gym has been full to bursting for hours now.

Josephine and I have one goal today: to score in the middle tier. Not good enough to attract attention, but not bad enough to attract attention either. Smack-dab in the middle.

Because there are two hundred students to test, they're dividing Initiation into four different days this year, with fifty students testing per day. We'll be broken into groups of five who will all go at once into different testing chambers.

They've transformed the entire stadium for it. I guess it's a pretty big deal.

"Oh my god," Cassie says. She's desperately flipping through pages of a textbook as though just touching the paper will transfer all the information into her head by osmosis. "I'm not ready. I am so not prepared. God, I should've reviewed this again last night."

Josephine catches my eye and silently mouths, *Are they all insane?*

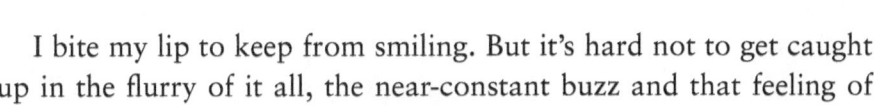

I bite my lip to keep from smiling. But it's hard not to get caught up in the flurry of it all, the near-constant buzz and that feeling of solidarity—everyone going through the same horrible thing together.

"When are they posting the schedule?" Mariam is frantically tapping a knife against her leg.

"I think I heard ten a.m.," says Cassie. She doesn't even look up from the textbook.

The school is posting a schedule of who's going when on a screen in the lobby today—in half an hour, really, since it's already 9:30. I'm not sure when I would want to go. I don't really think I have a preference.

Cassie and Mariam, on the other hand, have been talking about it nonstop for the past day. Early to get it over with? Or later so that you can learn from the mistakes that everyone else has made? Not to mention extra time for prep. I wonder how exhausting it must be to think about this day in and day out.

At 9:55, Josephine and I are standing in the lobby at the center of the Lotus, one giant circular room with hallways branching off in every direction. Up above, I can see the corridors on every floor winding around and around up to the top. Today, the lobby is choked with people. Two hundred students crammed in front of one huge screen, the light from it casting a blue glow on the white walls of the lobby and out onto all of our faces. And just beyond the screen, the short hallway to the stadium. The impatient energy in the room is *suffocating*.

I'm doing my best to observe everyone, take notes on everything so that I can report it back to Shanghai later.

People are pushing and shoving in a futile attempt to get closer to the front, to be able to see better, and it's making the entire crowd shift and sway in unison. I can feel claustrophobia rising in my chest, my throat, wrapping its arms around my torso until I'm struggling to inhale oxygen.

I wish they would just upload it already.

And then they do. It's up, groups and groups of names sorted first by day and then by hour. My eyes pick out my own name almost immediately.

Today. Group four out of ten.

Josephine's eyes flick to mine. "Fourth," she says. "Not bad."

She's not wrong. I guess I'd prefer going somewhere in the middle after all, rather than first or last.

I search the screen for her name. "When are you?"

"Tomorrow," she says. "Literally the last group. But like, it's whatever." She looks around and whispers, "Obviously, it doesn't really matter for us."

And even while I know what she says is clearly true, it's also inevitable, I think, to feel some nerves around this. It is a test, after all. And the energy in this room is contagious.

Eladine is changing Initiation up a little this year. They're having the praefectus watch us in case something goes wrong. In case we somehow hurt ourselves and need emergency help, however unlikely that is. Apparently, last year, there was a student who almost bled out after he accidentally shot himself in the foot.

I have no idea how that even happens.

But because of that little incident, we now have to wear headsets going in, with a button that connects to each member of the praefectus. It makes me a little more nervous, I think, to have someone watching me—what if they somehow figure out that I'm not exactly trying my hardest? At the very least, Paris is part of the praefectus group that is watching the first day. One less person who could have a chance to expose me.

The first two groups go in and come out almost too quickly. There are no screens for us to watch them, but the administration told us roughly what to expect in the stadium. Throughout the course of the past few days, they constructed temporary walls and corridors into the normally open space, converting it into a maze.

Too soon, there is only one group left in front of me.

I'm standing in front of my individual door that leads into the stadium, and I am almost certain my intestines are tying knots around each other. To my left and right, I can just see the remaining four members in my group lined up in front of their respective doors, eyes trained on the entrance. There is a red light blinking on the side, indicating that the other group hasn't yet finished.

In my head, I'm already imagining what it must look like inside, the hallway leading into the first exam room. I'm picturing the door opening, picturing the five of us rushing in. An entire swarm of butterflies have invaded my stomach, making their way up my lungs and my throat.

The room is swathed in nerves, coated with anxiety as thick as a block of ice on a winter morning, and I'm wishing we could just start already. I'm praying to god the button turns green. Everywhere around me are manifestations of nervous energy—bouncing feet, tapping fingers against pants legs, worrying at fraying hems.

I can't stand it anymore.

In my head, I'm thinking *green, green, green*. I am visualizing it so hard, so very intently I almost believe I can do it. Change it all by myself simply from wanting it enough.

Nothing happens. Obviously.

I am stuck standing in this in-between—this limbo of wondering when it will be my group's turn—for another ten agonizing minutes before it finally happens.

The red light blinks. It falters.

It changes.

It's green.

The doors slide open with a hissing sound and then suddenly, I'm in. It takes just one step to be swallowed by the darkness.

The first part of the test isn't about speed at all. It's the testing of physical abilities, the testing of technical skills. So I make my way down the hallway slowly, taking step after step through the dim passageways lit only by blue lights down at the bottom. Up about fifteen feet above, I can see where the constructed walls end. And even higher, the ceiling of the stadium.

It is so very quiet.

My heart is beating a fast, staccato rhythm in my chest and my ears are roaring with blood. I can't even hear the other people in my group. I have no idea where they are. It's almost as if I am the sole living being in this entire stadium.

The first hallway spits me out in an enclosed space—still part of the maze, I think—that is probably a quarter of the size of a football field. This room too is awash in the blue light spilling from the bottom of the walls, but it is brighter here. Bright enough for me to see my surroundings in clear detail—the weights on the left; the knives and target on the right. The gun. A door carved into the wall on the left opens out onto an indoor running track.

In front of me, a digital screen embedded into the wall tells me exactly what I need to do. It is a list of physical exercises: push-ups, pull-ups, lifts, sit-ups, run a mile. Do the listed amount, or until you fail. After that it's how accurately you can throw the five knives lined up on the table. How accurately you can shoot a gun. Different distances, each time.

I swallow. Pick up the barbell in the corner, and get started.

CHAPTER 15

I t takes me thirty-five minutes to make my way through the exercises. And by the end of it, I am dripping more sweat than I think
is possible. Even without having gone all in, I am beginning to feel
the tinges of exhaustion creeping in.

The second part of Initiation is the simulation, and this part is
actually scored based off of time, so I pass through the connecting
hallway into the simulation chamber almost immediately.

And then I stop.

I'm at a crossroads. I've arrived at a T in the maze; there is a path
left and a path right, and for a second, I just stand there. Staring.
Very much aware I'm wasting precious seconds because I have absolutely no idea which path to take. I am the most indecisive person in
the world and right now, it is biting me in the ass.

My heartbeat is bleating *make a decision, make a decision.* I want
so badly to shut it up.

My eyes catch on a very plain button—at least, I think it's a
button—in the wall directly in front of me. One press and two holograms unravel in front of me, one before each path.

I finally understand what this is. Paris said the simulation tested
our ability to read people. I'm guessing I have to figure out which
hologram is telling the truth.

Right hologram says: "Take my path down. I can guarantee you
safe passage and a shortcut through the maze."

Left hologram says: "Don't listen to them. They're lying. My path is the one that will offer you those things."

I'm running through the lying cues we learned in school in my head: sweating, looking away, fidgeting.

I think it's the left one. Maybe? Suddenly, I'm unsure and I start wondering how the others are doing, whether they've already gone past this first obstacle.

I hope I'm not last. God, I should've done *some* prep, at least. I make a mental note to remind Josephine when I get out of this so she's better prepared for her test.

I play it again, just to be sure, and then I kill the holograms and run to the left. I hope I made the right decision. I'm halfway down the hall—I can see the left turn into what must be the next obstacle—when I hear it. Voices speaking words that send icicles straight down my back, piercing my chest.

I hear my name. I hear Paris's name. And suddenly, the Initiation falls into the background and all of my attention is focused on listening.

A voice says, "Yesterday was extremely concerning. He said Paris and Anna killed Edenfield before the guards were able to get in."

A frozen chill shudders across my entire body. *Who are these people?* I realize I must be standing near an outer wall of the maze if I can hear their voices this clearly. They must be members of the faculty.

A second voice. "Yes, I did hear about that. Unexpected, but we knew we'd have to lose people in this. It's a necessary sacrifice. At least Edenfield was able to tell us what they came for before he was shot."

It takes me a minute too long to understand. Seconds tick by and I am still thinking that everything is fine, that it is okay, that our mission was successful. And then my feeling of safety crumbles. It crashes. *I* crash headfirst into horror and shock until I am up to my neck in it. I feel numb, rooted to the ground.

The first voice makes a noise in the back of his throat. "He said he's destroying the list the day after tomorrow. A little risky, in my opinion, but I suppose one doesn't just march into the king's study." He?

"What's the excuse?"

"There is no excuse. The king has his Circle meeting then, so the study will be empty."

"Good fortune."

I'm dead. I've died all over the floor, the simulation, the maze. I am almost convinced I've been shot in the head because I *cannot* believe what I'm hearing.

They're destroying the list.

I killed a man for that list. Without it, we have no leads.

I am swallowing the bile in my throat, bitter on bitter on bitter. I need to go. I need to leave. I need to *get out* of this stupid maze and tell the rest of them.

For a second, I consider using the headset, but I'm not sure if it's monitored. I'm not sure who else can listen in, if it's someone on *their* side. So I keep going.

I follow the hallway all the way down and I'm starting to realize that this maze is less about trying to figure out which direction to go and more about getting past these obstacles because it dumps me out into yet another room.

From what Paris said yesterday, I recognize this one right away. It's a poisons test. Mix potions to get the counteragent that's supposed to get you through the noxious gas in the next hallway.

I resist the urge to murder myself. Poisons is what I'm best at, but it is a meticulous, meticulous process. A precise science. Exact amounts to the milliliter and steps that can't be skipped or switched—and *god*, I am mentally shooting myself in the head.

I don't have time for this. I need to get through this simulation and warn the others.

Quickly, I grab test tubes, beakers, funnels, burettes, and different chemicals labeled by color. I'm reading the instructions, measuring everything to the milliliter, double-checking that I have the right ingredient because one wrong move and it's over. I will not pass. But I'm painfully aware of the seconds ticking by. The minutes.

By the time I'm done, my entire brain is mush. Jelly.

I take the resulting vial and shotgun it, tilting my head back, dumping the contents unceremoniously into my mouth. I am running out of time. Up ahead, I can see the gas beginning to seep into the hallway, ducking under crevices and leaping into the air in clouds of white.

I plunge headfirst into it, fanning the air with my arms as if I could push the gas away from me. In the midst of it, it's difficult to see. I am in a haze of white. A veritable snowstorm.

I'm beginning to get claustrophobic again. I have never thought of myself as the type, but I guess I am. I can feel my heartbeat rising, and in the absence of sight, it feels stronger. More potent. It is a bird, flying straight out of my chest.

The claustrophobia is also making it difficult to breathe—or maybe it's the sheer density of the gas. Difficult to inhale air. It is almost as if my lungs have become infant lungs, have shrunken to the size of walnuts and can no longer take in enough oxygen to support the normal functioning of my body. And the more rapidly I inhale, the more out of breath I get.

It isn't until my vision starts swimming that I realize what's happening. For the second time today, my brain is too slow—takes too long to recognize reality.

This is not claustrophobia.

It is the gas. Someone must have tampered with it because the counteragent isn't working. And even if somehow I messed it up, the gas used for this exam shouldn't be strong enough to cause this.

I am being poisoned. I know it.

This shouldn't even be surprising, really. It shouldn't. After all, I just heard two people talking about the Dawn Court infiltration. Two people who are clearly working against the court. It makes perfectly logical sense that someone would be trying to kill me.

Given my upbringing, I've always thought that in the event of dying, I'd be logical about it. I'd keep calm, stick to my lessons, figure out a way out of it. Except panic is making my head spin. Panic is the hand that twists the top of the dreidel that is my brain and I am going round and round and round.

I can't think.

I *should* be getting out of this gas, running straight until I am far, far away, except I can't remember which direction I came from. I have no idea which way to go and *oh god* I am seeing spots of black.

I can't die like this.

Lightning bolts of pain are shooting around my body, ricocheting off my skin like it's made of metal and just zapping, zapping, zapping around, unable to escape. In my desperation, I stumble straight into a wall and almost knock the headset off and—

The headset. I'm so stupid. It is almost humbling what this panic is doing to me.

I press the button. I press and press and press like my life depends on it—I suppose, actually, it does—until I hear Paris's voice crackling on the other side. He says, almost cautiously, "Anna, are you okay?" and I want, I want to die from relief. I am drowning in the wave of it that is crashing over my head, cool water in the summer heat that is my panic. My fear. My desperation.

"*No,*" I say. "I think the gas was switched out with something else." The words are tumbling out of my mouth, an incoherent stream I'm not even sure he can understand. But I can't seem to make my lips work in a normal way. I say, "I'm pretty sure I'm being poisoned by whatever gas this is, so please get me out. I would really appreciate it." I think I'm seeing more black than real life now.

A pause. "*What?* You're actually dying in a simulation?"

"Paris!"

"Yes, sorry. Give me a second."

The gas switches off.

"Just hold on a minute," he says. "People are coming to get you."

My vision's hazy. My *mind* is hazy. I think I'm becoming delirious. "Paris," I say, "if I die, do you think I'm going to heaven or hell?"

"Anna?" He sounds anxious now. It tints his voice and I'm thinking, *This is strange.* I've never heard Paris anxious before. At least, not recently. And then, "How long were you in the gas before you called for me?"

"Um," I say. I can't seem to remember anything very well. It's coming in flashes, in broken timelines and fragments of memories. "A while. I think."

A crackling sound like something moving on the other end. "Okay," he says. The thudding of footsteps and I'm thinking, *Thank god.* I'm feeling relief seeping into my brain, pushing against the mental fog. Paris must know they're close too, because he humors my question. "I think we're all going to hell. I think heaven is a fabricated concept for false reassurance."

I blink. "Oh."

"So you really don't want to die."

I fall backward into the darkness.

CHAPTER 16

Sometimes the screams and the blood, the sounds and the images all still haunt me. Still show up in my dreams like vindictive ghosts that just won't let me go. I was fifteen when it happened—the worst attack on the Midnight Court since the accords. Except, it wasn't even on Shanghai territory—it was in London.

Six years after the accords were finally signed, the leaders of our two cities decided to try something new. They put into motion something that had never been attempted before, never even dreamt of:

Integration.

They initiated the process of merging our two courts, having both cities open to Dawn Courters and Midnight Courters alike for the first time in centuries.

Starting with small groups, a dozen volunteers from each court were sent into the other city as an experiment.

Project Integration hinged upon the success of that experiment and it

did not

deliver.

Instead, it delivered this: Massacre.

I was dreaming, I remember, when we got the news. The dream I remember with frightening clarity. Everything else was a blur.

My parents woke me up, and it was written on their faces. Devastation. Pain that I hadn't seen since I was eight—since before the accords were even signed—and I knew, I knew something had happened. Something was wrong.

My mom prefaced it by saying, "Don't worry, Liang An Na."

Except that just made it worse.

When they told me, I couldn't believe my ears for a second. I remember scrubbing at them—my ears, I mean—figuring maybe there was something wrong with them. Maybe they were waterlogged—I had taken a shower right before bed that day, something my mother always cautioned against because she'd always believed having wet hair before you slept meant trouble.

I scrubbed for four minutes. Maybe five. Until they were red and raw and my mother had to catch my hands and hold them in hers and then, finally, I began to process.

Began to understand.

The Dawn Court had killed them. The entire group that had gone over from Shanghai—they had massacred them all. Brought in their shiny new guns, their pistols and rifles and whatever god-awful abomination to humanity they had, and buried them all with bullets.

This was what my parents told me. Later on, I saw it for myself. A play-by-play on a tiny phone screen so horrible it should've been a movie. Couldn't be reality. It must've been taken by one of the Midnight Courters there because it was from the perspective of someone in the group. You could see them all in the room, the six seconds of quiet, of peace, before the first shot rang out.

A bullet, shot point-blank into the forehead of the man in the foreground of the recording, blood oozing out—except it wasn't slow, like syrup, as you might expect. It was a huge flood of it, all at once, blood mixing with gray brain matter, and I wanted to throw up right there. Wanted to vomit out all the substances of my body until I could faint. Until I could erase these images from my mind.

And then the video grew choppy. Chaotic. Screams and gunshots blending together into some grotesque melody-harmony that lasted all of three minutes. At three minutes and twenty-two seconds, a splatter of blood on-screen. Like crimson paint, covering the camera lens, and then just a close-up of a face.

The very dead eyes of the person behind the camera, and I recognized that tiny mole just below the eye that I knew like some imprint on my heart because it could belong to no one else, only

my aunt.

CHAPTER 17

I am floating.
>   At

>   peace.

I have never known peace.

I wake up in a hospital bed. One so very similar to the one I was confined to a week ago that for a second, I am disoriented. I forget for the second time in so many days that I'm not home.

And then the rest of the room comes into focus, and I am reminded by its foreignness that this is not the Midnight Court.

I'm lying in what I assume is the school's infirmary. It's not particularly large, but not small either. To my left and in front of me are rows of pristine white beds. All of them are empty, except for mine.

I guess no one else was injured during Initiation.

"You're awake!"

Something collides into me and I realize, laggardly, that it's Josephine. Her hair is disheveled and her makeup is smudged and I realize she must have slept here overnight.

"Hi," I say. My voice comes out in a croak and I clear it. Surprised.

"You scared the *shit* out of me! You literally looked like you already passed into the afterlife when they brought you out. What the hell happened?"

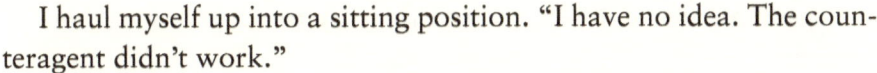

I haul myself up into a sitting position. "I have no idea. The counteragent didn't work."

Josephine's face turns solemn. "You think it's someone in here?"

I lower my voice, glancing at the door to make sure no one's eavesdropping before I say, "I heard two people talking about what happened in the Dawn Court when I was in the maze." I swallow. "About Edenfield. They said 'he's' going to destroy the list in two days and—"

Suddenly, I realize I have no idea what day it is. I have no idea whether I've been asleep for a few hours or a few days. I have no idea if the list has already been destroyed. Panic shoots through me like a blossoming flower in my chest and I bolt upright.

"Wait, what day is it? How long have I been asleep?"

"Just overnight," Josephine says.

Oh, thank god. I fall back. Close my eyes.

"And also," Josephine clears her throat, "administration's taking the poisoning as you failing to create the right antidote, so, um... you're not going to have a very high score."

"That's fine," I say. I can't be bothered to care. Not that it even matters; it's not like either of us are going to place for jobs after Eladine. The thought that Josephine must've already gone through her Initiation passes briefly through my mind, but it is immediately drowned out by the more pressing concern. "That means we only have one day to get that list." And then, belatedly I ask, "Where's Paris?"

"Oh," she says. "He came by for a couple hours last night." Grins. "We talked. Anna, he's so *cute*. I mean, he was always kinda pretty as a kid—but damn, he grew up. I can't believe you didn't tell me."

Sometimes, I think I want to strangle her. Truly. "Please stop talking."

The door opens.

And I am mortified.

Paris walks in. I can't tell from his expression whether or not he overheard our conversation before he came in.

I really, really hope not.

I shoot a glare at Josephine and then try to act as nonchalant as possible.

He says, "Good morning, Anna. Josephine."

"Hi, Paris," Josephine says. She smiles. "I was just leaving, actually." And then with a wink, she's gone.

I glare at her retreating back.

Paris is dressed in full Dawn Court white. White pants, white jacket. It's so very unlike him and I realize in the past week, I'd almost forgotten he was Dawn Court. Forgotten that we stand on opposite sides of this war.

He says, "Hey."

"Hi," I return. I watch him sit down in the chair Josephine was just in. Brace his elbows on his knees.

Looks at me and asks, "How are you?"

I shift in the bed. "I'm okay. All things considered. I mean, at least I'm still alive." I say it lightly, jokingly.

He doesn't laugh. Doesn't even crack a smile. His face is the very definition of a closed book; I have no idea what he's thinking. I have no idea why he's being so distant. Suddenly, I'm uncomfortable.

"Why are you—"

I stop. I realize I have no idea what to say because isn't this who he is? As long as I've known him and despite the sheer amount of time we've spent around each other because of this assignment, I realize I still don't actually *know* him anymore.

We were both forced to do this. We are not friends, something he made abundantly clear in Shanghai.

I'm not sure why I expected something else—*when* I even started.

"Never mind," I say.

He acts like I didn't even speak. Looks down at his palms. Says, "Anna, we need to talk."

I fall back against my pillow. Exhausted already, even though he hasn't even really begun. Not really. "Okay," I say. "About what?"

"I don't think we should work together anymore. I believe, at this point, that it's clear the Midnight Court—to the knowledge of the Emperor and your Council—wasn't involved with the theft. I'll let the Dawn Court know and you and Josephine can go back to Shanghai tomorrow."

I am—

I am in shock. And I think, *This is what it feels like to be hit by a truck*. No, not a truck—a battering ram.

I have no idea why this is hitting me so hard. Really, I should be happy to be going home except,

except...

I was just almost killed for this. I infiltrated the Dawn Court headquarters for this. And I refuse to go home before I find out who was really responsible. I refuse to return to Shanghai with failure cupped in my palms and etched into the skin of my hands.

"You have got to be kidding me," I say in disbelief.

"Anna—"

"No. You don't get to do this. You don't get to shut me out just because you don't feel like working together anymore. I don't care. If you care so much about it, *you* can stop investigating. I'll do it on my own."

Paris raises his eyes heavenward. "Anna, do you not understand the implications of the simple fact that someone tried to *kill you*? That you nearly *died*? You might be all right with that, but I am certainly not. Keep going and I'll be the one burying your casket," he snaps.

"But I didn't, did I? Do us both a favor," I say. "Don't pretend like you care. In fact, *you* were the one trying to kill me on multiple occasions in recent memory."

He shoots me a dirty look. "Oh, please, like I would've actually killed you. I very well could've, remember? I didn't."

"Yeah, peacetime, whatever." I wave a hand. "Point is, I'm not leaving."

Before he can say anything else, I slide out of bed, irritation offsetting the weakness in my legs, and leave the infirmary.

I need air.

CHAPTER 18

Twenty minutes later, I'm still angry.

I haven't completed any part of my assignment. Haven't gleaned any information on the Dawn Court. Haven't figured out who was responsible. All I know is, this isn't over for me. I cannot go back to the Midnight Court. I cannot see the disappointment clouding their eyes, perched on their shoulders.

What I do know is that I refuse to be second choice. Second best. Second, second, second to my perfect sister who has never tasted failure in her life. I am eighteen years old, so why, why am I still so afraid of her shadow?

As I make my way back to my dorm—not to pack, but to plan—I bump into Kyan in the hallway. I'm caught off guard, my mind dwelling on the need to get to that list, even if Paris won't help me.

"Hey," he says, blinking in surprise. "I was just on my way to visit you."

"Oh," I say. I'm a little lost for words. "Thank you. I was feeling a lot better, and there was no one around. I figured I'd just discharge myself."

"That's good," he says. "I hope it was nothing too serious."

My phone rings.

It is so sudden, so *loud* in this quiet hallway, that I actually jump. I didn't even realize my ringer was on.

"Sorry," I say to Kyan, wiggling my phone out of my back pocket. The caller ID is flashing: 妈妈. Mom.

I frown. "Sorry," I say again, beginning to speed walk away to find somewhere more private. "I just have to take this really quick." I have no idea what this could be about. My mother very rarely actually calls me.

"Ma? Hello?" I say in Mandarin as I enter an empty room, shutting the door firmly behind me.

"Anna, thank god. Are you okay? We just heard about what happened."

"Oh." *Of course.* "Yes, I'm fine. I'm sorry I didn't get a chance to call you guys yet."

"What happened?"

In a whisper, I give her the rundown. Everything that's happened in the past few days. Everything I heard during Initiation.

"Be careful," she says. "Keep your eyes wide open. Trust nothing and trust no one. Do you understand?"

"Yes, Ma."

"There's something else," she says. And I, I feel the dread pooling in my stomach before she even speaks. I think I must hate anticipation more than anything else in the world, because the sudden flash of anxiety finds my small intestine and large intestine tying instant little knots around each other until I am full of them. If you opened me up, you would see a knitting masterpiece.

"What is it?"

"There's been an attempt on the life of the Emperor's daughter."

My mouth

falls

open.

My brain is a sudden city of thoughts and a very loud, blaring fear that screams *This could mean war.*

I say, "Attempt, right? That means she's still alive?"

"Yes, but it was close. Too close. Anna, I think it might've been as much of an actual attempt to kill her as it was a warning for you. To stop investigating."

"You think it's the same person?"

"I think whatever it is you're doing over there, you're on the right track. But, sweetheart, if you want to come home we'd understand, your father and I. Tensions between our two courts right now are very, very high." She hesitates. "The Council's been talking about war. About launching the attack they had planned to do earlier. I don't want you to be caught up in it if that happens."

I shake my head, and then remember that she can't see me. "No, I need to stay. If it really is the same person, I can figure out who it is. Maybe prove that they were acting on their own. This doesn't need to become a war." *And prove myself too*, I think.

"Just don't get your hopes up," my mom sighs.

"I won't," I say.

"All right, I trust you, Anna. I love you. Stay safe."

"Bye, *Māmā*." There's a beeping sound as she hangs up.

Exiting the room, I see Kyan still waiting in the same place down the hall. "We need to talk."

Ten minutes later, we're in the common room in the Lotus. Kyan is calling the other three to tell them to meet us; I can hear the jumble of voices from his phone.

I'm still hesitant on whether I can trust them. This wariness, this ingrained distrust of Dawn Court members simply because of the side they belong to has been embedded in me since birth. But at the same time, I have a gut feeling that I can. And I have always been taught to trust my instincts.

Beyond that, I don't really have a choice. I need them.

"Yes, now," Kyan's saying, holding the phone directly in front of him. I assume it's a video call.

"Dude," Max grumbles. "It's fucking eleven a.m. I wasn't even awake yet."

"That," Dev says, "is your own problem. But also, why are we meeting again?"

"I concur." Paris. "What, exactly, are we being called for?"

"Anna has information," says Kyan.

"Tell Anna to go home."

I bristle. "Tell Paris to shut up."

Kyan blinks. Says, "I assume you two can hear each other."

"I believe they're having a spat," says Max. And then, in a high-pitched voice, "Shut up!"

"No, you shut up!" Dev adds.

"Both of you shut up," I snap. "And get over here." Kyan hangs up. Within five minutes, they're all here.

"Okay," says Max. He's sprawled on the couch, fully taking up all three seats as well as the armrests. I have no idea how he does it. "What's up, Anna?"

Before I answer, I turn to Paris, who's leaning against the wall a few feet away, arms crossed with a stony expression on his face. "If I tell you what I know, I get to be involved. You can't kick me off this assignment."

He sets his jaw. "Fine."

I smile. "Great." Turning to the rest of them, I say, "So, here's the thing. Right before everything happened during Initiation, I heard people talking. Two men, I think. Saying that someone's going to destroy the list of all the names soon. Tomorrow. Which means—"

"We need to get to it before they do," says Kyan, frowning. "That means whoever it is, their name is on there. Which means we're on the right track."

"Does that mean we have to infiltrate headquarters *again*?" Dev looks like he'd rather do anything else.

"No," Paris says, quietly. "We shouldn't risk it another time. I'll go. If it's in my father's study, I'll just ask him for it."

"I'm going with you," I say.

"For god's sake, Anna," he says. "*Must* you? What could you possibly need to come along for?"

"You agreed," I point out.

His voice is tight. "Fine. We leave tonight."

This entire day, I think, has felt like a series of broken, out-of-place moments—jumping from place to place, from conversation to conversation. And I realize I have no idea how I went from waking up in a hospital bed this morning to walking into the Dawn Court yet again.

Except this time, it's the actual palace. We're at one of the side entrances, the one closest to the king's study, waiting for the guards to change shifts again. As soon as it's clear, we enter.

The first thing I notice as we enter is the stunning interior of the Dawn Court palace—all white marble and gleaming gold. I have no idea how they keep it so polished. Even the carpet I'm walking on is golden.

Here and there, glass cases on stands line the wall, all filled with random objects. A semi-melted dagger, a rusted key. A book so old its pages are discolored, flecked with brown.

Artifacts, I realize. The Dawn Court sure loves its history.

We turn a couple corners, but only make it three feet down a hallway when Paris stops abruptly. He knocks on a door that doesn't seem any different from the others—maybe for safety reasons. When there's no answer, his gaze slides to me.

I shrug and the corner of his mouth quirks up. He twists the doorknob and opens the door.

The room we enter is a far cry from Edenfield's office. It is so big, so airy and spacious, it seems to be the size of an entire apartment loft. The wall opposite where we're standing by the door is lined with bay windows—huge panels of glass that I'm guessing are almost fifteen feet tall, maybe even twenty.

I can't quite believe I'm in the Dawn Court king's *study*. That I was let in so easily. It's almost absurd, almost comical how effortless it has been for me to carry out the Emperor's assignment so far.

On the left, I see a giant fireplace—one with an actual fire, which is surprising considering how many are fake these days—and a desk. Just as the boys had mentioned, the king's desk is piled with stacks of paper, pages strewn across the surface of it haphazardly. It's a wonder he can find anything.

Max wasn't lying when he said *understatement of the century*. I thought I was messy, but Gideon Ateş quite possibly puts me to shame.

I turn, taking in the remainder of the study. The floor is covered by a giant rectangular rug, and there's a worn leather couch that seems oddly out of place. On the right, the wall is made up of bookshelves. Bookshelves housing not just books but also *more papers*.

This man really needs to get himself some folders. I consider saying it out loud to Paris.

"Well," he says. "Do you want to take the desk? Or do you want me to?"

I have no idea why "I'll do it" comes out of my mouth.

Paris shrugs as if to say, *Have it your way* and moves toward the shelves.

I've only been searching through the piles on the desk for half an hour when Paris finishes with the shelves. He's coming over to the desk to help me when a sudden impulse pulls me by the wrist, drags me to the fireplace and I

really

hope I'm not looking at what I think I am.

Oh no. I think I *am*.

I swallow. "It's not here." I'm staring into the fire, at the white flecks of ashes that are scattered around the ground near it like snow—like the burned up remains of hope. And I'm thinking, *We're too late*.

"What? How do you know?" Paris's voice floats over from where he's standing near the desk, still rifling through papers.

"Because," I say, "I'm staring at the ashes."

The rifling stops. I hear quiet footsteps as he comes to stand behind me.

I point weakly to the flecks. "See?"

"Well," says Paris. "Shit."

I can't stop staring at it. My stomach is a stone sinking to the bottom of the well and my lungs are completely deflated. I can't seem to remember where my hands are, my head, my legs. I can't *think* and I can't

stop

staring.

"What now?" I ask.

"I guess we go update my father."

The king is in the boardroom.

I find myself wishing it was safe for the guards to just know who I am, because avoiding them is becoming increasingly exhausting. Paris checks inside first to make sure his father is the only one in the room before we walk in together.

Gideon Ateş is sitting at the very head of an oval table, wearing a clean white suit with his hair done to absolute perfection.

He is, I can tell, a man who cares very much about his appearance.

"Paris. Anna," he says. He doesn't seem surprised to see us. "What brings you two here?"

"An update," Paris says, "on the *assignment* you gave us." He looks at his father. "Someone here is connected to the theft. Possibly even responsible for it."

He explains how we were trying to find the list, how someone must've snuck into the study and burned it before we got there. The entire time Paris is speaking, I'm listening for any sort of noise outside, paranoid that someone's about to walk in, that someone's eavesdropping even though I know this room must be soundproof.

There is so much at stake here.

"I know this is a long shot," Paris says. "But is there any chance you remember who was on the list?"

Gideon is just saying, "Unfortunately not," when the door opens. Closes. And we all turn to find Darren striding in. My sigh of relief is almost audible.

He stops short when he sees us, a look of surprise flitting across his face. "Oh, hello again," he says. "I admit I was only expecting to see Father, but it's good to see the two of you, as well."

"Hey, Dar," Paris says, shifting his entire expression so that he just seems pleased to see his brother. He says, "Anna and I were just visiting Father."

"Of course," Darren says. He reaches out to pat Paris on the back and—

I see them. Right above a scar on his wrist: white flecks. They're stuck to the sleeve of Darren's dress shirt. Tiny pale dots of incrimination and I—I feel like I've been punched in the chest. Like someone has hit me with the full force of a truck and knocked all the breath out of my lungs.

I am afraid to move. Afraid that he'll see that I *know*—that I have put two and two together because there is *ash*, ash from the fireplace on this prince's sleeve and I simply cannot believe my eyes.

I cannot believe my mind.

He stole the poison? It doesn't make any sense.

My brain won't stop spinning. I swear I can hear the cogs and the wheels turning and clanking and screeching and it is almost a miracle that they can't. That Darren can't. I have no idea what to do. I need to tell Paris.

Or maybe I don't.

I don't know, I don't know, I don't know.

The king is saying, "Thank you for the update," to Paris but his voice sounds so very tinny, so very far away, like there is a glass wall that is separating him and us. I need to leave.

My heart is pounding in my chest, and it is not even a bird anymore: it is an elephant. A whole dinosaur—a pterodactyl, or maybe a Tyrannosaurus rex—and it is stomping all over my body. I can feel it in my *bones*. Like my entire body is a bell and my heartbeat is making it reverberate all over.

There is a smile plastered to my face, faker than anything I have ever said or done in my life, but I just keep smiling. Keep standing there until finally, finally we're leaving. Finally, we're being escorted out of the palace and I'm trying to elbow Paris as inconspicuously as I can, but he says tersely—

"I know."

Just two little words. I bite my lip.

I'm about to ask, "What now?" except we're stepping outside and—

A sound completely shatters, completely obliterates the silence, the stillness in the night around us, and Paris and I throw ourselves to the ground immediately, him grabbing for his gun and me grabbing for a knife, a dagger—*anything*—but at this distance, I don't think it would even do any good.

"Are they shooting at *us*?" I ask, frantically glancing around from our location behind one of the pillars.

"What do you think?" Paris hisses back. "They're definitely not shooting at each other."

It's beginning to get tedious, really, how often I'm finding myself in these situations.

I'm thinking, *I'm never coming back here again*. Either I'm shooting someone or I'm getting shot at. Not exactly situations I enjoy being in.

"Do you see anyone?"

"They're in the trees," he murmurs. "I can't get a clear shot."

"We're sitting ducks here," I say. "We're in the light and they're in the dark. We need to get out of here." I am running through potential strategies in my head, one after the other, but I can't think of a single way both of us can get out of here unharmed. It's statistically impossible.

"Our best shot is going back in the building," Paris says under his breath to me. "Sneaking out through some other exit."

"Lead the way."

"On three," he says.

"One...

"Two...

"Three."

We burst forward, emerging out from the cover of the pillar and racing toward the front door. The world is exploding, gunshots perforating the air until it's pockmarked with holes, with imperfections. It is complete and utter chaos.

I have no idea where the bullets are going, no idea if they're two feet or two centimeters from me, because right now, all I can feel is adrenaline. And it is drowning out everything else.

I keep my eyes trained on Paris's back and we are racing down hallway after hallway, flinging ourselves around corners, and for the second time in an hour, I feel déjà vu. Fuzzy around the edges.

On impulse, I ask, breathing hard, "Where's Darren's room?"

Paris turns around to look at me like I'm insane. "Really? Do you think now's the best time?"

"We're here, anyway," I gasp, following him as he ducks into yet another hallway. "It's a hell of a lot more convenient than sneaking in for the *third time*."

I think the last sentence is what gets him.

Paris's mouth tightens. He says, "Fine," and then he's grabbing my hand, whipping me around in the opposite direction and we very, very narrowly miss crashing headfirst into the guards who have closed in upon us.

The next two minutes are so chaotic I have absolutely no idea what's happening, no idea where we are in the palace, can't make out anything around me except a blur of the same white and gold, and then Paris is yanking open a door—not bothering to knock this time—and we're stumbling in.

He slams the door shut behind us.

Darren's bedroom. I'm scanning the room, taking one second, two, to process it all. King bed—all white—dark oak walls, empty desk in the corner. Another door that I assume leads to his closet. It is all so *bare*, so impersonal, as if he's only a guest here rather than an actual resident. Rather than someone who has lived here his entire life and for a second, it is disorienting.

Rapidly, we search through Darren's entire room, moving as fast as possible, and I'm hoping to god the guards don't find us and that Darren doesn't decide to walk in at this exact moment. I'm hoping he's having a nice, very long conversation with his father. He seems like a talker, anyway.

Paris says, "Try not to disrupt anything. My brother has excessively good eyesight, especially for someone who stares at a phone for at least half the day."

I shove the drawers back into the nightstand. Nothing there. "Only half a day? I remember you used to be attached to your phone the *entire day*."

I don't know what compels me to say this.

Paris raises his eyebrow at me from where he's crouched down at the desk. "Is that a joke you're telling, Anna?"

I flush and quickly look away.

Three minutes later, Paris says, "There's nothing here. We need to go, someone's bound to find us soon."

I'm about to agree, about to pull open the door, when my eyes catch on Darren's coat hanging from the coatrack.

Hm.

I ignore Paris's expression of confusion. Grabbing the jacket, I quickly shove my fingers inside both pockets until I find what I'm looking for:

A slip of paper, folded into fourths. I open it.

Bingo.

CHAPTER 19

It's a letter. Thinking quickly, I pull out my phone and snap a picture.

The letter is addressed to Darren, telling him exactly what needs to happen at a ball that I can only assume is taking place sometime in the near future. Telling him to hold on to the poison until it's time, and that is all I need to see, all I have *time* to see, because I'm suddenly very aware of footsteps getting louder outside and Paris is flinging open the door, ushering me out, and we are back on the run.

Hallway after hallway after hallway—clearly, whoever designed the Dawn Court was not particularly adept at their job—and then he's shoving open a door and we're outside again. Into the trees. Enveloped by darkness.

"Watch out," Paris whispers to me. "They're out here somewhere."

My stomach is back to tying knots. My fingers are gripping the handle of the knife so tightly my knuckles are white.

It's dark in the midst of all these trees. The very definition of pitch-black. I can just barely make out the outlines of the trunks and branches and leaves surrounding us—and the outline of Paris's body next to mine.

We're pressed into the trunk of a tree, the two of us, and the silence is so thick, so suffocating, that I am afraid to move a muscle. Afraid to make any sound because in this complete absence of it, a single snap or crack or rustle might as well be a neon sign blaring *Here I am! Come get me!*

I wonder how long a human body can go without moving.

My heart is pounding so hard, so quickly that I can feel it reverberate everywhere in my body. Every snap of a twig and whoosh of air through the leaves is making me flinch, and I'm thinking, *The gas was different.* The gas was maybe a minute, probably not even, of panic. Panic that was also slightly muted by the muddled fog in my brain. But this, this is pure panic. This is panic that I have rarely known before. I am almost painfully aware that my life is at risk right now. This is death so close it is kissing my cheek, brushing cool fingers through my hair. The devil is whispering in my ear, telling me *We will meet soon.*

I open my mouth to say something to Paris, to ask if they're even here anymore because I can't see anything, can't hear anything, but he shakes his head. Nods toward something to the right, and I squint into the darkness. I wish my eyes would focus—wish I could be like a cat or a bat or whatever else sees in the dark. And I'm taking an unconscious step forward—because that's what people do when they're trying to see better—when I spot it.

A very faint outline of a figure a couple yards away, the space where their body is just slightly darker than the surrounding area, and I am realizing too late that I shouldn't have taken that step. My foot is halfway in the air but it's too late to turn back, to say *never mind* because I know that this is going to give away our location, but it is almost like everything is moving in

slow

motion.

The way it is when you can see the end before it happens, but there's nothing you can do to stop it.

And then suddenly, Paris is yanking me backward, fingers around my wrist, and I'm colliding into his body. My back is flush with his chest and I stop breathing.

This, this is a different type of adrenaline, but it is charging through me just the same. Adrenaline and fear creating a mixture that is coursing through my veins like sweet poison and I...

I am losing control.

In the back of my mind, I'm very aware of the immediate danger that we're still in, but even as I'm staring out into the darkness, I know I'm not focused on that. I can't bring myself to care. I can feel Paris's gaze on me, and it is taking every last shred of self-control not to turn around. Not to face him.

I can feel his body heat all down my back, and his heartbeat is tangling with mine until I can no longer tell which one's which. I am lightheaded from sheer proximity, drunk off his scent, and I realize, bad habits die hard, and this is the worst of them all. He is.

My body falls back far too easily into this same pattern, this same cage, and I am there, I am watching, but I do absolutely nothing to stop myself from careening back into this disaster that already threatened to *destroy* me three years before.

I am not smart. I do not learn from my mistakes. I am fated to repeat every single error I have ever made in my life and this,

this is the only one I cannot come back from.

I want to empty my brain. Scrub it clean with bleach and soap and leave it blank. Make it new and pretty like a journal you might buy at a bookstore, before it is filled with scribbles and words and marred by history.

This tension. So stretched out, so brittle that I could touch it and it would break like a stick. I could snap it in half.

Paris brushes my waist—lightly, so lightly, almost like a breath or a kiss—and my own breath catches in my throat before I forget how to breathe altogether. His touch is *scalding* through the thin fabric of my shirt, and I am almost excruciatingly aware of his fingers as they travel down, graze my hip. Curve around my waist until his hands are gripping my skin and I can't even begin to understand how this heat doesn't leave marks behind, five identical brands on each side. Paris is breathing hard; I can feel the rise and fall of his chest against my back, can feel the heat of his breath on my shoulder, and it's injecting lighter fluid straight into my bloodstream, setting it alight, stealing the air from my lungs and the strength from my legs. This moment—this moment is stretched as taut as a tightrope. I am almost afraid to breathe.

All I know is, I want more. I want to feel his hand pressed against my skin—solid, hot. I want to touch every inch of him, and I can *feel* how close he is to me; if I just turned my head his mouth would be on mine,

but I stop myself. I realize the reality of what I'm thinking—what I'm doing.

"We shouldn't," I whisper to Paris, stepping away a little until there's at least a sliver of air between us. "We can't."

"I know." I can feel him swallow. "Anna," he says in a low voice and he too sounds a little out of breath. "It's one person, I think. We just need to find them before they find us."

"Oh," I say. I have no idea what I was expecting him to say, but it definitely wasn't that. "How do you know?"

"Just trust me," he says.

"Okay," I say, and I realize in this moment that I do trust him. Almost too easily. "So let's find them." Slowly, cautiously, I peel myself away from the tree—away from him—and venture a couple of steps into the darkness as silently as I can.

I don't hear him follow, but I sense his presence behind me, like a hot brand at my back. God, maybe this wasn't a good idea. This entire thing.

My eyes are adjusting to the darkness slowly. Too slowly, the outlines of the trunks and branches and leaves are taking shape.

The knife in my hand suddenly feels pitifully inadequate—it might as well be a plastic fork or spoon—and I'm reminding myself to bring a gun next time. To make it a habit—except the Midnight Court almost never carries guns around. I am too used to the Shanghai way of life, the swords and daggers and knives.

"Wait," Paris whispers, and I nearly jump out of my skin. "I think I heard something."

Stopping dead in my tracks, I think, *I was wrong*. It is not anticipation that I hate most in this world, it is this—this feeling like I am a rabbit being hunted by a person who I cannot see, cannot sense. It is an all-consuming feeling, and if I allowed myself, I could easily drown in it. I don't know what would happen if I did.

I'm starting to think that this hunt and this running are almost worse than the dying would be. I'm wishing I could just get it over with—that the knowing is better than the not knowing—when two simultaneous gunshots obliterate my entire world. My entire reality.

Completely shatters the silence, and the shards of it fly toward me. Pierce every inch of my skin. And it takes me seven full seconds to process what happened.

That the man—it was, it seems, a man—shot the first bullet and Paris the second. I see the outline of his limp form slumped on the ground and I am suddenly so extremely grateful for this darkness. Grateful that I can't make out a single detail of his body except for the silver glint of the gun that is still clutched in his hand.

I'm on the ground; my arm throbbing where it collided with the packed dirt, pulsing out steady beats, and I have no idea how I got here. No idea how I went from standing to lying flat on my stomach on the ground in the matter of a—

My gaze catches on another glint of silver in the moonlight. It's the bullet, embedded into the trunk of the tree, and it is just then that I realize Paris must have pushed me out of the way.

Paris.

In a second, I'm shoving myself off the ground. My eyes are frantically scanning everything within a ten-foot radius around me and there is a fear in my heart, a fear in my throat that is both unfamiliar and age-old at the same time. This feels like picking up an old book, dusting it off, holding it again in the same hands. Remembering the weight, the feeling of it all at once.

It feels strange to be in this position again, fearing Paris is hurt rather than wanting to be the one who hurts him.

My eyes catch on a flash of white. He's a couple of feet away, pulling himself to a sitting position, back against the tree trunk, and I know.

I know something's wrong.

Within two seconds, I am hauling myself up, running toward him.

He looks at me as I kneel down by his side, giving my body a quick, practical once-over, and asks, "Are you okay? Are you hurt?"

Leave it to him to be asking *me* this right now.

"No," I say. "Are *you?*"

Paris is already moving, already tearing a strip of fabric from his shirt. He says, "I'm fine."

"*Paris.*"

At my tone, he looks up and he must see something in the look on my face because his voice softens. "Anna, I'm fine. It's just a graze."

Distantly, I'm watching him work, watching him patch up the wound with an efficiency that startles me. "How many times have you done this before?"

"Too many."

When he's done, his head falls back against the trunk, eyes closed. He looks exhausted, completely still, except for the rise and fall of his chest, and suddenly, it is quiet. Too quiet.

In this silence, in this near darkness, I have a sudden urge to touch him. To brush his cheek, to intertwine my fingers with his, to release the tension from his body. And this desire, this pulse of *want*, is so intense it is almost painful.

I hurry to break the quiet. "Um."

He opens his eyes and blinks at me. "What?"

I look behind me. "What do we do with the body?"

Paris glances at the mass of black a couple feet away. "You can check, but I don't think he's carrying any ID. And I don't recognize him. I assume he's just a mercenary."

"So, what? We just leave him here?"

"Yes."

After a second, he taps a finger to my elbow and murmurs, "You have a scrape. You should probably get it checked out."

I hadn't even noticed. "I will," I say.

This moment, it feels so tentative between us. So fragile, as if one touch and it'll crack. Shatter.

"Paris." I realize that I'm staring at him and I forget, momentarily, what I was about to say.

"Anna." Paris is looking at me with raised eyebrows, with green-gold eyes so hauntingly familiar it hurts. In the darkness, they are

almost colorless. In the darkness, he is a study of contrasts, of black and white and no in-between—and god, I miss him.

I miss who he used to be. Who we used to be, and it is *destroying* me. It is tearing my heart completely into halves, into thirds, and I think, I was wrong.

I was wrong about hope. Because thinking everything had died between us three years ago and in the years since was better than feeling this, this unbidden and unwelcome hope that maybe, maybe it could be reborn. Brought back from the ashes like Frankenstein's monster that shouldn't ever have been created in the first place.

And I keep reminding myself that I have to kill him, that I was born a soldier for the Midnight Court and that this is my duty, and I must, I must fulfill it. That Katerina would never question this, never even consider it. But each repetition is wringing meaning out of the words as if made of water.

And at this point, I think, I need to admit to myself that I am terrified. Terrified that I am not strong enough to do what needs to be done.

I think the combination of fear and adrenaline is making me lose my mind and that exhaustion is making me insane. My brain keeps flipping back and forth, back and forth. Past and present.

You, I want to tell Paris, *are the sun and I am Icarus. Destined to die by your hand.*

CHAPTER 20

Memories are such strange creatures. They inhabit your mind—some are at the very forefront: obnoxious, loud, attention-seeking; while others, others are simply silent. Others you're not even aware are there—until you are. Until they jump out of the water—bright orange scales flashing—and force you to look at them. To greet them like an old neighbor. Say hello.

I think last night, last night triggered memories I didn't even know existed. Like someone inserted a skeleton key and they all just came rushing out, scenes and excerpts from my life that I barely even remember. An alternate timeline of my own reality.

Forgotten memories of me and Paris at ages nine and ten, biking down the Bund and celebrating this new accord that would finally bring peace to Shanghai. To our city. Chock-full of hope and naivete and rose-colored glasses.

Memories of us six months later and Paris is leaving, transferring to the Dawn Court for the first time in both our courts' histories. Because he belongs to both. Belonged. And I think I should be grateful, privileged, that this loss is the worst I've ever felt in my life.

And then they are us at fifteen and sixteen, and I'm thinking falling in love is like fire. Like pouring gasoline over our bodies and striking a match, watching ourselves burn. At fifteen, love felt all-consuming. Eternal. Novel.

I've been trying to wash the burnt smell of memories off my hands for three years. But no matter what, regardless of what I do, they hang on like iron hooks in my skin. In my heart. And try as I might, I cannot get them out because once they're there, you can never get rid of them. They're here to stay.

Three years ago, when we tore apart, when the fissure ripped through everything we were, everything that we had built in the past four months—past years, even—it was like a crack in my entire foundation.

A tear in my entire reality.

A breakup, I think almost selfishly, is worse than death. It is knowing that whatever part of your soul that belongs to someone else is still there, somewhere. In sight but just out of reach.

Time heals all wounds, it's true, but only ones that are finite. Only ones where the hurting is finished, where there's an end—but how can there be when that person is still alive? Still there, still digging knives into your skin and still entangled in every crevice in your body.

At least three years ago, I had anger as a brace. I had betrayal as a shield, the knowledge and belief that maybe this was what was supposed to happen. That maybe I was better off.

For six months after our breakup, I clung to the idea of fate. The idea that everything happens for a reason and, therefore, that our breakup was predestined. Meant to happen. And so was the massacre.

I believed that the Fates weaved destiny with black string and let it unravel, let the pieces fall where they may.

When the attack itself happened, Paris and the king were already gone, already back to London. I hadn't even known that he had left.

We broke up on a phone call.

It was 1:00 in the afternoon in Shanghai, meaning it must've been 5:00 a.m. in London, but I'd forgotten about the time difference. In my hurt, in my anger, in my overwhelming feeling of betrayal, I'd called. Again. Again. Again.

On the fourth try, he picked up. Clearly, I'd woken him up because when he said, "Hello?" his voice was still sleepy. A little soft.

And I said, "Fuck you." At fifteen, it was one of the only times I had ever sworn in my life, and god, did it feel *good*. I felt vindictive. Unforgiving.

I heard him pause. Figured it was guilt rather than confusion, and then he said—sighed, actually—"What did I do now?"

And that, I figured, was him covering up. Pretending not to know what I was talking about.

"I can't believe you. I can't believe I ever thought I knew you. I can't believe I ever loved you," and as soon as I said that I knew it was something I could never take back. That once it was out, it was out forever.

I asked, "Were you planning this the whole time? Was this whole thing a ruse? Get close to me so you could extract whatever information you wanted? Because good job. Seriously. I had no idea."

"Anna, what the hell are you talking about?"

"The massacre," I said a little impatiently. A little caustically. "Twelve dead Midnight Courters. Are you satisfied? I told you they were planning on staging an attack so that you could help *stop* it. Not so that your father could murder all of them before they even got settled in."

"You think I told the king." It was a statement. Blunt.

"I shouldn't even be surprised," I said. "I should've known you would do this. You're a Dawn Courter, through and through." I made sure disgust permeated my voice.

And finally, sharply, he said, "Right. Everything I did and said in the past four months was a lie."

"If I wasn't clear before, this is over," I said. "We're over."

His voice was quiet. He said, "There's no future for Midnight and Dawn Courters, anyway."

I retorted, "Go to hell."

And then I hung up.

CHAPTER 21

On my way back to the common room, my phone buzzes with a text from my mom. It says: *Huangdi's going to call you soon. Be prepared and make sure you're in a secure location.* And sure enough, as soon as I lock myself back in my dorm room, I receive an encrypted call on my laptop.

Hurriedly, I put in the Midnight Court encryption code and a window blinks into existence. The Emperor is sitting in a giant leather chair behind his desk. He's dressed, I notice, in the emperor's robes—yellow gold silk, embroidered with black and purple Midnight Court designs. Official business?

Behind him is the familiar view of the main Midnight Court building; I recognize the antique wood walls immediately, the dark red carpet so worn it's obvious it hasn't been replaced in years. In the eighteen years that I have lived there, not a thing has changed.

I dip my head slightly. "Huang Shang. You wished to speak with me?" I have never, I think, spoken to the Emperor alone. And without the presence of my parents, I feel more than a little unmoored.

"Yes, Liang An Na. How's the assignment going?"

I blink. I have no idea why he's asking me this. I can feel myself trying to keep a straight face, feel myself failing, frowning. I'm trying to read his expression, trying to figure out where he's going with this, but he gives away nothing. He is a blank slate, an empty page. And he's had years of practice keeping it this way.

"It's going well," I say. "We—*I'm* making progress. I'm hoping it will be completed soon."

"Good." The Emperor leans forward, steeples his fingers, and says, "There's something else I need you to do for me, Anna. I've recently received information from some of our...*jiàn dié*"—spies— "of the West's plans for their youngest daughter. Talia Ateş."

My heartbeat quickens, pounding in my chest, and I already feel the dread beginning to invade my veins. I think I know what he's going to say next.

He continues. "They are not sure exactly how, but the Dawn Court plans to use her against us. You need to make sure that doesn't happen."

Nausea is rising in my stomach, emptying gallon after gallon of murky black sewer water into my body until I'm choking on it.

"Do you understand what I'm asking of you?"

I do. I do, but I wish I didn't. I do, but there's no possible way he's asking this of me. There's no possible way he's asking me to kill Talia. Talia, who is Paris's only younger sibling, the only one he will protect with his whole heart. I used to think it was so endearing.

And a part of me, reluctant as I am to admit it, is *terrified* of what he would do if he ever found out. Terrified of what would happen to us, as embittered as we already are. You never know, in this period where the peace is so fragile, so delicate, who might be spying.

When I don't say anything, when he sees me hesitate, the Emperor says, "You understand why it has to be this way, don't you? Believe me, Anna, I don't want to go through with this either. But if it means that our court, our city, stays safe, if it means I can save the lives of our people, I will take it. I will make that sacrifice and *so should you.* I trust you will do the right thing."

I am speechless. Every word I have ever known has fled my mouth in this moment that I need them most. This moment when I am the only chance for Talia's survival, the only person who can beg the Emperor not to go through with this. I can't even hold on to some fraying thread of hope that another city, another country or jurisdiction would find out and step in, because for so long, they haven't. For so long, they've turned a blind eye to this war between the courts

under some unspoken agreement that as long as it doesn't harm them, we are free to keep attacking each other until we are all bathed in red.

Don't ask this of me. I'm screaming it in my head, everywhere but out loud. Everywhere but at him because I know there's nothing I can say that will change his mind. The Emperor, the Council even, was born in the age of war. Born in a time where morality didn't exist, where humanity didn't. And these are the consequences.

For me and for them.

I say, "I understand. And I will." But this time, I'm not so sure.

There is only one person who I know can talk me through this. Can convince me that this is a necessary thing that needs to be done, regardless of personal emotion. Regardless of misgivings.

My sister has always been the perfect soldier. She completes every task assigned to her without complaint. She is not encumbered by emotion, by morality, and sometimes, I wish I could be a little more like her.

The good thing is, I always have someone to go to.

When I call her, the phone rings six times before Katerina finally picks up. She's sitting in the Midnight Court library, the glaring light from the computer screen casting a blue glow on her face.

"Anna?" she says.

"Hi, Kat. Are you busy?"

Katerina shakes her head. Frowns a bit, says, "What's up?"

I pause. Now that I've called, I realize I have no idea how to phrase this. No idea how to ask her this, she who has never questioned her place in this court.

One second stretches into two. Three. She's looking at me, waiting for me to speak, but I am trying to string words together in my head. Struggling to. Failing.

In the end, I give up. Throw it all out the window and simply say, "The Emperor just called me." I exhale. I wonder, too late, if I'm even allowed to tell her this. He never said to keep it a secret, did he? "He wants me to kill Talia."

"Talia," Katerina repeats. "Talia Ateş?"

I nod.

"And you're not sure you can." It's not a question.

"Yeah."

She sighs. Rests her chin on her hand. Focuses on me. "Look, Anna, I know this is difficult. I *get it*. This shouldn't be our reality, one where an eighteen-year-old is asked to kill a child, but it is. It's the world we were born in, and at some point, you just have to accept it.

"Accept that things like morality and humanity don't exist here. Accept that it's *kill or be killed*. The Emperor's word is law. Do what he says, or"—she shrugs—"you're dead. Simple as that.

"Children grow up too. They become exactly like us. And believe me, given the chance, any Dawn Courter will do the exact same thing to you. They'll kill you without a second thought. Don't start thinking they're too human either. We were born with this responsibility. Our duty is to the Midnight Court first and ourselves second. Don't forget that."

I am a soldier, I am a soldier, I am a soldier. And in this world we live in, this world that I too was born into, there is no room for compassion. No room for weakness. I learned this lesson three years ago.

I think, *My sister burns as bright as a star*, and for once, I want that to be me.

CHAPTER 22

I'm back in the common room. At this point, I'm here so often
now that I almost wonder if I spend more time within these four
walls than anywhere else in the school—in the city—including my
own dorm. I'm lying fully lengthwise on the couch, head resting on
the armrest, staring at the ceiling and waiting for the rest of them to
arrive. It's so early in the morning my brain is still fuzzy, still full of
cotton, and I have no idea how I'm expected to think, let alone *con-
verse with people.*

One by one, they slowly trickle into the room: Dev and Max,
Professor Song, and then, finally, Paris and Kyan. I haul myself into
a sitting position. Say, "So, yesterday."

"Yes," says Dev. "Paris filled us in on the whole Darren thing. We
really think it's him?"

I bite my lip. "All the evidence points to him. He had the ashes
on his sleeve and the letter in his room. I took a picture of it," I say.

"Wow." Max's voice has a note of incredulity, like he can't quite
believe this. "Of all the people, I would not have expected *Darren* to
be the one behind all of this."

Kyan brings his legs up so that he's sitting cross-legged on the
beanbag chair and braces his elbows on his knees. His eyebrows are
scrunched together. "What motive could he possibly have to steal the
poison?"

"He's going mentally insane and suddenly thinks he belongs to the Midnight Court instead of Dawn?" Max offers.

"I highly doubt that," Dev inserts. "Maybe he's jaded and decided to turn to murder as an outlet." He looks pleased with himself for coming up with that idea.

"His family, specifically?" Kyan asks, dryly but smiling. "Anna, did the letter say anything helpful?"

I shake my head. "Nothing. Either way, we need to stop whatever he's planning."

Professor Song looks grim. Asks, "The letter mentioned that it would happen at a ball?"

"I think so." I pull my phone out of my pocket, scroll down until I reach the photo. "Yeah. Equinox Ball. What is that?"

"Paris?" Song prompts.

Paris looks over at us from where he's standing against the wall, green-gold eyes wholly unreadable. He's been uncharacteristically silent since yesterday. I wonder what he's thinking. I wish I could see inside his head.

He says, "It's a celebration, held on the fall equinox. All the Circle members are invited along with family and friends. A last hurrah before the colder months, in defiance of the Midnight Court."

Of course, because the Midnight Court's associated with fall and winter while Dawn is associated with spring and summer. An unfair assignment in my opinion, but one that holds because of the simple fact that the days are longer in the warmer months and the nights are longer in the colder months.

"Which means we're all automatically invited," says Max with a self-satisfied grin. "Being the offspring of important Circle members." And then, realizing his mistake, he adds, "Oh, sorry, Dev. You can be my plus-one, if you want."

Paris sighs and I know he's thinking the same thing: that Max can be so *dense* sometimes. But he's like a puppy dog, impossible to get mad at.

Dev just nods, and I wonder, not for the first time, just how he feels being the outsider in this group of Dawn Court insiders. The

only one who wasn't born into a position of power, who isn't from an established Dawn Court family.

"Paris, can you get Anna in?" Professor Song asks.

"Most likely. What are you thinking?"

"Nothing specific, but if the five of you can go in and isolate Darren, that's a start."

Max swivels in his chair to look at me. "Anna, toss me the phone, would you? I want to see the picture."

"I could just send it to you guys," I say.

"Nah. I just want to see something real quick."

"Okay, but if you drop it you're buying me a new one."

Max puts a hand to his chest. "That wounds me. Severely." He tips back in his chair. "Dev, can you believe she just questioned my hand-eye coordination?"

"Absolutely not. Absolutely unbelievable," Dev responds, shaking his head with faux incredulity.

"Okay, okay, I get it," I say and throw my phone to Max, who catches it with a wink.

"All right," he says, pinching the screen to zoom in.

Dev peers at it over his shoulder. "Yeah, it says the poison's going to be with him, right? So we find a way to get him away from everyone else like Prof said and then knock him out. Take the shit. Piece of cake."

The four of us look at Paris at the words *knock him out* but he doesn't even react. Just continues looking at Max and ignoring the fact that there are four pairs of eyes on him.

He says, "I would really appreciate if the four of you could cease staring at me."

Hastily, we look away.

"Can we maybe not jinx this before we even start?" says Max. "Also, how are we supposed to 'get him away from everyone else'? Say, 'Hello Prince Darren, mate, can I borrow you for a quick second?'"

"Maybe use your brain, Maximilian," Dev says.

"Shut up, Devaj."

Dev ignores him. "We tell him that someone's looking for him. The king or, like, a girlfriend. Does he have a girlfriend?"

"A fiancée," says Paris. "Everly."

I'm walking over to Paris, having absolutely no idea what's going through my brain except for the fact that it's too late to change my mind.

His proximity is like caffeine injected straight into my bloodstream. I feel like an addict back for another hit. "You're making really valuable contributions to this conversation," I tell him under my breath.

"Did you come over here just to insult me?" he returns in a low voice.

"No," I say. "You looked a little...isolated. I figured I'd grace you with my company."

Dryly, he says, "How generous of you."

"You mean, 'Thank you, Anna,'" I correct.

"Great, so we can have, like, someone he doesn't really recognize tell him that his fiancée's looking for him somewhere," Max proposes. "Like Anna."

At the mention of my name, my attention whips back to the conversation.

"Unfortunately," Paris says, "Darren would recognize Anna."

"Seriously? How?"

"We kind of bumped into him on our way out of the palace the first time," I say, cringing. "And also, he saw us yesterday."

"Good god," grumbles Max. "Well, it can't be any of us. He's known who we are since birth."

A thought takes root in my mind—it unfurls its leaves into my brain, and hesitantly, I'm thinking this might work.

If she agrees to it.

I suggest, "Josephine?"

Max blinks. "What's Josephine?"

"I don't think it's a *what* so much as a *who*," Dev tells him.

"Okay, fine. *Who's* Josephine?"

"The other Midnight Courter," Paris says. "That Anna came with."

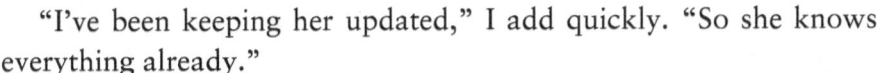

"I've been keeping her updated," I add quickly. "So she knows everything already."

"Oh. Well, I guess I'm fine with it," says Max. Dev and Kyan nod.

Professor Song says, "Sounds like a good plan, as long as you're certain we can trust her."

"We can," I answer, firmly. Then, "Paris?"

He glances at me with green, green eyes. Says, "Yeah, sure. Go ahead."

I call her. Ask, "Can you come here?"

When she arrives—seven minutes late because she kept walking past the door hidden in the wall—it takes another five to introduce her to everyone, explain everything we're planning for the ball, what exactly we need her help with.

When I'm done, she says, "Sure, I can do it. I'm pretty sure he's never seen me before, so it'd be a pretty safe bet."

I blink. Surprised. "Are you sure? You're under no obligation to help out with this, you know."

Josephine smiles. "I know, but it's so *boring* to be on the sidelines."

I shrug, looking at the rest of them. "I mean, she's not wrong."

Max says, "Sure." He pins his gaze on Josephine, echoes Professor Song. "You're sure you can be trusted?"

"If I couldn't be, don't you think it'd be an issue that I'm in this meeting to begin with?" she retorts.

"Actually, yeah. True."

Dev rises, striding over to the whiteboard and uncapping the pen with a flourish. "Great, let's put this on the board. So far, the plan is to use Josephine to draw Darren away and, uh, knock him out. Are we for real knocking him out?"

"Do you have a better idea?" Max challenges.

"Fine. Knock him out, take the vial—"

"Make sure he doesn't see any of your faces," Paris inserts. "Or hear voices. He can't know it was you guys."

"Right," says Professor Song. "Whatever the six of you decide to do, you must absolutely make sure that he does not know who was involved. He must not suspect any of you. This is imperative."

"Right," says Dev. "No faces, no voices. And then once we take the poison, we what? Leave?"

"We should have someone get the poison to Kyan," I speak up. "It might help with the antidote in case there's more of the poison somewhere. Better safe than sorry, right?"

Professor Song nods. "How far are you on that, by the way?"

"Pretty close, I think," says Kyan, pushing his glasses up in a familiar movement. He's wearing his usual serious expression. "I'd like to stay and keep working on it, if possible. Instead of going with the rest of you to Equinox."

Dev blinks. "Sure?" He looks around at the rest of us.

"Stay," Paris says. "We don't need six people to knock out my brother, anyway."

"Wait," I say. "Also, I think knocking him out the...er, traditional way is a little risky."

"What do you propose?" Dev asks me, one hand still poised against the board.

"We use gas. Some type of thing that can knock him out temporarily and we can just hide somewhere until it's done. Then there's no chance of him seeing any of us."

"Chloroform," suggests Kyan, catching on almost immediately. His eyes meet mine. "Except it's relatively difficult to control so there is a chance that you could kill him by accident, which probably isn't good."

"Probably not," says Paris, mildly.

"Okay, then an alternative is ketamine. It's not a gas, though. You'd basically just have to inject him with it. It'd take a couple minutes for it to take effect."

Josephine and I are staring at Kyan like he's grown three heads.

"What?" he asks, self-consciously.

"I just had no idea you were so well-versed with...chemicals," I say.

"It is his forte," Dev says, nodding.

"Where the fuck do we just get ketamine from?" Max questions. "I mean, hell, I'd like some ke—"

Dev whacks him on the head with the pen.

"There's some in the lab," Kyan says, placidly, as if he didn't just witness the altercation.

We all stare at him. Stunned. Completely nonplussed.

And then Max says, "Okay, then, that issue's solved."

Professor Song looks like she's trying to hold in a laugh. She clasps her hands together. Says, "Great. Then that's the tentative plan. We'll go over it again before you guys actually go in, but for now, expect that this is what's going to happen."

Meeting adjourned.

CHAPTER 23

The five of us are standing outside the Lotus, waiting for the cars to pull up. This late in September, the air already holds a tinge of chilliness and the faint, crisp scent of frost. Brittle brown leaves litter the grass, scraping across the pavement in the wind.

Max, Dev, Josephine, and I are taking one car there and Paris is taking another. If all goes well, we're not going to see him again until after the ball.

I feel like I should say something to him before we leave, like maybe, *Be careful* or *Nice knowing you* except that's ridiculous because it's not like any of us are going to die tonight.

Hopefully.

Not that this is particularly significant, in the grand scheme of things. I mean, we've infiltrated the Dawn Court headquarters—*twice*—so it's not like what we're attempting tonight is a particularly big deal. Discounting the fact that last time we went on one of these missions I almost died. And so did Paris.

I have no idea why that night left such a large stain on me, such a large mark. It's like Paris and I used to be connected by so many faded, tattered threads from the past but now there's a new one, and it's bright red. It's fresh. It shines as clear as a star on a moonless night, and as much as I desperately want to, I can't ignore its presence. I can't pretend that it's not there.

I think, also, that I get attached to people too quickly. Too easily.

That I am pushed and pulled, molded like clay by everyone else's hands, and I forgive too easily. I forget too easily. Sometimes I feel like a willow tree; I bend in whatever direction the wind asks of me because I am not strong enough on my own.

"Keep your guard up," Paris is telling Max and Dev. "If anything goes wrong, find me."

"Bet," says Max. "And don't forget to stay out of your family's crazy fights, man. Remember what happened last year?"

Paris snorts as his car pulls up, wheels crunching on gravel. "Right."

I wonder what happened last year.

He turns to me just before he ducks into the car. Says, "Try not to get shot at this time, Anna," and then disappears into the car.

I glare at his retreating outline.

We pull up to the venue behind a long line of cars that are exactly identical to our own. Shiny and white and new—like a rich man's toys.

The Dawn Court, I'm beginning to realize, is a fan of flashiness. Of showing off wealth in material goods that the Midnight Court would be horrified to see.

Yet another difference that separates our two cultures.

The building itself is not far from Eladine. It is large and swathed in glass and lights and opulence. Apparently, it's an offshoot of the Dawn Court palace, a location used for festivities and events like this one. And very, very secure.

There are dozens of guards patrolling the outside, gathered by the door when we arrive, and my heart is in my throat. It is still such an uncomfortable feeling, a foreign feeling that seems to go against the entire nature of my body to be walking among all of these Dawn Courters like I am one of them. To be staring at them and not drawing weapons.

Stepping out of the limo and walking up the steps to the door feels eerily similar to the Midnight Court, to the dozens of events just like this one. Except today, I am not wearing a *qipao* or *hanfu*. Today, I am in a white, Dawn Court–style dress and it's like a betrayal to my own court. Almost like stabbing a knife into the back of my own city.

Not for the first time tonight, I thank god that Josephine is here with me. They take our names at the door: Josephine, me, the two boys, checking the names against some list that's on their tablet screens and then we're in. Surrounded by a hundred of the Dawn Court's most trusted people.

I am almost sick to my stomach, praying to god that no one recognizes me for who I really am. For who Josephine really is.

"Well, what now?" she asks, scanning the crowd of people, and I can read the wariness in her eyes like they're words. Like they are letters on a page that mirror my own.

"We have to find Darren," I say. Except I have no idea how, because if I'm being honest, all of the Dawn Court king's six children look way too similar.

In the far-right corner of the room, I spot a flash of gold and my eyes focus on a blonde head. Talia. She's standing near her mother, looking suddenly so much more grown up than I remember in a white dress and a French braid.

Watching children you've known since they were babies, since they were five pounds of flesh and blood and happiness, sometimes feels like watching your own family grow up. Like they are your own children or maybe another part of yourself.

When I was fifteen, Talia was six, meaning she's around nine or ten now.

Still a child. I'm remembering, suddenly, the other half of the assignment the Emperor gave me. Remembering what exactly he wants me to do, who exactly he wants me to kill, and—

I don't think I can. Right now, she is so very real and human that I find myself rooted to the ground. Frozen.

Talia spots me seconds after I see her, cocking her head in innocent confusion. Kids, I think, are so pure. Not yet tainted by the stains of our world, not yet poisoned by the hostility and animosity so deeply ingrained it might as well be written in our veins.

Kids have no idea that they're supposed to hate, that there are some people they're supposed to kill on sight, no questions asked.

That there are people who will do the same to them.

I wave to her and she runs over to me, a grin splitting her face in two, and she launches herself into my arms. I squeeze her. She feels so tiny, so fragile in my arms, like a hummingbird. "I'm looking for your brother," I tell her.

"Paris?"

I shake my head. "Darren."

"Oh." Talia turns away from me and searches the room with an air of solemnity, in the way that little kids treat every task they're given with extra gravity, trying to seem as grown-up as possible.

Her face lights up and she jabs a finger toward the right wall. "Over there!"

It takes me a minute to find him, searching through blonde heads— god, is everyone in the Dawn Court blonde?

He's there, talking animatedly to a group of people and he's *laughing*. Looking so normal I almost can't believe that he's the one responsible. That right now, he's probably thinking about how best to kill his siblings.

My stomach is playing Twister with itself. I feel like I'm about to throw up.

I can't imagine how perverse you have to be, how much of a psychopath or sociopath—or whichever one it is—to think that. In the Midnight Court, family is everything. Family is your entire world and this—

—this would be treason to the highest degree.

I still don't understand his motives.

"Good job," I say to Talia, ruffling her hair. "Thanks."

Grinning at me, she yells, "You're welcome!" before scurrying back to her mother.

I turn to the others, murmuring, "He's right over there. In that group of people next to the wall."

"I see him," Dev says.

"You guys do know we look sus as hell, right?" Max interrupts. "Like we're just standing here staring at people." He nods at the mass of swaying people. "Let's dance and talk."

We carve our way into the crowd, venturing in until we're just past the outside border. Just a couple of feet into all of the twirling and laughing.

"Okay, so Josephine goes to get him next, right? And the rest of us need to be in position at the end of the hall," I say.

Max twirls me and I'm spinning for a second. Two. Watching the room blur into a brush of white and gold.

"Anna," he says, and I look up to find his gaze on me. There's nothing joking in his eyes for once, and it sends an immediate spark of curiosity down my spine. Max is so rarely serious.

"What is it?"

He suddenly looks uncomfortable, as if the suit he's wearing is a size too small for him. "I'm sorry to ask this of you, but would you be willing to go in with the syringe later? With Darren?" Max clears his throat. "It's just, if we do it and we get caught, the consequences are severe. Especially for Dev, given his situation. I just don't want to risk him getting kicked out of Eladine or worse, with his family so far away. I hope you can understand."

I blink. "Yeah, of course." I'm realizing that underneath his convivial, devil-may-care exterior, Max does have a soft side. Reserved almost entirely for Dev. The thought makes me smile.

"Thank you," he says to me.

From where he's dancing with Josephine, Dev asks, "Okay, great. Disperse now?"

"Wait, just to confirm," says Jo. "I just tell him his fiancée's looking for him, right? And then what do I do?"

"Leave," says Dev. "Or hide. He's obviously going to know that you lied once he wakes up, so you need to ensure he doesn't see you again."

"Oh. Right. Wait—" She frowns. "What if he sees his fiancée on the way to meeting her?"

Max smirks. "He won't. She's with Paris."

"Oh. Okay."

"Okay, great," I say. "Let's go?"

Dev nods. "Let's go."

CHAPTER 24

The hallway smells like lilies. Like cream and clove and a little citrusy. A little green, like spring. It makes me want to sneeze.

"They're really marking their territory," says Max.

Dev snorts. "They're not dogs, mate."

"Right, but you do smell this, yeah? It's like, burning my nose."

I bite my lip to keep from laughing.

I'm trying to keep track of where we go, trying to form a mental map that I can relay back to the Council, but a part of my brain is faltering.

A part of my brain is revolting without my permission and suddenly, I'm realizing that I don't quite *want* to.

I can't think about this right now, can't stop to dissect it, to wonder what it means.

It is a Herculean effort to shove it out of my mind.

We hide in one of the open rooms branching off from the hallway. It's completely dark, no windows except the one in the door, so it's relatively safe.

"All right," says Max, pressing his face into the glass. "Now we wait. Damn, I should've taken a shit before this."

"Seriously?" I ask.

"What?" he exclaims, indignant. "I'm nervous! Nerves make me need to shit."

"Okay, thank you, Max, but this is quite unnecessary information," says Dev.

"Agreed," I say.

"This isn't fair. This is two against one. That's unethical."

And then: footsteps. Immediately, the three of us fall silent.

I am unbelievably anxious. This should be easy. All I need to do is sneak up behind him and stick a syringe in his neck—and try not to hit any important veins—except I am so, so scared.

There are one hundred milligrams of ketamine in my hand. One hundred milligrams that might as well be a bullet in a gun because done wrong, I can very, very easily kill him.

And the consequences of that,

they're horrifying. They are war, and yet another stain on my soul.

"You've got this," Max whispers, nervously. "Right?"

"I really appreciate the vote of confidence," I shoot back.

"I am very confident. So confident. Zero percent chance this can go wrong. Anna, I believe in you irrevocably," he says.

"Thanks," I tell him, and the sarcasm is thicker than honey. It coats my throat like caramel on apples in autumn.

Anticipation, I think, is like an ignited firework in your stomach. It is a sparking fuse and a sudden flurry bouncing off the walls, trying to escape somehow, somehow. But it can't. It is trapped inside until you feel about ready to explode.

The nerves are drowning me. Filling my lungs and my entire chest and rising in my throat and somehow making their way to my brain. Nerves are everywhere in my body, tucked under ribs and under arms and in the very pit of my stomach.

When he passes by the mini-window in the door, I forget how to breathe. I am staring at him looking around, probably wondering where on earth his fiancée is, and I am almost stapled to the ground.

Until Dev says, "I think you should go now."

And then I'm nodding yes, right, taking five steps out the door and it's like I'm out of my own body. Not like I'm watching myself from above like some angel, but like my body and my mind are two separate things. Like I am disconnected.

Darren doesn't see me. He doesn't hear me. He's still searching around, and I'm struck, once again, by how absolutely flawless the Dawn Court royal family's beauty is. Perfect cheekbones, and perfect jawline, and perfect bone structure. He looks so much like Paris that, for a second, I almost falter.

Almost.

He sees me seconds before it happens, his eyes are widening and I'm so close I can even see his pupils dilating, but it's too late. I've already stuck the syringe in his neck and pressed down so that now all one hundred milligrams of ketamine are coursing through his system and I am really, really hoping that Kyan is right. That Kyan is trustworthy, especially when he said that there's almost no danger with this.

It doesn't really matter anyway because I've already ruined the plan. I've already crumpled it up and tossed it straight out the window because after the syringe was in, I was supposed to run. He isn't supposed to know who I am—except I am *frozen*, glued to the floor because I can't quite process what I just did and I am *shocked* that it worked.

Except now he's staring at me, staring at the empty syringe in my hand, and I think he knows what it is. I think he knows what's happening because he's looking at me with eyes that are not horrified enough or angry or frustrated enough for someone whose plans were just foiled, and that,

more than anything,

terrifies me.

Something is wrong.

And then he says, "You're too late, Anna. All of you." He's talking fast, words spilling out of his mouth one after the other and there is a hint of panic in his eyes—but I can't tell if it's real or fake. He says, "It was never me."

The word comes out of my mouth in a breath. A whisper. "What?"

I am painfully aware that even as we're speaking, the ketamine's taking effect. That really, this plan backfired because he'll be completely unconscious before I can even begin to make sense of this.

"I don't know how you figured me out, but there's a Midnight Courter too. His name is Liu Caihong. He was behind it. He has been, the whole time," Darren says, gasping, and he's already swaying on his feet. "There are two vials. I managed to steal one, but he still has the other. There's no time to explain. He's in there, somewhere, dressed like a Dawn Courter. Anna, you *have to find him. Please.*"

I am horrified. Utterly, completely horrified.

I think I might be in shock.

Liu Caihong. My first thought is: I know him. I know him from the Midnight Court; he used to be a teacher—fifth grade, I think. I met his daughter.

My second thought: I can recognize him.

I try to call Paris as Dev and Max come out to drag Darren's unresponsive form into the room. Shut the door.

The phone just rings

and rings

and rings.

I'm on my fourth attempt before the two of them come back out and I give up. I'm hoping to whatever gods that'll listen that I'll find Caihong in time. I doubt Paris can help me at this point anyway—I don't think he ever met him in the nine years that he was in Shanghai, nor would he even remember Caihong if he did.

I ask, "Did you hear what he said? About the poison?"

"Er, no," says Max. "Voices are a little muffled when they're traveling through wood."

I want to slap my palm against my forehead. "There are two vials. He only has one."

They are suddenly serious all at once. Grave.

"So where is it?" asks Max.

"He says a Midnight Courter here has it, and he's been behind everything. I need to find him," I say. I can hear the agitation in my own voice. I feel taut, like a rope—like stress and anxiety are pulling me apart and my body might as well be like some violin string, except all the noise that's going to be coming out of me will be a screechy mess.

"All right," Dev says. "You go find him. Max and I will check Darren, find his vial, and then we'll join you."

"Okay," I say. I'm breathing too fast. My breaths are coming in rapid inhales and exhales and I feel like there is *dynamite* under my skin. "Okay, I'm going to go. Call me if anything happens."

"We will," Dev says. "Go."

And then I'm running. I'm flying down the hallway in a body that is too slow, too weak, and I'm *dreading*. Dreading everything because so much can go wrong right now.

I can't even think about the worst-case scenario.

A part of me, in some back corner of my mind shut behind rickety doors and swathed with cobwebs, is thinking I should be happy about this. That this could be good for the Midnight Court. Really good. Have Caihong wipe out the entire royal family in London and let the blame fall where it may. It'd be so, so easy. Too easy.

Except I also know that I can't. I won't. My dedication to the Emperor's assignment is flickering, has been flickering like the weakest candle flame in the wind, and I'm thinking, for maybe the hundredth time since I was given this assignment, that maybe they should've chosen my sister for this. That maybe I am not as loyal to Shanghai as I should be.

That my parents, the Council, the Emperor would be so ashamed if they could hear the thoughts in my head. If they could *see* what's happening right now.

Except I don't really have time to think. I don't have time to make a pro-con list, so now I'm just running on pure instinct. And it terrifies me.

I slow down before I reach the main room so as not to arouse suspicion. My chest is heaving, my lungs expanding and deflating so rapidly I can't catch my breath. It is part anxiety, part exertion.

The room is packed with people—even more than there had been minutes ago—and I'm running my eyes over it, scanning the crowd in a vain attempt to pick out one person from a hundred, but it is absolutely useless.

Thankfully, at least, there is no commotion. Nothing that says that someone has died or is in the process of dying, so I still have time. I think.

I have no idea where to start looking.

Where would he go?

Where would I, if I were him? If I were a Midnight Courter crashing a Dawn Court event, trying not to draw excess attention to myself—the outskirts.

Near walls, near shadows, near corners.

As inconspicuously as I can, I disentangle myself from the crowd of bodies in the center of the ballroom and make my way toward the edges, scanning the walls while I'm walking.

It doesn't take me long to find him, and I suppose I should be grateful for the fact that at least this part wasn't difficult. Wasn't a mountain to climb all by itself.

He's standing half in shadow, rigid. So out of place that even his white clothes couldn't hide the fact that he is Midnight Court through and through. So out of place that even if I didn't know what his face looked like, I would have been able to recognize him without a doubt.

He doesn't seem surprised when he sees me.

I stop a couple of steps away. Ask, "Where is it?"

Caihong shakes his head, repeating exactly what Darren said to me earlier. "You're too late."

Desperation, I think, makes you lose all self-control. Desperation might be a drug in itself because I am now finding myself drawing a balisong on this man from my own court, in the middle of a Dawn Court ball, consequences be damned.

"Will you really kill me?" he asks. "To save *them?* This family who you hate? Who you *should* hate?"

"Don't tell me," I breathe, "what I should do. We're at peace. You're going to restart the war again. *Why? Is* this worth it?"

"Who would go to war," he asks, "if the entire royal family is dead?"

"New leaders will rise up in their place. Cut off one head and a hundred more will grow." It's a phrase my father has been saying my entire life.

I'm shaking. My whole hand is white from gripping my balisong so tightly I can't even hold it steady. I'm so *angry*—angry and terrified—and it's creating a mix in my chest that I'm not sure I like. That feels a little too dangerous, a little too out of control.

"You kill them," I say. "I kill you. It's your decision."

A muscle works in his jaw. He takes so long to answer that I'm beginning to think he simply isn't going to.

I have never been so impatient in my entire life. I stride up to him, shove the gleaming edge of the balisong against his throat. Say, "You have three seconds."

At the count of *one*, he says, "In the wine. It's in the wine."

Before I leave to get this information to Paris, I hit his temple, once, hard, with the handle of the blade and watch him crumple to the floor. Unconscious.

I'm taking no chances.

Impatience is suffocating me. It is ants crawling under my skin, it is time in my mouth slipping out from under my tongue, it is an hourglass in front of my eyes and I am watching the sand fall through so fast. So quickly.

I'm racing back into the throng, this time trying to find Paris and—

"Anna."

The voice comes from directly in front of me—more a surprised exclamation than anything—and I blink. Look up.

Richard Ateş, the crown prince of the Dawn Court, is staring at me like he can't believe that I'm here. Confusion is written on his face and I'm feeling like a deer in headlights.

"Um, hi," I say. "How've you been?"

"What are you doing here?" He doesn't sound hostile, just confused.

Great. Time to come up with another cover. I hesitate for a second. Two. "I came with Paris. Actually, do you know where he is?"

Now it's his turn to blink. "Paris?" Looks to the right. Points to the far end of the room. "Where the rest of our family is. Anna, are you all right? You look a little pale."

My mind is whirling, clanking cogs and screws, and I'm trying to decide whether I should tell him. Whether I can trust him.

I say, "I'm fine, must be the lighting." I begin pushing through the crowd, forcing my way toward the jumble of Dawn Court royalty in the back before adding, "By the way, don't drink the wine."

I hope he listens.

CHAPTER 25

Paris is standing in a group of Dawn Court Circle members, looking every inch the Dawn Court prince. It is times like this that I wonder what the hell I'm doing here.

It is so strange, I think, this feeling like 50 percent of the time, I know who he is. The other 50 percent, he is a complete stranger to me, and I'm wondering which version is the real one. Whether I'm deluding myself. It is so strange to have trusted someone so entirely, with your whole heart, only to now have to wonder whether you can even trust them at all. Normal people build trust through the years.

There is no rule book for this, I think, no guide. No person or sheet of paper or book to tell you what you're supposed to do when you've loved, then lost, then—what?

He catches my eye when I'm just inches away from his group of Circle members, and I'm praying to god that no one spots me. No one recognizes my face.

I watch his gaze darken, watch him excuse himself, and then he's standing in front of me, asking, "What's wrong?" Because why else would I be here?

"We were wrong," I tell him. "In short, Darren was under the control of a Midnight Courter—I have no idea how—but we were too late. The poison's in the wine."

Paris doesn't move. Doesn't react. Just swears once, softly, then says, "They just brought it in." His eyes flick to the table where they've just finished setting up the wine. Bottles of it in ice buckets, empty crystal glasses lined up neatly on the white tablecloth.

I feel a crushing wave of relief, so intense my head spins. It's like the anxiety was the tension in the strings that held me up and now without it, I am nothing but flesh and blood and jelly. No bones.

I want to sit down.

"Thank god," I exhale. "I thought maybe I'd be too late."

"Good work, Anna," Paris says and the corner of his mouth twitches. "All right, I can't tell my family in case anyone was also in Darren's position, so we're just going to have to remove the wine. People can survive without alcohol for a night."

"Are you sure about that?" I ask, but it is a half-hearted joke.

"Yes," he says. "Generally, I do believe that alcohol is not a necessity for living, but to each their own, I suppose. Why, would you disagree?" A glint in his green eyes. Amusement in his voice. "Are you a secret alcoholic, Anna?"

"Oh, shut up," I say.

We turn around, striding toward the wine table and grabbing both buckets.

"Are you sure he was telling the truth?" Paris asks me, shifting the bucket so that it's sitting in one arm.

"Well, I had him at knifepoint, so I assume he was."

Paris looks at me, surprised. He huffs a short laugh. "Right, of course."

I see the expression change on his face, see the exact moment he spots something, and suddenly, his features are spelling out confusion, dread, panic.

"There's a glass missing from the table," he says.

And I, I see it too, except it's not the glass I'm looking at. It's the crack in the gold foil at the top of the wine bottle in my hands—and I, selfish that I am, am realizing that I don't particularly care.

Definitely not as much as I should that a human being might be dying.

All I'm thinking is, *At least I know it is not Paris.*

I am a horrible, horrible person.

Except then I see who's holding the wineglass, pale gold liquid

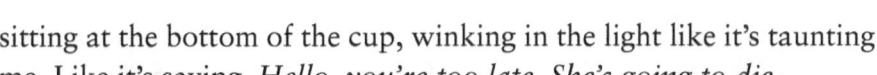

sitting at the bottom of the cup, winking in the light like it's taunting me. Like it's saying, *Hello, you're too late. She's going to die.*

Talia Ateş.

My mind is immediately thrown into pandemonium. My first thought, almost instinctually, almost like it's programmed into me, is how perfect this would be for the Emperor's assignment. How it would be completed without me even needing to get my hands dirty. How easy.

But even as I'm contemplating this, the thought is immediately drowned out by an overwhelming feeling of *Please, god, no.* Not her. I'm thinking nine is too young. At nine, you haven't even had a chance to live. At nine, you have experienced so little it might as well be nothing. Nine is a beginning, nine is preparation for twelve, eighteen, twenty-one. For thirties and fifties and seventies that she *deserves*.

I'm praying to every deity in the universe that she hasn't yet taken a sip. Or that maybe she hasn't had enough for it to do anything and I'm thinking this could not possibly have been what Caihong wanted. That if he saw what his plan had given birth to, maybe even he would be horrified.

Paris sees it at the same time as I do. He looks as if he's been shot, or maybe run over by a hundred-ton truck. All of the blood is rushing out of his face, but he doesn't even hesitate. Doesn't stand, superglued to the floor like I am.

He rushes to his sister and snatches the wineglass straight out of her hands. I'm watching them speak. I'm watching him say something to her, probably *What the hell are you doing drinking wine?* And then,

and then it just keeps getting worse.

I almost laugh at how insane this is, how ridiculous, because it really feels like I'm in some sort of drama. Perhaps a TV show or maybe a movie because there is no way this can be real life.

Caihong. *Caihong* is walking up to them like a man risen from the dead, except he doesn't look at all like he's been knocked out. Doesn't look at all like he was unconscious just a few minutes ago, and I have no idea how he's here.

I'm staring at Paris, trying to catch his eye, trying to tell him that *This is him, this is Caihong,* except Paris isn't looking at me.

And then, my phone vibrates. Once. I drag my gaze away from the two of them, away from the royal family for just a second.

Paris: *get the wine out of here.*

I have no idea how he typed that without looking at his phone.

I call Josephine. She picks up after one ring. "Hello?"

"Jo, I need you to come back in. It's a long story—I promise I'll explain later—but this is really important. Caihong's here. He's awake. I need you to check on Max and Dev—you don't need to come back into the main room, just around the hallways. Once you find them, I'm leaving two buckets with wine bottles in the hallway we were in. Right where it connects to the main room. I need you guys to dispose of them ASAP."

I can literally sense her brain processing on the other side of the line. "Okay," she says. "Got it."

"Thank you. You're the best."

"I know. You can make it up to me later." She hangs up with a *click*.

I grab the bucket of wine that Paris left on the table and make my way toward the edge of the room while Caihong is still distracted. Too preoccupied with Paris and Talia to notice that I'm stealing the bottles.

These past ten minutes have held more stress than I've felt in my entire life.

I drop the buckets off, trying to hide them as best I can against the wall, but I don't have much time. I can only hope that no one walks by and spots them.

And then I'm rushing back, pushing through people, until I'm a couple feet away from the trio and I hear snippets of conversation. Catch them in my open palms.

He says in broken English, "Let her drink it. It's a celebration, after all. Drinking wine is luck in this culture. Longevity, right?"

Paris looks irritated. His eyes are a stormy shade of green, closer to gray now—as if his irises sync to his emotions—and his jaw is set. He says one terse word. "No."

"Fine," Caihong says. In one quick motion, he shoves his hand into his jacket and pulls out a gun. Caihong has a gun. He has a gun and he's pointing it straight at Talia.

He says, "Then you should at least drink it for her. Drink. Or I shoot."

I think I've stopped breathing. I think the entire room has. *Caihong*, I think, *cannot be human.* He cannot *actually* want to kill a nine-year-old girl who is still too young to be a participant in this war. And I don't understand—the Emperor gave this assignment to me. Is Caihong going rogue? Working by himself?

And then, out of nowhere,

Darren. He's standing behind Caihong as if he's just materialized out of thin air.

What?

That ketamine should've knocked him out for at least a few hours—except here he is, standing a couple feet away from me alive and well and very much awake. He must've been prepared for this somehow, had some antidote on hand just in case.

People, it seems, don't want to stay down today.

And if he's here, what happened to Max and Dev?

Darren's holding a gun pointed straight at Caihong's head, but there is nothing he can do without decimating the entire cold peace. And his hesitation is one weakness that Caihong does not have.

And I am, I am horrified.

This, I think, *this is the definition of a sticky situation.* Paris can't drink the wine, but at the same time, if he doesn't, Talia dies.

I think I know Paris well enough to know exactly what he's going to do. The exact choice he's going to make and it is sending a tsunami of

dread

fear

into my stomach until I am choking on it. I know what this is.

Checkmate.

Paris looks at him.

Looks at me.

And tips back the glass.

CHAPTER 26

I have died. I have died all over the floor.

CHAPTER 27

I can't quite process what just happened. I am rooted to the ground, ice in my veins, and I am staring open-mouthed at the scene in front of me.

Caihong, grinning.

Paris, setting down the glass.

Talia, staring at both of them.

And I'm waiting. Waiting with so much fear, panic, anxiety, nervousness, horror, dread that I cannot breathe. I really, truly cannot breathe. It's like there's a paper jam in my lungs or a clog in my windpipe because I cannot draw in oxygen. I am a fish out of water.

Several thoughts invade my brain at once, colliding into each other like birds. 1. *I need to get Paris away from Caihong;* 2. *Someone needs to let Kyan know;* and 3. *We all need to hope to every god in the universe that he's figured out an antidote.*

The silence gives birth to chaos all at once. A dozen men corner Caihong, slap cuffs onto his wrists, and he doesn't even struggle. Doesn't even react.

He had one job and he completed it. Successfully.

I feel myself run toward Paris, yanking him behind me until we reach an empty room away from the celebration and I shove him against the wall.

"Are you *insane?*" I hiss. "What were you *thinking?*" I am a waterfall of emotion, an unending cascade of fear and anger that falls from my mouth in a stream of words.

"I had no choice, Anna, and you know it," Paris shoots back. He's leaning against the wall, chest rising and falling with alarming speed. "If I refused, he would've killed Talia. There was no decision to make."

I know he's right, I do. But right now, I'm thinking, at some point, the human body must overdose on too much adrenaline, too many emotions because my mind feels like it's made of jelly. Like all my brain matter has been whipped until it's batter, a whole pound of mush in my skull.

All I know is, Paris is dying. I need to get him back to Eladine, to Kyan.

My phone rings. Josephine, telling me she's found Dev and Max, and seconds later, they're barging through the door and the panic in the room rises a few levels. It is carved into every one of our faces, so deep it might as well be permanent.

"What the hell happened?" Max demands, staring at the two of us like we've been caught doing something other than arguing.

Dev and Josephine are open-mouthed, Dev in horror and Josephine in confusion. Her gaze flicks to mine, questioning.

"It's a relatively long story that we don't have the luxury of time to explain at the moment," Paris bites out. He looks pale.

Death, I think, is the elephant in the room. Thanatos—Death personified—is the sixth person, the sixth wheel, sitting on the desk with legs swinging, watching us all die with a smile on his face and lips that say *finally*. Thanatos is the cold breath on the back of my neck and the chills along my spine and the force pounding against my chest, forcing my heart to beat, beat, beat and my blood to roar in my ears.

"Paris drank the poison," I say, "so if Kyan doesn't have the antidote..."

"I'll greet you in hell in a few years, bro," Max says to Paris, straight-faced.

"Great plan."

I cannot believe my eyes. Or my ears, really. Cannot believe that

they could be *joking* at a time like this. I think my understanding of reality has dug its own grave and jumped inside.

"Are you guys *insane?*" I say to them. "We are all on the same page here, right? This is a literal life-or-death situation."

"That is a by-product of this life we live," Paris tells me, dryly. "We've all known we weren't ever fated to die of old age, to live to be in our sixties, seventies, eighties. We're slaves to our courts.

"Also," he says. "I have a theory."

"Which is?" I'm almost certain skepticism is practically written in bright red ink on my forehead.

"I am not fully of the Dawn Court royal family." He says this matter-of-factly, like it is no big deal that he doesn't truly belong. That for the better part of his life, he has been different. He says, "The poison might not actually be fatal for me."

We all stop. Freeze. Process the fact that there is some truth to his words, and it is like finally coming up for air after drowning in dark water. It is a twenty-ton steel block being lifted off my chest and for a moment, I can feel as if I'm not being crushed by the weight of my fears. Of my dread.

But it is a fragile hope, and I am almost afraid to touch it. To reach out a tentative finger and prod it like it's a terrified animal ready to flee.

"This is a gamble with your life you're taking," Dev says to Paris. He is so serious. So solemn. So grave.

"I know," Paris says. He leans his head back against the wall and adds, "But I'm simply suggesting we save the panic for later."

"Well, sorry if our concern was an inconvenience to you," I say.

"Thanks," he shoots back, lowering his gaze to mine. There's a glint in his eye that is part challenge, part taunting. "I appreciate the apology."

"Before you two start fighting again," Max interrupts hurriedly. "We should probably get out of here. And call Professor Song. And call Kyan. I mean obviously, best-case scenario is he's figured out the antidote."

I swallow the words rising in my throat. Bury them. Look around the room and then outside, trying to figure out some escape route that wouldn't require us to cut a line through the main room again.

"There's an exit at the end of the hall," Dev says. "I'll call the driver and tell him to meet us there."

And then we're on the move again.

I feel paranoid, spotting flashes of gold in every corner of my vision, and I am *exhausted*. My body feels like it's been running on fumes, on adrenaline for so long that I'm beginning to sputter out. A dying engine. This constant level of energy is beginning to give me a headache.

I am hyperaware of everything. Paris's presence behind me. The muffled sounds of our footsteps down the hall. The very real danger that anyone could come wandering in here, maybe as a reprieve, maybe to take a break from the noise and crowd of people in the main room.

I am full of tangled threads of emotion. Caught in them. Strangled by them.

When we finally break out into the night, the car is already waiting for us beside the curb. We pile into it: Paris, Dev, and Max in the back, Josephine and me in the middle. I'm praying we don't hit traffic. Praying we get to the school in time.

Praying, for once, that Paris is right.

CHAPTER 28

I'm sitting in the common room. Josephine's curled up on the couch next to me and we're both silent. Both buried under thoughts, but I have no idea what she's thinking. I'm also afraid to ask.

We returned to Eladine almost half an hour ago. Professor Song didn't even flinch when we came in, a bedraggled group of five suddenly so out of place in this mundane room with our evening wear.

Song just sent Paris—Max and Dev in tow—to Kyan, who apparently hadn't come up with a complete antidote, but at least had something that countered some of whatever the poison was.

Josephine and I have been sitting here, waiting for news. *Waiting,* I think, *is exhausting in and of itself.*

Josephine asks, "Penny for your thoughts?"

I glance at her. Rub at my eyes. "I'm not even sure what I'm thinking," I say. "My brain is a mess."

She's quiet for a moment. Silent. Then, "I've never asked you how you felt about this, the—assignment. Not just the face, or surface one. You know, after everything that happened."

Oh, god. I didn't expect her to bring that up. But really, I should've expected it weeks ago.

I think she can sense my hesitation, my wariness even though I trust her. I trust her completely. But this, this realization that's been growing arms and legs and vines and thorns in my head isn't something I want to say out loud.

Josephine says, "You don't have to tell me, but I won't judge you. Obviously."

I sigh. Heave a giant breath and expel it. Try to pretend that I could get rid of history and emotions the same way. "Sometimes I feel like we're inevitable," I say. "Not in, like, the cheesy soulmates kind of way. More like a disaster waiting to happen, you know? Like you can see it and you know what's going to happen but you can't stop it—and it *terrifies* me. I wish there was a way to just switch off your emotions," I add quietly. More to myself than to her.

Josephine shifts. Looks at me with a serious expression I rarely see on her face. "I trust you, Anna. I trust that in the end, you'll make the right decision. Even if you don't."

"And you know that, like you do, I believe in destiny. In fate. Maybe the two of you are endgame, maybe you're not. Whatever you end up doing, it'll work out in its own way. And you know I'll support you. Just be careful, okay?"

I almost laugh out loud. As if it's something I could control.

But I say, "I'll try." I will.

The click of the door opening startles me probably more than it should. I jump a little in my seat, a flush rising immediately to my cheeks.

Professor Song walks in, trailed by Max and Dev, and I'm desperately trying to read their faces. Trying to decipher if it is good news or bad.

I'm also wondering where Kyan is.

"Everything's fine," Song says to Josephine and me. "In case either of you were wondering." She sighs. "Not that I expect Midnight Courters to be concerned."

She says it without inflection and she's not wrong. It's just a fact. Expectations built from this world we live in.

She continues: "You can all get some rest now if you want to. Good work today. The mission seems to be completed—more or less. Caihong is being sent to a temporary Dawn Court prison as we speak."

"What'll happen to him?" Josephine asks her.

"To my knowledge, the Circle intends to hear statements from both Darren and Caihong over the next few days and, with the

Midnight Court, settle on the appropriate sentence."

"Did they ask if Caihong has more of the poison? Or is the vial it?" Dev questions.

Professor Song just shakes her head. "He won't say. And even if he does, I'm not sure we can trust his word."

"Right." Dev huffs a half-defeated sigh and I'm almost certain I know how he's feeling in this moment. That there will never be an easy win.

Professor Song clears her throat. "In the meantime, I think it'd be immensely helpful if we can assist on the side by finding evidence to confirm that it was indeed Caihong. Once it's certain," she looks at me and Josephine, "the two of you are free to return to Shanghai, to many congratulations and praise, I'm sure."

In my mind, I'm thinking I'm not *quite* done yet. I'm remembering my second assignment from the Emperor and there's a sudden inkling of unease in my chest that I'm not quite willing to look too closely at.

Talia.

Ignoring the nausea in my stomach, I say, "Thanks, Professor."

"Yeah, thanks, Prof," Max echoes.

She waves a hand at us, opening the door. Says, "Goodnight," and then she's gone.

"Where's Kyan?" I ask.

"With Paris," Max tells me. He looks tired, face drawn with dark circles staining the skin under his eyes. I've never seen him like this before—Max, who is almost bigger than life. "In the lab."

"I wouldn't go see them if I were you," Dev says. "Paris is a little... not his usual delightful self at the moment."

"Oh, yeah." Max nods. "I second. You might get your head bitten straight off."

"Oh." I think I'm well-acquainted with Paris's cruelty. The events of three years ago have at least taught me to build a wall of armor thick enough that it doesn't really touch me anymore. Almost.

"Well," says Max. "I'm about to faint from exhaustion, so I'm going to bed. See you all later."

Dev says, "Likewise," and then it is once again me and Josephine in the room.

"I think I'm going to go to sleep too." She arches an eyebrow. "I assume you're not doing the same?"

"I'll be there in ten minutes," I tell her.

She rolls her eyes. Smiles a little. Says, "Okay. *Xiǎo xīn.*" Telling me to be careful again.

"*Huì de, bié dān xīn.*" Don't worry, I will.

I hope.

For some ridiculous reason, Eladine's laboratory is on one of the highest floors. I'm walking along the edge of the Lotus and on the other side of the railing, I can see the white marble of the lobby very, very far below. Thank god I'm not afraid of heights.

The lab's frosted glass doors slide open with an almost imperceptible *hiss*, and I find myself in a space that might as well have been taken directly from some sci-fi movie.

With all the lights on, the room must be blinding white, but so late in the night, the sole area in the room that's not shrouded in darkness is the center.

I see test tubes full of colored liquids, and for a second, my fingers itch. The Midnight Court lab was a second home to me. Poisons and potions and antidotes. Except here, the space is marred by machines that I don't quite understand. Not for the first time, I wonder just how much of a genius Kyan is.

I'm also thinking, I am in a *Dawn Court laboratory*. In the heart of its spy school. I should probably be doing a better job of observing everything in closer detail right now, cataloging all of this information that would be so invaluable to the Midnight Court, but for the second time tonight I'm finding that I...don't really want to.

Kyan himself is sitting on one of the stools in front of an array of glass containers. He's wearing a white lab coat over a sweater vest, looking every inch the young scientist. Maybe even a professor.

"Hey," I say, not sure if he heard me come in.

His head jerks up, startled. Pushes his glasses up. "Oh, hi, Anna. Are you looking for Paris?"

"Just wanted to see what the situation is," I tell him.

"I was just leaving, but he's outside. Just out those doors." He jabs a thumb behind him to a second set of double doors like the ones I just came through.

"Thanks," I say. And then, because I'm suddenly not quite ready to go outside, suddenly weighted with uncertainty, I ask, "How's everything here going?" Gesture to the lab table.

Kyan sighs. "It's going, but I just can't quite get it right. I'm hoping I can use the rest of the poison in the vial to get past whatever this last hurdle is. I'm also trying to find a way to change the antidote into solid form. Less risky and easier to work with."

I think I like talking to Kyan because of how easy it is. No pressure. He's so nonjudgmental it's almost insane to me. He is so engrossed in this, the lab, his work, that everything else doesn't seem quite so important.

"Good luck," I tell him. "I'm sure you'll figure it out soon."

"You could help, you know," he says to me with a gentle smile. "I heard you're particularly adept with poisons."

"Oh." I'm surprised. Mostly because he wants to work with me. That he even trusts me to work on this antidote and not sabotage it. "Sure."

"Come by the lab tomorrow," Kyan says, shrugging off the coat and hanging it on the hook protruding from a wood bar in the wall. "I'll probably be here quite early, anyway, so whenever suits you."

"Okay," I say. I'm smiling. "Sounds like a plan."

He pauses by the door. "Fantastic. And good luck to you too."

I wait until his footsteps completely fade before I turn to the door. This, I think, feels like suffocating in a grave that I've dug—and this, this is nervousness sitting behind my eyelids, under my tongue.

I take a breath and I

walk

out.

I find myself standing at the edge of a mini-garden attached to the laboratory. It juts out a little over the edge of the Lotus and it might as well be floating in air. Hanging in the night sky, And it is

dazed with moonlight,

wedged among stars.

Paris isn't difficult to spot. He's no longer in his suit and tie, just a rumpled and untucked white dress shirt and white pants.

Sitting on the ground, back against the wall, head tilted upward. Eyes closed.

I know he heard the door open and close, heard my footsteps on the packed earth, but he doesn't move. Doesn't speak.

And I, I don't either.

I'm staring at him and I'm wishing I could wash the ashes of memories off my skin because the moonlight drinks all of the color out of his hair and it is far too familiar. Far too reminiscent of younger days.

He looks almost ethereal like this, all gleaming white and silver and cutting cold lines in the pale light. Not quite human. *This*, I think. *I prefer this.* This muted Paris I can handle. No glittering gold, no glittering title. This high up, this secluded from the world, it almost feels as if we do not belong to rival courts.

I have always known that Paris is part-Dawn Court, part-Midnight, but in this backdrop of velvet black and stars and moonlight, for the first time, he looks like it. He looks so very much like he belongs in the Midnight Court that I almost drown in this vision. This *intense* feeling of hope, of wishing for something that could never be reality and it—it is devastating.

"So, are you for sure not dying now? Is that confirmed?"

Paris's eyes blink open. He looks at me, startled, as if he wasn't aware I was here after all. Says, "With Kyan's antidote and the fact that I'm half-blooded, he and Song think there's most likely a ninety percent chance I survive the poison."

My eyebrows fly up. "And you're fine with this uncertainty? You don't seem particularly concerned that there's a chance you could be dead by morning."

He laughs a little. Amused. "Anna, there's always a chance we die. In fact, most of the time I'd say it's higher than ten percent. I believe these odds are preferable. Besides, I am not particularly afraid of dying."

My eyebrows go even higher. "Come again?"

He stares at his palms. Distant. "It's a very real part of this life we lead. I made my peace with it a long time ago. I don't particularly think the world would miss me either."

Silence. And then, "Did you come here for something?" His voice is not cold, but it is emotionless. Distant. And I falter for a moment.

"I…" I pause. "I was just checking on you."

"Checking on me," he murmurs. His gaze flicks to me and the green, the green and gold cannot be hidden by the moon. Cannot be doused, this part of him that is so Dawn.

I am unmoored.

He says, "How kind of you. I'm quite fine, Anna, but thank you for your concern."

It is clear he's dismissing me, but I ignore it. Push down this feeling of apprehension that's rising in my throat and walk over.

Hyperaware.

My body is thrumming with electricity, crackling with it, and it is so at odds with the peace of this night, this place. I sit down a couple inches away. A very real sliver of air between us that I keep there like a wall, a shield, but his body heat against my skin is like a hot brand of iron anyway.

"You don't look very fine," I say as offhandedly as I can. "In fact, you're looking a little like death."

"Thanks," he says again, sarcasm scorching his voice.

"Seriously. How are you feeling?"

"Dizzy. *Hot.*" He waves a hand in the air. "Hence, why I'm sitting outside. Please leave," he tells me. "You're making it worse."

Oh. I think I'm gaping at him a little.

Irritation, I think, *is this feeling of fire scorching your skin from the inside out*—at myself and at him. It is an iron chain wrapped around your chest until you can't breathe. My brief impulse for amicability very quickly melts into the night, the cold wind, and I'm beginning to wonder what the hell I was thinking. Three people warned me and I, I was so arrogant. I was so stupid, so naive in thinking that we were unfinished. So deluded that I'd forgotten—no, not so much forgotten as ignored—the precedent that has been sitting there and staring me in the face for three years.

I'm standing up, wishing to god that I could rewind the past ten minutes—except Paris also has risen to his feet, and his fingers are wrapping around my wrist and he says, "Wait."

My breath freezes in my lungs. I am almost afraid to move, very, very aware of his skin touching mine and

I

can't

breathe.

He says, "I apologize, I didn't mean that. Stay. Please. I think I'd like some company."

When I turn around, I think I might as well be about to fall off the face of the Earth. I think it might as well be flat because there is a very real cliff and I'm about to jump right off it.

He is so, so close. Close enough to kiss. And for a second, I think he actually might. Kiss me, that is. The tension between us is a tangible thing, as if I could reach out and run a finger along the taut red thread. Pluck it.

Except then, he drops my wrist and takes a step back and it eases a little. There is an odd flutter of disappointment in my chest.

Even poisoned, Paris is still self-contained. Still very much the perfect Dawn Court prince. Except when I look at him, his pupils are blown out. He's breathing faster than normal, and I can't tell if it's the poison or if it's...

this.

Maybe he's not so contained after all.

In the night, he looks a little wild, a little like chaos itself, and the combination of it all is giving me false bravery. Enough to say, "Can I ask you something?"

He regards me with wary eyes. "What?"

It spills out of my mouth before I can stop it, breaking through the rickety dams that are my common sense, my apprehension. "Do you remember that summer in Shanghai?" *Do you remember what we used to be?*

He blinks; I've caught him in a rare moment of surprise. "I—" He stops. Starts again and says, "What about it?"

I don't say anything for a minute. Then shake my head. Say, so quietly it might as well dip and dive into the wind. "I feel like I used to know you better than anyone."

And I did. I *did*.

They say the people you meet in your childhood all leave some of themselves imprinted on you like a fingerprint on your heart, and I think, *I have known Paris at four, six, ten. Sixteen.* You never really realize human beings' capacity for change until it hits you smack in the center of your face—winds you, blinds you, leaves you breathless and gasping for air that isn't there.

I can't quite believe I just said that. We have never, ever brought up the past. It is the elephant in the room that no one dare touch and I, I just have.

I not only touched it but pushed it right over. Anxiety is waiting for Paris to respond.

His gaze slides to meet mine. Looks away. The silence itself has a heartbeat, a pulse that is exactly in sync with mine. He says, "Maybe you did."

Oh.

I was not expecting him to say that. This feels tentative, this truce, this peace, this conversation. One tap and it shatters.

"Well," I say. I look at my hands. "Not anymore."

We are both quiet for a moment. Both unsure what to say and then he says, quietly, "Sometimes, I think I might miss those days. It was all much...simpler."

It is my turn to look at him, surprised. "Me too." I ask, tentatively, "Have you ever wondered what would've happened if you hadn't gone to the Dawn Court in the beginning? If you had stayed in Shanghai?"

His lips quirk, staring at me, and there is a glint of amusement in his eyes when he answers, "Do you mean in general? Or with us."

The words hit me flat in the chest, knocks the breath straight out of me along with my entire vocabulary, and I'm just staring at him, open-mouthed. Unable to move.

God, this past. These memories are so much more effort than they are worth, so much more pain and unnecessary emotion and it is so *exhausting*. They haunt me.

The shock goes down a hard lump in my throat when I swallow. "Either," I say.

A smile ghosts across his lips. "I don't," he says. "It'd do more harm than good, I believe. I don't see a point in asking what-ifs."

Oh.

"Right," I say. "Of course."

We're face-to-face. So close I might as well be breathing in *him*—his scent, his proximity, his warmth—instead of oxygen.

Except I have utterly forgotten how to breathe. My heart has forgotten how to beat, and I am standing stock-still in front of him—as if too much movement and it'll break this. Whatever it is.

I,

I have not been this close to Paris since that Shanghai summer. Our bodies are echoing us from an earlier time and this, this feels like I'm reliving a memory.

And this *wanting*, this *wishing* and hoping is a wave that is breaking over me once, twice, three times and—

It slips out before I can stop it. Slips straight off my tongue like ice on metal. "I don't want to be enemies anymore."

Paris's silence is agonizing. It's also something new, this uneasiness waiting for him to speak. I used to know every thought that ran through his mind, used to be able to read his every expression. He was an open book that is now slammed shut, wrapped around with chains of steel so many times over as to be unbreakable.

Finally, he asks me, quietly, "What *do* you want?"

Not exactly the answer I was hoping for, but it's not a complete rejection either. Except it puts the ball squarely back into my court and I am not quite ready for this vulnerability. I am not ready to let down these metal walls that I have built up over the years.

I am choking on the past, on history and unspoken words, but this proximity, it is making me heady. This close, I can see the pale green of his eyes in the moonlight. I can see the ring of gold, can see each individual eyelash, soot against his skin when he blinks.

The combination of his scent, the moonlight, the fragrance of the flowers—I feel drunk off of it.

This is a fever dream.

There is tension in the air. Tension between our bodies, in the string that connects us, and no matter how hard I've tried to cut it, snap it, burn it,

it refuses to break.

I am trembling, I realize, with the effort of keeping still. With the effort of maintaining this sliver of space between us. Holding on to this one last desperate thread of self-control in my body, trying to remind myself why I hate him. Why we don't work.

Paris is watching me with careful eyes, reading every expression that passes across my face like a book, and I am suddenly aware that I am very, very transparent to him. That he *has* to know what I'm about to say.

"Tell me what you want, Anna," he says again, softer this time and the words are on the very tip of my tongue. So tangible I can taste them—sweet and bitter and bittersweet.

Kiss me.

I can't say it. I can't say it, but he won't do anything unless I ask him to, and whatever game this is, I am losing. I know I am.

Darkness, I think, is such a lie. It lures you in with false promises of anonymity and this feeling of intimacy, of a veil behind which you can hide, a place where you can reveal all of your fears and demons and flaws and they will all just disappear, fade into the shadows like they are being absorbed—but it's all a lie.

In the morning, you realize that that veil has always been transparent.

But right now, here in the darkness, I feel as if I could fly. As if nothing I do matters and these seconds, these minutes will fade from the page as if they never really existed at all.

My blood is *simmering* in my veins and my skin is on fire and I let it all fall. All crumble. Let the world crash and burn, because the urge to self-destruct is engraved in every facet of my brain, every cell in my body. I say, "Kiss me."

And he does.

His lips crash down on mine in an instant, firm but gentle, and it is amazing, I think, that even after all these years my mouth remembers the shape of his. His taste. I feel like I'm drowning, drowning in sensation and emotions—or maybe I'm burning, maybe I have been lit wholly ablaze.

His hands move down my body, brushing my back, my waist, coming to rest on my hips. One hand slides up to cup my face and everywhere he touches, he leaves a trail of blazing flames.

I am, I am falling to pieces, flying away in the midnight wind one grain of ash at a time. I'm thinking, *This is pleasure bordering on dying*, this is heat so hot it is cold and it is burning me, every inch of skin on my body.

My heart is blazing hot, beating, frantic. It is a hummingbird caught in my chest, wings beating against the chambers of my heart, and it is like I am breathing sweetened air and it is making me lighter. It is making me float like I am not made of flesh and blood and bones, but clouds.

I'm pressed against the wall and everywhere, everywhere is his warmth—his scent—and it is transporting me fully back in time—except we are old and this, this feels new. Brand-new. At fifteen everything is soft and tentative and innocent, but this—

I bite his bottom lip gently and he groans, shudders rippling through his body. His hand flattens against my back, pressing me tighter against him while the other hand, the other hand is traveling up my bare thigh and I have never been more grateful to be in a dress. I'm thinking, *Thank god I didn't change after the ball, thank god thank god*. His fingers slip under my dress, curve around my waist, thumb brushing the ridges of my ribs and I gasp, a hot ache spreading from my core through my body, turning me into molten lava that is rushing through my veins, flooding through my body like a dam has broken and this—

—this is getting out of control. *I* am out of control, and the sudden realization is a bucket of ice water dumped on my head.

"Wait," I gasp, breaking away for a second. "Wait, I need to ask you something."

Paris looks at me, his chest rising and falling rapidly, still a little out of breath. His eyebrow is raised as if to say, *Really? Now?* But he asks, "What?"

I swallow. I'm suddenly unsure, uncertain, not quite ready to ask. Not quite ready for his answer. It's a peculiar sensation, like I'm sprinting down a hill I know ends in a cliff, but I can't stop myself. I say, "I just need to know. Three years ago. Why did you do it?"

And his gaze immediately goes wary. He pulls away from me, leaving a very noticeable space of cold air behind and I'm thinking,

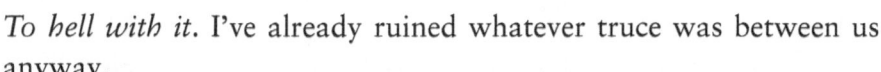

To hell with it. I've already ruined whatever truce was between us anyway.

Besides, this is not three years ago. I am not fifteen. And I cannot trust as easily as I did then. I found out a long time ago with Paris that trust gets your heart broken.

"Why did I do what?" he asks.

I swallow. "You know what. Why did you tell your father?"

He pulls completely away so abruptly that it shocks me for a moment. I stare at him, confused, watching his face shutter. Turn stony. Cold. Gaze hard.

"If you still can't figure that out, Anna," Paris says, "then maybe you shouldn't be here." He turns on his heel to leave, but I find myself reaching out. Grabbing his arm.

"No. You are *not* walking away again. What exactly," I say, "does that mean?"

I can't read him. Can't read his eyes, can't read his face. He says, "I don't think you want to hear what I have to say."

I narrow my eyes. "Just say it."

"Fine. Don't say I didn't warn you." A breath. A pause. And then, "You should know not everything is so black-and-white. I am sorry for what happened to your people, Anna, and I apologize for my court's role in it. But you—" He shakes his head. Lifts his eyes up to the darkness. "Out of all people, I thought you knew *me*. But clearly, I was wrong. I think I should thank you for it, for what you did. We never should have been together."

His words are knives flying into my chest. My heart. And I am stock-still for a minute, unable to move, and I am hyperaware of the pain that is now spreading to the rest of my body, turning my arms and legs numb and I am bleeding out, except instead of blood that is gushing out of me it is hope.

Yet again.

"You don't mean that," I say, and it comes out a whisper. Barely a breath. "*What* are you talking about?"

"Did you ever consider," he says, "that maybe your version of reality might not be the truth? That maybe you have it wrong?"

I shake my head.

Paris sighs. "Of course not. In hindsight, it was naive of me to have ever expected you to see beyond court biases. And I'm not blaming you, personally." He says, "I don't think I ever told you this, Anna, but I never really believed in love." He smiles. Looks down at his hands. At me.

Looks away.

"I spent my entire childhood seeing what it did to the people around me. I watched love destroy my parents. Watched my mother die more and more each year because of it, but you—" He stops for a moment. Laughs quietly. "You were making me change my mind. You were making me think that at the very least, maybe we were an exception. But there are," he says, "no exceptions. And I was naive to think that we would be different. I should apologize to you, actually, for allowing you to waste that summer with me. And for everything that happened afterward, I guess."

And I—I can't seem to draw air into my lungs.

I'm realizing now what I should have years earlier: He never had an intention of continuing this relationship. And this is enough to knock the breath straight out of my body.

But then, "You kissed me. Why?"

At this, he's startled. Surprise breaks through cracks in his mask, mars his features, and he says with a quirk in the corner of his mouth, with sardonic amusement, "I admit I don't have as much self-control as I should with you."

And this—

I can't handle this roller coaster of emotions anymore, can't handle this constant up-down, up-down and I think, any more and my heart will shatter from the stress of it. Crack fully in two.

CHAPTER 29

Sometimes I want to stop trying to fly. I want to stop trying to swim and kick and float on water because for the first time, I'm ready to drown.

I realize that I decided long ago I'm not going to go through with this assignment that the Emperor gave me. And that despite what happened last night, I know I'm not going to kill Paris. He is too much a part of me—my past and my present—for me to go through with it without destroying some part of myself in the process.

Except now I have no idea what I'm going to do. What I'm going to say to the Council, to my family when I return and they ask me *why*.

But I'll deal with that when I must.

Class the next morning is a strange return to reality. After the events of the ball and last night in the garden, it doesn't feel quite real to be back here in the classroom, sitting in these hard wood chairs among the other first-years, as if we didn't just discover who the culprit behind the stolen poison was. As if, because of that, this tremulous peace between the two courts isn't becoming more and more unstable, teetering on wobbly legs.

Today, we were meant to have another common room meeting. Go over what happened at the Equinox Ball, figure out how to confirm beyond a shadow of a doubt that Caihong was the one who stole the antidote—except Professor Song is stuck in faculty meetings for the next two days. And to be completely honest, something about it just doesn't sit right with me. Why would Caihong do this? Why risk reigniting the war?

But maybe it's just my bias toward the Midnight Court.

In the meantime, I try not to think about what happened in the garden last night. I try not to think about Paris.

We're in history class again. In the past month, we've made it past the prewar era and have moved into covering the period of war itself—why it started, how it escalated to where it is now. Today, we're taking a minor detour to focus on the Midnight Court.

"As you all know from the textbook chapter I assume everyone read yesterday," Professor Larne says from the front of the room, "the Midnight Court today is not what it originally was." I can tell the majority of the class is already not paying attention, but he plows on anyway. "The old Midnight Court was formed in Hong Kong, before it was moved to Shanghai almost a century ago. Does anyone know why?"

It is Josephine who raises her hand. Professor Larne seems pleased. "Yes, Ms. Jiang."

"A couple of reasons," Josephine answers. "The most obvious being that Hong Kong—specifically Kowloon where the Midnight Court ruled—was inundated by protests against British rule in the mid-twentieth century. There was just far too much chaos for the Midnight Court to effectively retain control. And also, because Hong Kong was never a seat of power. The Midnight Court may have been arbitrarily birthed there centuries ago—"

"Why?"

"As a result of the constant power struggles between warring families."

"Correct. Go on."

"But Shanghai, as a trading hub, was almost always more powerful. And especially starting from the nineteenth century onwards."

"Very good, Ms. Jiang," Professor Larne praises. "Indeed, you will find that wherever the concentration of power is, people tend to follow. But the original royal family—the Chen dynasty—didn't last long in the new location. Does anyone know why?"

Josephine raises her hand again.

"From the Dawn Courters in the class, this time." He looks around. Not a single person lifts their head to look back at him. I'm not surprised.

Larne sighs. "Okay." He tells us, "Take the next thirty minutes to read the textbook chapter, since it is painfully obvious that most of you have not read it. I expect an answer by the last fifteen minutes of class."

And in the end, it is a scrawny, light-haired boy who answers. "A bomb exploded in the main building."

Professor Larne nods. "Yes. In the commotion of the move to Shanghai, the Dawn Court was able to plant a spy into the Midnight Court's Council. And that spy, somehow, found a way to bring a bomb strapped to his body into an inner Council meeting where every member of the royal family was in attendance. And he detonated it, killing everyone in that room.

"The Dawn Court thought that would mean instant surrender from Shanghai, but the remaining Council members held an emergency vote that elected one person the new emperor. Xia Renfu. And that is how the new Xia dynasty began."

Later that afternoon, Josephine and I have combat training. Half of the first-years are being paired up into mock fights and the other half are either practicing on dummies or doing target practice. We are slated for the first rotation of the mock fights. They're hosting these in the stadium since there isn't nearly enough space in the gym where the other half of training is being held, and walking into a room has never been so nerve-racking.

Naturally, the praefectus are overseeing and I am terrified of seeing Paris. The events of last night are too fresh, a still angry brand on my chest, and I'm not sure I want to face him quite yet.

Maybe ever.

I hate this imbalance of power between us, hate that he's a second-year member of the praefectus and I'm just a first-year student.

Who also technically shouldn't even be here.

I think whatever has happened between us is a still-healing wound, and last night, last night ripped it freshly open—scab off, raw and trickling blood.

"Can you relax?" Josephine whispers to me as we file into the room, a steady stream of bodies.

"No," I say. My fingers are dancing across my leg, tap, tap, tap.

I haven't told her about the fifteen-minutes-that-shall-never-be-mentioned-again yet. By the time I got back to the dorm last night, she was fast asleep. Something that I should've been.

Passing through the threshold of the doorway, my first instinct is to look around, try to find him—in the same way it's better to know where the threat is rather than being blindsided—but a warring instinct tells me to keep my head down. Pray to god he doesn't see me. Avoid eye contact at all costs.

I usually try to avoid awkwardness like the plague, so this, this is torture.

Seventy-six of us are standing in a crowd in the middle of the stadium—an even number to guarantee that the pairings will work out. In front of us are the combat mats, lined up with incredible precision across the floor. Thirty-eight forming perfect lines, perfect squares.

There are three members of the praefectus standing in front of us. I'm fairly certain I recognize two of them—Khione and Ren, I think their names are. The other boy's face is familiar, but I'm not sure what his name is. I do know I've seen him before. Maybe at the praefect table in the mess hall. The rest of them are standing in a scattered clump in the back. They're talking among themselves, laughing, clearly very familiar in a way only people who spend every day together can be.

I spot Max, Dev. Paris.

He's wearing a white muscle tank and white pants, and his body is built like a blade. Like he has trained his entire life to be a weapon—which, I guess, he has. I can't rip my eyes away from the gold of his skin, the ridges of muscle in his arms, his shoulders, his torso, and my heart

constricts.

Slows for a second.

There's an easy smile on his face, a honey-warm look of amusement and I'm thinking, that expression used to belong to me. That smile was mine, reserved just for me, and sometime in the past three years, it became for everyone but me.

I know *he* knows I'm here. I know it. But he doesn't look at me. Doesn't even glance my way.

"First-years!" Khione's voice echoes through the stadium.

"As you should all know by now, the faculty is canceling classes for today to focus on combat training. In light of the growing tensions between us and Shanghai, they think that this is extremely important."

She clasps her hands together. "So, here's what'll happen. You're going to choose a partner. We'll be rotating a couple times, so you'll only be with them for half an hour at a time. Once you find your partner, take a place on one of the mats and we'll begin the mock fights.

"All of the praefectus are here right now, but once training starts, half will be going to the gym to look over your peers and half will stay here to oversee you. We'll be making rounds, so don't be surprised when we come by to watch your round. We'll be offering some constructive critiques, some advice, and then in a couple of hours you'll rotate into the gym and those in the gym will come here."

She turns to Ren and the other boy next to her, quietly asks, "Is there anything I left out?"

"Rotate when you hear a whistle," Ren tells us. "And try not to kill each other. Don't forget this is a mock. Save your energy for the real fights."

Khione turns back to us. "Great. Any questions?"

There are none.

"All right, choose your partners and get on a mat."

Josephine turns toward me. "Should we find a mat on the edge? Or the middle?"

I have no answer. My mind is flip-flopping between the two, both options on a seesaw that won't stop moving, won't stop going up and down, up and down, up and down.

In the end, we compromise: a mat that is technically in the middle but leaning toward the side.

Thankfully, Cassie and Mariam are next to us, meaning after the first rotation, at least there's someone else that we know.

The first whistle pierces the air, signaling the start.

"So, what exactly happened yesterday?" Josephine asks me. We're circling each other, waiting for the first strike. Gaze flicking up, down, arms, legs, torso. I don't even blink.

"Well," I say, looking around. Furtively, as if I'm about to expose myself for a crime. As if I'm about to say something that is illegal. "You know I went to find Paris after you left."

"Right."

She waits for me to continue. I don't. The rest of the story is stuck in my throat like a paper jam and I can't cough it out. I'm not sure I want to.

"And then? Did something happen?" she prompts.

I strike first, darting toward her and punching a fist toward her face, which she dodges.

"And then I found him. Did you know the lab is like all the way on one of the top floors? Isn't that insane?"

"Stop trying to change the subject." She attacks this time, swinging out a leg, except I've already seen it coming. Josephine and I have been practicing with each other for far too long for this to be effective. I know all of her tells. Some of them belong to me.

"I wasn't trying to," I say, rolling my eyes. "I was just relaying some information I found intriguing to my best friend." I hesitate. Suddenly, I don't want to tell her. I don't want to know what she's going to say.

"Out with it, Liang."

I look at the mat. The wall. Anywhere else. "We, um...we kissed."

As soon as I say it, I want to cringe. I want to take it back, swallow it straight from the air back into my mouth and wish that it never touched daylight because out of the cover of the night, of the darkness, of my own private thoughts, it is too lurid. Too forbidden.

Josephine's eyes widen into full moons—if full moons were dark

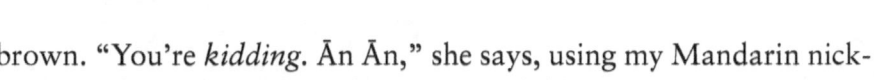

brown. "You're *kidding*. Ān Ān," she says, using my Mandarin nickname to chastise. "Did you kiss him, or did he kiss you?"

"It's a long story," I admit.

She's staring at me with eyes that practically bulge out of her head. "What the hell? I can't believe you didn't tell me first thing this morning. Actually, scratch that. I can't believe you didn't wake me up last *night* to tell me." She shoves my shoulder with mock offense. "What kind of friend are you?"

"Sorry, sorry!" I say. "I didn't want to wake you. Besides, it's not that big a deal." I'm trying to sound as nonchalant as possible, except it's so obviously fake it shatters by itself.

"Is that why you looked like you were about to jump out of your skin when we came in?" And then she pauses. "Wait, does that mean everything's fine with you guys now?" Her voice lowers to a whisper. "Did you talk about *you know*?"

At this, my stomach flips right over. Stabs a needle into itself until it deflates. Sinks in on itself.

"Um, no," I say. "Everything is not fine, and I guess we kind of talked about it? Actually, I think everything might be worse."

Josephine looks about ready to slap a palm to her forehead. "What?"

I shrug. "Point is, just pretend it didn't happen, okay? Pretend I didn't tell you."

She looks at me dubiously but doesn't argue.

CHAPTER 30

We're in mock fights for another three hours. Meaning by the time we make it to our second rotation, all seventy-six of us are sweaty and tired and probably look like we've just returned from hell.

I know I do.

I'm beginning to think maybe doing the gym rotation first would've been better.

I've pulled my hair into the sloppiest ponytail of my life. Strands of it are stuck to my forehead, my neck, and I have never been so uncomfortable. That's a lie. But I wish I could just go shower anyway.

I don't look at Paris when we file into the gym. Not directly, anyway. I can see him out of the corner of my eye, standing next to Khione on one side, and Max and Dev are on the other side. Waving to me. I wave back.

"Welcome, everyone," Khione says to us. She, I think, is the epitome of Dawn Court. White-blonde hair, amber eyes, dressed in a clean white jumpsuit.

"I hope you all made good use of that last rotation. We're going to continue with individual training now. So, some of you will be practicing hand-to-hand combat with the dummies that you see on the side. The rest will be doing some target practice—knives, mock guns, arrows. You know what I mean."

Khione is squinting at our group of first-years as if analyzing something in her head and then sections us off with her hands. "All of you on the left here, you're assigned to the dummies." She shifts her hands. "You guys are on targets. For those of you at the targets, we'll be doing half-hour rotations for each discipline, and then obviously once we're halfway through the session, you'll switch. Dummies go to targets and vice versa. All right, disperse."

Josephine and I break off from the group, taking up spots side by side in front of the line of pockmarked targets against the wall.

There are about thirty of them, thirty of us standing directly in front and thirty small tables covered in perfect lines of knives, arrows and a gun that I know doesn't shoot real bullets, but it leaves a metallic tang in my mouth nonetheless.

I can't help remembering the last time I faced one. The sound of bullets tearing into the silence.

The praefectus are making their rounds, weaving in and out of our group of first-years, stopping once in a while to offer some critique.

We start with knives—thank god, because out of the three weapons on the table, it might be the only one I'm actually good at.

Suddenly, I'm finding myself missing my *jian*, my balisongs, my *tie shan* and throwing stars. In the Midnight Court, your weapons are an extension of yourself. They are like companions, like lifelong friends, and sometimes, there are some that you've had for most of your life. Some whose grip is molded so perfectly into your hand it might as well be part of it. They are chosen both for functionality and for beauty, and the Midnight Court teaches fighting like a dance. A song of blades.

Dawn Court weapons are all about result, all about how much damage can be done and how efficiently and not at all about beauty. Not at all about skill and discipline and art.

It's almost blasphemous.

For half an hour, I'm feeling good. I'm feeling ahead. Each knife strikes the bull's-eye with almost easy accuracy, as if they have their own GPS and it's taking them directly into the center of the target.

And I'm smiling; I'm watching them all hit, watching Josephine's all hit, and watching the rest of our group whose residence in the Dawn Court means they spend most of their time working with guns rather than knives—and it shows.

"Nice job, Anna," Max says to me as he comes by on one of the rounds. "You have a particular face in mind when you're practicing with knives?"

I snort. "Don't need to, thank you very much."

He just laughs and moves on.

Five minutes later and we're onto the next rotation. Guns. Supposedly, they're made for practice so they just shoot these darts that embed into the targets the way bullets would.

I pick up the gun. Look at Josephine with trepidation and she's shooting a grimace back at me. Mouthing, *What kind of abomination is this?*

I shrug, mouth back, *Dawn Court abomination.*

It's not that I haven't used a gun before. Obviously, I have, but that doesn't mean I like it. It is everything about this war that I hate: deadly, crude, with no regard for the human lives that are being wasted in the process.

One touch and it is like the cold kiss of death, dark gray shiny metal as if it's trying to be beautiful. Trying to imitate the silvery glow of blades. But like all imitations, it falls short.

Slipping my fingers around the grip, I suppress a shudder at the foreign feel of it in my hand. Against my palm.

My stomach is roiling. I'm thinking, maybe this is what it feels like to be seasick, to be stuck on a still-sailing ship through a tempest and almost hoping it'd capsize. Hoping you'd drown just so this feeling would disappear. Erase itself from your body.

I think I know where this deep aversion to guns has suddenly come from. I have no idea when it got so potent, but I'm thinking PTSD is very much real. Maybe there's some milder version of it that's folding itself into the valleys of my body, the crevices of my brain.

Not that I'm a psychiatrist.

I get into stance, feet shoulder-width apart. Sight the target. Pull the trigger.

I don't even see the dart in the air, just spot it when it's sticking out from the target like a sore thumb. Nowhere near the center.

I let out a huff of frustration, only to hear Josephine swearing, and then I'm trying not to laugh. I'm staring at her dart that is barely better off than mine and she's saying, "God, I hate guns. I seriously don't understand the point of them."

I shake my head. Laugh a little. "Me neither."

We aim again, repeating the same exact process. I'm certain that I'm going to be doing this probably fifty times in the next half hour, and I am in serious danger of losing my mind.

And then, a voice is by my ear and it is piercing through the cracks in my skin and I almost flinch. Almost jump right out of my body.

I curse myself for losing track of Paris.

"You should keep a little more tension in your body if you're trying to shoot a gun," he says. His voice is quiet. Civil. Distant.

I swallow. I'm frozen. As if my muscles have locked themselves up, gone away for the holidays and all of the extra energy is going into my skin.

Every inch of my body is tingling from his proximity, can sense his presence behind me, and I am doing everything I can to keep my hands steady.

To force the gun still.

"What?" I ask.

He touches three fingers to my sides, to my stomach, and he's saying, "Engage your core. It helps with stability. Balance," except I can barely hear him.

He's touching me, but he is so cold, so aloof that I almost wish he would be angry. Bitter. *Something*. His skin is separated from mine by one very thin piece of fabric and this, combined with the scent of him, is sending shivers up my arms, my back, sending heat unfurling in my stomach.

The events of last night hang in the air between us, yet another skeleton on this chain of death that is wrapped around both of us, but neither of us acknowledge it. Neither of us bring it up.

Because no matter what, I cannot forgive him for what he's done and he will not let go of this grudge. We are forever fated to dance around each other, blades pressed to throats and neither of us able to pull away.

We are fated to die at each other's hands.

CHAPTER 31

I'm so distracted at dinner the next day.

They sent an announcement earlier in the day that there had been an attack on the Midnight Court embassy in London. The Circle made sure to stress that they had no part in it, that it was an unauthorized attack, and that they're investigating it.

I called my mom right after to ask her about it, but she didn't know much more than I did. Instead, she asked me about the events of the Equinox Ball. I told her everything that had happened, as vaguely as I could.

At one point, she asked me if I was able to gather any information on the layout of the building. I told her no—we had only seen the main room and the side hallway we hid in. I told her it was right next to the ballroom.

I lied.

Paris left for a Dawn Court meeting to discuss the attack a few hours ago, which means we're all given a reprieve from the planning in the common room for a day. It also means I'm stuck doing whatever else they have the first-years doing.

Currently, they're having some big feast for all of us after the six hours of combat training we've endured, but I have no appetite. Suddenly, I can't stand being here, in London. Standing on the ground that is soaked in the blood of my people, *my* blood, and is making me want to gag. Making me want to take off in whatever plane I find first and fly straight back to Shanghai.

Except I don't. I can't.

Instead, I find myself taking the elevator up to the thirteenth floor. Up to the lab. I'm tracing the exact steps I took last night and then I'm stepping through sliding doors. Listening to the wave of voices and laughter and clinking silverware down below fade into a smudge. Blur together.

Kyan's sitting at the lab table, straight-backed on a stool pouring liquid into a beaker when I walk in. I almost smile at the sight.

He looks up when I come in. Blinks. Says, "Hey, Anna."

"Hi," I reply, sliding into the chair opposite him. "Are you working on the antidote?"

He's still looking at me like he can't quite believe that I'm here, like I've materialized out of thin air and he's still trying to figure out if I'm real or not.

"Yes. I'm testing the poison, trying to isolate the elements so I can figure out a way to neutralize them."

I push up my sleeves. "Great. Put me to work."

In the back of my mind, I think I know the truth of what I'm doing. That I'm helping the Dawn Court create an antidote that would reduce the Midnight Court's power over them. That in effect, I am committing treason.

I can't really bring myself to care.

We spend the next ten minutes in silence—comfortable silence, surprisingly. Both of us working individually, occasionally pausing to exchange test tubes, pipettes, discuss something.

Half an hour later, I ask him, "Why aren't you a member of the praefectus like the others? Not in, like, a bad way," I add quickly. "Just curious."

"I didn't think you meant it in a bad way," Kyan says, smiling. He shrugs. "I just never really had a desire to."

"To…?"

"I don't know. Be in the spotlight. Lead people. Everyone—the students and the faculty—is always watching you as a praefectus.

Observing everything you do, because you're meant to be a role model. And I also just never felt that I was well-suited for the position. I'm not confident or charismatic or particularly people-centered, so..."

"Makes sense," I say. "The first part, not the second. I don't think I'd want to work with first-years either, if I were given a choice."

Kyan laughs lightly. "Right. That too." A pause. "Do you mind if I say something?"

I look at him, confused. "Sure?"

He doesn't meet my gaze. Says, "Anna, I've been friends with Paris for nine years. He's never really spoken to me about it, but I think I know more about whatever happened three years ago than I should."

At this, my mind falls straight off the stool.

Kyan continues. "Anyway, I just wanted to tell you to maybe give him the benefit of the doubt. Dig a little deeper. You might find he's not quite the person you think he is."

It feels a little bit like admonishment, but I'm not put out by it. For some reason, I think, I want Kyan to like me. His opinion holds some weight in my chest. Maybe because he's Paris's best friend. Or maybe it's just because of who he is.

Although, I have no idea what he means. I'm frowning at him, hoping he'll elaborate except he doesn't say anything else. Just goes back to whatever he's doing, and I'm left staring at the brown-black hair at the back of his head.

In the end we identify seven out of the eight elements of whatever the poison is made out of. One more and then Kyan will be able to create the antidote easily. He says he's going to stay in the lab until he can figure it out, until he can create the antidote, and we should have it by tomorrow.

We are so, so close and after this, after we figure out the antidote, the stakes are so much lower. No more concern over people dying; solely concern over proving that Caihong was the one responsible.

For the first time, I feel a semblance of hope. A small puff of it blown into my body by some wayward breeze, so ephemeral it fades right after.

But it was there.

CHAPTER 32

Maybe I spoke too soon. Maybe I was too hasty, because the next week, it's all over.

I'm already three quarters of the way to my dorm room when I realize I left my phone in one of the sitting rooms we were studying in earlier. I let out a half-frustrated sigh and retrace my steps back to the main building. I'm reaching for my phone when I feel it—the cold rim of a gun pressed against my back. A circle of cold metal seeping into my skin and I am

frozen.

My heart is banging against its cage, begging to be let out, but I am afraid to move. Every cell in my body is on alert.

In my head, I'm thinking this has to be one of the students, maybe faculty, maybe someone playing a practical joke, except, "Turn around, Anna. Slowly."

And the voice almost obliterates me.

This voice I have heard warm and cold, this voice has whispered sweet nothings in my ear, whispered *I love yous*, touched every part of my body late at night and it is achingly familiar.

I haven't seen him in five days. I wonder what happened.

I turn around slowly, so slowly, not because of fear of the gun pressed into my back now, but because I'm afraid to face him. Face this confrontation that I can feel is coming.

The first thing I see is the barrel of a gun now a foot away. Paris is standing behind it, coldly cut against the spluttering fire behind him. He's in a starch white jacket that must be some official uniform for the Dawn Court because I've seen it before. On the other princes. On the king.

"Paris," I say. "What are you doing?"

His eyes flick to mine, hard green and glinting in the light of the fire and he says, quietly, "You know what I heard when I went back home, Anna?"

I don't say anything.

"Did you think I wouldn't find out?" he asks me, quietly. So quietly. "That after ten years of living in the Midnight Court, I wouldn't have my own spies?

"You were going to kill me," he says. "That, I can live with. That, I can maybe even forgive. But my *sister*." At this, his voice shakes a little and I am startled, to say the least, at this tiny crack in his armor. At this admission of hurt that he allows to show through because I know Paris, and nothing he does is ever a mistake.

"How could you?" His voice is a whisper. "You've known her since she was born. Since you were nine years old. You know how much she means to me. Did you not care at *all* that it would break me? My family?"

I think, my own heart is breaking. It is cracking into halves, thirds, millionths and pouring out sand, tons and tons of sand until it is filling my nose, filling my lungs, and I am drowning in it.

But underneath it all, underneath this pain and regret for hurting him, is anger. It's flickering low in my stomach, licking up and down my insides and some self-destructive, chaotic part of me suddenly only desires to fuel this confrontation rather than resolve it.

I say, "I was going to kill you first."

His face is a twist of hurt. A myriad of emotions and I know what he's thinking. I know it because I realize that I was wrong. That despite everything, despite the years and the hurt and hatred, I do still know him. Better than anyone. But he doesn't know *me* anymore. Doesn't recognize me. And maybe it's better this way. After all, this is exactly what I thought of him three years ago.

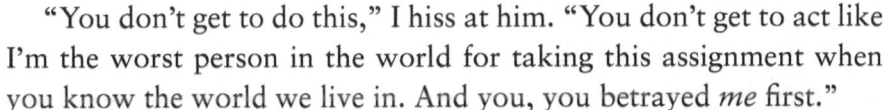

"You don't get to do this," I hiss at him. "You don't get to act like I'm the worst person in the world for taking this assignment when you know the world we live in. And you, you betrayed *me* first."

Paris stalks closer and I am taking a step back. Realizing I have to explain what he doesn't seem to know.

"I wasn't going to follow through on it," I say. "Not after... everything." I don't even know what to call what we've been doing. "There would've been no point except to make something out of nothing. Like what you're doing right now."

Another step back. Until my back is pressed to the wall and he is an inch away. Presses the gun to my temple, but even now, it is gentle. A light touch of metal against my skin. Even now, he can't hurt me.

And this, this makes me a little braver.

"You can't possibly think I could be that horrible, could you? That I could just kill someone that easily. Not just someone. *Her*. No harm, no foul, right?" I snap.

My body is a battleground of emotions, a knotted-up tangle of them and it is half-lingering fear, half-thrill that is almost unintentional, my body's natural reaction when Paris is near me and he is

very much

near me.

I want to touch him. I want to reach out, run my fingers through his hair.

I have no idea why I'm thinking this.

The icy cold of the wall is seeping into my back, but my front is all warmth, warmth from his body and it is such a sudden contrast of hot and cold it makes me breathless. And I hate myself for thinking this, for feeling this even as he's holding a gun to my head. I think, I was always right. Paris is my greatest weakness.

"If you want me to be scared," I say with a little gasp, "you should probably move further away."

At this, he narrows his eyes at me, lowers his gun slightly. Very deliberately moves closer until I can see the flecks of gold in his eyes and each individual lash, until we're practically breathing the same air and *god* he has stolen every breath out of my body.

Every working cell.

Every thought.

He whispers against my ear, "Who says I'm trying to scare you?" And then he kisses me, roughly and recklessly and I'm kissing him back, my fingers digging into his back. This kiss is all anger and lust, more like a battle than a show of affection. Paris takes another step forward until I'm pressed hard into the wall, so hard it almost hurts, but it only adds to the jumble of sensations all over my body.

The gun now safely tucked in his waistband, his hands grasp at my waist, my hips, everywhere he touches scorching hot and I feel like I am *burning*. Like I might as well be ashes. His mouth is on my mouth, my jaw, my throat and I'm letting my head fall, dying a bit as he gently bites my neck and then against my skin he murmurs, "Just answer me one thing, Anna. Were you ever going to tell me?"

We both pull away at the same time. When I look at him, he's watching me, green eyes steady. I open my mouth. Close it. There is no more oxygen in my lungs. No more words in my mouth and I find that I don't even really care.

"No," I say.

I can see with excruciating clarity the moment his face shutters. He says, "Of course."

I have the sudden urge to defend myself. "If you were me, wouldn't you have done the same?"

Paris sighs. He won't even look at me. "I don't know what to think anymore, Anna. I thought I knew you when I was sixteen—I was wrong. I thought I knew you again, now, and again I'm wrong. I can't let there be a third time. Even I have some semblance of self-preservation, you know."

I'm shaking, not from fear but from anger, from frustration. "I thought I knew you too," I fling back.

He says, calmly, diffidently, as if he has no stake in this conversation, no stake in whatever relationship this is now, "I'm going back to the Dawn Court tomorrow. I think," he adds, "perhaps it's best if you go back to yours."

CHAPTER 33

Professor Song sends for me the next morning—to her office this time, not the common room. She doesn't say why. After the events of yesterday, I have no idea what to say. No idea what to think.

I try my best to simply not think about it, shove it out of my brain because regardless of what happens between Paris and me, I still have an assignment I need to complete. I still have things to do.

Except I walk into Song's office and the universe must be laughing at me, must be so absolutely entertained at my expense, because there he is.

Paris, sitting in one of the two chairs across from Song's desk and I stop dead almost unintentionally. Slowly walk the rest of the way. Sit down.

Tension is already suffocating the room, stuffing sticks and stones into it until it is too full, until it's about to burst, and thank god Song's here too, because I don't think Paris and I can be alone in a room together right now.

He doesn't look at me. I don't look at him.

"Thanks for coming, Anna," Professor Song says to me. "And apologies for the late notice, to both of you. It was all rather abrupt.

"After the events of the past couple of days, the Dawn Court and the Midnight Court have agreed to cohost the opening day of the Grand Prix at the Hyde Park Polo Club as a show of solidarity. They want the two of you to go together, and make it look like you really are *together*. Send a message to the people that not only are we still in peacetime, that we're still allies, but that progress is being made."

I half expect Paris to laugh, to say no, but he doesn't. Of course he doesn't.

He asks, "When is this?"

Song sighs. "Tomorrow."

Oh.

"I know," she says, "This is extremely late notice. They didn't send a message until early morning today."

I clear my throat. "What exactly is the Grand Prix?"

They both look at me, and I can see the look of surprise that flits across Song's face before she says, "My apologies, Anna. I keep forgetting you're not from here. It's an equestrian event the Dawn Court hosts every year at the polo club. An antiquated sport, for sure, but... tradition. Every important leader or well-known figure attends.

"This'll be an opportunity to keep an eye on Darren, as well," she adds.

I blink. "Is the trial over?"

Professor Song nods. "A week or so ago, although the Circle just released the results to us. It seems Darren's standing firm on having been under Caihong's control, under threat of harm to the Dawn Court people or something like that—they didn't give us the details. Caihong objected, of course, but the courts sided with Darren"—not a surprise, I suppose—"and sentenced Caihong to prison in the Midnight Court." Song continues, "This is the chance we've been waiting for to find irrefutable proof that it was Caihong. And at the very least, we can make sure Darren isn't still under his control."

She's essentially telling us to spy on Darren. Which *I'm* completely fine with. I glance at Paris. If he's bothered, he doesn't show it.

"Paris, I know you have to head back to the Dawn Court right after this," Song says. "The two of you will just meet at the venue tomorrow." She asks, "Sound good?" but I'm barely listening anymore.

I forgot Paris was leaving. Heading right back to his home in the Dawn Court to tell the world exactly what I was planning to do, exactly what he had promised yesterday.

How could I have forgotten? I'm terrified he's going to tell Professor Song and the rest of the group too. I'm worried he already has.

Distantly, I hear Paris say "Yes." Feel myself nod.

Professor Song says, "That's it," and we're out the door.

I stop him the moment we're outside. "Paris, wait."

He looks at me. Says, "What?" And there's no animosity in his voice. No expression. I'm not sure what to make of that.

"You're leaving," I say, and it's not quite a question. "Right now."

"And you want to know if I'm going to tell them," and this isn't a question either. We're flinging statements back and forth at each other, flinging these things that we already know to be true and I'm thinking, *This is so pointless.*

So absolutely pointless.

He says, "I won't. Not yet. The courts need this moment of peace, but my family has to know." No malice. Just fact. "They deserve to."

He begins walking again, heading to the parking garage, and I follow. Refuse to let him go.

"This will put both of our courts back at war," I say. "And you know it."

"Then maybe," he says, "your emperor is to blame."

"Of course he is." I can hear the frustration coating my voice. "But there's nothing either of us can do about that. Paris, *you know* I would never hurt Talia. You can choose to let it go."

Somehow, we've made it inside the parking garage. We're standing next to the car and it is sleek and cold and uninviting. The garage itself is squeaky-clean, hospital-white and shiny. It is one giant space, and up above, the few lights on the ceiling are reflected on the floor. Temporarily blinding.

My fingers twitch, itching for the *emeici* piercers already in my hand, and Paris must've noticed me, because as soon as I grab it, he's raised his gun.

And here we are, deadlocked.

I almost laugh at how ridiculous this is. How many times we've been in this position, me holding a weapon on him. Him holding one on me.

It's like we're stuck in this constant circle, stuck in the same hamster wheel doomed to keep running in place. Doomed to never make it out.

We stare at each other for a couple seconds, weapons raised, and I can't believe what we've come to. How far we've fallen. Heaven to hell in not just the span of three years but the span of six days.

The irony.

I'm trying not to let the emotions show on my face, trying to mirror his expression so he can't tell what I'm thinking, but I can't tell if I've succeeded. I can't tell if I've failed.

One more second and he

very

deliberately

lowers his gun. Takes a step toward me, another one, until he's standing in front of my piercer and the point of it is pressed to the underside of his chin, the soft part of his skin.

He's calling my bluff.

And I am. I am bluffing. Because no matter how much I want to, no matter how much I don't, I know I can't kill him. He bleeds red.

I know because I've seen it.

"So?" he says, and his voice is quiet, a little breathless. "This is the second time you've threatened to kill me, and I am giving you the opportunity. Serving it to you on a silver platter. Take it."

"Paris."

I know he knows. I know he knows I won't push. I will my hand not to shake, will the burning in my eyes to recede, and pushing it back is like pushing back a wave.

He's staring at me expectantly, green and gold and incredibly, utterly beautiful and I realize he's waiting for me to continue.

Except there are no more original words in my mouth, no new thoughts, and I'm wishing someone would tell me how to speak, how to make him stay, because Paris versus my court, my family, will destroy me.

Tear me into a million pieces. Scatter them all across this earth.

And I'm thinking sometimes being alive feels like a chore. I'm thinking I have been searching for an asylum for my soul for eighteen years and I still, somehow, have not found it yet.

"Why are you doing this?" I wonder how many times I've repeated these same words to him. Both three years ago and now. Nothing ever seems to change.

Paris sighs. Looks at me. "I am..." He pauses. "So very tired. Tired of pretending I am someone I'm clearly not, of pretending like I'm not fully, completely rotten to the absolute core."

I'm already shaking my head. Already saying, "You're wrong. I don't believe you're willing to start a war just for this."

Then, "Why do you have so much misplaced faith in my morality, Anna? I've never thought of you as naive."

My words have abandoned me. Left me out on the street in the middle of the night, in the middle of the cold, uncaring that the wolves are coming.

Without them, I am weaponless. Worse, defenseless.

"That's because I'm not," I say, lamely. And then—furiously. "As much as you hate the world knowing who you are, as much as you want to keep a wall six miles wide between you and everyone else, I know you. And this, it's not you."

With two words, he punctures two holes in my lungs, in my reality. "Isn't it?"

In my head, I'm wondering, *What happened to him these past few years?* I think I've always known Paris had some piece of darkness within him, some part of the Midnight Court that Dawn couldn't hammer out, that his gold hair and Dawn Court title couldn't hide.

Now I'm beginning to wonder what having two warring identities does to a person, if it tears them open from the inside out. His parents' union two decades ago was the first spark of real hope for peace between our two courts, but even that couldn't fully save us. And the death of his mother nine years ago has slowly been tearing that peace apart—and him along with it.

"If you think about it," Paris continues, "we don't really know each other, none of us. You and I broke up three years ago and that might as well be eternity in teenage years. You don't know me. I don't know you."

His voice is quiet, detached because he's simply stating a fact. It only makes it hurt more, I think. I almost wonder if he'd intended it that way.

I feel myself take a step back, and then immediately hate myself for showing any kind of weakness in front of him.

But in this boy standing in front of me, I can see nothing of the Paris I know. Knew. Or maybe this is who he was all along, every horrible rumor I've heard about the Dawn Court made flesh and I had just simply refused to believe it.

"Fine," I hiss. "But while we're on the topic: You're right. I don't know you. No one does. You like it that way, god knows why."

"I've never asked you to try to understand me," he shoots back. "Nor my reasons for doing what I do. You bring it upon yourself."

In the distance, I hear voices, students getting up. Walking to class. Dread is pooling in my stomach like sewer water. Rising to my chest.

Paris steps away. Straightens the collar of his jacket. Begins walking back toward the car. I'm watching all of this happen, frozen, bombarded with the noise and the desperation and my own fear.

It isn't until I see him reach for the door, about to step into the car that I come out of it.

Grab his arm.

"*Stop*. Please." Desperation is rising in my throat, burning the backs of my eyes. "Paris, you tell them, and you know exactly what they're going to do. They'll attack my entire family first, in retaliation. My *family*." I take a breath. Say again, "Don't do it."

He touches my face with his fingertips, so lightly I almost think I'm imagining it, I almost think it's the touch of a feather. I shiver.

"It's my family too, Anna," he says. And then he's gone, swinging into the driver's seat and soon, all I'm left with is wind and dust.

CHAPTER 34

I'm late.

I know because it's practically noon and the event at the polo club started at 10:00 a.m.

Unfortunately for me, my languages class chose today to have a mandatory assembly in the auditorium and Professor Song decided it wasn't imperative enough for me to be there at the very beginning of the event to justify skipping class entirely. And also I've been skipping so much already it might become suspicious to the other students and faculty.

It's barely even a five-minute drive to the polo club in Hyde Park, but the administration insist on taking a car anyway. I don't argue.

Through the window, I stare at the yellow-brown blur of trees as we whizz past, watch the leaves drift to the ground and add to the ever-growing pile carpeting the park. In my head, I'm thinking about how different London looks now from when I first arrived. How much time has passed.

How quickly.

Paris meets me when I arrive; he's dressed in an untucked white dress shirt and khakis and I'm thinking, this is one of the only times I have ever seen him so casual. It throws me off a little. Cracks and replasters my reality.

This is strange. So, so strange. This is yet another section in the book that doesn't exist and neither of us knows how to act. Neither of us knows how to interact with each other.

A month ago, I was assigned to kill his sister.

Two days ago, he held a gun to my head for it.

Today, we're forced to go to this thing together. Put up a united front that is more smoke and mirrors than anything has ever been.

I have no idea what to do. What to say. For once, my brain is not a jumble of thoughts, but empty space. Fully blank.

Finally, he says, "You look nice."

Fine, if he wants to act as if nothing happened, so will I. "Thanks. So do you."

I know he's just being polite because I'm wearing a maxi dress they provided for me. It flows around my ankles—much longer than I'm used to. I have no idea how to move in this, let alone fight in it if I need to.

Paris takes me from the stables near the gate to the track. It is almost exactly like the one in the stadium back at Eladine, but this one is much, much larger. It's made of packed dirt, surrounded by grass on both sides.

On the right, I assume, is where the spectators sit. I count a dozen round tables under a giant white tent. White tablecloths. Dark oak chairs. The two courts must've put a lot of effort into the setup, because bouquets of lilies and jasmine and moonflowers from both courts adorn the center of each table.

Beside it, a small, two-story building opens out to a second-floor balcony where people are already crowded, dozens of conversations happening all at once.

Paris nods in the direction of the tent. Says, "People have just been mingling for the last few hours waiting for everyone to arrive, but it's about to officially kick off. They're giving the opening ceremony speech now."

I turn back to the tent and sure enough, people are beginning to make their way toward it, a steady stream and I'm watching it all. Fascinated for a reason I can't even fathom.

Paris touches my elbow, directs me to a table near the front. Retrieves his hand. He's doing his best to come in contact with as little of my skin as possible, for as little time as possible, as if touching me burns him. As if it hurts him.

And maybe it does. All I know is, every time his skin touches mine, it leaves me hollow. Leaves me remembering just how much has happened between us, how large a gap it has left in its wake.

I sit down, and it is just now that I notice the name cards on each table. Before each seat. Dark, cursive ink written over thick, cream paper.

Mine says: *Annabella Liang. Midnight Court.*

Of course they would make that distinction. Even in this event that is cohosted by the courts, which is meant to show solidarity, we are still separated. Together, but apart. Always.

Once we are all mostly seated, the king walks to the front. Stands before a microphone. Says, "Welcome, everyone. This annual Grand Prix we hold every year has been a tradition our court has recognized for almost a century and it is one that means quite a lot to us. This year, it's a little different.

"As many of you are aware, a few days ago there was an attack on the Midnight Court embassy, here in London. We want to emphasize that that was an unaffiliated attack. One neither sponsored nor endorsed by the Dawn Court as a whole. As such, the Emperor and I, along with the Circle and the Council, have decided that both courts will cohost this year's Prix.

"Emperor Xia wasn't able to make it in person today, but his daughter is here in his stead."

He gestures to his left and I'm wondering how I didn't see her before. Gwendolyn Xia, the Emperor's daughter. I have no idea if she knows I'm here. If she's spotted me.

At Gideon's introduction, she raises a hand to give a terse wave. Smiles. Even from thirty feet away, I've met her enough times, seen her enough times, to tell just how uncomfortable she is among all of these Dawn Courters. At nineteen, she is only one year older than me, but she has never traveled outside of the Midnight Court. Outside of Shanghai. And so far away from the bubble that the Emperor kept her in, she is very clearly uneasy.

But she hides it well.

The king continues: "We would like to emphasize that we are still in *peacetime*. That although tensions have risen in recent years, the accords still stand. And hopefully, we can all do our best to preserve that peace. That's all, thank you. Enjoy the Prix!"

CHAPTER 35

To be completely honest, I have very little interest in watching the actual competition, and neither does Paris, which leaves us stuck in a twenty-minute-discussion of what to do next. I'm in the middle of saying, "We should find Darren. Keep an eye on him from afar," when the king walks up to us.

Gideon Ateş, in all his Dawn Court glory. There's no crown on his head, or anything signifying his status, but it's indisputably clear from the authority he holds in his body, in the lines of his face, who he is. This man, the counterpart of our Huangdi.

I'm only aware he's near when Paris stiffens almost imperceptibly, eyes narrowing, and I turn around to see him.

Gideon says, "Hello, Anna. Paris. How are the two of you?"

Paris's voice is controlled. Neutral. There's a smile on his face that doesn't reach his eyes when he says, "We're fine, Dad."

Dad.

"Good." Gideon turns to me. Asks, "How has the Dawn Court been treating you, Anna? I hope you're at least enjoying it a bit."

He's being polite, but I've heard enough stories about the Dawn Court king to be wary. To remember caution. Remember that this man is not any less dangerous—and perhaps even more so—than the Emperor.

That he has made it clear he has no love for Midnight Courters.

I say, "It's been more pleasant than expected." *Make of that what you will*, I want to add.

"Good to hear. It's always great to see an interchange within the courts. Progress toward peace. Be careful though, Anna. Be very sure you can handle what comes next."

I have no idea if this is a threat.

"Anna," Paris says, and his voice is hard, "is very much capable of taking care of herself."

Gideon's eyes flash toward him. Then, to me. "Of course. My apologies, Anna." It sounds so flat, so ingenuine, and I know he knows it too. "My intention was not to offend you. I'm sure you are highly capable, as my son says."

"Don't worry about it." My voice is so artificially bright I don't doubt he can hear it.

He says, "All right, I'll leave you two to it." And then he's gone.

I let out a breath.

CHAPTER 36

Five minutes later, and I'm thinking this day is a never-ending stream of Ateşes. But this one I'm not particularly upset about.

Talia Ateş bounces up to us in a white-and-yellow dress, daisies embroidered on the hem of the skirt, and she looks absolutely beautiful. Absolutely radiant.

At nine, she has already begun to lose the baby fat that used to line her cheeks, her face. At nine, she is already beginning to shoot up like a sprout, almost reaching my chest. Green eyes, blonde hair, and it is so clear she's inherited every gorgeous gene that her siblings did. That she's going to be a stunning adult.

I'm thinking, When did I miss her grow up? She's so old now, practically a teenager. Practically double digits. I'm thinking, I missed her at seven, eight, half of nine. Three years of her life. She has gone from a chubby toddler to a young girl and there is a strange feeling in my chest. Half pride, half devastation.

When she comes up to us, she says, almost shyly, "Hi again, Anna."

To Paris, she says, "Can we go see the horses?"

He looks amused. Crouches down so he's eye level with her and their interaction is *killing* me. Shoving a red-hot poker right into my heart. I'm remembering Paris at sixteen, the older brother to this angel-faced six-year-old that he would do anything for. Absolutely anything.

At fifteen, I loved her like she was family too.

Paris indulges her, says, "The horses? Which horses?" The corners of his mouth are tugged up, biting back laughter. Talia points to the stables in the distance, not the ones near the gate but the ones past the track, on the other side.

Paris glances at me, and I say, "We have time. We can find Darren after."

"All right." Paris picks up Talia, hoists her over his shoulders. Says, "Let's go."

Halfway there, Talia wants to be put down. She runs toward the fence where the racetrack meets the edge of the forest and is suddenly fascinated by the wildflowers. I'm plucking one for her, putting it in her hair when she asks, "Are you moving here for good now?"

I'm frozen, my hand stuck in the motion of sticking the stem behind her ear. I have no idea what to say, but when I glance at Paris, he just raises an eyebrow.

You're on your own, he's saying.

So I shake my head. Say, "Just until December." I poke her nose. "But I'll visit you. Whenever you want."

Her eyes light up and *god*, it floors me every time just how innocent she is. How beautifully unaware of the horrors of this world. "Really? Like every weekend?" she asks. "And holiday? And birthday?"

"I don't think Anna has that much free time," Paris puts in, smiling at her.

Talia sticks her tongue out at him. Whispers to me, "He's just saying that. I bet he'd love it if you visited every day."

I feel myself flush. I have no idea why I thought she didn't know what happened between us. Or wouldn't remember.

Paris rolls his eyes, not at all bothered. He says, "If you're going to whisper, at least make it quiet enough so that I *can't* hear you from five feet away. Come on, let's keep going."

And we're about to. About to turn around, continue down the path when I hear it. The unmistakable sound of Darren's voice, and I'm wondering what the hell he's doing so far from the rest of the group. So far from the club and the actual competition.

One glance at Paris and it's clear he heard it too. He is silent, green eyes narrowed.

"You stay with Talia," I tell him in a low voice. "I'll go find him."

I don't give him time to respond. No time to argue.

Quickly, I slip away, into the trees, and all of a sudden, it feels as if I've been swallowed by the forest. By jewel-toned orange and yellow. Yellow grass below my feet, orange and gold leaves on the trees, save for the few spots of red and orange where fallen leaves mar the ground like drops of blood.

I track the sound of Darren's voice, expecting to see two people, but when I find him, he's alone.

He must be talking to someone on the phone because he's saying, "I have it under control. I'm sure you have more important things to do than worry about this."

I stop, crouch down behind a tree, and listen.

"Caihong's already left our hands. They sent him to some prison near Shanghai a few days ago. You should've been informed about this."

It's disorienting, not being able to hear whoever's on the other side of the call. It takes me far longer than it should to understand what's going on.

Silence as Darren waits for them to respond. And then, "No one knows. They all think your Midnight Courter was behind it—yes, including Anna."

I start at this, hearing my name on his lips. Bits and pieces are beginning to come together, mold together, fit into a very alarming picture in my head because I think I know what he's talking about. I think I know, and his next words confirm it.

He says, "No one knows I set him up. If they do, they're a hell of an actor. Feel free to move on with the plan. I'll do what needs to be done on my side."

I think the first thing I feel is shock. I think, because it's hard to separate that emotion from the others, from the sudden wave of them.

Shock is what slaps me straight in the face, hand across my cheek until it's bruised. Until it's bright red, then purple, then yellow and I can't quite believe my eyes, can't quite believe my ears. What I just heard.

Dread is what sits perched on my shoulders, at the top of my spine. It is heavy, unfamiliar, dragging me down to my knees until my palms hit the ground, until my back bends, breaks, shatters.

Anger tears me apart, pulls at my limbs, and I have to take my hands, grab pieces of myself, fit them all back together.

I can't believe this. I can't believe Darren fooled me, fooled us all into believing Liu Caihong was behind the whole thing. Fooled us all into believing he was merely a pawn in the game and not the king.

I should've trusted my gut.

I should've trusted my own court. I should've *known* Caihong was acting under duress. I wonder what, exactly, Darren did to him to make him follow every order the Dawn Court prince ever gave.

And now he's rotting away in prison for a crime Darren Ateş is responsible for.

Every day, I think I know the limit to humanity's cruelty. Every day, I'm proven wrong. And I'm so, so tired of this.

I leave just as Darren finishes his phone call. I watch him hang up. Stuff his phone back into his pocket. Glance around to make sure no one was watching and I almost wish he could see me, feel my rage.

He is every horrible thing combined. And he has dared to hurt my court. That I will never forgive.

When I get back, I don't tell Paris right away. Not with Talia just a couple feet away. Paris must know what I'm thinking because he doesn't question me. Doesn't ask what I heard.

For the next two hours, I'm quiet. Too in my own head to feel present at all and I watch Talia and Paris from a distance. Watch her raise up a tentative hand to pet the horses, watch him lift her up so she can sit on the pony near the stable door.

I feel like I'm seeing it all standing behind a wall of glass so thick I can't break through. Can't shatter it. I don't even try. In my head, I'm thinking I need to tell the rest of them. Kyan and Max and Dev and Josephine. Professor Song.

I'm thinking, somehow, I need to figure out how to expose Darren. How to stop him. How to hurt him back for daring to use someone from *my* court to fool *me* into believing he was innocent.

I won't make the same mistake twice.

By the time we return to the tent, night is quickly falling. The competitions are over for the day, and it is time for dinner.

We're all crowded into the tent, alight with chandeliers hanging from the ceiling, from metal rods they've somehow installed. Servers are coming around with platters of food, wineglasses, champagne. Up at the front, a band is playing music that is quarter notes and eighth notes, melodies and harmonies, crescendos and decrescendos floating into the air.

It is warm and lively and bright, and I am almost lulled into forgetting exactly what happened today. Almost lulled into letting go and simply enjoying the evening.

"So, Anna," one of Paris's brothers says to me—Parker, I think. We're sitting at a table with three of them. "How do you like our fair city so far? Thinking about moving here?"

That's twice in one day that I've been asked this question.

I blink. Remember that they think I'm here for diplomacy. That they have no idea what the real reason is.

So I lie this time. Say, "Maybe." Smile. "It'd be an interesting change of pace from the Midnight Court."

"Yeah? Change for the better, right?" he asks, grinning.

At thirty-four, Parker is already married with a child of his own. His wife, Maya, looks at me. Says, "Ignore him. He has excessive faith in London for someone who has never been anywhere else."

"Hey, Paris lived in both for years," Parker points out. He points a fork at Paris. "What say you?"

Paris's eyes flick to me. Away. A smile tugs at the corners of his lips. "Both cities have their merits."

Maya smiles. "That they do."

The conversation in the space ceases for a moment as the waiters come up, placing individual plates of the first course of appetizers in front of each of us. I wonder how many courses there will be. I don't think I've ever seen such a lavish meal. There's just *so much food* and I'm certain I don't have the space in my stomach for all of it.

Paris stares at the grilled asparagus on the plate in front of him.

Makes a decision not to eat it and instead leans over to whisper to me, "What's going on? What happened after you saw Darren? You've been acting off all afternoon."

I open my mouth, about to tell him when I see a flash of silver out of the corner of my eye and it is almost like déjà vu. Almost like I'm reliving that moment in the Midnight Court all those months ago.

Except this time, it isn't Paris. This time, I'm scanning the room, catching the glint of metal in the light of the chandeliers and I realize with a feeling of absolute

dread,

panic,

fear,

that it's pointed at Talia. *Talia.*

Paris must see the look on my face, follow the direction of my gaze, because he spots it a second after I do. But that second, that extra second is all I need.

Faster than I think I've ever moved, I'm running toward her, pushing her out of the trajectory of the bullet just as I hear the gun go off. Two guns. It's so loud it might as well be a bomb exploding in this tight space, this crowded room.

My eyes track her from the moment I hit the ground, roll a couple times, and *thank god* she looks perfectly okay, perfectly fine but I have no time to be relieved. To let out a breath because

I

am

on fire.

Every part of me is set ablaze and I can't even tell where it's originating from for a minute. It is pain like I have never known before in my life.

Pain I never even thought was possible.

Pain that can't possibly be real, can't possibly exist. People, I think, cannot possibly come back from this agony and survive, and I'm thinking, This is the pain of death. This is the pain that you feel when you're so close to hell you're burning from it. In it.

It is someone holding a lighter to the side of my stomach, grabbing a cast-iron poker that was just heated in the devil's fire and stabbing it into my body. Repeatedly. Unflinchingly.

This is worse than death. This is worse than anything I have ever experienced and *oh*, how I wish I could die just so that I can stop feeling this.

It is very clear to me, suddenly, that I was shot. That the man who was aiming for Talia hit me and someone must've killed him. And now he is lying on the ground, feeling nothing, while I am *falling* to the same ground, feeling everything in the world.

I cannot even hurt him back because he is in the bliss of death.

Dimly, I'm aware I'm slumped against the side of the tent, that my lungs are screaming in agony and maybe my mouth is too. That I am heaving in air through my lips so rapidly that it doesn't seem real. In and out and in and out except I can't ever seem to get enough.

Pain is making me see stars. Real, honest-to-god stars dancing in my line of sight and everything is a complete blur. A smear of color like some watercolor painting, and I'm thinking I used to like watercolor, really loved it, except now I hate it. I hate it so much that I think if I manage to survive this, I will tear apart every single watercolor painting I own.

I think I'm going insane. I must be delirious already.

Suddenly, I see a flash of gold and green and white and I can barely make out Paris's face in my shrinking vision. But I can see enough to make out the pure, unadulterated horror on his face. The fear.

He's saying, "Hold on. Try not to move. I need to put pressure on the wound before you bleed out."

And I try to say something, try to do something, except my limbs are no longer working. I am a broken machine, except instead of oil seeping out of me, it is blood. Hot, scarlet blood and I am really, really not liking how much of it I can feel soaking the front of my dress.

This is real fear. Fear like I have never known. This is a very new experience that I never, ever want to repeat in my life. I'm trying to say, "Paris," except my mouth won't listen.

My lips won't follow my brain and he's shushing me, he's saying,

"You're okay. I'm right here." And then, "This is going to hurt. I apologize in advance."

A hot, branding pain. So intense I'm gritting my teeth in an attempt not to scream. So intense my vision turns to static, black and white and gray dots swimming before my eyes, and I think I might faint. I really, really do. At least in this in-between state, the pain has dimmed. I'm pretty sure it's not a good thing that my body is becoming numb, but at this point, I'm not sure I care.

"I don't want to die," I tell him. I'm staring, can't stop staring at the way his hair is so golden, gleaming in the light from the chandeliers, at his eyes that are so, so green, can't stop thinking just how beautiful he is and I have no idea why my thoughts are drifting this way, no idea why my brain is deciding to go in this direction at this very crucial moment in time.

He says, "I'm not going to let you die."

And I realize I've been lying to myself, force-feeding falsehoods to my brain because right now, the truth is, I have never, ever felt safer than I do in his hands.

He stops, keeping one hand pressed to my side, and says, "Just hold on, Anna. I'll be right back."

My hand shoots out of its own accord. "Wait, don't leave—"

He stops. I can hear him telling someone to call Kyan, to call Professor Song, and then he's back beside me. Says, "I won't. I won't leave until you're ready. You're going to be fine, Anna. I promise."

And I believe him. I trust him. Turns out, I always have.

CHAPTER 37

I wake up in the infirmary for the second time since I arrived in London. Except this time, it is not Josephine that is here when I wake up, but Paris.

He is sitting on the chair next to the bed, scrolling on his phone, and I take this moment, this moment when he's not looking, to stare at him. To drink in all of the extra adjectives and adverbs of his face because I still cannot reconcile these two versions of him.

"I know you're awake," he says. And I flush, heat creeping into my cheeks, singeing my insides with hot embarrassment, and I'm praying he didn't see me staring.

Paris puts down his phone. Looks at me. "Your breathing's different when you're asleep, you know. I thought it was common knowledge."

"Whatever," I say. My voice comes out scratchy. "How's Talia?"

"She's fine. Perfectly unharmed, thanks to you." At this, I feel a crushing wave of relief.

Paris asks, "How are you feeling?"

I can't read him. Can't read his face. "The medics completely healed the wound, by the way. It shouldn't be more than a scar now."

I blink. Shift. Realize, astonishingly, that he's right. I feel absolutely no pain. It's almost like yesterday was a fever dream.

Yesterday. All of a sudden, images and memories and sounds and smells flash through my mind, pieces of my consciousness after the gunshot. Me, hitting the ground. Paris's face above me, his hands pressing fabric to my body, urgent. Frantic.

"Thank you," I tell him, quietly, "For yesterday. For not letting me…bleed out." For saving my life, but I don't want to say that out loud.

He looks at me, gaze catching mine for a quick moment. "Of course. Always."

Always.

This—

This I have given up understanding. This hot and cold, this warm and then distant. He is so, so utterly unreadable. Utterly unknowable, and every time I think I finally understand him, have finally figured him out.

I'm proven wrong.

Maybe it's the shock of last night, maybe it's the exhaustion from these past few *months*, because suddenly, this agonizing silence is absolutely suffocating. It is shoving a pillow in my face, telling me to breathe, and I'm thinking just how small this space is.

Air.

I need air.

I sit all the way up, ignoring the twinge in my side as I move to slide out of the bed, when Paris reaches over, saying, "Anna—wait, I don't think you should get up just yet—"

And I interrupt him. Cut him off, say, "*Don't.*" I feel myself backing up, trying to put as much distance between us as possible, but only because I'm afraid of what I'll do if we're too close.

Paris is my Achilles' heel.

He stills. Asks, "Don't what?"

"Act like you care what happens to me when you've made it so abundantly clear you didn't three years ago, and in all the years since."

This time, I watch it happen like turning a page. Watch all traces of emotion disappear from his face like ink bleeding off a page as he sits back down.

Says, "You still don't get it, do you?" Sighs. "You have no idea how incredibly frustrating this is."

"Get *what*?" I demand. "You keep alluding to something as if it's so obvious, but you don't say what. Can we talk straight for once? We used to."

At this, a ghost of a smile dances across his lips. "There are a lot of things that are used-tos between us," he says. And then he clasps his hands loosely in front of him. Crosses one ankle over the other knee and asks me, "What exactly do you remember about what happened three years ago?"

The question is so out of the blue that it catches me off guard. I hesitate for a second. A minute. Say, "You told your father that the Midnight Court was thinking about an attack on the Dawn Court, and then you guys attacked first. In retaliation."

Paris leans back in the chair. Looks at me steadily. "And how, exactly, did you know that it was me who told him?"

I'm confused. I have no idea where this is going, but I answer anyway. "Because the only people who knew were members of the Council. Except I told you. A horrible decision, in hindsight."

He ignores my comment. Asks, "Are you sure?"

I huff out a breath of exasperation. "Paris, what exactly are you trying to say? Just say it. We don't have time for this."

He smiles, his mouth quirking up at the corner. Looks down at his hands. Says, "It wasn't me, Anna." His gaze raises to mine and disbelief is flooding through my system, fueling the blood that circulates through my veins, the beating of my heart, and I refuse to think that he is right.

"No."

Paris continues as if I hadn't spoken. "If you recall, I warned you once that my father was spying on us. That he had someone tailing us and I was going to try and trap him. Expose him."

I do remember. The memory comes to me like a conch drawn out of water. Surfacing from the back of my brain into the very forefront.

It was the end of July, almost two months into whatever we'd been doing and the two of us were in the garden, reclining in a bed of grass, only green because it was under the shade of the giant tree to our right.

It was a rare, peaceful day. Honey-sweet air and the buzz of bees, bird chirps. Sunlight dappled through leaves. Not too hot either, now that summer was beginning to wind down, July giving way to August and finally, the hottest month of the season would be behind us.

I was sitting up, weaving dandelion stems together to create a bracelet. An activity that I had done all the time as a kid and was far too old for now, but I didn't care. No one was around to scold me, to judge me. My parents were stuck in meetings all day and my sister was on assignment in Cheng Yang. It was as if someone had taken every perfect element and stuck it all together, glued or meshed or melded until it fit perfectly into this one day.

At fifteen, you still haven't found out that perfection doesn't exist.

Paris was lying on the ground, propped on one elbow, the mid-morning sun setting his gold hair and his green eyes ablaze and I thought

he was the most beautiful thing I had ever seen. And he was mine.

Paris was watching me with a light amusement in his eyes and a faint smile on his lips and I remember basking in it,

his attention,

his love.

It was a heady feeling, to be loved by someone for the first time. Someone that wasn't your parents or your siblings or relatives, some-one that had no obligation to love you but did anyway. It was a novel feeling.

"What are you doing?" he asked me.

I held up the string of yellow flowers. Said, "Give me your hand," and he did. It was still such a weird feeling then, being able to touch someone so casually. As if they half-belonged to you. The touch of his skin against mine still made my heart beat, so fast it felt like falling. Falling too fast but it felt good nonetheless and I didn't care. Refused to look at it too closely, because there are flaws in everything if you look hard enough and I wouldn't.

I slipped the bracelet on him and it should've been illegal, how well it matched the white and gold and dawn. I remember being about to say something to that degree except I was interrupted by a rustle.

A whisper of a sound so faint I would've missed it except Paris shot up, straight into a sitting position with narrowed eyes, and suddenly, he was not languid, lazy. He was alert, body drawn like a bow and I remembered that we were both made to be weapons.

I asked, "What is it?"

And he said, "Someone's watching us. A spy sent by the king, I think."

I frowned. "Watching us? Why?"

Paris glanced at me. "He knows about us. He hasn't said anything, but I know he knows." He looked away. "I've been seeing the same man multiple times throughout the week. At first, I thought it was just coincidence, or my own brain playing tricks on me, but I think I recognize him from the court." Wryly, he adds, "Gideon's never really trusted me, since I'm half Midnight Court. He's keeping an eye on me. On us."

And that, that shattered the entire illusion of it. The entire afternoon.

CHAPTER 38

"I assume you remember," Paris says, and I blink. Tear myself out of the claws of the past and its memories. Rip the hooks out of my skin.

"Maybe," I say. "So, what? You're saying that the spy heard our conversation and told your father?"

"That is," Paris responds, "exactly what I'm saying."

There's a weird undercurrent of something in the air, a thrum of it. It's like when a star dies and out comes a giant black hole because this past minute has torn down everything I thought I knew. Destroyed every principle that I have lived by for the past three years, leaving this gaping feeling of uncertainty, of not knowing what comes next, in front of me.

For my entire life I have known exactly what Paris is to me. When I was six, before we became closer, he was just a friend. Someone I knew existed, someone I saw once in a while, said hi to in passing, but also someone I didn't really care about. Someone who had no imprint on my life.

When I was fifteen, he was everything. He was half of me, half of my heart, half of my identity, and I almost believed that that was the way it should be. The way it would be.

After that, he was my enemy. The giant scar of my past, my greatest weakness, and I have lived to this song of betrayal and revenge, listened to it so many times it is embedded into my brain and now he is telling me that it was all false.

All an illusion.

And I have no idea what we are anymore. We are no longer ene-mies—that, I have already believed—but we cannot go back to what we once were.

Suddenly, I think I have never been in more danger of falling. The foundation of my entire life is breaking down, crumbling, and I have no idea what to think of this anymore. Of him. Of myself.

"Why should I believe you?" I whisper, but it is a futile attempt. I know it is. And he does too, because he doesn't even answer.

Instead, he says, "I lied, you know, that night in the garden. After Equinox. I thought that after all of those weeks, you would've fig-ured out at least that it wasn't fully the truth. I thought that was why I was sensing some shift in you. A shift in your anger, your hatred, and I was maybe ready to forgive you too. I couldn't believe how wrong I was."

I hear myself say, "Oh." And then after thirteen seconds and twenty-three heartbeats, "I'm sorry. I guess I should've known the king had lied to the Council. I should've known that wasn't some-thing you would've done."

He smiles a little, shakes his head. "I'm sorry too. I suppose I did the exact same thing with Talia. I feel like I consistently give too much credit to the Midnight Court, thinking you've changed, that you have become exactly the soldier they wanted to mold you into, and not nearly enough credit to *you*. You who have always defied it."

Coming from his mouth, in words shaped from his lips, my inabil-ity to be what I need to be doesn't sound so bad.

"I should've believed you," he says. "I should've believed that you wouldn't hurt her. I should've believed *in* you and I will never stop apologizing for not doing so. I will never stop *regretting* not doing so."

His eyes are so green, so sincere. So absolutely genuine, I want to reach out a hand. Touch his face. Tell him it's okay.

"I understand," I say. "I think maybe I would've done the same thing, if I were you."

Paris smiles. Shifts in his seat. Says, "Well, anyway. I just wanted to say thank you. If not for you, Talia would most definitely not be here. I owe you everything."

"You owe me nothing."

He doesn't respond for a moment. Doesn't speak. And then, softly, "You have no idea how many times I wish I had just told you."

Oh. My voice is quiet. "Why didn't you?" The question hangs in the air between us for a moment, strung onto the back of a semicolon. Evaporating into white smoke.

Paris is quiet for a minute before answering. There's a small, sardonic, almost self-deprecating smile on his face when he says, "To be completely honest, I was hurt. I thought you, you were the one person who knew every part of me. The good and the bad. The one person I didn't need to hide parts of myself from, because you loved me not in spite of them, but for them."

I'm afraid to breathe. Afraid to make any noise.

Paris looks away from me. Leans back against the chair. "When you called—" At this I cringe. Maybe that call was overly aggressive. "I was so surprised. I had no idea you thought of me that way. So—" He takes a breath. "I decided to let you go. To let *us* go. I realize now that I shouldn't have. That I had given up too easily."

"I shouldn't have let you," I say. "I wish I had believed in *you*, the way you had always believed in me."

At this moment, I'm realizing just how much our blind loyalties to our individual courts had hurt us. How I am so willing to believe the worst in the ones I love because this is what the courts dictate. This is what they tell us, from the moment we are old enough to listen.

I'm thinking, I don't want to talk about this anymore, I *can't*. We can't keep beating this to death, every mistake we've made with each other, everything we've done to hurt and betray.

So when Paris says, finally, "Let's just agree to move on. Leave the past in the past," I say,

"Yes."

And when he kisses me, for the first time, this truly, sincerely feels like a new beginning.

CHAPTER 39

My mother calls me early the next day. Says, "You haven't been calling much, Anna." I can hear the faint undertone of accusation in her voice.

"I'm sorry, Ma," I tell her. "It's just been really chaotic, recently."

She sighs. "The Council's impatient. The worry of impending war is hanging over all of our heads. I don't want you to get in trouble with the Emperor."

"Sorry. I'll be more consistent," I say. Yet another lie.

That afternoon, I tell the others about what happened at the Prix, exactly what I heard Darren say. That we were wrong. That Caihong was set up. That Darren, Darren Ateş, third prince of the Dawn Court, has always been behind the stolen poison.

There isn't much we can do, planning-wise, since both Max and Dev have gone home to visit family for the long weekend, and having waited this long, what's a few more days? But I can feel myself getting antsier by the second.

At least it's also midterms season. I'm sitting with a textbook splayed open in front of me, studying in the library, and I think it's the first time I've ever been here. It's situated in the west wing, a giant, dome-like space that's ringed with shelves of old and new books. Sunlight filters in, warped through the glass wall of the academy, and in the light it's casting, I can see the individually illuminated dust particles floating past me.

The light falls on Paris, who is sitting across from me; his head is down, eyes flickering across the screen of his laptop, and he's absent-mindedly twirling a pen around his fingers. In the sun, he is lined with a hard edge of gold. It sets his hair ablaze, illuminates each individual eyelash, turning the green in his eyes so bright it is almost like jade.

"Stop staring at me and start staring at your textbook," he says, and then looks up. A light, teasing smile flits across his mouth. "You haven't turned a page in at least fifteen minutes."

I can feel my cheeks flushing, blood rising to my face. I had no idea he was watching me.

"It's not like this actually matters for me," I put in, but we both know it's a weak excuse.

Paris looks amused. He says, "Mhm."

To be completely honest, I've already spent the past day setting up my studying schedule for the week. History on Sunday—today— Cryptography tomorrow, Poisons & Potions on Tuesday, Languages on Wednesday, and Combat & Physical Training on Thursday. And then I would have an extra three days to go over anything I'm not too confident in and do a full review. Paris promised to help me once he's done with his finals tomorrow, since he's already taken the classes that I'm in, and I'm realizing I have no idea why I'm putting aside so much time for these exams at a school where I'm a fake student.

I'm also not quite sure what we are now, Paris and me. Not quite sure what this is. We have gone back and forth and back and forth so many times it is all so completely tangled. But I think, for now, for once, I am satisfied with this tentative peace.

Right now, I'm reading about the pre-courts era, a time when London and Shanghai were not so separate. When it was common-place to travel between the two cities, almost without restrictions. A time when you were free to go where you pleased.

It's almost inconceivable to me.

The words escape my lips before I can stop them. "Have you ever thought about what it would be like if the courts merged? If we were integrated?"

Paris raises his head to look at me, warily. "What?"

Well, too late to stop now. "If Shanghai wasn't known solely as the territory of the Midnight Court and London wasn't the Dawn Court. Imagine if this school"—I wave a hand around for good measure—"was half Dawn Court, half Midnight Court. Or if the entire court system was just abolished."

His gaze is completely unreadable. And then he looks away, says words that I'd never thought would come out of his mouth. He says, "Of course I have."

I blink at him.

"I don't think I've made it a secret how much I hate this," he says. "Especially to you. I hate the way my father controls this court. I hate the way my siblings follow every order he gives like robots." Paris's voice is hard, but steady. Controlled. "You have no idea," he says, softly, "how many times I've dreamed of changing it."

"So why not do something about it?" I am sharply aware of the words that I'm saying, the way I'm bordering on traitorous. A bright scarlet label right across the chest.

Paris smiles at me. Looks down at his hands. Says, "It's a dangerous thing to say. A dangerous thing to think. And in this court, in both of our courts, you have absolutely no idea who you can trust."

He's right. I know he's right.

I stop talking about it.

CHAPTER 40

At noon today, I had thought, this day has been too close to perfect. Too peaceful to last, and at night, I realize I was right. Absolutely right, because the world comes crashing down at midnight.

A loud whistling sound—like the kind that invades your ears before you faint—and then, crashing. Rumbling. An explosion that sets the night on fire, tears the darkness completely in two and unravels the black into reds and oranges and yellows.

Fire.

I sit up immediately, scrambling out of bed and shoving my feet into boots, I rush to the window. Josephine and Cassie are awake too. Only Mariam still sleeps.

The three of us stare at each other for a minute, all wide-eyed. All confused.

"What the hell was that?" Josephine asks. Her voice is hushed. None of us are willing to speak too loudly, make too much noise as if too loud and something breaks. Something shatters.

"It sounded like..." Cassie hesitates.

"A bomb," I finish. The gravity in my tone sends the word ringing through the air.

"Well, shit," says Josephine, and she's scrambling out of bed, coming to join me by the window, and together, we draw the curtains open.

And I am astounded.

Horrified.

Stunned into silence.

In the night, fire is stabbing the darkness. Huge, terrifying blazes of it, glorious red and orange and yellow, staining the horizon like some oil painting gone wrong and I—I have never seen anything like it.

It is almost awe-inspiring, how savage it is. Fire, devouring the grass, all the oxygen in the air, everything around it like a natural disaster, licks of it whipping into the air and we are all slack-jawed, all staring outside like it is some scene on the screen in a movie theater rather than something that is only separated from us by a slice of glass. A few yards of space.

I can't quite believe my eyes. And Josephine too is staring open-mouthed outside like she can't either, and in my head, I'm wondering, Was this intentional? Is this some Midnight Court attack?

There's no way they would do this, knowing we were here. There's no way.

Except even I am not sure.

"*What*," says Josephine, "is going on?"

Cassie looks uneasy, a little queasy, like dinner isn't sitting well in her stomach, and she asks, echoing my thoughts, "Do you think this is the Midnight Court?"

Her eyes are darting from me to Josephine and back again, probably wondering if we're in on this.

I shake my head. "It can't be." I don't think. At least I sound more certain than I feel.

Josephine nods her agreement. "Yeah, absolutely no way in hell. If it was, they would've said something to us, at least. Would've gotten us out."

She looks nervous and I realize, really, we should be hoping that it is the Midnight Court. That they know we're here and, therefore, we're not in danger.

Because if it isn't, then there is a very, very real chance that death is once again standing on our doorstep. Knocking on our door.

An alarm goes off seconds later, blaring and piercing and destroying my eardrums, and suddenly, everyone is awake. Everyone is scrambling and out of breath and it almost gives me déjà vu from the morning of Initiation, except this is different. Very different.

We're rushing toward the door, carried by the momentum of the stream of people heading for the exit and there's a franticness in the air. A sense of urgency, panic, which is tainting everything around us with black ink and I'm struggling to stay calm. Struggling to breathe in the midst of all these people.

I need to get out of the crowd.

Confusion is muddling my brain, tying the tail ends of each of my thoughts until they're a tangle, wrapped around each other like snakes. And instead of fading, they are filling my brain until there is no space left. Until I feel ready to burst.

Apparently, Eladine has had drills for this. For bomb raids. Everyone knows exactly what to do. It would've seemed like military precision, except fear blurs the edges. Transforms it all into chaos. We're taken from the dorms into the main building, into the Lotus, and my hand is grasped tightly in Josephine's. We can't lose each other. Not now.

I imagine that my heartbeat is melding into the collective, one in hundreds, and for once, I feel I am in solidarity with these people. These Dawn Courters that surround me, that I live with, and it is a strange feeling. A peculiar one. And not entirely unwelcome.

In the Lotus, the praefectus are directing us. They are stationed at intervals in every hallway and I'm thinking, there's another aspect of it, of being a member of the praefectus that Kyan didn't mention so many days earlier.

It is putting everyone else's safety before your own and I realize I...I admire them.

What is happening to me?

"Where the hell are we going?" Josephine whispers, and it is Cassie who answers.

"The basement. Supposedly, they built it to be bombproof after"— she flushes slightly—"the Midnight Court bombed us like twenty-five years ago or something. The question is if they can get us all in in time."

At this, I swallow. The praefectus will be the last ones in, and if they can't, if they don't get us all in, all of *them* will be the ones in danger.

Paris.

Panic is alight in my blood, panic sending little flaming sparks into my veins, and I find myself telling Josephine to keep going without me, that I'll catch up in a second. I find myself reaching for my phone, tugging it out of my pocket so violently it almost flies straight out of my hand. I force my fingers to be steady as I jab at the screen, inputting the numbers I know from memory, and then it's ringing.

And ringing.

And ringing.

Paris picks up after the fourth ring, voice crackling on the other side and he says, "Hello?"

I think I almost keel over with relief. "Paris. Where are you?"

"The lobby." Then, suspiciously, "Why?"

"Just stay there," I tell him. "I'm coming to find you."

And before he can respond, I hang up, shoving my phone into my back pocket and heading toward the lobby.

My first piece of advice to anyone in an emergency: Never try to run *against* the stream of people all heading in one direction. Especially when whatever lies at the end of said direction is most likely what's going to keep them alive.

It takes me four times longer than usual to reach the lobby, even though I do my best to stick to the sides of the hallways, against the walls, where the traffic is not so thick.

The bombs are whistling down more frequently now, and from the hushed conversations that I picked up on the way, one has already destroyed the stadium.

I'm one hallway away from the lobby when I hear it: the unmistakable whistling of a bomb and it is so loud it might as well be screaming into my ear from three inches away. My heart rate kicks faster, the panic in my brain sharpening, shooting from synapse to synapse, and for a moment, I feel lightheaded. As if I'm floating.

It's an eerie sensation. For a split second, everything is muted. I'm wondering if this is real, if this is reality, and then I'm crashing back down to earth. To my body. And it all comes rushing back in so fast it feels like vertigo.

This is the third time my life has been in danger and it is no less terrifying. But this time, I have no clue what to do. No clue where to go. All I can hear is the bomb whipping through the air above me, careening closer, but I have no idea where it's going to hit. No idea what direction I'm supposed to be running, or where I'm supposed to hide.

Every thought in my brain is jumbled together, wrapping around each other, a tangle of webs, and I am barely processing everything that is happening around me—shouting, running, *screaming*.

And in my numb state, I'm thinking, this—this is pure chaos.

When it hits, I'm still frozen—not just my body, but my brain. I'm rooted in place, feet pinned to the floor beneath me and I have never thought I'd be the type of person to freeze up in this situation, but here I am.

Practically a statue.

The collision shakes the entire building, sending the walls crumbling, the ground cracking, and all I can think is, Thank god it didn't hit me. But immediately, I feel guilty because judging from the sound, the damage, it must've destroyed the entire east wing and there might've still been people there—students or teachers or custodians and—oh god. I have no idea where Kyan is.

Please let no one be there. *Please tell me he made it.*

I'm watching plaster break from the ceiling in chunks, tumbling through the air and into the ground, bits of it flying upward and I still have no idea what I'm doing. Fear and panic are sending adrenaline lancing through my body, saturating my veins with nowhere to *go*. No exit.

The noise is deafening.

I'm about to run in whatever direction, who cares which, and hope for the best when fingers wrap around my wrist. Suddenly, I'm being yanked into an empty room.

I hear the click of a door being shut and instantly the noise is muted.

"What the *hell* are you doing?" a voice asks furiously, and I turn to find Paris staring at me, anger written on his face, and I realize that he's making no effort to hide his emotions from me for once. "Are you *trying* to get yourself killed?"

I stare at him for a few seconds before I shake myself. Recover enough to say, "No. I think you're about to, though."

"You should be heading to the basement, like everyone else."

"So should *you*."

He lifts his gaze to meet mine, looks right at me. Says, "I can't do what I need to if I'm also worrying about you, Anna. I need to know that you're safe." And then, "Please?"

I'm stunned straight into silence. All the words that I was going to say have died, piling up in my throat and the only thing that comes out is, "Oh."

Two letters.

I'm about to say something else, maybe "No," but maybe "Okay," when there's another shriek, an earsplitting whistle that cuts the air cleanly in two, and Paris's head jerks up with alarm, eyes suddenly alert and he's looking at me, lips mouthing words but I can't hear above the noise of the incoming bomb.

I can already tell that this one's going to be close. Closer, even, than the last one. That if even the sound is this awful, I don't want to know what happens when it hits.

Paris is running toward me, a flash of something in his eyes that looks suspiciously like panic and this, this small admission makes me *terrified*.

If I had to choose a way to go, being bombed into oblivion is not it.

And then he collides with me just as the bomb hits, the impact sending both of us rolling for a couple of feet as chunks of plaster and stone and whatever else these walls are made of begin to rain down, white and gray coming down in sheets around us and the sound,

the sound is deafening. It is a deep roaring that is a knife shoving its blade into my ears, it is a thousand people screaming at the top of their lungs until it all gives out, until their voices break.

The front of my body is flush against the floor; I can feel every tremble, every shake of the ground as the world cracks just a little bit more. I can almost imagine the fissures delving into it, spidery lines snaking into the dirt and the earth and rock, reaching for the core.

Paris is hovering above me, propping himself up on elbows next to my head and I can feel his heartbeat against my back, the whisper of his breath on my skin, and I withhold a shiver. Try not to think about what would happen if I flipped over.

I'm becoming over-aware of him. Of the heat of his body against mine and the scent of him that has never left my skin. I'm thinking, There is so much that I haven't said to him, haven't told him. That my tongue weighs so heavy from all the words I've left *unsaid* and I'm thinking how fragile human lives are, how capable we are of being finite. One touch and we're gone, and I don't have the luxury of time. I open my mouth, about to tell him everything, everything, except—

It's over almost as quickly as it started. The rumbling and the noise and the falling debris slow to a standstill and Paris rolls off me immediately, pulling himself into a sitting position with his back against the wall.

The sudden silence is so quiet it almost doesn't seem real. I flip over, too exhausted to get up, peek up at Paris and ask, "Are you okay?"

His eyes meet mine. "Are you?"

One word: "Yes," and in this moment, that is all that matters.

He smiles slightly.

"Good. Let's maybe try to keep it that way."

CHAPTER 41

Since half the first-year dorm buildings were destroyed in the bombing, we're all relocated to the spares a little ways off from the main campus. Meant for emergencies, which I guess this is. At the very least, given how much destruction there's been and the fact that we're now on high alert, the administration doesn't expect any more rounds of bombing.

But I'm not at the temporary dorms. Instead, I'm in the praefecture wing, which was somehow, incredibly, untouched. I'm in Paris's room.

The praefecture quarters are so much nicer than our first-year dorms it's almost immoral—but I suppose it makes sense, to a degree. They have their own individual rooms, for one—as part of a suite of two—large mahogany furniture, and giant glass windows. Through it, I almost swear I can make out the dark outline of a small balcony jutting out into the darkness.

"Are you sure you're okay?" Paris asks me—not for the first time tonight. He's lying next to me on his bed, the light from the small table lamp casting a warm glow over his skin, his hair. It still feels so novel—him in such close proximity. *Us.* Something both age-old and brand-new at the same time.

Distantly, I'm remembering the last time we were in the same bed, that fever dream–like night in Edenfield's cabin. I'm remembering how tense it had been, how strange we were to each other after so many years apart and so much bloodshed. How different it has become.

"*Yes*," I say, nudging him with my elbow. "Just like every other time you've asked."

He smiles. Shakes his head. "Sorry, I'm just concerned. Maybe a bit too much."

"Maybe," I return, but we both know there is no substance behind it. And then, softly, I say, "There was a moment...I really did think that that was it. That I would die ingloriously from some ceiling chunk falling onto my head."

Paris lets out a faint laugh that sends butterflies fluttering around my stomach on quivering wings. "You did always have a flair for the dramatic." I punch him lightly on the arm and he backtracks. "Okay, you're right, you're right. I thought so too. Would've been maybe one of the worst ways to die." He shudders. "They'd probably make a ballad about it too, to make children laugh."

"Your worst nightmare," I agree. It's quiet for a while, both of us a little lost in thought. Absentmindedly, I reach across the space between us. Play with the red string bracelet on his wrist. And then I say, "But seriously, it made me realize just how fragile everything is. How easily it could end."

When I glance up at Paris, I find him watching me with steady green eyes. Waiting for me to continue.

"Sometimes, I just hate how we wasted so much time."

He pulls his hand back from me for a moment, intertwines his fingers with mine. Squeezes my hand lightly. Says, "I don't think it was a waste. I think if anything, our time apart was necessary for us to become who we are, independent of each other. And it showed us how much we can overcome."

I don't think I will ever get used to this gentle side of him. This side that I haven't seen since the last time we were together. I didn't realize how much I missed it. This. Us. "And aren't you the one who believes that everything happens for a reason?" he asks me, teasingly.

"I suppose," I answer, smiling. And then the words spill out of me before I even have a chance to think, to weigh the pros and cons and talk myself out of it. "I missed you. A lot."

Paris doesn't even hesitate. Just says, "I missed you too, dummy."

This time, when he kisses me, it feels like home. Like safety and belonging, comfort and familiarity all in the touch of his lips against mine. And I'm reveling in it, reveling in the warmth in my chest and the heat on my skin, in the floating feeling of contentment that fills my body like helium, so close to bursting.

And then he pulls back for a second, bends his head to kiss the inside of my wrist, and the moment his lips make contact with my skin, fire erupts like a wildfire low in my stomach.

It feels like a fuse has been lit under my skin, as if I am made completely of matches and he has set them alight, all at once. In a second, I've moved closer to him until we are only inches apart, reaching up to kiss him again, but this time, it has transformed into something deeper. Something heavier, more fervent. And I'm thinking, I never want to let go. I never want to let this second go. Paris pulls me roughly against him, his hand tightening in my hair, and butterflies erupt in a chaotic frenzy in my abdomen.

His shirt has ridden up, revealing a flash of his stomach and the arch of his hip bone and I can't stop myself from reaching down, brushing his skin with my fingers, and the effect is immediate. Instantaneous. He stills against me, his breathing uneven, and he's whispering in my ear, "Anna."

I don't answer. Instead, my fingers travel down, lower, and my heart is pounding so fast I can't quite believe it hasn't beat straight through my chest. I am dizzy with anticipation, with nerves, with desire all blazing through my body, and I find myself grasping the fabric of his shirt. Tugging it up over his head, I'm staring at him, running my hand from his shoulder down to his chest and stomach and—Paris grabs my hand. Flips me over so that my back hits the mattress and he is hovering over me, desire written in the heat in his eyes and the tension in his body and it is

still absolutely incredible what his touch does to me.

I can't help myself. I slide my hands down the velvet expanse of his back, marveling at how soft his skin is over the muscle, how solid his body feels beneath my fingers. I touch his face, his chest, let my hands roam free because finally, *finally* I can.

"Anna," he gasps out, and the heat of his breath on my ear sends shivers dancing through my body. "You're really testing my self-control here."

"Self-control?" I repeat, a little breathlessly as he traces feather-light kisses down my jaw. My throat. "Why in the world would you have that?"

Paris laughs against my skin. "You're not funny."

I don't even have the brain cells to form a cohesive response. Before he can say anything else, I pull his mouth back to mine, hook my legs around him, and there's a newfound urgency in the air, a newfound urgency in the way he kisses me, the way I kiss him back.

Paris's hands travel down my body, fingers gripping the sensitive skin at the backs of my thighs, and time loses all meaning. *I* lose all ability to think, all ability to form a single thought, because all I can focus on is the shivering feeling of his skin against mine and the scorching ache that is spreading through my body. Almost impulsively, I bury my fingers into his hair, feeling each individual strand like cool silk in my hands, and the hot and cold contrast is almost too much.

I kiss him hard, once, on the mouth. Guide his hand to the hem of my tank top and my heart is beating so rapidly it is almost winged, could almost transform into a bird and fly away into the night.

Paris stills for a moment. Looks at me with green, green eyes. Murmurs, "Are you sure?" And I nod. It's not like this is the first time, anyway. Even though it might as well be. Even though it feels like it is.

Gently, he slips it over my head, trails kisses down my body and I'm thinking I am truly, undeniably on fire this time. That every touch of his mouth against my skin is setting me ablaze. He kisses me everywhere, both gentle and rough at the same time, and my breath escapes my lips in gasps that tremble in the air.

"Anna," he whispers in my hair, tightening his grip on my waist. "You are my entire world. You always have been."

Seconds dissolve into each other, form minutes before they too collapse, blown away in the wind. In this one moment, he is undoing my entire reality. Undoing *me*. In this moment, nothing matters, nothing is real except the touch of his skin against mine and the feeling of his kisses on my body.

I think, there is nothing better than this.

Afterward, we lie on the bed, facing each other. I'm staring at him, taking this moment to drink in every detail of his face, commit it all to memory.

"What?" Paris asks me, a little self-consciously. "Why are you looking at me?"

"No reason."

He rolls his eyes. Kisses me one more time, briefly. Asks, "Do you want to sleep?"

I nod and he reaches over, switches off the light. The darkness envelops us immediately, comforting. Soft. Paris settles back into bed and wraps an arm around my waist. And finally, for the first time in either court, I feel

safe.

CHAPTER 42

It's a full three days before they're able to process the damage. The stadium and the east wing have been completely reduced to rubble; the garden is pockmarked with so many gaping holes and scorch marks it looks like a battleground. Which maybe it is.

Classes are canceled for the day, maybe even the rest of the week, while they figure out what to do. How to fix this. In the meantime, they've already announced that once they resume, any classes that were once held in the east wing are now being relocated elsewhere. Combat training classes will be outside.

They're blaming the bombing on the Midnight Court. The Circle released an official statement a couple hours ago stating they were going into a daylong meeting to decide what to do. Whether war would be reignited.

I'm thinking, this peace was never meant to last. That we have all—both courts—taken the past nine years for granted and now it is over. There has been far too much rocking the boat, far too many thrown stones cracking the glass for it not to shatter. Soon.

The Circle meeting today is a full one, meaning all its members and all of the members of the royal family have been called to the Dawn Court building to discuss what they plan to do. Paris left this morning.

Gossip fills every crevice, every corner of the halls and the class-rooms, whispers and hushed conversations and nervous faces. I have seen people in the halls eyeing me and Josephine as if they're just now recognizing who we are. What court we come from. Only Cassie and Mariam still treat us as before, but there is one thing that almost everyone agrees on: The cold peace is over.

The courts are going to war.

It isn't official—not yet, anyway—but it seems to be the widely accepted consensus around here and it's injecting dread into my stomach.

I don't believe the bombs were the Midnight Court. I don't believe that they would do that, knowingly risk my life and Josephine's. Even the Midnight Court cannot be that monstrous.

But I also understand the Dawn Court's reasoning. I understand why they would blame the Midnight Court—because who else could it be? Neither of us have any quarrel with the other countries, and the Dawn Court would not bomb itself.

I have been drowning in this constant not-knowing, this constant fear, this constant anxiety for the three days since the bombing. Hindsight, I think, is twenty-twenty, and right now, I wish I had it because I have no idea what I need to do.

The Midnight Court embassy contacted me this morning too, asking Josephine and me if we wanted to go home. If we wanted to leave our positions, leave our posts to go back to Shanghai. They promised there was no shame in that decision. But I think shame is something that cannot be avoided when you're fleeing with your tail between your legs.

And it is not so much me trying to prove myself anymore as it is my desperate hope, this need to figure out not just whatever it is that Paris and I are, but also the truth about the poison. If Darren was really the one behind it. Why.

And Josephine too is not quite ready to go back to Shanghai. I think, in some way, both of us have fallen a little in love with this city. With London.

"What do you think they're going to do?" she asks me. The two of us are in the common room, Max and Dev—and *Kyan* for once—all sprawled around the pool table.

I told her about last night the moment we met up this morning.

She wasn't even surprised. I guess I shouldn't have expected her to be, given I never made it back to the dorms.

"I think you guys are fucked," Max calls, cue in hand.

Dev elbows him so hard he jostles the stick so that the ball misses the pocket by a wide margin. "Don't listen to him," he tells us over Max's stream of swearing. "He enjoys being pessimistic."

Kyan and I exchange a glance and I watch both of them with narrowed eyes. Max and Dev have been sharing quite a lot of touches lately. Light taps on the arm, hands grazing each other, pats and prods and nudges. I wonder if they're even aware.

"Does it concern you guys at all," I ask, "after the bombing, that the two of us are from the Midnight Court?" *Do you still trust us?* is what I want to say.

"I think I speak for all of us," Kyan tells me solemnly, "when I say that by now, we've all recognized that court allegiance doesn't define anyone. And I feel like the two of you have done more than enough to prove that we can trust you."

Dev and Max nod in agreement.

I can feel a smile spreading across my face. "Thanks, guys. Kyan."

"Of course," he says.

"Okay, but for real," Josephine cuts in. "Do you think we're going to be at war again? Because if we are, I really don't think we should be here." This, she directs at me.

"I have no idea," I say. In reality, I've been thinking about this too. Maybe obsessively. I have no idea what to do if our two cities actually end up destroying the accords. If this is it. "If they do declare war, I'm sure the embassy can get us back in time."

"Or they send everyone to kill us. We're literally sitting ducks."

Kyan says, "You're most likely safe within Eladine. The professors and the headmaster don't really do things under the umbrella of the Dawn Court. They're a bit of their own entity, if you know what I mean."

"Well," says Jo, "I *really* hope so."

"Do you guys think it was the Midnight Court?" Max asks. "The bombing?"

There's a pause, a dragged-out moment of silence that seems to last far longer than it should, before Josephine says, "No way. The Midnight Court would never risk war like that. Not to mention they know we're here—it would make literally zero sense for them to choose Eladine specifically to bomb."

I take a deep breath. It crosses my mind for barely a second that it might not be a good idea to say out loud what I've been thinking, but I disregard it. "I think it was Darren."

They all look at me.

"What?" Max asks.

I pored over this for *hours* last night. I say, "Think about it. What parts of the school were destroyed during the bombing?"

"Some of the dormitories, the stadium, the east wing. Why?"

"Maybe it wasn't random," I say. "Maybe the bombs were targeted."

Max raises an eyebrow. "If they were, it definitely wasn't for the stadium."

Dev pats him on the back. "So smart. So intelligent."

"No one cares about a training area," Kyan adds. "So it was either the dorms or something in the east wing, which is..."

"The history and languages classrooms? And electives?" Josephine offers.

Kyan's frowning, and I see the exact moment he comes to the same realization that I did. I knew he, of all people, would get it.

"The poisons lab," he says. "The antidote."

I watch it all dawn on their faces: understanding mixed with a sort of horror. It all clicks, fits together so perfectly it's like putting in the last piece of a puzzle. Watching the edges all line up.

Max says, "Oh, shit."

"What do we do?" Dev asks. He's taken to pacing the length of the room, back and forth and back and forth and back and forth. It must be a new habit because I've never seen him do this before. Or maybe he's just never been this stressed.

"We need to talk to Liu Caihong," I say. "The man Darren set up. We need to confirm that it's him, and then figure out a way to tell the king and the Emperor."

"Where is he?"

At this, I smile a grim smile. Say, "He was extradited back to the Midnight Court. And imprisoned."

"Great," says Max. "So, what? We're going to barge into the Midnight Court prison?"

I shoot him a dirty look. "It's not as crazy as you make it sound," I say. "I'll get permission from the Council."

"And the Council's going to let you bring three Dawn Courters into a Midnight Court prison?" Kyan asks, but there's no inflection. Just genuine curiosity.

"Maybe," I say. "It won't hurt to ask. And if they say no, we'll just sneak you in. It's not like we haven't snuck into the actual Dawn Court like fifty times."

"Twice," Kyan corrects mildly.

"Same difference," I say.

"Well," says Dev. I see his Adam's apple bob in his throat as he swallows. "I mean, Eladine has a plane."

"A *plane*?" I ask, flabbergasted. "This school has its own plane?"

"And a hangar," Max adds, nodding vigorously. "It's for emergencies. And for flight training for the upperclassmen who want to potentially pilot once they graduate."

"Well," I say. "Why not?"

"Hey, now that you've lived in both courts, what's your opinion?" Max asks me, curious as we make our way to the hangar. "Like, which one do you think is actually more fucked-up?"

I blink. "Seriously?"

"Well, yeah." He shrugs. "I mean, if you're able to remove bias and all that."

"I think they're equally bad," I say, and hope to god karma doesn't charge me with treason for saying so. It would've been so easy, I think, to lie. To say that obviously the Dawn Court is worse, but I can't anymore. Not with good conscience.

"Well, shit," says Dev.

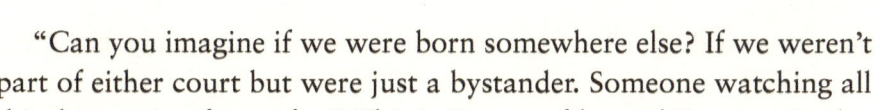

"Can you imagine if we were born somewhere else? If we weren't part of either court but were just a bystander. Someone watching all this destruction from afar." This is Kyan, softly, and I'm surprised.

I didn't expect this from him. But I guess out of all of us, he'd be the one to say this.

"I have," Josephine says and *this* one actually startles the oxygen right out of my lungs. Makes me pause and take several seconds to process.

She says, "I used to wonder what it'd feel like to live in some rural part of China. A place so out of touch with the rest of civilization that people don't even know the courts exist."

"Or another country," I let slip before I could shove a filter into my mouth.

"I don't mind the courts. Much," Dev says from where he's sitting by the door. He's almost lost in thought. "I just wish they were more open to outsiders. Well, I can't speak for the Midnight Court, but the Dawn Court, I mean. It'd be so much easier if they'd just let my family move here."

I cock my head. "If you don't mind me asking, Dev, how are you part of the Dawn Court if your family isn't?"

"My dad was," he says. "But he fell in love with my mum when he was visiting family in Mumbai, and she wasn't a part of the Court. He tried to move her and some family out here too, but the Dawn Court wouldn't allow it. Apparently, there's some excessively long process you have to go through to become a member—security reasons, I guess, and they just didn't have the money for it.

"He was my only family here," Dev adds, quietly. *Was.*

"We're your family," Max says, and his voice is fierce. I don't miss the appreciative smile Dev shoots at him.

We steal the plane.

Or rather, a plane. Apparently, Eladine has a hangar full of them a few minutes off campus and Max and Paris are well-acquainted with aircraft theft. They've done it many times, supposedly. Not Dev, because of his...situation.

I don't argue. Just scramble into one of the seats in the back and attempt to ignore whatever the two of them are doing to disable the tracking device.

In the meantime, I call my mom to let the Midnight Court know we're coming in advance of our arrival.

She picks up on the first ring. "Anna? Is something wrong?"

"It's a long story," I tell her. "But I think Caihong might have been set up."

"By Darren?" She knows exactly what I'm talking about before I even have to say it.

"By Darren," I confirm. "I would like to talk to Caihong, if possible. Or, we, rather."

A pause. "We?"

"Me, Josephine, and three Dawn Courters. Friends," I tell her.

Another slight hesitation. And then, "Okay. I trust you. I'll alert the Emperor and the Council that you're coming."

"*Xièxiè, māmā,*" I say, thanking her, and hang up.

"All good?" Max asks me.

"All good."

Five minutes later, Josephine says, "God, I hate planes." We haven't even taken off yet and her eyes are closed, fingers squeezing the armrests of her seat, and I almost laugh. If there's one constant, it's Josephine and her aversion to flying.

Kyan says, "You better prepare yourself, then. Max and Dev aren't exactly known for their smooth flying."

"Get ready," Max calls from the cockpit. There's a giant grin on his face that I can see reflected in the windshield and I gulp. Try to swallow my heart in my throat. Begin to wonder if maybe this wasn't the best idea.

And then suddenly, with a deafening roar of the engine, we're on the move. Speeding down the runway.

It's nine in the morning when we arrive in Shanghai. It seems the Emperor and the Council wanted to keep this arrival of Dawn Courters into the Midnight Court as quiet as possible, because they make us land a little ways off from the heart of the city. We are an hour from the Bund, on a tiny helipad at the edge of Shanghai.

But the moment I step off, it all comes rushing back in, a flood like some internal dam has broken.

I hadn't realized how much I missed Shanghai.

It's like stepping back into the sun after freezing in the dark for too long, like taking that first gasping breath after being underwater. The familiar glint of Pudong's skyscrapers in the distance, the faint hum of traffic and car horns, the metallic smoky air of the city mixing with the salty tang of the breeze coming in from the sea are all the same and a smile is tugging at the corners of my mouth before I can even stop it. Before I can even process it.

Home.

But, I think, there is also this strange feeling of *missing*. I can't help comparing these two cities, my two homes, London and Shanghai and I'm—

I'm finding myself missing it. London. Missing the peace of mornings in Hyde Park, quiet afternoons in the common room, the hustle and bustle of Mayfair and Westminster and Spitalfields and it is like my heart is split in two. London and Shanghai. Dawn Court and Midnight Court—and maybe that makes me a little bit of a traitor— but maybe I don't really mind. Maybe loving shouldn't be a crime.

Apparently, even the pressing need for secrecy can't keep parents away, because when we step off the plane, there they are. Waiting for us. Josephine's dad and my entire family: mom and dad and sister and all.

It is like a homecoming, this welcome. Like we're war heroes coming back from abroad and now they're welcoming us back home, saying congratulations, thank you for your service, except the difference is, we're not done. We haven't succeeded quite yet.

My mom crushes me in a hug so tight I forget how to breathe for a second. She smells exactly the same: cherry blossom shampoo and whatever lotion she's been using for the past fifteen years. No perfume. My mom doesn't believe in perfume.

My dad hugs me too, not as long but just as tightly. "*Huānyíng huíjā*," he says. "*Wŏmen xiăng nĭ, le.*" *Welcome home, we missed you.*

Katerina is standing at their side, smiling a little, asking me if I'm so sick of London, and I don't respond. I know what she'll say if I tell her the truth and to be honest, I don't really care at the moment.

To my right, Josephine is hugging her dad and there is a giant grin on her face that makes me smile again. Harder. I used to feel bad for her, guilty that I had—in comparison—such a loud, giant family and hers was just her and her dad, but they only need each other. And somehow, the loss of Josephine's mother has made the two of them impossibly close. I'm almost jealous.

Suddenly, I realize with a flash of guilt that the three Dawn Courters are standing awkwardly behind us, watching these little reunions, and I drag them over to my family.

Say, "This is Max, Dev, and Kyan. Guys, this is my family."

My parents are guarded. It's probably not visible to the untrained eye, but I've had eighteen years of studying their expressions, their faces, wondering if they're mad or just mildly ticked off, if they're hiding something. I can see it almost immediately, the tightening around their eyes, but they welcome the three of them warmly. Say, "What a pleasure to meet you."

My sister is not so good at hiding her distaste. She hasn't had a lifetime of practice the way my parents have, but she tries anyway. Dutifully greets them, says "Welcome to the Midnight Court." She's so stiff and I know for a fact that the three of them notice.

I almost feel bad for her, how quickly she believes and how tightly she clings to the propaganda the Midnight Court has fed us. How unwilling she is to be open to the possibility of something different.

Max glances at me with an eyebrow raised and I just shake my head. Glance away.

"Be careful," my mom tells me in Mandarin. Her eyes are dark, piercing mine. "You have a lot of eyes on you, especially now that you've brought three Dawn Courters into our home. Don't give them a reason to persecute you."

I swallow. By *them*, I think she means the Emperor. "I won't. I promise," I say, but there is no heart in my words. I know even as I say it that it's a promise I can't keep. I decided long ago to let go. Dive off of my own accord before I get dragged down. She, of course, doesn't know this. She never could.

My only reassurance is that no matter what, even if they lose me, they will still have Katerina.

"Should we go?" Dev asks. It's a genuine question, not an attempt to rush us into leaving.

"Yeah," I say. "Let's go."

The Midnight Court prison used to be in the Midnight Court itself, in Shanghai. Except two years ago, one of the prisoners escaped— killed three people and injured seven—so now they've moved it to Gulangyu Island.

The last time I was there was three years ago. Summer. August.

A lifetime ago.

It's a three-hour train ride and then a ferry from Shanghai, three hours of rural land, occasional small towns, mist-covered mountains straight out of one of the paintings in my parents' house.

Paris is meeting us there—a couple hours later, since he took off a little bit after us, as soon as the Dawn Court meeting ended.

It's supposed to be an unusually warm day today—low seventies when it's usually fifties or sixties in a Shanghai November, but I guess this is what global warming does to a place. At 10:00 a.m. though, it's still a little chilly outside. The early-morning mist and dew still cling to the air, to the grass like they're trying to hold on for dear life, both hands forming a death grip.

"China is so much more rural than England," Dev comments, staring out the window with a boy-like curiosity I've never seen on him before.

"No shit, dude," Max says, "It's always been this way. Don't you listen in history class?" But he's smiling, staring outside with his face smushed against the glass in a way that makes me laugh.

They're looking at the rolling hills and farmland like they've never seen anything like it before and I realize, with a jolt, that maybe they haven't. Maybe they've been in the city their entire lives, and *that* is kind of a depressing thought.

In a perfect world, I think, I'd move out of the city. Leave the courts behind and find someplace rural. Quiet. Unblemished by the scars of the past and the seeping black poison of history. Someplace that has only ever known peace. That is still pure.

I'm not even sure such a place exists.

"So, what do we do when we get there?" Max asks me, moving away from the window for a second to look at me. He leaves a smudge on the glass.

"The warden will take us straight to Caihong," I say. "And then..." I frown. "We should probably come up with a list of questions or something to ask him."

"Are you sure he's going to talk to us?" Kyan asks me, quietly. Sunlight strikes his left eye, setting it alight until he looks like he has heterochromia. One eye black and one eye honey brown.

"No," I say.

"Torture," Josephine says. "Obviously."

The word hangs in the air like acid, like a weighted blanket, except instead of a blanket it's a thousand tons of poison.

Torture wasn't something that was even looked at twice nine years ago. In fact, it was so commonplace I remember memorizing the exact square of pavement where I could begin to hear the sound of screams near the prison as I walked past.

I avoided it as much as I could.

But we, we are the younger generation. We are the ones that the adults consider spoiled. Too young to really experience the trauma and tragedies of war when it was going on and now it's over.

We've grown up softer. Nurtured by peace, shaped and molded by it rather than hardened by war and violence.

Torture is unfamiliar to us. Completely out of left field, and I am seriously doubting my ability to extract information from someone with a literal scalpel into their flesh.

"Um, not it," Max swallows, echoing my thoughts.

Gulangyu is right off the coast of Xiamen, in the heart of the Fujian province that inhabits southeast China. The island's been ruled by so many different countries—Britain, France, Japan—in the past couple hundred years that it is a mosaic of clashing cultures. A kaleidoscope of traditions and people and architecture that somehow fit together perfectly like it was fate. Like it was meant to be in a way that is beautiful.

It is completely secluded, vehicle-free for centuries. One of the only places that the dirty fingertips of modernity have not yet stained.

The town has not changed at all in three years—same colonial houses, same narrow alleys, same tiny shops lining the streets—but it doesn't surprise me. It's barely changed in a hundred.

Looking at it
hurts a little.

Because I remember every moment from the last time I was here and it is an overwhelming sense of déjà vu, so much so that I almost wish it had changed. It is a raw, fresh pink scar, a constant reminder of love and loss, and it will never, ever let me forget.

But it also gives me hope, hope that maybe we can return to this. Maybe there is still a whole book with empty pages, waiting to be written.

CHAPTER 43

The last time we were here it was August, three years ago. Summer winding down, blending into a pre-autumn interval where it wasn't quite fall—the air wasn't yet crisp, the leaves not yet vibrant—but it wasn't exactly summer either. There was a stillness in the air, a languidness that was almost entirely *August*. As if people were trying to make the most of this break before everything started up again full force in September. Before the school year began and Paris left for London.

I knew our time was finite; I'd been counting down the weeks since mid-July, but it was like all of a sudden, they were passing by faster than ever. They were passing *me* by, two hundred miles per hour faster than what I could keep up with, and without warning, summer felt practically over.

It wasn't something I liked thinking about. In fact, I avoided it as if just having the thought could cut me, and there was a certain bliss-fulness to feigned ignorance, to pushing away problems rather than facing them head-on.

We had decided to go to Gulangyu on a whim, a spur-of-the-moment decision you almost always only make when you're young, when you're too impulsive and reckless to know any better. I had done some quick research on my phone, and four hours later, we were here.

The ferry to the island felt like freedom. Tasted like it. The feeling of wind in your hair and the roar of the boat as it carved a foaming white path through the murky blue-green water. The tinge of salt in the air.

Five minutes in, the euphoria started leaking out and reality began settling in. "My mom's going to kill me," I said. "I promised her I would start preparing for school today."

Paris glanced at me, a hot dog he had just gotten at the food cart at the dock halfway to his mouth. He shrugged and said, "I'll just tell her it was my idea. I kidnapped you."

"Then she'll kill you."

At this he smiled angelically. Said with conviction, "No she won't. She loves me."

He wasn't wrong. Although my mother had been wary from the start—and was a little still—because of Paris's connection to the Dawn Court, she adored him. She had known him since we were kids, after all, and there's a certain security, a certain safety to knowing a person for so many years. Knowing them since they were young, because not even someone who tries to hide every part of themselves can hide everything. In time, almost everything comes out whether you want it to or not.

Plus, she was friends with his mother.

"Yeah, whatever," I said, but it was faux-irritation and we both knew it.

By the time the ferry docked on the island ten minutes later, Paris had long since finished his hot dog. "Do you think this place has an ice cream shop?" he asked, eyeing the row of buildings in front of us that were almost entirely residential apartments.

"Is this trip entirely about food for you?" I responded.

He ignored me. "Or anything interesting? Are you sure it was the right decision to come here and not the place a little further away?"

We had had a fifteen-minute argument this morning about whether we should come here or go to Shenzhen a little further south. A four-hour train ride rather than three, but the hours were fading too quickly already and that precious extra hour of transportation felt like a poor way of spending it.

"*Yes,*" I say. "Be patient." Paris was never patient, always itching to go somewhere else, do something else, and I had no idea if it was a boy thing or if it was just him. I, for one, could be perfectly happy sunbathing for hours, watching the occasional seagull venture so far from the coast that I could see it from the park. Or spending an afternoon reading a book by the window.

Paris obliged, but only for me. He was always active, always on the move.

We ended up finding an ice cream parlor half a mile from the dock. It was small, definitely family-owned, with a yellow and white awning and a huge wooden sign with the words *bīng qí lín* hanging below it.

The inside was small—maybe not even three hundred square feet—with a seating area with six tables on the side. The chairs were rickety wood. So were the tables.

"Well," I said in between licks of ice cream. We had both gotten cones and mine was beginning to melt down the side. I was trying my best to avoid getting it on my fingers. "What's the plan? What are we doing?"

He looked at me sideways. "What do you want to do?"

I stopped eating for a second. Hesitated. To be completely honest, I knew exactly what I wanted to do. Where I wanted to go. I had spent the three hours on the train googling the island and someone had said Sunlight Rock was nice. It was the highest point on the island, formed by two boulders side by side, and the absolute best view.

I wanted to sit and admire it. Not really Paris's cup of tea and I knew it. I also knew he had spent the past few days accompanying me—reading on a bench next to the Bund, taking walks around Tan Garden, feeding the fish in the pond—and I didn't want to ask him to do it again. Didn't want to ask him for more.

"Persimmon. Just spit it out."

At this, I was so surprised I stared at him with the ice cream cone frozen in front of my mouth. Two months ago, I had decided that I was sick of never knowing what he was thinking, of him never telling me. So, "persimmon." Every time one of us invoked it, we were compelled to say exactly what was going through our mind.

I wasn't expecting him to use it.

I glared at him. "Fine. I want to go to Sunlight Rock."

He raised an eyebrow at me, and I knew without him having to say it out loud what he was thinking. *What the hell is that?*

I sighed. "It's the highest point on the island. It has a really good view. Before you say anything, I *know* it's not exactly what you love doing. I'm sure it'll be fun to be that high up."

I waited for him to argue, to shake his head and say no, but he just stood up. Said, "Let's go, then."

CHAPTER 44

The prison is on the eastern edge of the island, literal steps away from the beach, and I almost wonder if this was intentional. If the tiny window that overlooks the sand and the pale blue water is there just as another reminder of what its inhabitants have lost, a reminder of consequences.

You would never know it's a prison from the outside. The building itself is incredibly nondescript, pale yellow and made completely of cut stone. It is almost indistinct from the surrounding colonial buildings.

For a second, it feels like Italian summer—or the way it looks in pictures, anyway. Leafy trees still green even though it's this late in the year, pastel-colored balustrade balcony railings, great arches like windows.

The prison is three stories and a gorgeous blend of Western and Chinese architecture. So very fitting for Gulangyu.

"Damn," says Max. "The prisoners must be living good here. It's legit like a vacation home. I would live here."

I glance at him. "Not on the inside."

"Plus," says Josephine cheerily, "they only get two portions of disgusting food a day. And limited outdoor time."

Max gags. "Never mind."

The warden comes out to meet us; he's a man in his fifties, fully

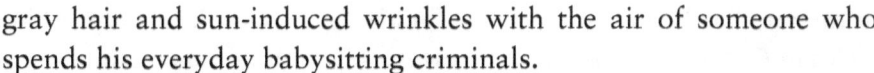

gray hair and sun-induced wrinkles with the air of someone who spends his everyday babysitting criminals.

"*Nǐ hǎo*," he says when we walk up to the door. "Liang An Na?"

I nod. "We're here to see Liu Caihong." I say it in English for the benefit of the three Dawn Courters behind me. I know Max, at least, is horrible at Mandarin.

The warden's English is choppy, infiltrated by the flat intonations of an obvious Chinese mother tongue, but at least he can speak it. This far from Shanghai and the major cities, it's a wonder if someone can speak English at all.

He says, "Follow me."

The warden walks up to the door. Unlocks it with an actual, physical key that is so out of place, so written off in history, forgotten, obsolete, that it almost feels like a breath of air.

Sometimes I think I was born in the wrong era. Although I am, self-admittedly, horrible at opening doors with keyholes. Utterly inept. Every key I've ever used seems to magically not work in my hands, so maybe I wouldn't have survived anywhere else.

The inside of the building is a hot-cold contrast, a reintegration into modernity with its impeccably clean white linoleum. Both sides of the walkway are lined with identical cells, so sparsely furnished— with a single tiny cot and threadbare blanket—that I wonder if it's even humane.

I wonder what their meals look like.

Each cell is separated from us by a thin slice of glass. It is a wall that is completely see-through, as if this prison is a zoo and the prisoners are here for entertainment. For us to gawk at, laugh at, watch as though they're not human, but animals. Something beneath us.

I make a point not to stare at the people inside the cells—both because of some fleeting sense that it doesn't seem moral and also because I'd rather avoid their leering gazes. I can feel them on me already; like a sheen of oil on my skin, like the feeling of poorly made sunscreen that suffocates your pores.

"Good god," Dev murmurs. "This place is so weird."

"Yeah," Max agrees, and they're right. I feel it too, this twinge in the air that I can't quite place. Suddenly, it doesn't feel at all like we're in Gulangyu. The sunlight from a few minutes ago is miles and miles away, so far it might as well be on another planet altogether, because there is a very real chill around us.

They must regulate the temperature in here, I realize. Keep it a couple degrees under what's comfortable so that the prisoners always feel some slight level of discomfort. Constantly keeping them a little off-balance. It is a manipulation tactic as old as time.

Thankfully, the man we're looking for is on the lowest level, meaning we don't have to parade ourselves before yet another floor of prisoners.

On the way, Kyan says, "Paris touched down. He just texted me."

I'm opening my mouth, in the middle of saying, "Tell him to meet us here," when the warden stops abruptly. Looks at us and I'm just realizing we've arrived in front of a cell. He says, "You have fifteen minutes." And then he's gone.

We stare.

The last time I saw this man, he was dressed in Dawn Court finery, white velvet and gold embroidery, gleaming leather shoes.

Today, he is the opposite. He's dressed in the classic prison uniform—loose, dark gray shirt and pants made of rough polyester. It is the color of smoke. Of typhoon clouds. It is black stained by white until it is no longer pure, no longer wholly black and a very loud symbol of dishonor.

But the alternative, I think, was death. Without extradition, he would've been executed in the Dawn Court, but maybe death is worse than dishonor. In most old families like the one Caihong comes from, like those of the Council, the ones still clinging to the traditions of the old ways, it is.

When he looks up, I can see with almost alarming clarity what these weeks in the prison have done to him. It is painted in stark, black watercolor, acrylic, Sharpie, written in the paleness of his face; the drawn, sallow skin under his eyes, the splotches of dirt and stains that mar the gray fabric of his clothes like a diary of time. The growing scruff on his face is another.

People die in here, not physically but emotionally. Mentally. Perish and rot away like forgotten food and I want to throw up at the sight of it. I want to upheave all the contents of my stomach, but thank god it's only just hit noon and the only thing I've had today was a cup of coffee.

My eyes slide away from him, jolted away as though my gaze and his entire being are magnets with matching poles, created to repel, pushed by some force that is invisible to the eye. My gaze catches on a flash of glass in the corner, and I find myself staring at a tube. The vial—empty now that the poison has been spilled.

I wonder why he still has it. I assume the Midnight Court didn't care enough to take it away. After all, they know he is innocent. This prison sentence is just for show. Just to appease the Dawn Court.

Max, of course, is the first to speak. He says, "Hello?"

Caihong doesn't look directly at us, his gaze never resting on our faces, which I'm not complaining about in the slightest. He doesn't say anything.

"Do you mind if we ask a couple of questions?" Josephine asks, gently probing. In some other life, she used to want to be a doctor. When we were younger, she used to dream of working in the hospitals, bringing our people back to life, but now the war is over. Now there isn't as much need for doctors and medical staff—and there is more need for spies. For people on the front lines so well-versed in espionage that they might as well live and breathe it.

Our society shifts with our relationship with the Dawn Court. No matter how much our Council tries to rid themselves of our other half, no matter how much they declare themselves above London, independent of it, we are irrevocably intertwined.

"*Wèn*," he says. His voice is so low, so quiet we need to lean in to hear it. *Ask.*

Josephine glances at the rest of us, makes some motion with her hands like, *well?*

I clear my throat. Finally force myself to look at him again. Swallow before asking, "Are you guilty?" I ask the question in fast Mandarin, a jumble of intonations that step on each other's toes, fronts ramming into backs until only Josephine can understand.

I want to make sure of this, that Caihong was set up, before we really begin this questioning. Otherwise, I'd probably look like an idiot.

His gaze slides to mine, locks in. "*Wŏ dāng rán bù shì.*" *Of course I'm not.* It comes out in one violent stream of words, a cocktail of pent-up anger, of frustration that has been clawing at the edges of a wall too smooth to find purchase on, that has been building and building and nothing else for a week.

"What did you ask him?" Kyan asks me, but I just shake my head.

Say, "It wasn't important," and he just shrugs in response. I know he, of all people, won't push me.

"Who set you up?" Josephine asks Caihong, having heard our conversation.

I know what he's going to say. I know exactly who and I'm waiting for him to confirm it. I'm holding my breath and anticipation is burning a hole straight through my stomach.

I almost don't want it to be true.

But I do.

"I don't know the name," Caihong says. He looks exhausted, hopeless, as if he's already resigned himself to sitting in this prison forever. To carrying out this life sentence he should never even have gotten in the first place.

"Give us a description," I urge. "Anything. Anything helps."

"Blonde hair. Green eyes. A member of the royal family, I think." He frowns. "There was a scar or tattoo on his left wrist, I couldn't tell."

But that, that is all I need to know. I saw that scar on his wrist, a slight marring of the skin like an old burn mark, and it is enough for me. Enough to confirm it.

Darren is and has always been behind this.

I still don't know why, but Paris needs to know this before the Dawn Court does something they can never take back.

The three Dawn Courters know it too, recognize his description like it's a brand, like in three words, he has described the Dawn Court prince perfectly.

I can see it in their faces, not just recognition but disappointment too, as if they were hoping against hope that somehow, maybe it wouldn't be Darren. Maybe for once he was telling the truth and maybe things could be easy, just another thing to attribute to this age-old feud between our two courts, but for once, it isn't.

For once, the fates have woven something different, something strange.

"Do you know why?" Dev asks him. He walks forward, ignores Max's warning hand, until he's practically nose-to-nose with the glass. Crouches down until he's level with Caihong and I find myself admiring his courage. I'd say I wish I was more like him, but I'm happy keeping as much distance between me and the man in the cell as possible. Something about him, all of this, unnerves me.

Caihong shakes his head. Says, "I asked. He didn't say. Just told me he'd kill my daughter if I didn't do as he asked."

His voice is flat, an overtone of listlessness that is spilling fear into my belly, painting me over with a dawning horror in wide brush-strokes.

And then, shaking, angrily, he says, "Not that it even mattered. He shot her anyway. Three times." It's almost as if he's in a trance. "Two in the stomach. One in the head. He made me watch as he did it, the bastard."

His entire frame is trembling, every part of him practically vibrating with anger and grief and I'm thinking *oh god, oh god, oh god, please let it not be true, please let it not be true because—*

because.

Nausea is poisoning my stomach once again, stretching obsidian black tentacles through my body, multiplying until I'm choking on them. I shove a fist in my mouth, pinch the skin between my thumb and my pointer finger, which I'm pretty sure is to stop yourself from crying rather than throwing up, but I can't think. I'm doing everything, curling my fingers so tight my knuckles turn white, blood draining from my body somehow, somewhere, evaporating into pure horror because I'm finally realizing why he looks this way. Acts this way.

It wasn't all because of the prison.

Darren killed his daughter anyway.

This girl that I remember seeing when she was three years old, running around her father's legs.

"She was...twelve?" I ask and my voice trips out of my mouth, stumbles into a whisper.

He nods. "Twelve years old. *Míng tiān shì tā de sheng rì.*" Tomorrow, tomorrow is her birthday. Would've been.

My hands rise to my mouth of their own accord as he says, "He killed her." The ring of finality that accompanies death. They are the true peas in a pod, I think. The original. The only one that lasts through history.

Twelve years old. Barely older than Talia.

And for the first time: pure, undiluted fury. Fury is pooling at the bottom of my chest cavity, unfurling red-hot wings and begging to break free—no—fighting to break free. It is burning my insides like acid and I

can't

breathe through the anger that is gathering at the pit of my stomach. In my lungs. This man dared to hurt my own. The people I love. And for once, I am not quite so uncertain because liquid fury cools and hardens into this: decisiveness.

Resolve.

I can't imagine what it feels like to be Caihong. I don't even think—no, I *know*—I don't even want to try. Family is everything in the Midnight Court and a parent losing a child, a parent burying a child, it is wretched. And it makes me sick to my stomach.

"I'm sorry," I tell him. "I am so, so sorry. I promise you we'll find a way to get you out of here. And he won't get away with this. You have my word."

Josephine throws me a sharp look and I know what she's thinking, what she's doing. I can read her silently telling me to be careful, to not throw promises around so cavalierly, but what she doesn't know is, this isn't cavalier. This promise I will keep until my dying breath.

CHAPTER 45

I need to find Paris. I need to tell him. Not just because he needs to know, but because I am fraying at the seams. The edges. *Something*—horror, disbelief, a crumbling view of humanity—is beginning to flood the hallways of my mind, tear me apart, pour poison in.

I'm walking out of the prison, one step, two steps, three steps into the open air, but I am only dimly aware of the sound of Max and Dev whispering to my right. Only dimly aware of my horror mirrored on all of our faces.

I am sleepwalking through reality.

When I grab my phone, it is with shaky hands. When I type out the text, it is with trembling fingers.

meet me at the top in 15

He doesn't even question it. Doesn't ask. Just says,

okay

Sunlight Rock is exactly the same as it was three years ago. Maybe *rock* isn't the best name for it; it's one giant, towering cliff that rises above the rest of the island, above the trees and buildings like a sentry.

It overlooks the entirety of downtown Xiamen—the coastline, the red rooftops—and once you're up there, you feel on top of the world. It's a heady feeling. A dangerous one.

It takes me fifteen minutes to climb up the steps, fifteen minutes of staring at gray stone, the occasional scarlet Chinese characters engraved in rock. Fifteen minutes of blind climbing and hoping time erases this new stain because I can't stop thinking about it. Can't stop thinking about the fact that she was just *twelve*. A child.

It's so ironic, I think, how the temple built atop this rock was meant to worship Guanyin, the goddess of mercy, when all I have left in my body is vengeance.

When I finally reach the top, I don't fool myself into thinking I got there first. Paris has always been the faster climber. But expectation still does not prepare me for this, this wave of emotion when I see him—surprise and exhilaration, and most of all, relief.

He's standing a couple yards away, weapons strapped over jacket, practically set ablaze by the sunlight, outlined in it, and for the first time, I think I see the beauty in Dawn. The power of it.

It is almost obliterating, this feeling, relief so strong it threatens to numb my knees, my legs until I can no longer stand. I think, I search for home on every crevice of this earth, but this is it. He is it. He has known me at nine, fifteen, eighteen, has watched me through my formative years, been by my side during some. He is the imprint on my heart that will never fade, that refuses to leave, that will always stay.

And my body is running of its own accord, colliding into him so forcefully that it pushes him a step back. I read surprise in his eyes and a little bit of concern, but his arms are coming around me anyway; he's holding me to him, asking me what's wrong, what happened as I finally let go.

The hyperventilating finally begins to steal all the breath from my lungs, replaces it with panic instead, and I can't stop thinking about what this war is doing to us, this rivalry. Can't stop thinking about the miles and miles of bodies left in our wake, blood staining the dust, the air, everything it can touch and it is so

meaningless.

Because no one wants it to be over. We are all killing ourselves, each other, as if we're feeding blood to this monster that needs it to survive. It is an endless cycle, a torturous one, and I am suffocating in it.

How has it come to this? Murdering twelve-year-olds as some kind of sick, twisted joke? Or maybe this is what it has always been.

We live in a world where anyone can betray anyone, where anyone *will*. And no one questions it. No one even blinks an eye.

Paris doesn't say anything at first, just brushes a quick kiss on my forehead that sends shivers down my spine. He frowns at me. Asks, "Anna, what happened? What's going on?"

I shake my head and I'm shuddering; my entire body is shaking and I'm staring at my hands when I say, more to myself, "What are we doing? Our two courts, we spend our entire lives, our everyday, planning attack, revenge, some way to hurt each other. It's so useless." And then to Paris, "We went to talk to the prisoner."

He nods. "Liu Caihong, right?"

"Yeah." I squeeze my eyes shut. "He confirmed that Darren was the one pulling the strings. The puppet master." I suppress another shudder.

And then, suddenly, I don't want to tell him the rest. I don't want to be the one that breaks it to him that his brother—this person that is irrevocably connected to him by blood—murders children. Is barely human. Took the life of an innocent person, shot them three times too many. Twice in the stomach. Once in the head.

And it makes me sick to my stomach.

"Anna, whatever it is you're trying to spare me from," Paris tells me, and his eyes are hard, solemn, "don't."

Words, I think, have more power than anything. More power than guns, swords, daggers, because those can only physically hurt you and these, these little bullets on my tongue have the ability to break you emotionally, to tear you apart from the inside out and make you wish you were dead instead.

"He told him, the Midnight Courter, that if he didn't follow orders his daughter would be killed. And so obviously, he did what he was told, but it didn't matter in the end."

I don't look at Paris as I say this. I don't need to see the rising horror in his eyes that even he, this time, cannot conceal.

"Darren killed her anyway. Three bullets, point-blank. Right in front of her father. And he made him watch."

Slowly, Paris sits down, perched on the edge of a rise in the rock. Braces elbows on knees.

He's silent for so long I start to think maybe he's gone mute out of shock, and then he says, "I need to tell my father." His voice is hard, masked again, but this time, I think, it is unintentional. This time, it is more a survival mechanism than anything.

"Wait," I say. "Your father isn't just going to believe a Midnight Courter, especially with allegations like this. You and I both know that."

"Then what do you want to do?"

I've thought about this since I spotted the vial in Caihong's cell. I say, "We can test the vial for fingerprints. Darren said there were two vials—one which he stole from Caihong, which we took, and the one that Caihong had. Which means Darren's prints shouldn't be on there, but if he's lying, if it was him all along, he would've given the vial to Caihong. Fingerprints."

Paris raises an eyebrow. "Do we have the vial?"

"Caihong does," I say. "I saw it in the room. Cell."

His mouth quirks up a little—a mirthless half-smile. "Good."

"Paris," I say. He looks at me. I think he knows what I'm about to say. My voice is hard, firm. Unflinching. "If I'm right about Darren—and I'm almost certain I am—I *will* kill him if it comes to it. If he forces my hand and the accord rules no longer apply. He has hurt too many people that I love."

A brief smile flits across Paris's mouth. He says simply, quietly, "I know you will."

For the next five minutes, neither of us move. We're sitting at the edge of the rock, feet dangling off the edge of it, but it's been three years since I was last here and I am not so wary anymore. Not so cautious. The drop down isn't so much daunting as it is freeing.

"I'm surprised you remembered this," I say, glancing sideways at him. "That you knew what I meant."

"Are you kidding?" he asks me. "It's only been three years, Anna. Clearly, my memory isn't as deficient as you think it is."

It's not quite peaceful, this moment, not with this bomb that Caihong has dropped on me and that I, in turn, have dropped on Paris, but it is as peaceful as it's been recently. As peaceful, I think, as it's going to get.

Here, so far removed from everything else, it is easy to forget. Easy to drop this weight crushing our shoulders, pretend that for once, all of these flaws with the world do not fall on us.

But it's wishful thinking. A temporary reprieve.

"Persimmon," Paris says to me, suddenly, and I stare at him.

"Really? Now?"

He shrugs. Says, "Tell me what you're thinking."

"You did this to me last time and now it's only fair that I ask you."

"You never do," he says, and it's true. Paris ended up using that word a lot more than I did, but sometimes, I was scared to know what he was thinking. "But fine," he says, "I was thinking about that too. The last time we were here."

"And?"

"*And*," he says, shooting me a look as if to say *if you would let me finish*, "in some ways, everything's changed. But in others, nothing has."

He looks at me, fixes green-gold eyes on me. Says, "I meant every promise that I made to you back then, Anna."

I forget how to breathe.

CHAPTER 46

It took us forty-five minutes to hike up the stairs to the top of Sunlight Rock.

Mainly because I kept stopping for pictures.

Despite the crowd of people on the island, there was absolutely no one at the top. Maybe because of the heat. It was supposed to reach a hundred degrees that day, definitely the hottest of the summer.

But up here, this high above it all, it felt cool. Just right.

I remember thinking just how strange it felt to be so high, high enough to be able to see the rooftops of all the buildings down below, high enough to be able to see the river and the ocean. Miles and miles of it.

Of course, I had been this high up before, but in the city, in Shanghai, every building was tall. You could be three hundred feet up—even six hundred—and all you would see were the windows of the other office buildings. Maybe the Bund, if you were lucky.

Paris went straight for the cliff, sat right down at the very edge of the rock so that directly beneath his feet was what felt like miles and miles of air and I, I loved heights, but not recklessly. Not like he did.

He didn't force me to go near the edge, didn't pressure me, but after a few minutes of standing in the safety of the center of the rock, curiosity got the best of me.

I ventured out, slowly, cautiously, and he reached out a hand.

Offered it to me. And it wasn't until I was gripping it, until he was holding me steady, that I walked the rest of the way. Sat down next to him.

"Don't let me fall," I told him.

He said, "I won't. I promise, I will never let you go."

CHAPTER 47

We have to go back to the prison, Paris and I. Max, Dev, Kyan, and Josephine are somewhere exploring the island, waiting for us to finish up so we can leave.

Somehow, it always ends up being just the two of us. Three months ago, it felt so strange. Foreign, awkward, tense. Strangers, but not really, after three years of silence. But now, it is comfortable again. Familiar.

And I find that it doesn't quite scare me anymore.

"This," Paris says, glancing up at the facade of the building, "doesn't look like a prison. It looks like a vacation home." He sounds halfway to indignant.

"Well, it's not," I say. "It's disgusting on the inside and keep your head down. Unlike the rest of us, the Emperor did *not* give permission for you to be here, which means if you're recognized, we're both in trouble."

Paris ignores me, keeps examining the outside of the building and asks, "What kind of architecture is this? It's superb! It doesn't look fully Eastern."

"You're not funny," I tell him, and he sends me back a smug smile.

The prison looks exactly the same as it did a couple of hours ago, despite the dying sun outside. I realize, abruptly, that it's because it has no windows—not on the first floor, anyway. The entire space is closed off, isolated from the outside by every means possible and it's a wonder the prisoners aren't all pale ghosts.

Isn't vitamin D part of survival? I'm pretty sure I read somewhere that it is what keeps bones healthy, the very foundation of your body, and without it, without the foundation, what happens to everything else?

Answer: it crumbles.

The warden meets us at the door. "Back again?" he asks. I can't read his expression.

"We just need to talk to him one more time," I tell him. And then, as an afterthought, I add, "Please."

With a grunt, he gestures to the hall. "You know where it is. Don't take too long."

"Jesus," Paris comments under his breath, sober again, as we walk inside. "This place puts the Dawn Court prison to shame."

"I'm sure the Emperor would love to hear that," I say.

"You're not proud of it."

"No. I don't think it should be a competition, who treats their prisoners worse," I say.

"Maybe," he responds. "But to the Council and the Circle, it's a show of strength. Who can discipline lawbreakers the best. Who scares people into obeying."

"And then there are people like Caihong," I say. "Who's being punished for something he was never guilty of."

"True," says Paris. "Corruption practically runs rampant in both of our cities. It's nothing we don't know."

"Yeah, but maybe it's something we start doing something about."

It is the first time that I'm daring to say this out loud—daring, even, to think it. And it is a far more liberating feeling than I'd thought it'd be.

We stop in front of a familiar cell.

"Liu Caihong," I call.

He turns around to look at me, gaze sliding toward me and away, but it is Paris's face he catches on. The transformation, I think, is incredible. How expressive human faces can be, how many emotions it can show all at once—anger, fear, disbelief.

In a low voice, he asks, "Who is this?"

I open my mouth to speak, to reassure him that this isn't Darren, that he is nothing like Darren, but Paris beats me to it.

"I'm Paris Ateş," he tells the prisoner. "Darren's"—winces—"half-brother."

"Paris," Caihong repeats. "I've heard of you. You're one of the youngest of them."

"Yes. I apologize," Paris says, quietly. Composed. "For everything that my brother has done to you and yours. I know it doesn't make up for anything, and definitely doesn't bring back your daughter, but I hope it eases some of the pain. Maybe some of the guilt. Rest assured," he adds, "my brother *will* be brought to justice for everything he's done."

Caihong nods. Says, "*Xièxiè*,"—thank you—and some of the tension is erased from the air.

"Of course," Paris says. And then, intently, "There's something we wanted to ask you. Something we think can help corroborate your story." He is all business.

"What is it?" Caihong asks.

I point to the empty vial on the floor, next to the scrap of fabric the prison wardens call a blanket, and say, "The vial. We were thinking we could run it for fingerprints, prove that Darren was at least involved in whatever happened. Unfortunately, I don't think that the Dawn King will believe you without some semblance of evidence."

Caihong is staring at the three-inch piece of glass like he can't quite make sense of it. "That vial," he says, "reminds me of everything I went through. Everything I have lost. It reminds me of my anger, when I am too tired to hold on, reminds me that there is still one thing I must do before I can die." His eyes flick up to mine, to Paris's. Hard and black and unforgiving. "Get revenge.

"Take it," he says, "But promise me that you will not let him get away with this. Promise me you will not let him go free."

So again, I say, "I promise." And it is yet another weight on my shoulders.

The empty vial is burning a three-inch hole in my pocket as we step out of the prison. I'm staring at the sun as it disappears under the horizon, drowns under the water and dyes the blue with the blood of its dying rays. Only to return to repeat the process again the next day.

Sometimes I wonder if the earth ever gets tired of orbiting the sun. If the sun ever gets tired of rising.

I call my mother again to let her know we're going to need access to a lab. I tell her everything that happened, everything that Caihong said about Darren. Everything he told us about his daughter. What we intend to do now that we have the vial—the only damning piece of evidence that we need.

I can hear the quick clicking of the keyboard as she types and short snippets of conversation before she says, "I contacted the lab in Xiamen. Ask for Dr. Tang when you get there. They're expecting you."

"Thank you." I hesitate before adding, "Also, Paris is with me."

A brief pause. And then, "Like I said, I trust you, Anna. Just be careful. Keep both eyes wide open."

"I will."

"Okay." I can hear the undercurrent of resentment simmering in her voice when she speaks again. "Do whatever you have to," she tells me in a low voice. "*Make sure Darren pays for what he did.*" This is spoken in rapid Mandarin, the syllables all crashing into each other. "I will support whatever you choose to do." Her anger mirrors my own. That is one thing that will never change—the urge for Midnight Courters to protect their own. To avenge them.

"I will," I say. "I promise." And then I hang up.

There are one, two, three minutes of silence before Paris says, suddenly, "I think I hate my family, sometimes."

I blink at him, unsure of how to respond for a moment. "You mean because of Darren?"

He sighs. "Yes, Darren, but not just him. My father can pretend to be good, pretend like everything he does, he does for our own good and the good of the court, but he is"—Paris searches for the word—"insane. Certifiably insane at times and sometimes, I think he takes loyalty too far."

He shakes his head. Says, "We shouldn't have to do all of this, run tubes for fingerprints, prove that it matches with my brother's, just to get my father to believe that the Midnight Court isn't to blame for every misfortune the Dawn Court experiences."

I sigh. "Yeah. It's the way of the world."

He says, "Maybe it doesn't have to be."

The abrupt buzzing of an incoming call interrupts whatever slippery slope this conversation is going down.

Paris slips his phone out of his pocket, says, "Kyan, what's up?"

I can barely hear Kyan's voice on the other side, just lengths of crackling, a low murmur.

A second later, Paris turns to me, says, "They're asking if we should just split up. The two of us can go to the labs and they can do some recon, figure out what the current situation in Shanghai is. If the Midnight Court's planning something."

I nod. "Let's do that, then."

"All right," Paris says, attention back to the phone. "I'll see you later. Yeah, bye." He hangs up.

"Your phone calls are so dry," I tell him. "You should've asked them what they're doing. I bet they've already walked past that one ice cream place on the island."

Paris rolls his eyes. "Where's the closest lab?"

"Off the island," I say. "We're probably going to have to take the ferry back to Xiamen." Thank God that enough Shanghai Midnight Courters are so sick of being in the center of it all that they've migrated down south, even to island cities like Xiamen.

We fall into step, walking down to the ferry terminal, and it's like we've gone back in time, like the past few years have been whited-out from the page that is history. But part of this also feels shiny and new. Part of this feels like carefully removing the cellophane from something that has never been touched.

In the distance, the sun has finally set. Across the water, on the other side of the river, lights are flickering to life in the city's skyscrapers and high-rises, tiny specks of yellow pulsing from windows, lines of blue, red, purple. They are reflected in the water, an exact

mirror, save for the occasional ripples that disrupt the image and send it scattering; but this, this is the city coming alive.

We step onto the ferry, making our way to the edge and away from the crowd of people. Neither of us moves to sit down.

"Do you ever miss Shanghai?" I ask, watching him stare at the rush of black water and the coastline of the city as we draw closer.

He glances at me. Glances away. Murmurs, "Sometimes."

I wait for him to continue, to say something else, but he doesn't. Just falls silent. So I say, "Persimmon."

Paris huffs a laugh, shakes his head and says to me, "*Now* you're using it? Fine, I'm thinking yes, I missed Shanghai, but it was mostly because I missed *you*, dumbass."

"Oh," I say.

"You had to have known that," he tells me. A smile ghosts across his mouth. "My father offered me every opportunity to come back—I figured he was testing me. He wanted me to say yes, act like whatever happened had no effect on me anymore, but I refused. Declined every single one. Most likely disappointed him, but it wouldn't have been the first time."

"Your father is an ass."

"Believe me," Paris says, "I know."

"For what it's worth," I say, "I really am sorry I believed him so quickly. Believed the Council. I shouldn't have."

He shakes his head. "I know. I think I forgave you a long time ago. Before I was even consciously aware that I did."

We step off the ferry, touching down onto downtown Xiamen. In the distance, the twin towers rise up, so far above the other buildings they're like two sticks marring the skyline.

It takes ten minutes to walk to the labs, passing by symmetrical office buildings until we stop in front of one. It's a stout building, square and cut in geometric lines. Made of glass.

The lobby is all shiny black marble and warm wood. Very generic, in my opinion.

"Hi," I say in Mandarin to the receptionist behind the desk. "We're looking for Dr. Tang? For the fingerprinting."

"Oh, yes. Right this way." She leads us up the stairs and down the hall, opening the door into a lab that looks remarkably like the one at Eladine. "Dr. Tang? They're here for you," she says, and I turn around to find a man walking toward us. He looks like he's in his late forties, graying hair, thin-frame glasses, smile lines etched into his skin.

"Hi, yes, welcome! Your mom called to let me know you were coming," he tells me. "You needed to run something for fingerprints?"

I pass him the vial. "Yes, this. Last contact was probably around a week ago, maybe even earlier. And it's gone through a couple of hands since then."

"Not to worry," he says, examining it in the light. "There's still enough substance for the machine to pick it up."

"What are we going to do after he gets the prints?" I ask Paris in a low voice as Dr. Tang begins pressing buttons on a sleek white machine a few feet away. "The Midnight Court wouldn't have any records of Darren's prints to match it with."

His voice is hard. "We're going to ask him for them."

At this, I turn around fully to face him. "Really? He's just going to let us take his fingerprints?"

Paris smiles a humorless smile. "I'm going to confront him. I'm going to call his bluff."

CHAPTER 48

It's midnight by the time we get back to Shanghai. Tucked into Paris's jacket pocket is the empty glass vial and a physical copy of the prints Tang pulled off of it. He sent both of us a digital scan too as a precautionary measure.

I don't even realize that I've fallen asleep until Paris rouses me, shaking me lightly by the shoulder, and I'm blinking my eyes open to the warm amber lights inside the train.

"You better be glad I was here, otherwise you would've slept straight through Shanghai and most likely woken up in Russia," he says, pulling me to my feet.

"Thanks," I say, rolling my eyes. "You're really a lifesaver."

A brief grin flashes across his lips, and then he's serious again. "We can stay the night in Shanghai if you're tired. Go back in the morning."

I shake my head. "No, we're in a time crunch. I'll just sleep on the plane and hope to god Max and Dev don't crash it."

He laughs. "All right. Let's go."

The four of them are waiting for us back at the helipad, each of them clutching plastic cups and straws in their hand—all of them empty.

I raise an eyebrow. "Really?"

Josephine shrugs. "We waited for you guys for *hours*. We had to do something."

"So much for recon then, huh?" I ask.

Josephine sticks her tongue out at me.

"But seriously," Max says. "What took so long?"

"It took an hour to get the prints," I say. "And three hours to get back here. I'd say that's a pretty reasonable time frame. Right?" I nudge Paris with an elbow.

"Right," he says.

Max rolls his eyes. "Yeah, whatever." He eyes us. "So, are you guys good now? I struggle to keep up with your relationship."

"Me too," says Dev.

"I struggle to keep up with *yours*," I tell them both, which shuts them up immediately.

On the far right, Kyan winks at me. Mouths, *Nice.*

Thanks, I mouth back.

Paris asks, "What are you guys saying?"

"You'd know if you weren't so oblivious," I tell him.

"That doesn't clarify anything."

The six of us board the plane in single file, two in the cockpit, the rest in the back. Paris and I go in the cockpit first; suddenly, after everything that happened today, I don't think I can sleep. My mind is crowded with thoughts, emotions all jamming into each other, collision after collision.

Paris enters first and I follow, sliding into the seat next to him.

We are both quiet until we're in the air, on a direct course back to London, and in the blanket of darkness, in the stillness of the hour, it is as if the entire world is holding its breath.

Silence has crept in, slow and prowling, invading the cockpit. I can feel it sliding around my chest, brushing a tail against my neck, but neither of us make any move to speak.

Finally, we're flying to what feels like the end. We will either come out alive, triumphant, or we will have failed. There is no in-between.

In the darkness, Paris's voice seems to float on air. He asks, "Are you ready?"

"For once," I say, "I think I am." And it's the truth. For the first time, I feel prepared. Ready to do what I need to because I am just now realizing that everything I have witnessed and been involved in, everything that I have seen being done to the people I love, has made me recognize that sometimes, there are things you need to do for the good of the whole. Even if you don't think you have the strength to.

Finally, I think I understand *me*. Myself. I'm understanding that maybe I am fueled by something other than duty, the way my sister is and maybe,

maybe that's okay.

"This entire time I was afraid," I say, "that maybe I wouldn't have the strength to follow this through. To do what needs to be done."

Paris glances at me, surprised. The blinking lights of the controls cast a pale blue sheen on his face, reflecting in the irises of his eyes. In the darkness, the green is only a thin sliver around his pupil.

"I think that might be the most ridiculous thing I've ever heard."

I shoot him a dirty look. "I mean it." I sigh and for the first time, I voice it out loud. I say, "My entire life, I've lived in Katerina's shadow. For years, I blamed her for being so controlled, so disciplined. Blamed myself for not being the same. She is exactly what my parents hoped for, exactly what the Emperor wants us to be. What the court needs. She doesn't question orders, doesn't question the system. Our way of life. Doesn't waste time daydreaming like I do."

Paris cuts me off. "Anna, you—" He stops. Shakes his head and there's almost a disbelieving smile on his face. "I can't believe you've been thinking this. Your emotions have always been your strength. Our world doesn't need more soldiers. We don't need more mindless drones—not to say your sister is one—who don't bother to wonder why our system is so broken. Who only add to the violence and the bodies that are piled so high we can't see above them anymore. What we do need," he says, "are people who are brave enough to ask why. To wonder how to fix it and you…" He touches his fingertips to my cheek, so light I can barely feel it. "You are exactly that.

"I have always admired the way you have the courage to be compassionate in our world which doesn't quite value it," he says. "It's one of the reasons why I loved you."

"Loved?" I ask.

At this, a fleeting smile crosses his face. He rolls his eyes. "Do you really need me to say it?" he asks. "Love. I love you. I always have.

Even," he says, "when you're shoving a blade to someone's throat. Or mine."

I laugh, but I'm barely paying attention anymore.

I think I'm falling. Falling or floating or something in-between, I'm not sure. I have no idea. In this moment, every broken part of me, every shattered piece of history and memory, is fitting together perfectly. Seamlessly. Every hurt, every loved and lost has been rewound. It is still not fully erased, but it is fixed. And that is all that matters.

When he kisses me, I'm thinking, it was all worth it. Everything we have been through and gone through, together and apart, for this moment. This kiss is why the sun and the moon chase each other day after day, endlessly, hoping for the one moment they finally meet.

CHAPTER 49

Half an hour before we land, we're all gathered in the back of the plane—hopefully, there will be no disturbances while the cockpit is empty.

Dev called Professor Song earlier to tell her about everything we found out on Gulangyu, and she wants to hold a meeting to figure out what to do next.

"I think we should head straight to the Dawn Court palace," Max says. "Confront the bastard. Call his bluff." For once, he doesn't look like he is joking. Just grim, almost angry.

"I second that," says Dev. "Give him as little time as possible to do whatever it is he's planning next. We have no idea how much time we have, so better safe than sorry."

"Then you all need to figure out exactly what you're going to do when you get there," Professor Song warns. Her face flickers on Dev's phone screen. She looks tired, face lined, and I realize with a sort of shock that it's already early morning in London. We've flown through so many time zones it's hard to keep track.

Not to mention the six of us have been awake since yesterday morning, other than the irregular naps here and there, and it's almost as if time has lost all meaning. As if it no longer exists in this space.

"There's an event going on at the Dawn Court last night and this morning," Paris speaks up from beside me. "Daybreak." This I've heard about—the Dawn Court's mirror celebration to the Moon

Festival, a commemoration of dawn and the court itself. "We'll land just in time to make the end of it. Everyone—my entire family—will be there. Most likely if he's planning something he's going to do it today. Tonight."

"So, we have one chance," says Josephine. It's barely even a question.

"Yep," Dev affirms.

"We just need to find him, get him away from everyone else," I put in. "And then confront him. Ask for his fingerprints."

"And then what?" asks Josephine.

A pause.

"I have no idea," I say. "Open to suggestions."

"We're running out of time," Max says. "We might have to just play it by ear."

We all stare at Song's disapproving face on the phone screen.

"Or," Dev says, "it's six against one. We'll find some way to tie him up or something—"

"Some bondage action," Max says, nodding. Dev shoots him a dirty look. Paris hides a smile.

"Anyway, as I was saying before I got rudely interrupted, we tie him up, get his fingerprints, and then take him to the king. And your father can figure out what to do with him next."

He says the last part to Paris, who nods. "Works for me."

"Should we split up?" Josephine asks. "If we're tight on time, it might not be a great idea for all of us to go searching for him together. We can cover more ground individually."

"It'd be more dangerous too," Max counters.

Almost unanimously, we look at Professor Song.

She says, "It's up to you guys. If you think the risk is worth the reward."

"Wise as always," Dev says, nodding.

"We might as well," I put in. "If anyone needs help, just call."

Max seconds. "Agreed."

CHAPTER 50

It's almost sunrise by the time we arrive.

I half expect whatever event the Dawn Court is hosting to be over, but I can see the lights flooding out of the palace windows even from a distance.

We land the plane on an airstrip a mile away—better safe than sorry—and walk the rest of the way to the grounds.

It's so strange, I think, how quickly something becomes familiar to you. How quickly foreign things become *un*foreign, written into your memories with red and black ink that you can't miss, can't erase.

After the past three months here, the Dawn Court building has become almost familiar. It is not quite so foreign, not so mysterious. It is not this cloak-and-dagger entity, this place that houses the deepest secrets of my enemy court.

It is, simply, just a building.

This time, we walk in with no preamble. No ploy, no game, no cover-up. It doesn't matter who sees us anymore—we know what Darren's doing and I'm sure he knows we do.

The guards make no move to stop us as we step in, pause in the lobby. Look at each other.

"Should we split up here?" Dev asks.

There is a moment of silence, a moment that feels heavy, weighed down by so many previous moments, so many words left unsaid.

And then, Paris says, "I suppose so."

"Remember, if you find him, call," Dev reminds us. "And if you need help, call. The palace is big, but it isn't that big. It should be fine."

As the six of us disperse, out of the corner of my eye I spot Max walking up to Dev. They're conversing in low, rapid tones, shooting words back and forth. I watch Dev reach out, squeeze Max's hand before I look away. Give them this moment of privacy.

I'm about to leave when Paris speaks up from beside me. I didn't even realize he was still here. He says, "Wait." I watch in confusion as he pulls out the gun in his jacket. Flips it in his hand so that he's gripping the barrel and then holds the handle out to me. "You never remember to bring a gun. I can't take any chances."

I look at the gun. Look at him. Take it because I know there's no use arguing with him in this moment. "Don't die, Ateş," I say.

He grins, presses a brief kiss against my lips. "I'll try not to, Liang. Just for you."

It feels strange to be walking the halls of the Dawn Court by myself. Every other time I've been here, it was with Paris by my side; I was a stranger in a court that was not my own but now, now I'm alone. Now I'm here and it feels not like I belong here, but close to it. Terrifyingly close. No guards reach out to stop me, no one even gives me a second glance and I'm wondering why. If it's just my clothes or if it's something else altogether.

If something about me, after all these months, has become more Dawn Court than I realized.

I see him before he sees me. Darren.

Of course I'm the one that finds him first. How fitting.

He's striding down the hallway, speaking in a low, urgent voice to someone on the phone and I'm almost certain he's probably just been told about what happened. About our visit to the prison, what Liu Caihong told us. Gave to us.

But it's too late. We're already here.

He spots me four seconds later; I watch his eyes widen slightly, watch his features shift into something that looks almost like surprise, like panic, before it shifts back. Before his face closes itself off and I'm thinking that this talent, this ability to hide emotions, must be a shared trait within the Dawn Court family.

"Anna," he says, stopping in front of me. "What a...pleasant surprise to see you here."

I plaster the fakest smile I have ever conjured on my face. Say, "Paris invited me. It's great to see you again."

Behind my back, I'm trying to unlock my phone. Trying to call the others, but before I can hit the button, Darren's grabbing my arm and I'm so surprised I drop it. Watch it and half my hope clatter to the ground. I should've expected that. I had no idea he was going to reveal himself so soon.

Darren picks up my phone, keeping one hand on my arm and his grip is like a vise. Like iron. I can't pull myself free. He yanks me into a random room and I'm trying to regain my balance. Trying to act normal.

"What is this?" I ask, forcing my face into a neutral expression, trying not to give anything away until he says it. Until I'm absolutely certain he knows.

Darren shuts the door behind him. Locks it and an unbidden, uninvited flash of alarm goes off in my stomach.

"I saw the way you looked at me just now," he says, eyes narrowed and watching me. "What do you know?"

I can't help the anger that is exploding in my chest, unfurling bright red petals, sending off bits of pollen into the air—except instead of pollen, it's reckless rage.

I spit out, "Everything. I know you were the one who stole the poison, who forced the Midnight Courter to put it in the wine at the ball, who murdered a twelve-year-old and bombed an entire school just to destroy an antidote."

He doesn't react the way I expected him to. Instead, he lifts his head. Raises a brow and there's a smile that I *really* don't like playing about his mouth. "Is that what you think I was doing?"

My face morphs into a frown before I can stop it. "Isn't it?"

He laughs. And then laughs harder. I think I might've waited for a full thirty seconds before he finally says, "Unfortunately, you're wrong, my dear." He lifts his gaze to mine. Says, "I was actually trying to kill *you*."

I stare at him.

Shell-shocked.

"What?" I ask.

"Yes, sorry," Darren says. "I was trying to kill *you* with those bombs. It was part of the deal I made with the Emperor."

I'm dizzy. The room is beginning to spin slightly, but instead of moving horizontally, it's moving vertically and it's like the world keeps falling from the sky. Endlessly dropping, only to drop again.

This, I think, is the actual bomb. This is obliterating my entire being, everything I thought I knew to be true. This is obliterating my entire reality and I realize I have no idea whether he's telling the truth or not.

But all I know is this: If Darren was going to lie, he wouldn't have said this. It is too ridiculous to be false and I am melting onto the floor. I am almost stunned to see that somehow, I'm still upright. Somehow, my knees haven't buckled yet and I'm still standing here. Staring at Darren. Almost completely still despite the magnitude-ten earthquake happening in my head and my body right now.

Darren sighs, rubs a hand across his mouth. "Really, you shouldn't know this, but it wouldn't do all that much damage." He's silent for a minute, tapping his fingers against the table almost absent-mindedly, as if he's determining the best way to deliver this.

And then he says, "Do you remember, in history classes, when the textbooks talked about the old Midnight Court?"

I rewet my lips. Say, "Yes. Of course I do."

"It seems you have some old Midnight Court royal blood running through your veins," Darren says to me. "And despite how diluted it is, despite the fact that the new family's been in power for almost a century now, the Emperor's still a little concerned. You're a liability."

And for the second time in two minutes, I drop dead all over the floor. This time, I actually do have to sit down.

"That's insane."

"Is it? It is entirely possible, and more than likely, that they missed someone in the takeover. Entirely possible that that person cloaked themselves as a commoner and was never discovered. Until recently, of course."

"Okay," I say. "Say you're right. Say you're telling the truth. So, what? The Emperor sent me on this assignment just so you could kill me? Why couldn't he have just killed me himself?"

Darren shoots me a look as if wondering how in the world I could be so naive.

"Too messy," he says. "If it somehow got traced back to him, the murder of his deputy's daughter, it would be grounds for a possible coup. Much cleaner to have it be executed in the Dawn Court, blame it on yet another casualty of war."

"And what about my family? Are you somehow going to find a way to kill them too?"

Darren laughs loudly. "Oh, Anna. How oblivious you are. Don't you think that if either your mother or your father came from that bloodline, that the Emperor would've found out already? That they would've long since been wiped from existence?"

My brain is whirling, spinning around and around and I can't quite process this. Can't quite bring myself to understand what he's saying. This is *madness*. And I am mad to believe him.

Darren sees the dawning comprehension on my face. He says, "Yes, Anna. Your parents aren't actually your parents. Or, I should say, your *biological* parents."

I feel sick. "*Do they know?*"

He just shrugs. Says, "That you're adopted? Obviously. The truth of your bloodline? You'll have to ask them, but I would assume not."

I am silent. I am speechless. It's so strange how shock can suck all the strength out of you, out of every single muscle in your body until all that you're left with is blood and bones. In the past five minutes, my world has been heaved upside down, right side up, and upside down again by a man I have never spoken more than a few words to in my entire life.

I'm thinking, It is always, always the ones you suspect the

least—because if you asked me which of these two Ateş brothers would be more likely to turn my entire world on its head, make me question everything my life has been founded on, I would've said Paris.

This I never saw coming.

I almost wish Darren never told me. That I could continue living this lie of a life, never knowing the truth about myself. My family. Never knowing the extent of how corrupt my city is because—don't get me wrong—I've always known that it wasn't lined in gold, that this system wasn't flawless, but this?

This is beyond my comprehension. The Emperor claims to hate the Dawn Court, but just as much as he hates them, he is willing to work with them for personal gain. And he is every bit as bad as Darren.

Maybe even worse.

And I have spent all this time, my entire life, trying to be the flawless Midnight Court soldier. I have spent so much energy trying to fix what I thought was wrong with myself, trying time and time again to prove my loyalty to this court that is so undeserving.

And right now, I'm finding that I don't quite care anymore. Every expectation that I have built myself around is crumbling straight to the ground and it is

almost

freeing.

"So what exactly did you get out of this little arrangement?" I finally ask. "The poison? But that was already in the Dawn Court's possession."

"So it was," Darren agrees. "But that doesn't mean I could've just easily stolen it." He rubs at his chin. Smiles. "A rather funny story, actually. It was on one of my many attempts to steal it that I bumped into a couple of Midnight Court spies doing the exact same thing. Crazy how small the world is, isn't it? Seems like the Emperor was preparing for the resumption of a certain war. Anyway, I had them contact the Emperor for me, told him my terms, and in return, I wouldn't expose his whole operation. A pretty good deal, in my opinion."

"It wouldn't even work now," I point out to him, "if you still had any remaining. We have the antidote."

He just says, "I don't need it anymore."

A creeping feeling of apprehension is beginning to slither down my back. *Anymore?*

"You look like your entire world just crashed down," Darren observes, sick amusement dancing in his eyes.

God, do I want to slap that smug smile off his face.

"Maybe it has," he adds. "Here, I'll give you a little pick-me-up." He leans against the wall, crosses his legs at the ankles. Says, "I was planning on finally executing my plan today, now that I have my entire family with me, but I'll give you a choice. One chance to save someone."

And here it comes. "You want me to choose one person in your family," I say, flatly.

"No." He's smiling again, a full, open-mouth smile with perfect white teeth. My stomach drops before he even says the next part. Falls all the way to my feet.

He says, "I'm asking you to choose between Paris and the rest of the family."

CHAPTER 51

Darren has a particular ability to kill me, I've decided, because for the third time in this one conversation, I'm reeling. It's like he's punched out my consciousness and now I'm just floating in the air, staring down at my frozen body in utter shock.

"No," I say. "Why the hell would I do that?"

He sighs, focuses on something that I can't see. Says, "It's amazing how much you believe in humanity. How much you believe in morality," and this sentence sounds so much like Paris I'm dizzy for a second.

I have to remind myself that regardless, they are nothing alike.

His face hardens. "Choose, Anna. Or I'll kill them all."

"You're sick. Who's to say you'll succeed, anyway? Someone *will* stop you."

"It's too late, Anna. My plan was in motion long before all of you arrived. You have," he says, pushing himself off the wall, "until I reach the door to give me an answer. Five"—he takes one step toward the door—"four"—two steps—"three, two, on—"

"Wait," I say. "I'll play your stupid game. On one condition."

He raises an eyebrow. "You're in no position to be requesting *conditions*, but go on. I'm intrigued."

My heart is pounding uneven, staccato beats in my chest and even though I haven't done anything, have barely moved in the past five minutes, I'm out of breath like I've run a marathon.

My head is spinning at a hundred miles a minute and I am trying *desperately* to find a way out of this, a loophole, but there is none.

I am trapped in this tomb of my own creation and now Darren is dumping in the dirt.

Paris will never forgive me for this, but I, I have no choice. And I would rather him hate me than be dead.

So I say, "Paris *and* Talia. Don't touch either of them."

Darren grins. "Fine." He opens the door, halfway out, halfway in. "And by the way, Anna, try to stop me—kill me, tell anyone—before I do what I need to, and I *will* make sure your entire family doesn't see tomorrow. I have the Emperor under my control, in case you've forgotten, and I've already put safeguards into place that will ensure this if you try anything. I would advise against attempting to call my bluff."

And then he slips out the door, leaving me propped against the desk, wondering what the hell I've done, because for the first time, Paris and I are fine. We're *good*.

Except I've just destroyed it all over again and this time, it feels permanent. It feels real.

It takes me far too long to force myself to get it together. Still too long to make it out the door.

There is a metal band around my chest, tightening and squeezing until I can't breathe. Every scrap of fear, anger, disgust—hopelessness—is twining together, forming a stone that sits heavy in the pit of my stomach, and I think, I need to follow Darren. Part of me has already accepted this, that almost all of the Dawn Court royal family is about to be wiped out and—

I am torn in halves. Straight down the middle.

The Midnight Court part of me is telling me I shouldn't care. That this is a good thing, something that will weaken the Dawn Court and raze it from the inside out.

But the *human* part of me, the one that says humanity equates with morality, is telling me that I should care. I should care more, and I am going insane trying to reconcile these two parts of myself. Two parts that don't make a whole, but all I know is:

I have no doubt that Darren will make good on his threat. But even if I can't stop him, I need to see it. I need to see what he does with my own eyes and know that my hands are just as red, just as bloody. That no matter how hard I try to pretend I am not this, no matter how hard I try to avoid violence and bloodshed and almost everything this war means,

I can't. And I have an idea.

The entire lower floor of the Dawn Court palace is surprisingly empty when I leave the room. Every member of the Circle and the Dawn Court royal family is missing and I am, suddenly, terrified that I've missed it. That it's already happened, and I am too late.

Except the logical part of me is thinking that if the king and queen and four of the Dawn Court princes were just murdered, there would be a lot more chaos.

And then I spot them.

They're all standing in the courtyard, one side illuminated by the yellow light spilling out from the bay windows. It is a small expanse of green, surrounded on three sides by a square hedge speckled by pale white flowers. And in the center, a crowd of people stand in a loose circle around a figure that I know, without a doubt, is Darren.

I see the King and Queen, Richard, Theo, Parker, Tyler, Paris—no Talia, thank *god*. She must already be upstairs asleep, too young to be awake this late. At the very least, the universe has granted me this tiny reprieve.

But my heart is still in my throat.

In two seconds, I break into a half-run, half-walk in an attempt to wed speed with inconspicuousness. I am hoping to god that no one questions why I'm speed-walking to the courtyard and all I'm thinking is, the few yards separating me from outside is the longest of my life. That these seconds are dragging by, five in one, and I might as well be running underwater, might as well be wading through air that is quicksand, and I am both hyperaware of everything and not.

And then I'm bursting outside, barely aware of the sudden impact of cold air on my legs, my arms. It takes me a few seconds to find

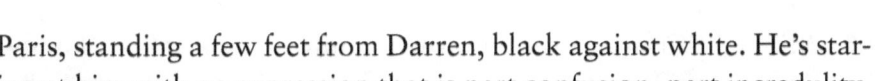

Paris, standing a few feet from Darren, black against white. He's staring at him with an expression that is part confusion, part incredulity.

I feel a sudden pulse of hatred for Darren, so intense it almost numbs my knees, obliterates every cell in my body, leaves me momentarily breathless.

He has hurt and threatened the people I care about, the people I love, and I have already made up my mind. I think, *Maybe I was born for this world after all.*

I make my way across the grass to Paris, stopping by his side, and he glances at me briefly, says, "Hey."

"Hey," I say. "What's going on? When did you get here?"

His gaze flickers to Darren. Back to me. "I was searching here after we all separated. And then *he* appeared." There is unmasked disgust in his voice, and I'm wondering how it must feel for him right now. To hate his own brother.

"Do you know where the others are?"

Paris shakes his head. Says, "I called them down here just now, but I haven't seen them come in yet. Just you."

Just me.

Part of me is almost relieved, relieved that they, at least, won't see what I'm about to do. Won't witness firsthand the worst betrayal I have ever perpetrated. I'm thinking, at least they will be spared that.

"Paris," Darren says, and we both look at him. Paris's face is unreadable.

"Anna says I'm responsible for stealing the poison. What do you think? Do you believe her?" He seems to actually be waiting for Paris's response, but I have no idea what Darren's getting at, no idea what he wants Paris to say.

"I think I believe her without a doubt. Always."

I look at Paris, about to say something—I have no idea what—but he's not done yet. He says, "I think you're a liar, a child murderer, an asshole with absolutely no morals, and you, you are *not* my brother." His voice is harsh.

The entire garden is staring at the two of them, shocked into silence just like me.

Darren says, softly, warningly, "Look at you, believing the words of a Midnight Courter over your own family. In *front* of our family. Imagine if our whole court could see you now. I'm sure Father's disappointed."

"He's been disappointed in me my whole life," Paris says, emotionlessly, carelessly, ignoring the fact that the king is standing not ten feet away. "It doesn't exactly faze me anymore."

This I already knew. This Paris had told me about when we were together, but I'm surprised it's still the same. That nothing has changed.

Darren lets out a laugh, begins pacing around the garden. "But you could change that." He stops. "You could change his mind about you."

Paris looks like he's running out of patience. Says, "Darren, say what you have to say and stop wasting my time."

Darren smiles, taps his fingers against the fabric of his pants and—

I realize, too late, what he's about to do. In a movement almost too quick to see, he's drawn a gun from the waistband of his pants. How he hid it there so completely I have no idea. In another flash, he's pointed it at Paris, and I—forget how to breathe.

I'm watching the scene unfolding before me and my heart is stuck in my throat. I'm thinking *no*, I'm thinking *You promised, not him* and I'm beginning to wonder why no one's doing anything when I see the shock and alarm and confusion painted messily across all of their faces.

They have no idea what's happening. They're too confused, too frozen to do a thing. Dread almost brings me down to my knees.

From where she's standing near the edge of the garden, the queen says, "Darren? Paris? What's going on?"

They both ignore her. Darren is looking at Paris, and Paris, Paris is just standing there. He's staring at his brother pointing a gun at his head with a calm that is almost concerning.

"Put it down, Dar," he says. "You and I both know you're not going to shoot me. Enough with the theatrics."

I'm not sure I'd have that much faith if I were him. If Darren was shaking, even if he acted a little bit *not mentally all there*, I'd trust him more. Instead, he's just standing there, holding a gun to his brother's head and he is utterly, completely still. Composed.

My fingers tighten on the grip of the gun Paris gave me, squeezing so hard my knuckles are white. I wouldn't put it past Darren to break our agreement.

Even this is not fazing him. Instead, he is just as calm—almost dangerously calm—and there is a glint in his eye that tells me maybe he's smarter than he should be.

"Did you ever even question," Darren says, "why I'm doing all of this? Why I'm bothering to funnel in so much effort, so many resources into making this happen?"

"You mean killing our entire family?" Paris's voice is saturated with acid.

Darren doesn't react. Doesn't even blink. "Yes."

"You're disgusting."

"You're naive," Darren shoots back. "Our two courts are killing themselves, trying to one-up the other. At some point, we'll both die out."

I'm shivering at how similar his words are to what I said just yesterday. His thoughts are practically an echo of mine.

"We have to make sacrifices, something *Father* isn't willing to do."

At this, I glance at the king. See several people do the same. He's standing next to his wife with an almost resigned look on his face and that, that drops yet another stone in my stomach. Ten pounds of dread. Panic.

"Yeah?" Paris asks. "And what's your grand plan?"

"Unite the courts."

I think I gasp out loud. I think we all do, the entire garden, in unison. We're watching this like it's some kind of soap opera. I almost can't quite believe my ears because this, not only is it unheard of, almost too ridiculous to even think, much less say out loud, but it is treason. Especially for a Dawn Court prince.

But then, he continues. "Can you imagine our combined strength if we come together?" He's addressing all of us now, looking at me and Paris and every member of his family. I can't tear my gaze away from him. "The power of the Dawn Court entwined with the power of Night. We would be invincible. Think of the improvements to our economy, to innovation, if we pool our resources. We could cure all forms of cancer in weeks. Beat any disease before it even has a chance to rear its head. Tell me," he says, "that this isn't something you want. Tell me this isn't a future you would live for."

I find myself almost agreeing with Darren—with this depraved *killer*—and I resist the urge to throw up.

"And what does this have to do with murdering the entire family?" Paris asks.

At this, Darren's face becomes more muted. "That's the sacrifice. You don't think Father would ever agree to this, do you? And can you imagine Richard and Parker agreeing to this either?

"I am third in line for the throne, brother, which might as well mean I will never get it. And for this, I need it." He cocks his head. "And even if, by some miracle, or by my own hand, I do become king, who's to say it won't be taken from me? By Tyler or Theo or even *you*? The poison was a preventative measure, a safeguard, if you will. Simply put, familicide was meant to make the process smoother. More efficient. Root out any obstacles and dispose of them preemptively."

"You're fucked up," Paris says. His voice is a hard, angry lash and Darren's face twists in rage for a second before he's able to rein it back in. "Did you even consider *asking* any of us before you just decided that the best way is to just kill first, ask later?"

I know Paris well enough to recognize the signs of fury, in the cadence of his voice, the tightness in his body. He is practically vibrating with anger and I'm almost afraid of what he'll do. What he's capable of, in this moment.

"Think about it as removing variables from the equation," Darren says. "Uniting the courts would be an unbelievably large project. Conflict and disagreement among the leaders would inevitably lead to conflict in the rest of the court. Rebellions, uprisings, even skirmishes between opposing factions, and you can imagine how many people would be killed or injured in those."

His voice intensifies. "I'm sacrificing a few lives to save so many more. And I'm not asking you to do anything. You don't even have to get your hands dirty at all if you don't want to. But…" He looks at Paris. Looks at me. "Join me. Think about all the people we could save, the rise to power we can give birth to."

He fixes his attention on me. "Annabella, you remember the days of the war, don't you? You would've been—what, nine—when the accords were finally signed? You lived through nine years of war, nine years of bodies piling up in streets, too many for them to even clean them all up in a day. Do you remember the stench of rotting flesh?"

My blood is turning to poison in my veins. I have been trying to forget these memories for almost ten years.

"The Midnight Court and Dawn Court are back on the brink of war. We could stop it," he says, and his voice is earnest. Intent. "We could put an end to this centuries-long war and finally achieve lasting peace. Tell me you've never wished for this."

He and Paris both look at me and I'm scared. I'm terrified they can read it on my face, this considering the impossible, and I am so afraid of whatever dark feeling is blooming inside me.

I'm shying away from this realization that maybe a part of me sees the logic of his argument, maybe even *agrees* with him, and I can't stop wondering what the hell's wrong with me. I think maybe, finally, I've gone absolutely mad.

Darren can probably read whatever my inner thoughts have translated to on my face, can probably see it clear as day, because he asks, "Just answer me this: Do you want peace?"

And I say, "Yes."

CHAPTER 52

"Yes, but not like this. Not in the way you're trying to achieve it. What kind of peace," I breathe, "comes at the cost of so many lives?"

Darren shakes his head. "This is the only way in which it can be done. This is the only way that the court system allows it to be done."

"But that's not all, is it?" Paris asks. His voice is so quiet. "You might say you want peace, you maybe even deluded yourself into thinking that's why you're doing this, but that's not the whole reason, is it? You have always hated being the third-born. Third in line for the throne. You, out of all of us, have always craved power."

Darren's expression doesn't even change. He doesn't even react. Only says, "And so what if that's a collateral benefit?"

I think the other members of the royal family are finally beginning to understand, beginning to process it all, because Richard speaks up. His voice is shaking with barely restrained anger, barely reined-in rage.

"You bastard," he spits out. "What are you doing? This is insane, even for you."

"*You*," Darren snarls, rounding on him, "have no right to judge me. You, who have spent your entire life trying to be Father's clone. Doing everything he has ever asked of you. You have *no right*."

Richard ignores him. Asks, "How do you even plan to kill us all? It's seven against one."

And the smile, the sudden smile on Darren's face kills any and every hope I had remaining. Slaughters it in a single breath.

He says, "What beautiful timing you have, brother. In a few seconds, you all"—he turns around to address the group—"should be feeling the effects of the tetrodotoxin that I put in the champagne. Don't worry, it's just a temporary paralysis. You'll all come out of it in a few minutes, after I finish what I need to do."

I look around, horrified, and sure enough, they are all still.

Frozen in time like wax statues except they are not made of wax. They are made of skin and bone and blood. Muscle and sinew. And none of them can do a thing to stop what's about to happen.

Paris and I are the only ones who haven't drunk the champagne and for a minute, I'm thinking, Thank god we came late. Until I realize it doesn't matter anyway. Because Paris gave me his gun. Because he is too far away without it to stop what Darren's about to do.

Darren says, "You'll see in time that I'm right, little brother." He smiles. Raises his gun. Points it at the king and I know, in this moment, that I'm the only person able to stop him. The only unparalyzed, unfrozen person close enough to Darren to be able to prevent this disaster from happening.

Paris has shifted his gaze from Darren to me, and his eyes are so very, very green. For the first time, he is pleading with me. "Anna, please. I know you don't owe me anything, I know you have no reason to help me, but," he says, "please. This is my family. Save them."

I want to say yes. God, I want to say yes. My hand is clenched around the rubber grip of the gun and my finger is on the trigger and all I want is to *pull it*. To see the bullet tear into Darren's body, to watch him bleed out until there is nothing left and he can no longer harm the ones that I love—I *want to*. So badly. My entire body is trembling with the pure force of it, but I have already made my choice.

I chose him. And I chose my family. And as much as I wish it were different, I cannot risk them just to save the ruling family of my enemy court—even if it is Paris's.

So I break my gaze away from his and it feels like something tearing, like whatever it is we finally built between us isn't so much crumbling as being torn in half by my hands. I stare at the gun in my hand, but I'm unable to move. Unable to do anything. It might as well be a prop for all the use it's doing me.

I can't bring myself to look at Paris because I know what I'd see: incredulous green eyes, like I have finally, truly become absolutely insane, and a look on his face I can't stand. A look that looks terrifyingly close to betrayal.

I have hurt him too much already. And for some reason, it is like I am fated to keep doing it. I can't stop myself.

I am realizing something that really, I should have realized sooner. That Josephine saw three years ago, and it is this: We are not good for each other. We were both born to hurt, to destroy, to kill and this world, this world is not kind to those who stray. Those who dare to dream.

When Darren pulls the trigger the first time, I don't move. I just watch as it rips through the air, hits Gideon directly in the chest and he crumples to the ground like a rag doll. I don't even have time to process just how small he looks, this man that was always so imposing, so much larger than life. Distantly, almost as if through a dense glass wall, I hear Paris shout. I watch him start toward Darren as if to stop him. Watch him realize that he can't possibly get to his brother in time.

I'm fighting the urge to squeeze my eyes shut, to plug my fingers into my ears like I'm still a child as three more bullets sear through the air. Richard, the queen, and Parker all collapse, blood already forming a dark puddle around them and bleeding like veins into the grass. It spreads fast, scarlet devouring the green until it looks like some watercolor painting, a grotesque blend of colors.

My stomach is full of black tar, my lungs forgetting how to breathe and I'm watching this all unfold in absolute horror, as if it's a scene out of a movie, because there is no way this is real life. I don't dare look at Paris next to me, frozen, wholly powerless to stop this horror from unraveling its glistening crimson threads.

Two more gunshots slash through the entire fabric of the night— giant, gaping tears into reality, into the utter silence that has fallen over the entire courtyard. They are, I think, the most grotesque sounds I have ever heard, but I don't let myself react. Don't even let myself flinch because I know I don't deserve it. I let this happen.

All of a sudden, Paris, Darren, and I are the only ones left standing. The only ones left alive. I can tell Paris is frozen in shock, in the way stiffness is written into his body, in the way he's staring, eyes wide with disbelief. I watch him fall to his knees and it is *breaking* me.

I can feel the moment the anger simmering in my blood transforms into rage; rage, surging through my veins, a torrent crushing my chest until it's hard to breathe.

I don't even stop to let myself see the aftermath, to stare at all six twisted, contorted bodies lying on the ground with identical, blossoming scarlet stains on white like hideous, crimson carnations.

I don't even think.

Just shoot a bullet through Darren's chest before he even has time to react, while he's still careless in this high of victory, and it is liberating. Letting go. Breaking free.

He staggers back, eyes wide, but it is disbelief mixed with resignation. As if he isn't really surprised that I did this. After all, the condition to his threat was only that he be allowed to carry these murders out without interference. He never said anything about after.

When he falls to the ground, sprawling onto the grass, he laughs a little, spits out red blood. Says, "I always knew you had a little bloodthirstiness in you, no matter how hard you've tried to hide it. You can't deny who you are."

I straighten.

Completely numb.

Darren's blood is all over the ground, splattered over my dress and I realize, I'm standing in the heart of the Dawn Court with the blood and the life of a Dawn Court prince on my skin and I have committed a sin so horrible.

And I know the consequences of this, the punishment in the Dawn Court for a Midnight Courter who has taken the life of a royal.

It is death. And I am ready, I think, to face it.

Nobody moves. It is like the entire world has been shocked into silence, into motionlessness. And this, this feels almost surreal: moonlight, grass, champagne flutes.

Now synonymous with death.

CHAPTER 53

Paris is the first to move. He gets to his feet, slowly, carefully and his face is wholly unmasked. I can see every emotion clear in his expression and I almost—actually, I do—wish I couldn't.

He's standing six feet away, but it feels like an entire ocean. It feels like he is worlds away, watching me with cool eyes and I had never realized that whatever remaining affection he had for me was a crutch until it's gone.

Until he is facing me, so very, very distant. So very emotionless.

It is no longer betrayal in his eyes. Not even hurt. Instead, it is a cold fury that terrifies me and I know, I *know* that we are broken.

That this time, it is actually, truly over. I can't swallow whatever it is in my throat that I am choking on.

"Paris—" I start, but—the words dissolve on my tongue. I could say it, I could tell him what happened in my conversation with Darren. What he made me do. What he threatened me with, but maybe, maybe this is what was meant to happen. Maybe all we do is hurt and it's time to end that cycle.

Maybe it's time to let go.

I'm ignoring how uneasily the thought is sitting in my stomach, how cold it burns and how potently it is exuding this feeling of *not right*.

"Don't," Paris says to me. His voice is harsh, lashing. "Don't, Anna."

We're staring at each other, separated by a few yards and it feels exactly like that. It is us and a few feet of space, of grass, but everything is shattering. Breaking apart. Tearing at the seams and I am just now realizing,

the king is gone. And so is every single one of his brothers, every single next in line, meaning...

Paris is now the king of the Dawn Court.

I think he realizes it at the same time I do.

Suddenly, he looks years older. Suddenly, the black of his clothes means nothing because even with it, there could be no doubt what he is. What court he belongs to. It is almost like the Midnight Court part of him is fading, dissolving in acid, and I wonder how I've never realized just how much Paris looks like his father.

Because he does, in this moment. I'm realizing that I've never really seen him as just another prince of the Dawn Court because for ten years of his life, he was Midnight Court. But we are never the same people we were as children.

And I have spent so much time trying to reconcile these two versions of him that I never realized that maybe I can't. Maybe they are like oil and water, meant to be separate.

In the distance, the sun is beginning to emerge above the horizon, slaughters the night, and in the light of this wretched dawn, he says, "I, Paris Ateş, king of the Dawn Court, exile you, Annabella Liang, from this court. Forever." His eyes are so green. Hard like shards of pale emerald and he doesn't look away. He meets my gaze. "I'll make one more promise to you, Anna. If you ever come back, I won't hesitate to kill you."

完

ACKNOWLEDGMENTS

Since before I can remember, I have been reading other authors'
acknowledgements—acknowledgements of books that I had fallen in
love with, books that had become a part of me. As a thirteen-year-old
girl, I don't think I ever could have dreamed that just nine years later,
I would be writing my own.

I have so many people to thank who have supported me and listened to me and encouraged me—that I don't even know where to
begin.

I suppose first, to Kathy, my sister, the one who has been here
years and years before anyone else. Genuinely, since day one. Thank
you. I don't say this enough (or actually, ever) but I am so grateful
that you were born into this world two minutes before I was and
have always been by my side since. You really are my other half - the
person who I started this whole journey with, who fell in love with
books at the same time as me at age five or six or seven, who read
my first (horribly written) novel at age fourteen and who loved it
anyway. I couldn't have asked for a better sister and best friend.

To my parents who were just as excited for this as I was, who—
when we were children—drove me and my sister to the library every
weekend and waited for us to browse for hours. Who bought the
million books that are now taking up (a lot of) space in their house
because we refused to take them all with us. You are the ones who
even made this possible at all by cultivating my love of books and
words since childhood. Thank you both for everything you have
done for me.

To Kaipo. I will never stop feeling lucky to have met you, someone who parallels me in so many ways. There is so much to thank you for—for listening to me yap incessantly about this book daily and never complaining once, for always supporting me unconditionally, for being my rock when I have always had to be my own. There are not enough words in the English dictionary to tell you how grateful I am for you (多谢, 胖猫!).

To my agent Esty, none of this would have been possible without you. You quite literally made my dream come true and I couldn't thank you enough! I am eternally grateful for your constant encouragement and kind words, for the way you love this book just as much as I do. Thank you for believing in me from the very beginning and for being my guide in this very grand, very confusing publishing world!

To my editor Amanda as well as Ashlyn and Kendal and the entire Turner team—I appreciate all of you more than you know. Thank you for having faith in me and my words, for pushing me to make this book the best it could be, and for all of your work and effort into making it what it is today. (And for answering my million questions with lots of patience!)

To Bhoomi and Emma and Ari and so many other people in the writing community and all of my friends outside of it—and of course, my entire street team—thank you all so much for your friendship, for all of the unwavering love and support and belief in me and this book. Thank you for sharing in this extraordinary journey with me—it means more to me than you could ever know, and I wouldn't have wanted to do it with anyone else!

And of course, to every single person who has picked up this book, who has taken the time to read these words. I am so grateful to have been able to share Anna and Paris's story with you—I hope you loved reading it just as much as I did writing it!

ABOUT THE AUTHOR

MELINDA GONG is a recent graduate from NYU with a degree in business. Born in New Orleans and raised in New Jersey, she grew up constantly surrounded by tales of Chinese mythology, forbidden love, and girls with swords taking over the world. She is now based in NYC and, when not busy with work, can be found with her head in the clouds, taking excessively long walks, or drinking far too much coffee.